ETERNAL

POSSESSION

ETERNAL

POSSESSION

An Eternal Novel

Book 2

K.G. INGLIS

ACKNOWLEDGEMENTS

Once again, I'd like to give a special thank you to my wonderful husband and my two awesome teenage kids, without whose support and encouragement this series of books would not be possible. They have suffered through many nights of eating pizza and fish and chips so I could get this book ready for release.

To Glen who has spent many hours editing this book for me. Your keen eye picked up the typos I couldn't see.

I would also like to thank all my friends who followed my books online for so long, Clint, Shelley, Macy, Dakota, Ana Maria, whose efforts helped make the launch of the first book in this series, Eternal Covenant, a success.

And, to everyone who has taken the time to read my books. Thank you all so, so much.

<u>The Eternal Series:</u>

Eternity Begins (prequel)

Eternal Covenant

Eternal Possession

Waking The Eternal Dragon (short story)

Heart Of Eternity

Eternal Temptation

Eternal Craving

Eternity Is Forever

Eternal Youth

Hunt For Eternity

Eternity Unveiled

Eternity Unbound

Eternally Entangled (novella)

Coming Soon:

Eternity Bites

1

Abby stretched, slowly becoming aware of her surroundings. The cold musty air raked her lungs with the sleepy intake of breath, and the hard lumpy mattress beneath her felt familiar in an abstract way. Yet, these things no longer gave her any discomfort.

No longer gave her discomfort? What a strange thought. Her sleep leaden mind teased her sense of reality, such that for a brief moment she was unsure where, or even who she was. She almost believed she was sleeping in one of the abandoned tunnels beneath the streets of Oxford as she often had, when she lived as one of the homeless. Although, there she had never felt this deep anxiety, a gnawing feeling which stayed with her no matter how deeply she slept. It was a feeling of desperation to find something. No, not something,...someone.

Alex.

The cobwebs in her mind cleared in an instant and she was up on her feet and heading for the door in the next.

She had wasted too much time already, and she still had another night of travel ahead of her before she reached the compound where Alex was being held. What she was going to do once she got there, she still had no idea. No doubt she'll work it out as she goes. If living on the streets had taught her anything, it was to be resilient, think fast, and never assume anything. Survival often depended on it.

Abby's stomach twisted in on itself with the anxiety that had driven her for the past two days.

For the first time in two months, since she became a vampire, she felt as though her new *'condition'* was a hindrance, slowing her down, since she was limited to travelling by night.

Unlike older vampires, she was constrained by her inability to remain awake during the day. What she wouldn't give right now to be a day-walker like her vampire sibling, Saladin, an eight hundred year old, arrogant nightclub owner. He might be an arsehole but fortunately for her, he employed an intelligence expert with connections here in the Ukraine.

Abby made a mental note to thank him properly for his help when she got back home. If she lived that long of course. Where she was headed there was no guarantee of a return ticket.

Truthfully though, she might be able to tolerate the sunlight as well as Saladin, she hadn't been able to stay awake long enough during the daytime to find out. It was so damn frustrating.

Abby ran her fingers roughly through the short length of her brunette hair, fluffing out the flat, bed bedraggled appearance. Unwilling to be caught off guard she had slept fully clothed, right down to her boots.

It wasn't the fact that she was a single, white female travelling alone in a strange country that made her uneasy. Not at all. She was used to being a recluse, and she was more than capable of taking care of herself. Finding herself holed up in a WWII underground bunker, filled with strangers who called themselves her allies, was what made her feel a little on edge.

However, the bunker itself was a pleasant surprise. It had recently been converted into a restaurant, complete with WWII memorabilia, making it popular with tourists. Not much about the place had changed since it was first built early last century. The domed stone ceiling and walls had certainly retained their original, rustic condition. The only thing drastically altered was the uneven blue stone floor, replaced by flat, grey slate tiles to meet public liability requirements. While the premises' primary use was as the Alliance's Baltic and Northern European Headquarters, it was also a legitimate business and had to conform to strict regulations.

The irony of the bunker wasn't lost on her. The Guild of Ascension was, until two days ago, controlled by Ahriman, an evil fallen angel whose recent incarnation had been that of an English homicide detective, hell-bent on making himself the world's most powerfully evil immortal. Fortunately, he failed miserably. However, previous to that, he had incarnated as a man infamously remembered for his war crimes, Adolf Hitler. This bunker, which had once housed the Nazi resistance, was now home to the current fighters against the legacy of his evil regime.

Abby checked over her cache of weapons hidden beneath her jacket. With everything that had happened recently, she wasn't prepared to take any chances. Trust had to be earned. Experience had proven that even those who you thought were your allies could in fact, be your enemy.

Abby's unique ability to read people's thoughts gave her an edge, which she intended to take full advantage of, but she would be a fool to put her trust solely in her gift. It wasn't infallible.

Regardless, she had no one to rely on except herself. That is the way it had always been and that is the way it would stay.

Until she got Alex back, nothing else mattered. And, there was nothing she wouldn't do to get him back.

He was her *Mate*.

To complicate the situation, their bond was incomplete and she feared that if his genetics were the same as his sister, Cassie's, he was likely to become weaker with each passing day that Abby was separated from him.

Would he die if she couldn't get to him? She had to assume, yes.

That wasn't an option.

Abby prayed that Lilith, the traitorous bitch who betrayed them and kidnapped Alex, would be at the compound when she arrived. There would be nothing she'd love more than to peel the flesh from Lilith's bones, one paper thin strip at a time.

Swallowing the lump in her throat, she re-adjusted her weapons. Her mind drifted back to the night before his kidnapping when they were ambushed by Ahriman's minions. Alex had been severely injured, he had almost bled to death in her arms from a severed femoral artery.

The healing hormone in her saliva had repaired the artery and sealed his wound, but he had lost a great deal of blood in the process.

Those precious minutes it had taken to staunch the bleeding had changed them both, bonded them irrevocably.

Although Abby didn't have much experience feeding from humans, she knew it was a pleasurable experience for both the vampire and their donor under normal circumstances. With the strong attraction she and Alex already felt towards one another, and the intensity of the situation with his injury, their blood bond had connected them more intimately, creating something...deeper. It bound them on a soul level. They became a part of one another.

For all that, their bond wasn't complete, and it would remain that way until Alex tasted her blood. Until then the physical separation from her would drain him of energy, slowly weaken him a little more every day, like a battery without a power supply to recharge it.

A couple of bags of blood replaced some of what he had lost through his leg wound, but it wasn't enough. He was still weak from his blood loss. Combined with his separation from her...

A surge of fear pulsed through her veins, perfusing every cell in her body with a violent shudder as she relived the memory of that night.

She nearly lost him then. She wouldn't let it happen again.

What was happening to him now? She could only guess. One thing she knew for sure, the Guild didn't plan on hurting him, at least not right away. They went to a lot of trouble to get him. They needed him for something.

Abby stepped through the doorway into the supply room at the rear of the restaurant, the hidden panel sliding seamlessly back into place. It was still early and the building was almost deserted. The Chef ignored her as he searched the shelves for ingredients, giving her no more than a passing glance as he muttered to himself.

Gustav's deep baritone voice carried to her sensitive ears, even though she could tell he was doing his best to speak quietly. The heated tones of the conversation had Abby instantly on guard. Her fingers nervously stroked the handle of the blade hidden beneath her jacket.

"Abby. Hello, I'm Nadia. I've been dying to meet you." The young woman bounded over to her holding out a pen and notepad for Abby to take, her thick Ukrainian accent contrasted with her perfect use of English.

Abby took a step away in surprise, taken aback by the young woman's enthusiasm. Her hand latched onto the dagger reflexively, itching to unsheathe it.

Gruff protests in Ukrainian and severe glares threatening reprisal were fired at Nadia, who stubbornly ignored the three men completely, pushing her notepad and pen at Abby a second time. Bouncing on her toes with excitement, Nadia seemed oblivious to the danger of her internal organs becoming external accessories.

"Sorry," Gustav offered apologetically. "We tried to talk her out of it."

"Could I have your autograph, please?" Nadia begged.

Her autograph? Why would she want *her* autograph?

Had she stepped off the plane into an alternate universe where telepathic vampires had somehow become the equivalent to movie stars? Not that this girl would know she was telepathic.

Abby stared dumbly at Nadia who once again pushed the notepad and pen toward her.

Abby opened her mind to the girl's thoughts and inwardly groaned.

As it turned out, she had become a celebrity of sorts, by proxy at least. Video footage of her with the legendary, first vampire Sammael, or Alaric as he preferred to be known now, at Saladin's nightclub on the night of his so-called *'resurrection'* back into the world, had apparently been forwarded around the globe to practically every supernatural on the planet.

Abby had spent the best part of her life shunning contact with people. All people. She had gone out of her way to avoid them, to the extent that she had deliberately taken up residence on the streets. She felt suffocated by people's attention, their thoughts bombarded her mind with torturous monotony. It was quiet on the streets. Nobody came near you if you looked like a dirty vagrant. You simply slipped into obscurity. It wasn't always an easy life, but it was peaceful, just how she preferred it.

To find out that she had inadvertently become famous was enough to make her hyperventilate.

Alaric had also been a recluse until his *'coming-out'*. He hated his new Hollywood status among the supernaturals, all the whispers and open ogling he now endured. Abby had chided him for his snarky remarks and eye-rolling groans whenever he went into public.

It wasn't so amusing when the shoe was on her foot.

Humour her and she'll go away, Abby thought to herself optimistically.

With a shaky hand Abby discretely released her grip on the dagger and swapped it for the pen, scribbling a short message on the pad and signed, Abigail Dresdan.

"Thank you," Nadia squealed as she raced back to the table to show the three men who continued their disapproving glares at her.

"Abby. I want you to meet Klaus and Sebastian," Gustav said, ignoring Nadia's squeals of delight. Gesturing first to a heavily built man, Klaus, his beard almost as grizzly as the nasty scar that stretched the length of his face from the edge of one eye, reaching down to just below his jaw line. Klaus flashed a pair of golden eyes to appraise her of his lycan geniality, in case she didn't already know.

Next to him sat a fresh-faced blonde man with a mischievous sparkle in his eyes, Sebastian. His lithe frame and nimble movements gave him away as a vampire, even before he flashed his pearly white fangs when he smiled.

"They'll be travelling with you to the Guild's compound. Klaus was raised in that region and can guide you through a few shortcuts." Klaus gave her a lopsided mock grin, deliberately scrunching up his face around the tethered scar, giving him an evil 'Chainsaw Massacre' look about him.

"Sebastian has a few tricks he can use that might come in handy to get into the compound." The blonde vampire dipped his head and winked, his opalescent eyes sparkled darkly with playful devilment.

Great. A road trip with two of Snow White's dwarves, Grumpy and Happy, if dwarves were around six foot tall, that is. Ha, there was an oxymoron, giant dwarves.

"Abby, is it true that Sammael is your sire?" Nadia interrupted, scooting across the bench seat and motioning for Abby to sit next to her, clearly unwilling to let any of them have a serious discussion until she had her fill of 'Groupie Session Time'.

"Yes. That's true," Abby answered simply.

"That's so cool."

"Nadia," Gustav growled. "Enough. We have more important things to discuss. Go and make yourself useful in the kitchen." His deep gruff voice took on an edge of warning. Nadia frowned and pouted but was gone a moment later, muttering to herself as she stomped away.

"Sorry about Nadia," he explained, a little exasperated by his daughter. "She is a good girl, but a little ah, ah…" his forehead furrowed in heavy corrugation, pulling his thick eyebrows together until they almost touched. His finger tapped the table in an automated fashion as he searched for the right word in English. "Excitable."

"I don't mind," Abby lied, doing her best to keep the smile on her face.

Gustav shifted in his seat, pulling a map from a bag beside him and laying it on the table.

"Here," he pointed to a densely forested area, "Is where the Guild is holding your friend. There's an old fortress converted into an Army outpost during the war. We believe the Guild is now using it as their headquarters," he explained in disjointed English.

"They have been shipping in supplies along this river." Gustav's finger snaked along the length of the tributary that ended a mile or so from the compound. "Unfortunately, we only have satellite photos of the shipments, although we have reports that they have been accruing radioactive isotopes and large amounts of scientific equipment."

Abby had already heard this much from Dray before she had left England.

"Why haven't you had confirmation of this?" Abby asked. She wasn't an intelligence expert, she hadn't even played any of those ridiculous, time wasting computer war craft games, but even she knew the saying *"Know thy enemy like thyself"* was the first rule in battle.

Gustav balled his hands in front of him, his eyes darkening with frustration. Klaus growled, a fierce guttural noise that would freeze an angry bull in its tracks in fear.

"No one we've sent in there to investigate has ever returned," he answered grimly, their loss weighing heavily on his shoulders. Even though the men he had sent had volunteered, he still felt responsible for them.

Abby knew this trip was dangerous, and she was prepared for any eventuality, but she didn't want to be liable for the lives of anyone else.

It was her duty to free Alex, no one else's. The last thing she needed was to be held accountable for the loss of more of Gustav's men if things went pear-shaped. She was already burdened with enough guilt to sink a battleship.

"No disrespect to any of you, but if this is likely to be a suicide mission, I'm going alone," she stated, eyeballing each man with determined resignation.

"No," Klaus growled. "You find your friend. I find my brother," rolling his r's with a thick accent. He leaned across the table menacingly, daring her to deny him his right to go.

Abby didn't flinch a muscle, holding his glare for a moment longer before giving him a slight nod.

"And what's your excuse for going," she asked Sebastian whose eyes glittered with roguish glee. "I'm bored," he grinned, steepling his hands in front of him. "And, Gustav tells me I annoy the customers," he said with a dark chuckle of proud satisfaction. "So, I think it's time I have a change of scenery," he added, casually thrumming his fingers together with carefree disregard.

"You realise this could turn out to be a suicide mission, don't you?"

"Ah, yes. I am well aware of that. But that is what makes it so much fun."

Abby gave Gustav a questioning look. "I don't need any foolhardy thrill seekers on this trip," she grated out, her eyes shifting to Sebastian with a disapproving glare.

"Don't worry about Sebastian. He likes to joke around some, but I am sure he will do nothing to compromise your mission, will you Seb?"

"Of course not." His shocked look of indignation and disappointment that anyone should doubt his dedication and conviction was almost believable. Almost. Except, Abby could read his mind.

Was he willing to put any of them at risk? No. Was he willing to toe the line and behave? Again, no. However, the most interesting thing she discovered ploughing through his mind, was that Dray had specifically requested he go with her. If Dray trusted him, then maybe, just maybe she could too. Heavy emphasis on the *maybe*.

After a four-hour drive, Abby was dropped off in the middle of no-man's land with her two new travel buddies, very aptly nicknamed Grumpy and Happy.

"Smell that glorious fresh air," Sebastian stretched his arms out wide, expanding his chest to take in a deep breath. "So much better than your God awful doggy stench. What do you call that cologne, month old road-kill?" he taunted Klaus.

"You want to die blondie?" Klaus growled, taking a swing at Sebastian.

"Already did that. What else do you have in mind, but nothing kinky," he jibed, taking a leap aside to avoid the baseball mitt sized fist heading in his direction. "I'm not into any man-on-man shit. So, I suggest you put your paws away before you give the lady the idea that you're after a bit of slap and tickle."

Klaus' eyes took on a golden glow with murderous rage, peeling back his top lip to reveal a vicious set of carnivore hardware, his fingers stretching into lethal claws. "I'm going to kill you, little cockroach," he snarled, adding a string of foul curses in his native tongue. His ebony brows slammed down over eyes which darkened with dangerous intent.

Pivoting, he swung at Sebastian once again. Sebastian blocked the punch, then caught him with a kick that knocked Klaus backwards, but only for a moment. Despite his size he moved with the grace of the wolf inside him, smooth and fluid, dancing lightly on his feet. Every powerful blow controlled with devastating accuracy. But it made no difference.

"You won't be so smug when I separate your head from your body," he said in a painfully calm voice, as though performing a decapitation was a routine job.

"Good Lord. If you two don't tone down the testosterone, I'll kill you both myself," Abby yelled, the storm brewing in her eyes gathering strength.

The two men stopped and grinned at each other, clasping forearms in mutual appreciation.

"Don't mind us," Sebastian said. "We're just limbering up. We need to be ready for whatever nasty surprises the Guild might have waiting for us."

A sparring session? Abby threw up her hands in frustration. "We don't have time for this. Let's get moving," her voice cracked like a bull-whip. She didn't intentionally mean to sound so harsh, but she was unaccustomed to men behaving like Neanderthals and her nerves weren't exactly at their best right now.

"Sorry," Klaus apologised sheepishly. "The liddle lady is right. Get moving," he said to Sebastian, slapping him hard enough on the back to send him stumbling a few steps. Getting the last blow in on their friendly scrap.

Six freaking hours of trekking with this pair? Good God, give me strength, she inwardly thought in frustration.

Maybe she could ditch them.

Wishful thinking.

At least she knew they could fight. It would be better if they focussed on the enemy though, not each other.

Snow flurries fluttered around her face, getting into her eyes and tickling her nose as they started their long hike.

For the next few hours they moved in silence, scaling steep craggy mountain sides and walking along obscure muddy trails barely fit for mountain goats. The only sound came from skeletal trees rustling in the breeze, muted marginally by the mountain of snow that coated the ground.

Nearly there. Abby told herself over and over with each step.

2

Astrophysicist and Theoretical Physicist extraordinaire.

What bullshit.

Here he was, with the brains of a super computer, and he couldn't figure a way out of this Godforsaken room.

What he wouldn't give right now to have a few practical skills. You know, be one of those guys who could pick a lock with nothing more than a hair pin, or re-wire circuitry and open electronic locks with only the internal workings of a pen light. Actually, that part he could probably do…if he only had a fucking pen light.

Fuck, this is frustrating, he thought as he threw himself against the heavy door for the zillionth time.

Alex sank to the floor in an exhausted heap. Breathing heavily, his muscles shook from his fruitless efforts to escape. Escape really wasn't the right word. But, if he could at least get the guard's attention…maybe.

Nope, it wasn't happening and there was no point fooling himself. He was a prisoner here until whenever his captors choose otherwise.

Two very large guards were stationed outside his door at all times, that he knew for certain. Apart from that, he knew nothing. Not where the corridor outside his room led to, nor where the building was situated. He wasn't even certain he was still in England. Listening to the muffled sound of accented voices, he doubted he was.

The last thing he remembered was being hauled into a helicopter. Then, nothing until he woke up in this meat locker.

The room would give any alcoholic an instant hangover. White washed walls and ceiling, polished white linoleum floor and extra bright fluorescent lighting. A single bed with white linen was pressed up against one wall and opposite, what he assumed was originally a storage cupboard was now, you guessed it, an all white bathroom.

If he ever got out of this monotonously bleach-bland room, the only colour he wanted around him was black, and that was only until they invented a darker colour.

Dimly, he registered the sound of the lock turning in the door. As the door began pushing at his back, he slid sluggishly to the side, sitting behind it as it was pushed fully open.

"Where the hell is he?" the male said.

"I'm behind here, moron," Alex said, lifting himself off the floor. He barely had the energy to move. Regardless, he wasn't going to give this tosser the satisfaction of seeing him on his knees.

"I know you. You're the fuck knuckle I KO'd at the airport," Alex said. "And, you..." his eyes narrowed on the dark skinned woman next to him, his weight shifting to the balls of his feet ready to fight, "You're Ahriman's brown-nosing, chicken-shit assassin. Obviously, not a very good one since you high-tailed it when your buddies had their heads removed. Are you still working for Ahriman or have you found someone new to leach off?"

"How dare you, you sniveling little gutter snipe," Mira snapped, her fangs descending in anticipation of fresh blood.

"Your loyalty is cheap, Mira, admit it. You change your loyalty like you change your clothes. You work for whoever is paying the most or whoever wields the biggest stick."

"He's right you know," the male said when Mira growled dangerously.

"The truth hurts, suck it up," Alex added, swaying a little on shaky legs.

"A couple of days of solitary confinement hasn't improved your manners at all," came a familiar voice from Hell, as a second woman stepped through the doorway.

A couple of days? Is that how long he had been there? Being cut off from everything and everyone, it felt like an eternity. The only thing Alex had to occupy himself with was the meditation Narayan had been teaching him. It filled in a few hours here and there, but it wasn't enough to pacify his overactive brain or his burning need to feel Abby in his arms. To feel her skin beneath his hands, so soft and smooth, like the most perfect alabaster, her body all graceful curves. Nor could meditation lessen the memory of her decadent scent of vanilla and orchids. If anything, it heightened it, making him light-headed and really homesick.

"I see you brought Ahriman's lap dog," Alex bit out. His bitter contempt at seeing Lilith was only dampened by his fatigue. Inside he seethed with hatred that bordered on psychopathic rage. "Where's your master, whore bitch, and what did you do with my sister?"

It felt strange using that word, *sister*. For his whole life he had believed Cassie was his cousin, and not even blood related at that. Neither of them had any idea they in fact shared the same father. Not until a couple of days ago. He had been surprised by that revelation, but not disappointed. Cassie had always felt like a sister to him and it gave him a case of the warm and fuzzies to know he had blood relatives living in this world with him. Not just one but two and a half.

Cassie was his sister, which made Alaric his great grandfather, sixty-three times removed. He and Cassie were descended from Alaric and his daughter. Alaric was also soon to be his brother-in-law and the couple were expecting a baby, hence the half.

Alex had no doubt they would be out there somewhere right now planning his rescue.

"I'm right here," the blonde male standing in front of him responded. "I'm Ahriman. And, I killed your sister," he smirked with iniquitous delight.

"What the fuck?" Alex gave the male an intense visual scrutiny. Credibility for his statement didn't ring true. There was no way in the world this guy would be standing here if he had killed Cassie. Alaric would have hunted him down and torn him limb from limb. There would be no rock in the world this snake could hide under where Alaric wouldn't find him.

"Cut the bullshit. What's going on here," Alex bit out in an acerbic tone. He was tired, and he had no interest in their twisted mind-fuck games.

"I can see you don't believe me, I assure you though I speak the truth. I had a minor complication when I had my big show-down with Sammael. My old body got a little damaged and I needed a new one. So, here I am," he said in a forced chipper tone.

Alex gave a mock *'woo hoo'* and punched the air. There was nothing like inciting a psychotic demon into violence. Although, the threat of retaliation had never persuaded Alex to keep his mouth shut before, so there was no reason to change now. Maybe that made him an arsehole. Okay, that definitely made him an arsehole, but he had every intention of pushing the boundaries of fate until fate pushed back. *In for a penny, in for a pound*, as the saying goes. "So, Alaric killed you, you satanic freak show. I'm glad to hear it. But, that doesn't explain how you became a parasite infesting this cock sucker," Alex said, waving his hand in an exaggerated flurry.

"Actually, Sammael wasn't strong enough to kill me. I was almost fully transformed by the time he found me. It was that pathetic professor." Blood stained spittle flew from Ahriman's lips, his face flushing with anger, pulsing veins bulging in his forehead and neck. "Who knew that Guardian's were real," he mumbled to himself.

As for how he came to be inside Stedman…Well, he was saving that pearl for later. He intended to let Alex find out firsthand.

"So, you up-graded to a new model of douche bag, but I think you got duped numb nuts." Alex looked over the sorry form of Ahriman's host body. His eyes were blood shot, his face pasty white with a fine beading of perspiration on his forehead. "It must be Hell inside that rotting maggot sack, you must feel right at home," Alex quipped.

Ahriman's temper kicked up a notch.

"I hate to break this to you doofus, but you seem to be leaking," Alex said, running a finger under his own eye and pouting with a mock sad face.

Ahriman touched his cheek, his fingers coming away with blood. His eyes, nose and ears were bleeding in a steady trickle. Not only were his organs now at the point of failure, it appeared his veins were now liquefying too. Like a form of radiation sickness, his new body was degrading at an alarming rate.

Regrettably, the average human body was not made to sustain the high vibration of a soul such as his. Ahriman stared at Alex, a small curve lifting the corners of his mouth into a smug grin.

But then, Alex wasn't an average human, was he?

"So, what am I doing here? You got Cassie's blood. Obviously that didn't work out so well for you. I'm assuming I'm your back-up plan?" Alex refused to believe that Ahriman had killed Cassie. They had a close bond, if something had happened to her, he would know, right, get some sort of *feeling*?

"Originally it was only your brains I was after, not your blood. But, I have to admit your genetics are an unexpected bonus."

"What exactly does that mean?"

"Your research. It means you're going to put your research into practice."

"What? What the hell are you talking about? My research is theoretical. There's no practical application for my research."

"Ah, but that's where you're wrong, dear *boy*," Ahriman boasted. "You're going to build me a device that will open a portal to the Underworld."

Ahriman had an overgrown sense of his own power. The egotistical bastard would suck his own dick if he could, Alex thought.

"Let me guess, you were dropped in the ugly and stupid bucket when you were being created and it stuck? No wonder you were sent to the Underworld, you're an embarrassment to your own kind."

Ahriman slapped Alex across the face. "Shut-up," he snapped.

"Oh, sorry, I left out socially retarded. I thought only girl's slap. I guess that makes you ugly, stupid *and* retarded. You're the trifecta of losers."

It was official. Alex was his own species. The Death-wish-osaurus and extinction was calling.

Ahriman raised his hand again in a fist but dropped it almost immediately, his lip curled in an uncivilised snarl as he warred with himself not to pummel Alex senseless.

Lilith stood back with smug satisfaction. She was *sooo* looking forward to Alex getting what was coming to him, and she intended to be there to watch.

"You *will* do what I tell you, because you're nothing but a pawn in my game, and I play to win," he snarled through clenched teeth.

A pawn? A fucking pawn? "You're out of your fucking tree if you think I'm going to cooperate with you," Alex bit back.

"There wasn't an option in my statement," Ahriman growled. There wasn't an ounce of kindness or warmth behind those cold, callous eyes either.

"Ahh, hmm." A deep voice from the hallway drew their attention. "Sir, we have a report of intruders scouting the borders of the compound. Would you like us to eliminate them or recruit them?"

"How many are there?"

"Only three that we can detect, Sir."

The Alliance, Ahriman deduced. They'd taken longer to get here than he had expected, and only three of them? Either Alex wasn't that important to them after all, or they were up to something.

"Send out some men. Capture them if you can, if not…well, C'est la vie." He gave a flick of his hand. "And report back to me."

Without so much as a glance in Alex's direction, Ahriman, Mira and Lilith left his room, the lock clicking into place behind them. Alex let out a long, weary breath as the last of his energy evaporated away and he sank back down the wall to sit hugging his knees on the floor.

Not long now. They were coming for him. He would be out of this hellhole within twenty-four hours. He hoped.

"Mira, get Morganna. Now!" Ahriman barked at her.

"What do you have in mind?" Lilith asked suspiciously.

Ahriman ignored Lilith's question, instead gave further orders to Mira. "Tell her to get the chamber ready for the ritual."

"Yes Sir," she answered and quickly marched away.

"You're not thinking of taking Alex's body as a host, are you?" Lilith snapped in a disapproving tone. "You can't. His body is still weak. If Stedman's body only lasted you two days and he was healthy beforehand, how long do you think Alex's body will last? I won't allow it. You can use one of the guards until Alex is back to full strength."

Ahriman's temper was already on a hair trigger and Lilith's little tirade snapped the last thread.

His huge body turned and slammed her against the wall, his enormous hand gripped around her throat like a vice, cutting off her air.

16

Lilith's eyes bulged wildly from fear and oxygen deprivation. She stared into the dark abyss of his soul, flinching as his searing power slashed through the air.

"How dare you take the liberty of presuming you can tell me what I can and cannot do," he roared. "Your usefulness is wearing thin, Lilith, along with my patience. You warm my bed and that is all." He released her throat and allowed her a gasping breath. "Do not question my judgement again, or you may find out firsthand what I do to those who piss me off," he added sweetly, trailing a finger down her throat, along her collarbone and dipping lower between her breasts.

Lilith whimpered as he pressed the heavy length of his arousal into her belly. As much as he scared her sometimes, she couldn't help melting at his touch. She was a Class A moron, she was the first to admit it, but she would do anything for him, no matter what it cost her, so long as he kept her in his bed.

Ahriman pushed himself off her with a contemptuous snort and waved an impatient hand to keep her silent. He could feel the relentless ticking of the clock beating against him.

The enemy was at his door and he had a job to accomplish.

"Impatient much?"

"I thought we'd already established that. Yes," Abby huffed, pushing Sebastian aside to take a look herself.

Inside the compound walls the weeds clung to the courtyard surface, growing over abandoned WWII heavy artillery. Moss covered the walls and the external timber doors were rotting and decrepit. The premises could easily be mistaken for being deserted if it weren't for the shiny new hidden surveillance cameras. The interesting thing was that these cameras were trained to monitor inside the compound, not beyond, and there was no one guarding beyond the inner walls. The battlement on top of the run-down building was unmanned and no dogs patrolled the parameter.

Klaus hissed. "Someding is wrong."

His warning came only a moment before the courtyard filled with men.

There seemed to be an endless supply of brawny, fierce men in the compound now. Maybe they grew them in a garden out the back somewhere. There was something odd about them though, something….not right, but Abby couldn't quite put her finger on what it was that seemed out of place.

The Guild knew they were there. But how? Sebastian thought. He was an elite hunter. He didn't leave tracks, he was careful not to carry any scent on a hunt, and he moved soundlessly through the terrain. Even his shadow was indistinguishable from his surroundings.

He would bet his left nut that the compound was warded with perimeter spells. Although he'd never come across one before, there was no other explanation. There was barely any security on the outside of the building, no razor wire fences and no alarms or trip wires.

This place was getting weirder by the second.

Abby, Sebastian and Klaus retreated back into the forest. A handful of guards in hot pursuit.

Half a mile from the compound the first guards caught up with them.

Sebastian watched Abby dance on the balls of her feet, dishing out a succession of blows with brutal efficiency, like a beautiful Valkyrie.

He would love to get her in the gym, where they could spar until he took her down on the mat and…Well, okay, that wasn't going to happen. She already had a *mate*. The story of his life.

He wasn't the only one watching her though. Just beyond a bush to her right, another guard stalked her, waiting to pounce when she came within his reach.

Sebastian slipped around behind, tapping him on the shoulder he offered him a biting smile, his fist raised ready to deliver a blow.

Holy crap! It can't be.

"Where da hell you come from liddle cockroach?"

Only two men he knew used that term of endearment, Klaus and…

"I would say your mother's bed, but I've seen your mother," Sebastian quipped, his tone tainted with disbelief.

Klaus' head snapped up. That voice. He knew that voice.

Klaus laid out the last two psychopathic guards, flipping the blades in his hands and plunged one into Mr Creepy Buzzcut's heart and the other through the neck of his sidekick Beelzebub's inbred cousin, and leapt toward the scuffling men. Sebastian may have been half Dieter's size but he packed a mean punch, catching the larger man in the temple, dropping him like a sack of potatoes.

Dieter. Klaus' brother was fighting for the enemy?

Could this night get any weirder?

Yes. The night was almost over, and Sebastian and Abby weren't wearing their infinity-plus sun block.

The biting wind lashed his large frame as Klaus carried the dead weight of his brother through the foot-deep snow back to their base camp, a small hunter's cottage several miles away. Very few people knew of its existence hidden away in one of the densest parts of the forest.

Dieter began to groan, then wiggle on Klaus' shoulder, his movements becoming more aggressive and louder as he came to.

"Dieter. Behave," Klaus growled, dropping him on the ground and pinning him face down in the snow.

"We're here to help you, but we don't need to make it a pleasant experience. Got it?" Sebastian's chastising words with their blatant threat had no effect.

Dieter's eyes were blank, vacant. There was no sign of recognition for his brother or Sebastian.

The lights were on, but nobody was home.

Until this moment Abby would have believed that these soulless mercenaries were imported directly from the Underworld, willing to perform any job for the right price. Now? What the hell was going on?

"What a head fuck," Sebastian muttered.

"What dey do to him?" Klaus looked to Abby and Sebastian for answers who both shrugged and shook their heads.

"I don't know, but I'm going to kill him if he doesn't shut the fuck up. He's going to let his new buddies know where to find us," Sebastian muttered.

"I'll help you hide the body," Abby promised.

"Just kidding bro," Sebastian quickly apologised when Klaus's eyes began to glow dangerously in warning. The hand gestures and accompanying comments, although in his native tongue, suggested that Sebastian perform various sexual acts on himself, most of which would be physically impossible. "Sheesh."

Over the years Sebastian's unique sense of humour and perverse grasp of honesty may have led to some hurt feelings and long-held grudges. But overall, he was a pretty likeable guy.

"I fix dis." Klaus curled his hand into a tight fist and thumped his brother with enough force to keep him unconscious for a week. The echo of the punch reverberated through the trees, dislodging a flurry of snow from their skeletal branches.

"We need to get moving. The sun's almost up," Abby urged.

They also needed answers.

Time was running short for Alex. She could feel it in her bones.

She had to find a way to get into that compound, although now she had to wait another freaking twelve hours before she could make an attempt.

Arrrrgh!

3

Teagan removed her heavy coat, her outfit shaped itself to her lush body, the V of her blouse, although buttoned conservatively, outlined her full breasts and lower, her hips and belly, which she probably thought was too ample. But damn, she was built the way a woman should be – sensuous, with curves that excited the primal male inside him. Without a doubt, her body was made to buffer a man's lust.

His body hardened, primed for just that.

Saladin had watched her throughout the funeral, drawn to the way the frigid winter breeze tugged at her long, ebony curls, caressing the pale ivory skin of her face. Her cheeks flushed a soft pink from the wind's bite, and her eyes, the warmest shade of chocolate brown, dipped as she attempted to avoid his intense gaze.

Now, inside the Drunken Duck Pub where the mourners had gathered, it was Teagan who stared in awe of the man standing next to her friend, Cassie.

Saladin turned in her direction. Sharp angles defined his face, from his high cheekbones to his strong jaw and pencil-thin anchor-style beard and moustache. And when one corner of his mouth lifted into a half smile, revealing a gleaming white fang, her pulse did an excited flutter.

He had been carved from a stone slab of danger, power and grace, and if she exposed even one ounce of softness, he would devour her, probably literally.

Saladin walked toward her, clearing a path through the crowd with nothing more than his presence.

"Teagan isn't it?" Saladin asked, as a way of a conversation starter, his smooth voice liquid silk in its hypnotic perfection, his eyes thoroughly surveying every luscious curve her body had to offer, from head to toe.

"Yes?" She swallowed hard, her mouth suddenly dry. All her bodily fluids seemed to have instantly pooled between her thighs.

"I'm told you're a friend of Cassie's, as am I. I think it would be prudent that when this little party is over, you and I should get to know each other better." His charming smile sent the whirlpool of desire deep in her soul, slowly spiraling up to the surface as his hand slid to the curve of her waist, encircling it and pulling her closer. "I could make you feel in ways no female has ever dreamed possible," he promised, his low-pitched voice caressing her from the inside out.

Teagan's scent was ambrosia. It was filled with a heavy dose of feminine musk that bled through him like an erotic poisoning. It burned through every cell in his body.

He wanted her.

Teagan stared at him, unsure how to respond. *Get a grip girl*, she scolded herself. *He's a vampire.* "Um, if you don't mind, I'll take a rain check," she finally told him, her arching tone, taunting and haughty.

"You'll never get this opportunity again…."

Well, la-de-da. Didn't that make all the difference. He's still a vampire. Even as she reminded herself of that fact again, her lusty body continued to respond to his seductive advances.

Saladin stared at her with his piercing blue eyes, the light of victory already dancing within them. He thought her acceptance was a given, and God, he really was tempting.

Teagan's lips parted for a retaliating jibe as his head swooped down and took her mouth in a bold kiss.

She gasped, shocked by the jolts of pure pleasure that ricocheted through her body, practically causing her insides to liquefy in a gooey hormonal puddle. It was like being struck by lightning. Dazzling and electric, pulsing directly into her moist core, heating it until the need to clench her thighs together and swallow her moan all but overwhelmed her.

Saladin released her lips, although continued to hold her body tightly against his, giving Teagan just enough space for the mood barometer in her mind to flip from lusty fog to ticked-off.

Her chin lifted, and while she was shorter than he was by several inches, she somehow managed to look down her nose at him, her intense gaze filled with superiority.

Interesting. Usually females batted their eyelashes and gave him smoky bedroom eyes when he turned on his charm. Instead, her confidence and defiance sent a rush of heat through his veins, piquing his interest even further.

"You're delusional. I know who you are, Yusuf Saladin. And I wouldn't lower my standards to be seen with someone like you," she told him tempestuously.

"Someone like me? Do you mean, a vampire?" his silky smooth voice rolled over her, weakening her knees.

"No. I,...I mean...man-whore," she accused. Turning on her heel she attempted to disappear into the crowd, except Saladin's vice-like grip latched onto her hand and held her in place for a moment longer.

A look of frustration crossed his face. No, wait...anger. No...disappointment? Whatever, it was a bad look.

Was he deciding whether or not to *compel* her, to get his way?

Teagan snatched her hand back and scuttled against the bar trying to assess the situation. For a man who didn't *need* to breathe, he seemed to take all the oxygen from the room. She forced breath into her lungs as she reminded herself that for her at least, breathing mattered.

"Until later then," he offered with a slight bow, his cocky grin still firmly in place.

"In your dreams," she bit back.

"Oh, most definitely beautiful lady. I'll look forward to it."

As Saladin turned his back on her, Teagan wasn't sure whether she wanted to run out of the pub screaming or run after him, but as it turned out, hyperventilation worked too.

"Man-whore?" Saladin muttered to himself with a chuckle as he headed across the room. He couldn't deny it, the term did fit quite well.

He really liked this woman. She stirred something inside him that excited him.

"Explain to me again who this friend of yours is?" Saladin asked Cassie.

"If you explain to me *again* who exactly Gwynn ap Nudd and Raif are, and how they fit into the whole Alliance gig. I must have suffered some brain-fade earlier when Alaric was explaining it all to me, because they don't look anything like what I expected." Cassie watched the two men in question talking to her *mate*, Alaric. Although Alaric was an impressive six-foot six-inches tall, he was almost dwarfed in comparison to Raif and Gwynn who had to tilt their heads slightly to avoid banging them on the light fittings, their stature a striking seven-feet in height, each.

"They're Fairies. What were you expecting?"

"I don't know, but not...them." She got that fairies weren't a species as such, it was the term to describe where they were from, like people from Earth are known as earthlings, the people from Fey were fairies, but still...

After everything that had happened to her in the last couple of months, you would think she'd be prepared for anything, yet she just couldn't seem to get her head around these two.

"Raif is a wyvern. A dragon," Saladin explained slowly in a slightly patronising tone. Although his arrogant manner tended to piss her off, Cassie chose to ignore it, this time.

"Which would explain his slightly reptilian slit-like pupils instead of round ones like ours," she observed.

"Exactly. And, Gwynn ap Nudd is a nephilim. Half-angel and half-human, their race was banished to Fey thousands of years ago, at the same time as the Watchers, the angels who'd fathered them, were sent to the Underworld for their betrayal."

"I know that part," she said impatiently. "Get to the good stuff. How do they fit into the whole Alliance thing? Do they all look like him? You know, the pointy ears, silvery white hair down to his waist and the most amazing violet eyes. At least I know where fairy tales got Elves from."

"No, dear *girl*." There was that patronising tone again. Okay, so maybe she had earned that one, prattling away there like a school*girl*. "They don't all look like him. Each angel who fathered a child was different, therefore their offspring had different physical traits and

24

different gifts too. The nephilim's more primitive human halves make them slightly temperamental and irrational, which at times also makes them dangerous to be around. For the most part though, they're well-meaning people with good hearts. But some…" Saladin pursed his lips and raised an eyebrow.

"Well, don't leave me hanging," she coaxed, backhanding him in the stomach.

"Fine," he griped, lowering his voice he tipped his head down closer to her ear. "The nephilim broke off into two groups. The majority of them stayed with Gwynn, but the others followed a woman named Morganna le Fey, a sorceress with exceptional powers. They became known as the rephaim…the evil ones. There was an uprising when the rephaim tried to cross back to earth. They lost. The nephilim called on the druids for help and between them they banished the rephaim back to Fey where they were imprisoned. Stripped of their ability to *sift* between the dimensional barrier of Fey and Earth."

"And? Keep going. Is that how the nephilim and wyvern became part of the Alliance?"

"Sort of. They were already guardians against the Underworld."

"I don't quite follow."

"You would if you let me finish," Saladin told her, irritation grating through his tone.

"Well, get on with it then." Now Cassie was deliberately trying to piss him off. She didn't have much else to do these days. Locked away at the manor with only the same handful of people to talk to, and her new dog, Tilly, formally the pet of Brian Harlow, the man whose funeral they were currently attending. Her sequestering was for her own protection, or more accurately, for her baby's protection, so she didn't complain about it. She, herself was now an immortal, but they had no way of knowing if her immortality was also transfused into the baby she carried. They knew it carried the gene that would make it possible, but whether the gene was active or dormant was anyone's guess. As a result, Cassie's life tended to oscillate between mildly boring to mind-numbingly, bat-shit crazy boring. So she took every opportunity that came her way to liven things up a bit.

Saladin gave another impatient huff and looked her in the eye for a long moment to make sure he had her full attention. "There are many separate dimensions: Earth, Fey, the Underworld and the Higher Realms are the main ones. Each dimension is sealed off from the others. The elders created a portal for human souls to pass to the Higher Realms only two millennia ago and created the vampires to keep the universal balance. Besides Earth, there are other physical worlds whose occupant's souls feed into both the higher and lower dimensions. Depending on the soul's vibration, the more evolved souls head upwards, the evil and depraved souls are sent to the Underworld. But there is only one world that borders each dimension directly, Fey. The wyvern guard the border between Fey and the Underworld to make sure the creatures it contains don't break free. The nephilim guard the border between Fey and Earth."

"You still haven't told me how they fit into the Alliance."

"I'm getting to that, woman, just hold your horses." At this point, Cassie could tell he was only finishing his story because he wanted to know more about Teagan. If he had any other way to learn more about her friend, Cassie knew Saladin would be pursuing that option, rather than enduring the frustration of talking to her any longer. "Earth too has its protectors. The lycans. They protect the borders into Fey from this side, which also sometimes includes protecting humans from themselves. Anyway, after the rephaim's uprising, the leaders of each of the races got together to form a network of information, which we now call the Alliance. That's it. Now, what can you tell me."

Yep. She was right. "Fine. Although, you realise that nothing I tell you will help you get into her pants, don't you?"

"I'll be the judge of that," he argued. He couldn't help his eyes from stealing another glance at Teagan's tempting figure at the bar, downing a shot of something alcoholic.

"Okey-dokey. Well, you know Alaric and I came here yesterday to pay our respects to Mrs Harlow and the family?" Saladin nodded. "As it turned out Teagan and her sisters were here too. I hadn't seen Teagan since I got fired from Meg's a couple of months ago, and I had no idea she knew the Harlow's, but it just goes to show what a small world we live in, doesn't it?"

"Hurry up and get to something interesting," he sniped, his thinly veiled annoyance having the opposite effect on her than he had obviously intended. For a moment Cassie considered prattling for the next ten minutes about serving cold coffee and inedible food at the café, but the iridescent glitter in his eyes was a sure sign that his *good* mood was balancing on a razors edge. Who would have guessed that an eight hundred year old vampire could still feel the humiliation of rejection so keenly.

"Alright, alright. As it turns out Teagan and her sisters are druids. Their mother died giving birth to their youngest sister, Elise, and their father abandoned them to their grandfather to raise. About a year ago, their grandfather contacted Teagan and two of her sisters, twins, Paige and Kaitlyn, who'd all moved away from home. He let them know he had to go away for awhile, and he'd arranged for Oliver Harlow and his family to take Elise in while he was gone. He didn't give an explanation why, just up and disappeared. They've only heard from him twice briefly since."

"And?" Saladin prompted testily, probing for more personal details on Teagan.

"Annnd…while we were talking, Alaric asked her if she was skilled enough as a druid to create the new ward on the manor."

"So, *she's* the druid Alaric was talking about earlier?" his eyes now glued to Teagan's back, mischief dancing in his eyes. Now things were getting interesting, he thought.

"Yes. She and her sisters are going to do it together. She said her grandfather was the one we really need, but no one knows where to find him. Apparently, he's the most powerful druid in the world. I think they're descended from Merlin. *The* Merlin, can you believe it, he was a real man."

"Yeah, fascinating. What sort of things does Teagan like, music, food, books, movies?" Saladin asked, unimpressed by Cassie's fascination for the family's druidic ancestry, and annoyed by the lack of relevant information he could use to lure Teagan into his bed.

"Cassie, love." Cassie melted against Alaric's large frame as his arms came about her waist. "Are you ready to leave?" he asked in a husky voice, spearing Saladin with a warning glare to save his interrogation for another time.

Alaric had been so busy over the last few days, between Brian Harlow's death, Oliver's ascension to Alpha, Ahriman's attack, Alex's kidnapping and all the Alliance business…not to mention the fact he was still on high alert for another attack. All he wanted now was a few quiet moments alone with his *mate*.

Saladin wasn't about to object, even if it did piss him off a little. Besides, Cassie's brain wasn't the only one he wanted to pick for information, he had a whole village of people to interrogate, and he was in the perfect mood to do it.

During Ahriman's attack, Alaric had killed the mercenary who had remained behind with Ahriman. A few hours later when they returned to the gardens to retrieve his body in the hope of learning who he was, they discovered he was gone. Every single piece of him.

Everyone talked about it in hushed tones of secrecy, but the missing body had all the hallmark signs of a lycan clean-up job, which of course pointed to another traitor amongst them. Not an appealing prospect.

Saladin slapped Alaric on the shoulder, offering him a weak, but genuine smile. After all the recent dramas, Alaric and Cassie were well overdue for some *private* time together, and by the look of the direction his hands were headed, he wasn't prepared to wait any longer. Much to Cassie's delight.

"Saladin, what are the plans for this evening?" Alaric asked him.

Cassie excused herself to do the rounds and say goodbye to a few people while they talked shop.

"I have a few people to talk to here, then I have to go to the club tonight, but I'll be back before dawn. I've arranged for a couple of my people to stay for a few days, Pan and Hawke."

"I remember Hawke." The buzz-cut, ex-Marine who manned the door of his club was hard to forget. He had intimidation down to a fine art form. "Who's Pan, I don't recall seeing him."

"You wouldn't. He stays out of sight most of the time. His real name is Philippe, but everyone calls him Pan. His brother turned him when he was only thirteen. He's been thirteen for the past one hundred and fifty-six years. Don't let his stature fool you though, he is one of Dray's best spies, and he can fight like the Devil himself."

Okay. Alaric wasn't quite sure what to make of that, but he trusted Saladin and Dray's judgement. So...he'll give him a chance. With Abby in the Ukraine looking for Alex, and Narayan now back in India returning the *Cup* to its appointed Guardian, the Dalai Lama. He was grateful for any trustworthy help he could get to help protect his family.

"They'll arrive an hour or so after sundown," Saladin said. The dusky sky was moving toward a dark crimson on the horizon. The sun's blush for the day was passing quickly.

Saladin followed Alaric outside as he waited for Cassie.

"Alaric, before you go, I want to talk to you about the new ward on the manor..." he began.

With a twinge of envy, Saladin watched as Alaric swept the woman he loved into his arms, spread his wings and flew her home.

He may never know love like theirs, but returning inside the pub he set his sights on the next best thing.

Saladin stared at Teagan, intrigued as she downed the shot in her hand and pushed her glass to the bartender for refill number...whatever, she had lost count. Life was so unfair. She watched her sisters. Kaitlyn was busy batting her eyes at the wyvern Raif, while Paige was batting her eyes at several men. Even her thirteen-year old sister seemed to be fixated on Oliver's son, Callum, following him around like a love-sick puppy. Teagan groaned at the injustice of it. Her sisters were free to choose any man they wanted. But not her.

"Jeepers creepers, can't you leave me alone?" she grumbled as Saladin deposited himself on the barstool next to her.

"No, I can't. Especially since we'll be spending so much time together in the near future. I'm staying with Alaric and Cassie for a while and I've volunteered to oversee your progress with the ward on the manor. I believe we will be spending a great deal of time together over the next few weeks," he chuckled, his voice thickening. So did his petulant cock, as it began to throb at the enticing thought.

Teagan groaned softly as she banged her head against the bar in frustration. "Kill me now. Better yet, why don't you go and pick on one of my sisters? I'm sure one of them would be happy to scratch your itch, because that's all it would be to you, wouldn't it? You're the proverbial one hit wonder. Play with the new toy once, then throw it away and move onto the next one? Uhh uhh. No, thank you."

Teagan had enough on her plate without a horny vampire hot on her tail. She had a pathetic menial job, a dysfunctional family, a business course to finish and she was next in line for the family curse. It was a complicated juggle which she balanced precariously on the path to barely functional adulthood.

"Leave me alone," she growled when he continued to sit there and just stare at her, his eyes glittering with amusement. "There's not supposed to be any *fun* in funeral."

At this point she wasn't beyond using animal control techniques to keep him in line, you know, a poke in the eye, just like they suggest you do for an attacking shark. After all, wasn't that what he was? A land shark. He had the teeth for it.

Arsehole.

4

"Fred. Wilma. Back so soon?" Alex addressed Ahriman and Mira. "Oh, I see you brought Dino with you again too…complete with a new tramp stamp," he said to Lilith, indicating the dark purple blemishes on her neck. Compliments of Ahriman's strangling grip.

Lilith cast her eyes downward. Her hand lifted to her throat and pulled a lock of her blonde hair around to cover the marks.

For the first time his consistent use of trenchant canine insults toward Lilith failed to get the desired effect. That was no hickey on her neck. Trouble in the camp? Hmm. Time to change tactics, widen the rift between them, he thought with delighted enthusiasm.

Alex couldn't resist tweaking their tempers.

Ahriman's searing power flowed about him like a river, its surface calm and unbroken, but its fast flowing current beneath waited to drown the unwary. His dark eyes glowed with smothering power.

For all that power, the body which contained it was barely standing. Ahriman stood with a wad of tissues held to his nose as the earlier trickle of blood had become a torrent flowing readily, his pale face was streaked with trails of crimson, oozing from his ears and eyes, and when he smiled…Alex shuddered. His teeth were blood-red from bleeding gums.

Not a pretty sight.

"Time to become my partner in crime, Alex." Ahriman's sardonic smile sent a shiver down his spine, chilling the blood in his veins.

"What are you talking about now, snot wad?" Alex had no idea what was going on, but it wasn't good. Nothing that made the three of them happy could be good for him. "I already told you I'm not making your demon portal device, so if that's what you're here for, piss off or kill me. I. Won't. Do. It!"

Stubborn determination wasn't going to get him anywhere today he could see. In fact, it only seemed to get them more passionately enthused.

Not good. Oh, so not good.

"We have no intention of killing you, Alex," Mira put in petulantly. The sudden hammering of his heart was music to her ears. The arrogant prick was about to get the make-over of his life.

"Your determination is very quaint, but quite ineffectual. You have no choice," Lilith drawled, scornful menace backlighting her eyes.

"I always have a choice!" he asserted in a caustic rebuttal.

"Not this time pretty boy. As you can see, Ahriman's current body isn't faring very well and…."

"He needs a new one. Me," he croaked in a barely audible whisper. The world tilted on its axis and began moving at a glacial rate. Sweet Heaven's mercy. How did he get out of this one?

Alex's jaw set in a hard line of tension as he was led from his room into a wall of well armed, stony-faced guards waiting to escort him away. Their affects, so devoid of emotion Alex wondered if they hadn't all been submitted to a lobotomy or were in fact cyborgs, who'd had their humanity replaced with apathetic machine parts, since not one of them seemed capable of an original thought. Maybe they weren't android, but they were definitely adroit, and Alex was reluctant to provoke them, even in their cognitively deficient state. However, not all the guards in the compound were like these. Senior ranking guards like Mira were the exception.

It was beginning to look like the odds of escaping were hovering somewhere between pigs flying and hell freezing over, but he had to try something.

He could take the two guards nearest him and run, or he could hit the fire alarm and hope the noise distracted their teeny tiny brains long enough for him to get away.

As escape plans go, this one was pretty lame, but what other choice did he have. Sandwiched between Bill and Ted or Bing and Bong, whatever their names were, in the middle of the Conan conga-line, Alex was marched to a fate worse than death.

Alex eyed the stairwell doorway just ahead, hastily putting together an escape plan. He could take out the two on either side of him, snag their weapons, and then hope to God he could mow down the other four before they caught up to him.

"Hold that thought, pretty boy," Mira chuckled. Her icy fingers pinching the back of his neck in warning. Really. How dumb did he think they were?

With each new stairwell and corridor he was led through, he calculated all the possible avenues to freedom. Until the last dour passage came to a brusque end.

Panic seized him as that final doorway came into view, rooting his feet to the floor. Evil tainted the air, licking at his senses. Alex had always been sensitive to electromagnetic energy, and the static emanating from that room was almost enough to bring him to his knees. An acrid taste filled his mouth, bitter and sweet at the same time. He didn't know it, but it was the taste of dark magic. His heart pounded fiercely in his chest as Mira unceremoniously pushed him through the opening with acrimonious triumph.

The chamber was like every other ancient evil crypt on the planet, or so he assumed. Dark. Dusty. Smelled like the air had been filtered through a dried corpse.

A myriad of flames filled the room from wall sconces, the effect giving the room a muted glow, pulsating in time with the flames.

There, in the centre of the room was an altar, the platform raised a foot above the floor, a pair of thick columns supporting a wide, smooth slab of stone on top. Fighting the reflex to gag on the bile rising from his stomach, his heart hammered in his chest as he was pushed nearer to his fate. One step, then two.

Alex waited for the very second when the guards shifted their hold to get him onto the slab. When they did, he sprang into action. He jerked down, slammed his fist into one groin, a foot in another, then rocketed back up to head butt whoever was in his way of escape.

Their groans of pain and spurts of blood were his signal to run and his feet started moving of their own accord toward the doorway.

Only feet from escape he came to an abrupt halt, caught by an invisible hand clasped about his throat, squeezing the air from his lungs and bringing him crashing to the floor in an instant.

Turning his head around slowly, his eyes locked with Morganna. Her insipid voice mumbled an incantation, her fingers curled in the air to grip her prey. Him.

Stars hijacked his vision, then darkness closed in on him.

As Alex came to with a groan, he attempted to sit up but only managed a few inches. He was stretched out and strapped down onto the stone slab, his arms and legs held by heavy thick leather straps.

Fuck! It had been worth a try.

"Alex. What a feisty little man you are," Lilith accused, her irritating face only inches from his. "And, I do mean *little*." She waggled her little pinky finger at him with a condescending pout.

"Your flattery makes my balls twitch," he said, pushing his chin at her. "Now, fuck off."

Her upper lip curled in a snarl as she leaned in and whispered. "Your balls will do much more than twitch in my presence after your body is playing host to my *boyfriend*. You'll be having hot, steamy sex with me," she scoffed with a gleeful titter.

"I wouldn't be so sure about that, *pumpkin*," he said, imitating Ahriman's term of endearment for her, "I wouldn't do you even if I had a bucket full of disposable dicks."

That actually got Ahriman laughing, coughing and spluttering on the blood that filled his lungs.

"You and I are going to have lots of fun together, Alex," Ahriman crowed with a throaty wheeze, his pitiless eyes as cold and hard as ever as he climbed up onto the slab beside him and laid down.

"You're going to regret this, arsehole," Alex promised in defiant contempt. He tugged against his restraints once again, rattling off a string of multi-syllabic tongue twisting words that only someone who'd swallowed a dictionary and thesaurus would understand. For all anyone knew, Alex could have been spewing a load of poetic nonsensical horse twaddle. A symphony of it in fact. When those ran out he resorted to the usual colourful colloquial terms, repeatedly…in seven languages. When his well of clever facile words finally ran dry, he flipped them the bird.

"Everything is ready. Let's begin," Morganna said as her hooded form moved to stand at Ahriman's head. Her body appeared to glow faintly as she recited ancient words of power, building the tempo until the moment she plunged her dagger into the heart of Ahriman's host, Stedman.

Alex grimaced. No matter what kind of low-life arsehole Stedman had been, he didn't deserve this fate.

Reality struck hard. That was his fate too!

Alex frantically pulled against his restraints with all his strength. He didn't want this. This wasn't his fate, it couldn't be. His fate was to be with Abby.

Oh, Christ. Abby. Even with only half a bond between them, losing him would destroy her.

Alex couldn't let this happen. A silent howl of fury ripped through his soul.

Lilith took an instinctive step backwards, warily watching the shimmering form of Ahriman hovering over the altar, directly above what was left of Stedman's body, and moving slowly toward Alex.

Morganna lifted her hands, a slow malevolent smile curling her lips. "You might want to brace yourself," she chuckled.

That was the only warning Alex had before the spell she was casting slammed into him. Bowing his body until he thought his spine would snap in two. His whole body jack-knifed as pain shot through him. His limbs convulsing out of control, his head banging against the stone beneath him. Wave upon wave of searing pain ravaged through him, hammering through his skull. Powerful shocks burning his limbs, right down to his fingers and toes.

It felt as if he was being scorched from the inside out.

White spots floated in front of his eyes and darkness surrounded him, sucking him into a spinning vortex of oblivion.

Ever so slowly, voices filtered through his mind as Alex came to in a fog once again. He seemed to be making a habit of this, he thought apathetically.

Sensation moved through every cell in his body, pulsed, ached.

He blinked back the terrible light that assaulted his sensitive eyes. It was like viewing the world through a blazing kaleidoscope of colour, and it was as painful as all hell.

Everything was shaken up, loose, even his skin felt disconnected from his bones and muscles.

His first attempt to lift his head was an epic failure. He might as well have been trying to lift a bowling ball with a rubber band, the effort causing a pain that pierced his brain, making him wish he was still out cold. At least his eyes worked, he thought, rolling his neck to examine his surroundings.

Why was his head moving in the opposite direction of where he wanted it to go? Why were his legs moving without his instruction? And, that voice inside his head, what was it saying?

A cold sweat appeared on his overheated brow, his muscles wouldn't respond to his commands even though he pulled every ounce of mental strength together to make his body move, move, *move!*

It was to no avail.

It was like being born again inside a frame he didn't recognise, couldn't escape from and couldn't control.

Ahriman's sadistic chuckle echoed inside his head.

Oh, crap. He was royally fucked.

5

Abby came awake with a shock, her heart palpitating hard enough to drill a hole through her chest wall.

"Liddle lady, you okay?" Klaus asked as he patted her cheeks gently.

Abby sat bolt upright in an instant, her eyes darting about to get her bearings. She often woke not knowing where she was, the feeling of disorientation always managed to set her off kilter for a minute or two. It was an annoying legacy of her previous life on the streets.

"What happened?" she asked him, a feeling of anger and pain lingered in her body like a phantom's touch, creeping along her nerve endings all the way to her bones.

Klaus sat back cautiously, watching her carefully. "Dat's what I want to know. You were yelling in your sleep. You okay?" he asked again, concern in his voice.

"Yes. Ah, no. I don't know…Give me a minute," she answered as she ran her hands through her short hair several times, her mind sifting through her own haunting memories from sleep and the reality which now surrounded her. What was real?

That feeling of pain remained. It wasn't fading like dreams normally do. This was deeper, stronger, although at the same time it felt like an echo. A pain so intense it set her teeth on edge.

Abby opened herself to her gift and searched for the mind that was torturing her. It wasn't Sebastian, nor Klaus or his brother Dieter, who still lay unconscious in the next room.

"I've got to go," she burst out in panic.

Klaus moved to block the doorway. "No, liddle lady. You can't go now," he admonished, glowering down at her with his arms crossed, his bulky frame blocking the doorway not giving her an inch of room to get past.

"Let me pass you big oaf before I break your knee caps. You don't understand, I have to go. Now!" she berated. "It's Alex's pain I'm feeling," she tried desperately to explain, appealing to Klaus' compassion, unsuccessfully. "Something has happened to him. I have to go. *Let me go!*" Her voice rose and octave in frustration. "I have a silver dagger and I'll use it if I have to," she promised, her emotion barometer oscillating between panic to pissed off.

"No. You go out dat door and you die." Klaus was a crusty, cantankerous beast. For all the gruffness in his voice though, his eyes were gentle, sympathetic. He too had lost someone he loved. It seemed his brother was still lost to him even though he lay in the next room. The Guild had done something to him too. His mind was gone. He had become a highly functioning killing robot, with no thoughts or feelings.

"Just watch me."

"You can try to kill me if you like, liddle lady, but you still die. It's midday, not midnight."

"What?" How was that possible? She shouldn't be awake for another five hours. Regardless, she had to leave now. Alex needed her. She couldn't wait around until sunset, she would go insane.

Scratch that. She was already going insane. Abby knew how irrational she was behaving, but she couldn't help herself. Not even when her parents institutionalised her after her grandmother died, did she feel this unstable. Living inside that place, mentally bombarded twenty-four hours a day by a multitude of minds who truly were crazy, only strengthened her resolve to escape the human world that was so painful to her. Abby thought living on the streets was the answer to her prayers, as she discovered though, it was becoming a vampire that had finally freed her of what she had believed to be her curse. For the first time ever, she could block out or dim down the endless barrage of thoughts in her head.

Right now, she wished her gift was even stronger. Strong enough to reach Alex in the compound several miles away. She thought being separated from him was frightening enough, but the thought of losing him altogether had her perched on the edge of sanity. One little nudge and she would be lost into that dark abyss too, just like all those poor souls at Dorland House.

"I help you get him, but not til dark, okay?" Klaus told her.

Abby gave a slight nod. Despite her determination to regain her composure, her obstinate emotion barometer swung again. Abby quickly sniffed back tears threatening to escape her clouded eyes.

Klaus moved away from the door when he was sure she wouldn't try to make a run for it. She would be no good to anyone as a pile of dust.

He sat on one end of the bed and motioned for her to sit beside him. Slowly, in his broken English he filled Abby in on what they had learnt in the few hours she had been sleeping and of their plan to get her inside the compound.

Sebastian had informed Gustav of what they had discovered and the situation with the guards. Another team was on their way to hunter's cottage, some would stay with them, others would retrieve Dieter and return him to their headquarters. With any luck they would find out what was done to him and fix him, although Abby wasn't holding her breath on that.

Time dragged through the afternoon. She tried to sleep some more but found it impossible, she was just too worked-up, at least the pain she felt from Alex had subsided. Instead, she called Alaric. Not surprisingly he had already been informed of the situation via the Alliance phone tree. While he couldn't be of direct help, it was comforting just to hear a familiar voice.

Abby's bag was packed by the door just waiting for the moment she could leave. She paced anxiously back and forth through the main room of the cottage, her eyes firmly glued to her bag as though it might suddenly grow legs and leave without her if she so much as took her eyes off it for a second.

"How much sunlight can you tolerate?" Sebastian asked her as he calmly whittled a piece of wood he had rescued from the fireplace, into a fine point.

"Huh? Oh, um, I don't really know. I've only been in the sun for a few minutes once before," she replied distractedly. "Why?"

39

"It's an hour to sundown, if you're willing to test your endurance, we could leave now."

The hope that suddenly lit up Abby's face, sent a twinge of sadness through him. He envied her. To have someone in his life who meant as much to him as Alex did to her, it would be a gift from God himself. He even envied the distress she felt. He had nothing, no one in his life who he cared for or who cared for him. He had been alone since the day he became a vampire at the age of twenty-six, two hundred and thirty years ago. But, today for the first time, he truly felt lonely.

The guards listened warily from the hallway outside the lab as Ahriman appeared to have a conversation with his new host.

"You're just the talented visionary my project has been looking for," Ahriman proudly boasted to Alex, pleased with the timely procurement of his new host.

Alex saw what Ahriman was studying. The device wasn't terribly big, maybe the size of a small television set with a bunch of platinum-iridium wires, electron tubes and coils scattered about the work bench and the kind of equipment he had only ever dreamt of using. He doubted there was another facility in the world that had this much high-tech equipment to play with.

Accelerators, spectrometers, free electron laser, photo electric vacuum cells, heating chambers and a computer system impressive enough to give even him some serious wood in the hideous trousers Ahriman had dressed him in.

Of course, Ahriman's excitement that he now had the knowledge to use all this equipment killed Alex's buzz stone-cold.

It felt bizarre, not only to be sharing his body with another person, but also his thoughts, emotions, knowledge and his memories.

All of which was against his will.

He had never been so exposed and so hidden at the same time. He was a prisoner inside his own body. That sharing went both ways though, to an extent. Alex had access to Ahriman's thoughts and emotions, although he had no access to his memories. He could however, feel the protective barrier encasing them like a steel strong box.

Alex pushed against that barrier a little harder, putting all his mental fortitude behind it. He had to know what happened to Cassie. Was she really dead or had Ahriman been bluffing? If he could access his memories…

"Ah, Fuck!" Alex reeled from the sudden stabbing pain in his mind.

Ahriman chuckled. "If you want to know what happened to your sister, you only need to ask."

Opening up the pathway into his memory, Ahriman let Alex watch as Cassie was swallowed by a poisonous mist, suffocating the life from her, and felt every bit of Alaric's pain and grief as he fought to break the barrier that contained her.

So, it was true, the bastard killed her. Pain and loss ripped through him, creating an open wound Alex was sure his parasitic nemesis would take full advantage of.

"You're a sick fuck, you know that?" Alex was working himself up for another verbal tirade so toxic it would peel the lining from his colon as he redirected his pain into hatred.

"Save your slander," Ahriman drawled. He had heard it before and as much as he enjoyed tormenting Alex, he didn't have the time. He had a deadline to finish the portal device and time was running out, not to mention his energy.

Unlike his possession of Stedman whose body began to decay from the moment he became his host, Alex's body only felt fatigued, a lethargy that was bone deep and continued to slowly decline.

"Your sister isn't dead, *now*. It seems that somehow her immortality gene was activated before she died," he divulged begrudgingly. He assumed that if he gave Alex that last tidbit, it would appease him enough to get some peace and quiet for a short while.

He assumed wrong.

Bereavement turned to relief and coalesced with antagonistic rage, and the tirade Alex had been building up to a minute earlier, turned into a deluge. Ahriman truly was an evil, sick fucker. Alex could feel the enjoyment that his pain and loss gave him. It was like a drug to him, his very soul fed on the misery he caused in others.

"Shut up, for one minute," Ahriman roared.

The guards weren't the only ones watching Ahriman warily as he paced, ranted and fumed, pulling at his own hair in frustration as his argument with Alex escalated.

"Ahh hmm."

"What?" Ahriman bellowed.

"Sir? I have the research papers you asked for. Would I be right to assume you're suggesting we attempt a spectrum shift?" Dr Leon Greenville asked nervously. Expecting retaliation for his interruption he hovered near the door and the relative safety of the guards. It was a false sense of security, he knew. The guards would sooner remove his head if Ahriman commanded it, than protect him. But right now they were the lesser of two evils.

Ahriman cursed under his breath as he tried to rein in his temper, refocussing on the more important task at hand. "I'm suggesting going beyond the light spectrum, below the infra-red. We need a quantum casket laser or a gyrotron."

"That's impossible. There's not enough time to get one here."

"Well then, we're just going to have to build one," he sniped sarcastically.

"But I thought the aim was to reverse the magnetic polarity to bring down the veil."

"It is, but there is more than one layer to the veil, we also need a synchotronic light source."

"That's going to take a hell of a lot more power to make the device work than we've got access to."

"Let me worry about that. Get back to work," he snapped.

Dr Greenville turned away from him but didn't move.

"Is there a problem, Dr Greenville?"

"No. No problem, Sir. But, I believe Mira is here to speak with you," he gulped, quickly side stepping the woman in front of him, who was sizing him up for her next meal, like he was the juiciest lamb chop in the farm yard.

Ahriman's lip peeled back in an angry snarl. More God-damned interruptions. Wasn't there one imbecile in this facility who could solve a problem by themselves?

His head was beginning to ache from fatigue, and Alex's non-stop rhetoric chatter in his brain.

Mira approached him as her comm-link beeped.

"We have movement outside the compound," the guard reported.

"How many?" Mira replied.

"Only one. And, they're heading straight for the gates. Were you expecting anyone?" he asked her.

"No. The compound is in lockdown." Mira's voice was angry. "Bring him in and send out a patrol. Make sure he doesn't have any friends out there with him."

"I believe it's a *her*, not a *him*," the guard told her.

"What? Are you sure?" The guard took a second look at the console in front of him. It was definitely showing a female life presence, not male. And a vampire to boot, he reported.

Intriguing. An unaccompanied female vampire out here? Could it possibly be...? If she was right, things around here were about to become very interesting.

"Bring her in. I'll deal with her myself," Mira snapped.

"We're on it," the guard confirmed.

"No, you won't," Ahriman told her, his callous tone like a razor through the air. "Take her to my rooms."

"I don't think that is advisable, Sir. I'll take her to one of the cells and interrogate her myself. If she's got any subversive plans, I'll make sure she tells me all the details," she suggested eagerly.

"No, you won't," Ahriman repeated slowly as if speaking to a child. His low tone and merciless stare left no room for compromise.

Mira pushed the issue impetuously. "Sir, we don't know who she is or why she's here. Considering you are still in a human body and she is a vampire, I don't think it is a viable risk to be alone with her."

"I know who she is, and why she is here, and I can assure you I am in no danger. Take her to my rooms and do not question my orders again. Do you understand me?" he hissed at her through clenched teeth.

Mira stood her ground for a moment longer, eyeballing him. The defiance took more effort than she let on. Alex's body may be weak, but his immortality gene was certainly compatible with Ahriman's higher vibration, giving him a new edge to his power. It coursed through the air in waves of heated electricity, causing every hair on her body to stand at rigid attention.

"Yes, sir." Turning on her heel, she swiftly left the lab, rubbing at her arms to relieve the feeling of ants crawling over them. The electrical charge he seemed to emit wasn't a reassuring development. It was disturbing and a timely reminder to stay on his good side.

Mira was never one to follow orders blindly, nevertheless for now she would do just that, or at least she would let it appear that way.

She was almost one hundred per cent certain that their visitor was Alaric's progeny, Abby. If so, she had a score to settle.

"What the hell are you up to?" Alex demanded.

"Alex, you're a fountain of information, did you know that? If you're right and it's your *mate* here to rescue you, and I suspect you are, then I intend to play a little game," he answered maliciously. "Let's see how long it takes her to work out that I'm not you, shall we?"

"You fucking bastard. If you so much as touch one hair on her head, I'll kill you." Just as soon as he could get him out of his body, he thought.

"My dear boy, the only way to get me out of your body is for *you* to die." That condescending drawl was really beginning to irritate Alex, although not nearly as much as no longer having a single thought or feeling of his own. That, really, really pissed him off.

Abby dropped her bag on the ground at the front gate of the compound as two guards came out. The sun had now dipped well below the tree line, stretching the twilight shadows into darkness. She and Sebastian had travelled at top speed for the last half hour, covering the last mile on her own. Her skin still prickled and itched from the pressure inside her veins. Fortunately, the burning heat was now beginning to recede. Being exposed to sunlight wasn't the most unpleasant of experiences but certainly not one she wanted to repeat too often. It was worth it though to finally be standing at the threshold of the Guild's compound.

It appeared that Klaus' bold plan was going to work. He theorised that the guards would show no sign of aggression towards her unless she herself became aggressive. So far, so good, Abby thought as a guard picked up her bag and calmly escorted her through the main gates towards the run-down building, passing another half dozen guards leaving to patrol the surrounding forest.

With any luck, they had no idea there was twice the number of men waiting for them in the forest, not to kill them, but capture them. It stood to reason that Dieter wasn't the only mercenary inside the compound who was there against his will. Gustav had lost several men out here, and who was to say more hadn't been taken from other areas too.

It was a risky tactic capturing the guards, they had no way to know how many more guards the compound held. It could be like stirring up a hornet's nest, steal back a few of the hives drones only to have the whole colony of angry hornets swarming after them. What other choice did they have? Most of these men probably didn't ask to be here any more than Alex did.

Crossing the threshold Abby shivered, a nervous reaction.

The building's interior was dank, mildewed, reeked of mouldy furniture and droppings from various small animals who had claimed the space as their own. Plaster crumbled and floorboards creaked with rot. Tattered sheets of wallpaper coated the walls in equal parts grime and despair.

The deeper into the building she got the less derelict it became, ending at a shiny stainless-steel elevator door, in what she assumed to be the centre of the building.

Before the doors even opened, Abby's hackles raised themselves on the back of her neck. The elevator's occupant projected a cunning intelligence and sadistic hunger that made her skin crawl.

Abby discretely adjusted her leather pants. The satellite phone in her back pack would be confiscated, that was to be expected. But, with any luck the micro version hidden in the gusset of her panties would go undetected. But geez, it was uncomfortable.

As the elevator door slid open, Mira practically purred with satisfaction.

"Abby. So nice to see you again," Mira greeted with artificial friendliness.

"Can't say the same," Abby disagreed. She was still irrationally fixated. Nothing was going to calm her down until she saw Alex with her own eyes, felt him with her own hands. "What have you done with Alex?"

"Straight to the point. I like that," Mira replied, her lips curving into a smug grin. Her eyes however, remained as cold as two chips of black ice. "Alex is still intact, I assure you. In fact, I believe he is waiting to see you," she sniggered, as the guards ushered her into the elevator. Their large bodies filling the remaining area, bringing the two women almost nose to nose in the confined space.

The elevator stopped at sub-basement three. Butterflies tied her stomach into a tight knot and her heart pounded in her ears.

What condition was he in? Would he be happy to see her? And, the biggest question on her mind, the one that was turning her into a jittery mess and had shut down the higher levels of thinking in her brain...

Would he want to complete the blood bond with her?

After all, they never had the opportunity to discuss the subject before he was kidnapped. What if he didn't want her?

You picked a bad time to get cold feet and start second guessing things, she scolded herself.

As they approached a door guarded by two men, Abby drew in and held her breath. Alex was on the other side of that door, she could feel it.

Her nervousness turned to excitement as the door swung open.

"Alex!"

6

The waves in his thick, jet-black hair framed the strong contours of his features as he raked it back with careless fingers, falling lazily against his high cheekbones. His full lips stretched into a welcoming smile. He had sinfully kissable lips, making her mouth water. His chocolate brown eyes with their enviously long black lashes, locked onto hers.

Ahriman was nothing if not cruel.

Excessively, spectacularly cruel.

The thought whispered through his mind with delight as his eyes skimmed the length of Abby's succulent body. Long shapely legs, small waist and pert full breasts pressed hard against her stretchy top, all covering what he assumed would be deliciously soft smooth skin.

She was ripe enough to pluck.

His ebony brows slammed down over eyes that darkened dangerously. Riveted by curiosity at the mere sight of her, he watched as she closed the distance between them.

Curiously, every step closer she came, his body began to feel different, regain energy.

Abby's mind raced with excitement and relief. The only coherent thought was to get to him as quickly as possible, wrap her arms around him and hold on for eternity. Never let him go.

Coming toe to toe however, she stopped as he looked down at her, his expression was a curious mix of hunger and something else that Abby didn't understand. A cautious twinge crept into the back of her mind. She would not have survived on the streets for so long if she had taken everything at face value. Dangers lurked around every corner just waiting to catch the unwary. Even in her excitement induced fuddled mind, she was aware she was in enemy territory. Why had they taken her to Alex so easily, without interrogation?

"Run. Abby, get out. Run!" Alex yelled. She couldn't hear him. Somehow Ahriman's presence in his body blocked her from hearing him.

"Fuck. Fuck. Fuck."

Ahriman snickered contemptuously in his mind.

"Alex? Are you okay? What did they do to you? You were in pain this morning, I felt it," she blurted in a rush.

The concern in her eyes was very touching. Pity it was wasted on the one person who couldn't give a damn.

"Abby. Don't worry about it. It was nothing. I'm fine, see?" Ahriman answered calmly, a gentle smile alighting his face.

"Run! Abby, run!" Alex screamed again. Why did he even bother trying? In the hope of finding a chink in the demon parasite's armour, that's why, he reminded himself.

Alex mentally paced inside his mind. He had the IQ of a genius, he *could* think of a way to save Abby. He had to.

Taking Abby's hands in his, Ahriman smoothed his thumbs over the backs of her cold fingers, still half frozen from her brisk run through the wintry forest. The moment their hands touched, his body jerked from a sudden injection of energy. It was like being plugged into a live power socket, an exhilarating charge, setting fire to every cell in his body, not only making his hair stand erect, but also the flag pole between his legs.

"Alex. What's happened? I can't hear your thoughts."

"It's nothing. I'll be fine. They did a couple of experiments on me because of my immortality gene, that's all. I promise I'll be fine."

"But, I can't hear your thoughts. Can you hear mine?" Her pretty brow furrowed delicately on the question. Her hand lifted to touch his face gently, lovingly.

"Don't worry about it. I'm sure it's just temporary," he reassured her. "Why did you come after me? It's too dangerous out here by yourself. I'm not worth the risk."

"Alex. You're my *mate*. I wasn't going to let you die."

"Did you come alone?"

"Sort of. I had a couple of guides who brought me here, but they've gone back now," she lied. If she couldn't communicate directly with Alex's mind, she wasn't about to tell the truth out loud and expose the team in the forest. Alex was a prisoner here and now so was she, which meant the room was probably bugged.

"Is Alaric coming to get us out?"

"Yes. If they don't hear from me in a couple of days, he'll be coming." That, was not a total lie. There were no firm plans in place as yet for Alaric or anyone else to swarm the place, although she did need to either get herself and Alex out within the next forty-eight hours, or at the very least contact them by then, or they would make plans to rescue them.

"Wait up. What do you mean…die?" Ahriman asked, as it occurred to him that she may not have meant *'die at the hands of the enemy'*.

"The blood bond," she answered a little sheepishly, a slight blush colouring her pixy-like face and her eyes dipping with embarrassment. "I know we didn't have time to discuss this before you were kidnapped, but I knew if I didn't find you quickly you would probably have died."

"What exactly do you mean?" he asked again, this time picking through Alex's brain at the same time for answers. "I need to take your blood to complete the bond, is that it?"

"Yes," she said, the colour in her cheeks deepening.

"What would happen if we don't complete the bond?"

"You would die," she replied tightly, her throat barely able to let enough air pass to voice the necessary words.

"And, how often would I need to take your blood?" he asked her, taking her hands in his once again, his cold mind calculating the consequences of such a move.

"Every day," she lied once again. At this rate she would need to change her name to Pinocchio. The blood bond itself only needed to be completed once, but it was her intention to give Alex every opportunity to survive his kidnapping, no matter what happens. If, for any reason he should die before they could escape, with her blood in his body, death would not be the end for him. He would become a vampire too.

Maybe she was being presumptuous in assuming Alex would want to become a vampire like her, but in her heart she knew that given the option between being dead and undead, he would choose the latter. Once again though, she couldn't afford to discuss the matter out loud with him until she was sure they weren't being watched or overheard.

"Don't even think about it, mother fucker. Send her away. I don't care if I die. You can find yourself another host, but don't you dare touch her," Alex threatened heatedly.

Well. Wasn't this an interesting turn of events. Ahriman had expected to torment Alex by manipulating his woman into his bed, maybe a bit of physical torture…Now, how much misery would it cause Alex, if he completed the bond knowing that she would need to give her body to him every day, even after she discovered the truth. Oh, this was good.

Abby began chatting, idle gossip from back at the manor, blah, blah, blah. Useless twaddle he had no interest in.

Ahriman's plans with Abby did not include talking.

It was time that Alex learned his place. And, that place was cowering away in a distant corner of his mind, silently.

Tentatively, he leaned down and kissed her, but she hesitated to kiss him back. His hands moved to her waist, then to her taut backside. He swiped his tongue over her bottom lip as he pulled her closer, lifting her hips until he could grind the heat of her mound against his erection, making her gasp and open to him. Instantly, he penetrated her mouth, the hot, wet slide of his tongue against hers demanding her reciprocation.

A slow burn heated the blood in her veins, loosened her up so that when he dragged his lips along her jawbone and down her neck, she threw her head back and thawed completely.

Abby found it hard to concentrate. To try to dampen down her nerves, she smoothed her fingers over his broad shoulders and along his strong sinewy biceps. His muscles tensed beneath her touch.

Violence throbbed through Alex's mind, along with the unwanted heat of arousal she always triggered in him. Ahriman was using his bond with Abby against him.

Alex felt every touch, every heated pass of their tongues together. He could taste her and sense the essence of her innocent soul and howled with fury.

What manner of creature could have spawned a demon as evil as Ahriman.

Ahriman called her name. "Abigail." His voice, a sensual purr against her skin which rumbled through the weakest parts of her. The parts that were aching for his touch.

She swallowed, ignoring the nagging feeling that something wasn't right. This was Alex, her *mate*. The only thing wrong was their current predicament, being held hostage in the Guild complex. It was messing with her senses.

Abby thought her heart might burst from her chest it pounded so fiercely. His lips seduced hers, first gently, then hungrily, speeding her pulse further. Fire danced through her as his thumbs stroked the sides of her breasts, straying ever closer to the sensitive peaks. Heat blossomed within her, as did fear. She was inexperienced, and the intensity of his advances were a little overwhelming.

As a freak and an outcast in human society, Abby had only ever been kissed once in her life, an experience which had set her on a path to isolate herself from the world which taunted her, tormented her. Survival had been her focus. The idea of sex had never crossed her mind, not until she met Alex.

Alex was open and honest, and he loved her, and he accepted her for who she was, warts and all.

Abby closed her eyes and tried to control the tremble rippling through her body, as he expertly stripped away the layers of their clothing, admiring the visual display before him. There was satisfaction in his eyes, but they lacked the warmth that she had expected.

What exactly had they done to him?

Where was the hungry need that had always burned in his eyes when he looked at her? Where was the caressing touch that made her melt into a hormonal puddle of desire?

"Alex, what the hell is wrong with you? Alex? Please, stop. Don't do this," she begged. She wasn't comfortable with this, not at all. The words fell from her in soft, short, breathless bursts, confusion filled her voice. "I'm not ready. I need a bit more time. We can complete the bond without sex," she begged again, attempting to back away from him.

"I think you are." To illustrate his argument he lifted his hand, his thumb skimming over the taut thrust of her clearly aroused nipple. Abby practically melted under his touch, her body arching into his of its own accord. A barely audible groan of pleasure escaping her lips as his hand moved to cup her full breast in his hot palm.

Ahriman was going destroy to Abby's innocence and there wasn't a damn thing Alex could do to stop it. Despite her age, she was innocent, shy and timid in her interactions with others, and completely unprepared for what Ahriman had in mind. He was the one who should be touching her, kissing her and exploring the depths of her body, but not like this. Never like this.

He couldn't even warn her. Ahriman's occupation of his body blocked Abby's telepathic abilities. He was totally cut off from her. Shame and fury lashed him to his soul.

"Stop this, you fucking bastard!" Alex screamed. He raged on with no effect. Ahriman wasn't listening. He was having too much fun. Oh, he knew Abby was a virgin, he read that straight from Alex's mind. That was what made his whole game all the more enjoyable. Her enemy was taking her virginity, not her *Mate*.

Alex felt his heart clench at the emotion in her gaze, a loving swoon that she meant for him. He felt her body tremble at his touch, could feel her need for him. But it wasn't *him* who was holding her.

He could not protect her, could not save her from the misery he knew was coming, the shame he knew she would feel when she learned the truth.

Alex was furious with Ahriman, with himself and with Abby. Ahriman for his cruelty, himself for his weakness, and Abby for her blind belief in him.

Ahriman guided her to the bed, laying her down, coming over her like the stealthy predator he was.

Ahriman tightened his grip on her, nestling himself in the V of her thighs, pinning her beneath him. With purposeful movement he slid the length of his steel hard erection intimately through the slick folds of her arousal, making her gasp as he rubbed over her sensitised clit.

Abby felt a slight tingle in his touch and a jolt of electricity pulse through her body, flaring the slow burn deep in the core of her body into a blazing inferno of need.

Instantly her hips reciprocated the grinding movement, the moist cap of his heavy length sliding closer to the entrance to that glorious channel, promising a haven inside her tight confines and a need for fulfilment he couldn't explain.

"Wait." Her breathy voice barely registered in his lust filled mind. He was so ready to take her, just one more slide through her heated folds and he'd thrust himself home.

"Wait," she repeated. "We have to finish our blood bond. If you don't take my blood and we're separated again…" she couldn't finish the thought, the fear and desperation she had felt over the past few days was something she couldn't bear to live through again.

Ahriman forced himself to still his motion against her, the loss of sensation eliciting a groan of disappointment.

He had to admit, from the moment she entered the room, his new body had regained its energy, he had felt more alive and every nerve hummed with the need to become a part of her. Should he complete the blood bond? How much stronger would he become with her vampire blood in his body?

Alex screamed all manner of obscenities at him. He would rather die than have Abby tied to him now. Tied to them both.

If he could send Abby away, he would die, he knew he would. If not from the physical effects of the unfulfilled bond, then from a broken heart. But it would save Abby from the agony he knew she would feel when she discovered she had bonded herself to a demon.

"Yes," Ahriman replied. He would complete the blood bond.

Abby made a cut with a finger nail just above her right nipple. "Now," she encouraged when she saw him hesitating for one last moment.

A fragment of her mind fought the tangle of physical sensations, her subconscious trying to tell her something important. But all coherent thought had abandoned her on the surge of primal need.

"No. Don't do this. Please, I'm begging you. Please, No!"

Ahriman's tongue snaked out and licked at the bead of blood trickling down her breast. The moment her sweet nectar touched his tongue he shuddered with pure delight. His hungry mouth latched onto her breast and sucked for all he was worth as the bond between Alex and Abby exploded through him. Emotions he had been so long denied swamped him now. His chest tightened, an all-consuming rage of need sent sensual daggers of erotic sensation through his body.

53

Pure driving need, sharper, more intense than anything he had ever known, took over his body with primal urgency.

With no prior warning, Ahriman plunged himself deep into her core in one powerful stroke. Entering her was exquisite, pure adrenaline. Untamed. Raw. It was a free fall of sensation, demolishing coherent thought.

Abby gasped as his thrust broke through her virginal barrier. A twinge of pain, followed by the most incredible pleasure.

It was unlike anything she had ever experienced. She could feel him pushing the tender muscles apart, stroking the delicate tissue, and sending almost unbearable pleasure whipping through her body.

She held onto him as he continued to suck on her breast.

Their combined cries echoed about them as he thrust inside her to the hilt. One long, smooth stroke into the very heart of her as her muscles parted, then clenched down on his shaft like a velvet fist. Control became a fragmented idea as her heated silk enveloped him. He held her hips, steadying her, holding her in place as he began to pound inside her.

Gasping cries rippled through his chest as his hard length throbbed and pulsed. Her powerful legs tightened about his waist locking him inside her, clear to her soul.

As he raised his head from her breast, he shifted his body over her more fully, her fangs scraping over the soft flesh of his neck as the pressure began to build inside her, the pleasure coalescing, tightening with every desperate lunge of his steely erection into her snug depths.

He had never known such sensations in his life. A pleasure that tore through his body, his soul, wrapping him in warmth and in peace, despite the agonising need for release.

Abby experienced every sensation, every emotion in Alex, her *mate*, as he filled her, catapulting their bond to a whole new level of intimacy, but still his thoughts were silent to her. She arched into him further, meeting his rhythm, trying to take more of him with every thrust until the world dissolved around her.

Primal need engulfed her.

As her fangs sank into flesh, pleasure swamped her with a fever so intense it blistered her skin and set a fire burning from the inside out. Her climax swept her away on a torrential tide of ecstasy.

The inner muscles of her tight channel clenched around him, tight rippling caresses washing over his thick length as he worked it into her, fucking her with uncontrolled pounding lunges, all the strength and desperation of his hunger surging through him.

"Abby." He howled her name as he exploded, coming inside her with hot, vicious jerks of his shaft. Her fangs deep in his vein intensified the orgasm tenfold and he emptied himself inside her in what seemed like an endless orgasm.

Locked inside his prison, Alex cried silent tears. He had failed her. He had failed his *mate*.

Rolling off her, Ahriman chuckled and waited until he had her full attention. There wasn't going to be any loving postcoital caresses or cuddles today.

Not ever.

His eyes flashed, evil chips of ice.

Ahriman watched her eyes widen. Saw the surprise that filled her expression.

"What the hell?"

On a burst of adrenaline Abby leapt from the bed, pacing on the spot as she stared lamely at Alex in disbelief. Her heart raced even as it sank into the pit of her stomach.

Slowly, Ahriman followed her from the bed.

Swallowing hard, she looked up as he towered over her. She dropped her eyes to his manhood which was already hardening for her once again.

He placed his index finger under her chin, tipping her head to meet his cold sadistic gaze. Abby reeled from what had just happened, from what she saw in his eyes now.

There was cunning intelligence in his eyes, a vicious hunger in his glare as it slid slowly down her slender body.

"Alex? What's going on?" As hard as Abby tried, her mind couldn't process what was happening. This was Alex, her *mate*. She could feel her connection to him, but the man speaking to her, looking out through his eyes was definitely not Alex.

Casually, he straightened to his full height and crossed his arms over his chest, staring down at her in lofty amusement. One corner of his lush mouth tilted into the cockiest grin she had ever seen. A half-smile of superiority and arrogance.

"Well pumpkin, it's like this…I'm not Alex. My last body wore out and Alex very kindly offered me his."

Her eyes widened. "Ahriman?" The word was barely more than a strangled whisper.

Ahriman watched as the wheel of emotions spun in her mind and featured on her pretty face. Shame? Astonishment? Desperation? *Click! Click! Click!* Ah. There it was. Horror. Ahriman chuckled with delight.

"Yes, in the flesh," he chuckled again, impressed by his own pun. "But don't fret about your *mate*, he's still in here, but he's just a spectator now, and I can tell you, he enjoyed the little show you just gave, almost as much as I did."

"You bastard!" Abby narrowed her eyes on him with soul sucking, ball shriveling hatred and contempt, her chest blooming with pain.

Alex continued his relentless tirade of venomous curses at Ahriman as Abby hurriedly dressed and ran from the room into the wall of guards waiting to escort her to Alex's old cell.

Pain, anger, fear and unadulterated hatred poured from Alex, which unfortunately only served to fuel Ahriman's enjoyment.

Alex fell silent, the suddenness took Ahriman off guard, although he could still feel his seething anger rolling through him. Ahriman waited a moment, then another, waiting for Alex's next caustic, useless threat.

"I will make you suffer, every moment of every day that you're in my body," Alex promised with calm resolution. *"Payback's a bitch."*

Ahriman laughed. "You have no power to do anything to me."

"Free will is a primal power. You may have power over my body but not my mind, I still have free will and I promise you, you'll regret ever setting foot in this world by the time I'm through with you, arsehole."

Alex had spent the best part of the last two months with Narayan, a Tibetan vampiric Buddhist monk, who had a penchant for philosophical sayings. One that sprang to mind at that moment was: *'The happiness of your life depends on the quality of your thoughts'*. If he only had his thoughts at his disposal at the moment, he was going to make sure every

56

one of them tormented Ahriman until he fell into the abyss of insanity. Maybe then he could reclaim his body and find a way to expel Ahriman's parasitic soul.

"Game on, cocknut!" Alex's hostility now had somewhere to go, he thought with satisfaction.

Alex desperately wanted to pull Abby into his arms, to nuzzle her soft body against him, comfort her and tell her everything would be okay, that he would make it right. But, he couldn't get so much as a single finger to move at his command.

Then again…who was it who called Abby's name when he came so explosively inside her?

It was *him*, not Ahriman. *He* had been the one. At that moment Ahriman had retreated into himself to a small degree. And, Alex knew why.

Ahriman took a shuddering breath as he stood alone in his bedroom, his control over Stedman had been total, but Stedman never had even half the determination that Alex had. Not to mention, Alex was born with the genetic make-up of a fighter, combined with his immortality gene, although dormant, made him even stronger.

The intensity of Alex's wrath had thrown him off his game and rattled him. But that on its own was nothing compared to the shock he felt from Alex's blood bond with Abby. Ahriman swallowed hard.

From the moment he tasted her blood, he felt as though he had no more control of Alex's body than Alex did. The soul deep connection between them was so strong, so overwhelming to his senses, it felt as though his own soul was being ripped apart from the intensity. Ahriman shuddered. The thought that he had to endure their bonding daily to keep his new body from failing, terrified him.

He couldn't help the feeling that he was chained to a slow moving train wreck. One he had no control over, he could only stare and wait for it to happen.

Too late now. What's done is done.

It would be better to keep his focus on his main objective. The portal device. As soon as he could get that finished he would happily sacrifice Alex and return to the Underworld, if for no other reason than to be free of Alex and Abby's bond.

It didn't matter that Alex had promised to make his life hell. Whatever Alex could do, he could do better. He'd had thousands of years more experience.

Right now however, he was too rattled to return to the lab, he needed something soothing to calm down, or at least numb all the frazzled nerve endings that continued to zing from the newly formed blood bond.

Grabbing a glass and decanter of scotch from the bar he poured himself almost a full glass, no ice. Slammed it back, then poured himself another. By the time he finished the second, the block of ice that was currently doubling for his stomach had begun to thaw as his mind flipped the reality switch into denial.

Alex was not going to get the better of him. *Denial.*

He could survive their blood bond. *Denial.*

He could complete the portal device on time. *Maybe.*

7

Teagan walked at a sedate pace along the lengthy driveway. Its distance was so protracted, she was beginning to wonder if she had accidentally taken a wrong turn down one of the unmarked roads so famous in this part of the countryside for their anonymity. Yet, she had never seen a road maintained as immaculately as this avenue of huge old-growth oak trees which she was now passing under. Their thick limbs rippled outward in twisted sprays, interlocking with one another in a magnanimous canopy of bare wintry branches above. Below, at their base grew an equally impressive and impenetrable avenue of azalea bushes with their new buds just beginning to form, readying for next spring's blush of colour.

Teagan gasped in awe as she rounded a bend in the driveway, opening up to a large circular area, with a three tiered fountain in the centre and the most magnificent house, or more correctly, palace sized mansion she had ever seen.

An old red sandstone building stood timeless with its backdrop of Savernake Forest bordering the property on three sides, and perfectly manicured gardens between. Ivy vines wove their way up the textured walls, finding footing in the mortar between each stone, rising three floors, almost the full height of the front façade, only a foot or two short of the moss covered tiled roof. Several chimneys were visible from the front aspect on its steeply pitched roof, one of which emitted soft plumes of smoke. Circular turrets dominated the corners of the building, rising level with the peak of the roof. Bordering it all were narrow battlements, extending the length of the walls between each turret. It was stunning against its picturesque backdrop and the early morning sun.

"Did you get lost getting here?" Cassie quipped, greeting her friend with a hug.

"You say that like your driveway isn't longer than most roads."

Cassie shrugged her shoulders nonchalantly, although it wasn't too long ago that she had first been enchanted by this house in the same way Teagan was now. It's amazing how quickly something can become familiar to you, she thought with a sigh of contentment.

"I'm so glad you're here. I've told Alaric to give us some girl time before he hijacks you to talk about the ward on the manor. I hope you don't mind?"

"No. Of course not, I'm glad. We didn't get much of a chance to catch up yesterday," she answered, a broad smile twinkling in her eyes. "This place is amazing. I can't believe you live here. It's nothing like your poky little flat back at Oxford," she chuckled, giving Cassie another excited hug.

"Yeah, well. There was a bit of an incident at my flat and I'm afraid the place is still in pieces, fortunately though, fewer pieces than it was a couple of months ago. Alaric destroyed my flat when he fought Jarvis, the vampire assassin sent to kill me. Although, I'm starting to think I'm a magnet for psychopathic men with murder and mass destruction on their agendas," Cassie said as she grabbed the crook of Teagan's arm, leading her along the flagstone path which led around to the back of the house. Yet again, the distance was so vast, Teagan wondered if she had crossed time zones, at the very least she should have brought a cut lunch to eat on the trip.

"What do you mean?" Teagan's brow furrowed with concern.

"You'll see."

Reaching the corner of the building, Cassie stopped and pointed to what used to be the manor's back garden covering the western aspect of the estate.

"Wow. Alaric did that?"

"Yep. With the help of Ahriman." *May God rot his festering soul,* she added silently to herself.

In the space of an hour, the two had fought with preternatural speed and strength, as well as their other unique abilities. The end result was meteor sized craters divoting the ground. Not to mention all vegetation either being burned, frost bitten, pummelled to sawdust, or now dangling from the branches of trees in various other parts of the manor's gardens and adjacent forest. Everything was completely destroyed, except for an enormous seven hundred year old Yew tree. Its long, heavy branches broken into pieces, its thick trunk fallen, but remarkably still intact. If she stood beside it, Cassie still wasn't as tall as the tree's trunk was thick. No doubt they were going to have a devil of a time removing the tree, even with the use of vampire and lycan strength and several chainsaws.

Beyond the garden, Teagan noted the picturesque Savernake Forest was still intact, untouched by the garden's devastation. She doubted it was luck that had saved it. The forest oozed land magic, to a degree that would have made her grandfather giddy with excitement. Being a druid, she was more in tune with nature and all the natural elements of earth, but her ability to sense it and manipulate it was less than half of what her grandfather could do. You'd think she would envy him, but in fact it was the opposite. She didn't want his abilities, she feared them. It wasn't the power itself that scared her. It was knowing that one day she would inherit his power and *everything* that went with it.

Teagan shivered and wrapped her coat around herself tighter.

The sun slowly burned away the early morning's drizzle, evaporating the moisture which shrouded the wood in a ghostly, shining mist.

"Do you feel like a walk through the forest?"

"Sure." Teagan had walked through the forest several times over the past few days during her stay with the Harlow's, never tiring of it. Like Cassie, the woods held a special fascination for her, an element of peace and harmony she couldn't find anywhere else.

Teagan squealed and jumped back against the wall as an enormous wolfhound bounded around the corner, tail wagging furiously and jumping at Cassie. Its huge paws resting on her shoulders and her whimpering barks intermingled with her lapping tongue against Cassie's cheek.

"Tilly. Down," Cassie growled. Her once pristinely clean cream angora sweater now destined for Mrs Philpot's washing basket. "Crap."

"This is Brian Harlow's dog, Tilly?"

61

"Yes. '*Silly Tilly*'. She's a nice dog, but she's got way too much energy. At least with her around, Alaric lets me walk outside on my own. Any sign of something unusual and she starts barking, and with his hearing…," she huffed in frustration. "Well, let's just say he likes to give me the illusion of having some privacy, but in reality, one bark from Tilly or a squeal from either of us and thirty seconds later there would be half a dozen vampires and lycans surrounding us, each sporting their own particular brand of fangs ready to kill something," Cassie said as they navigated their way through the least devastated part of the garden towards the tree line beyond.

As they entered the forest, Tilly loped ahead, rolling in the rotting leaves and dirt and digging at rabbit holes, but never straying too far from them.

Once again Tilly bounded back to them, kicking up a clump of mud into Cassie's face. "Goddamn it," she grumbled. "I'm a magnet for psychopathic men and menacing dogs," wiping it away with the sleeve of her already grubby top.

"I don't know what you're complaining about, your skin is so perfect. Do you even have pores?" Teagan commented, hoping the dark circles under her own eyes didn't stand out too much on her pale skin. In comparison to Cassie's glowing, radiant skin, she probably looked like a raccoon.

Cassie's complexion wasn't the only thing she could tell that was different about her after she became immortal. She had attained flawless skin *and* lustrous hair like a vampire, otherwise she had pretty much lucked-out with the whole super human thing. She didn't get amazing hearing or telescopic eyesight, she still couldn't run faster than a motorised wheelchair, and she was still as uncoordinated as ever.

"You can talk. What I wouldn't give to have breasts like yours. They could be used as a flotation device."

"You could get them too. You only need to put on another forty pounds," Teagan grinned.

"So, there's hope for me yet," Cassie laughed, rubbing her belly which was still flat. She had only been pregnant for a couple of weeks but since virtually every waking moment of that time had been spent thinking about it, it felt much longer.

"Did you know Tilly rarely leaves my side? She even sleeps on the floor next to my bed," Cassie said, changing the topic back to her current aggravation.

"That's not so bad."

"It's when she drops whopping big smelly farts all night. If I lock her out of the room, she howls until I let her back in."

"Okay. I can see how that might be annoying. Better you than me," Teagan sniggered.

"Thanks for your support, friend."

"You're welcome."

It seemed so long ago since Cassie had a normal conversation with someone, she had almost forgotten what it was like. The last person she talked like this with was Alex.

Almost as though someone had let all the air out of her balloon, she suddenly felt deflated and flat. She really missed her brother.

Word had reached them early that morning about the situation in the Ukraine and that Abby planned on going into the compound at sundown. She really liked Abby, she was like a sister to her. Now she had to worry about both of them.

"Maybe we should head back," she suggested. "No doubt Alaric and Saladin will be pacing the floors waiting for us."

Saladin. For a brief time Teagan had actually forgotten about him.

Beyond being a vampire, Saladin was everything she disliked.

He was annoyingly gorgeous, too obscenely rich, and worst of all, arrogantly over confident.

Secretly she envied his confidence. Even if she lived to be a thousand, she doubted she could achieve even half his measure of self-worth.

"Saladin is judgemental, arrogant and frankly, just obnoxious."

"Yeah," Cassie agreed. "What gave him away?" she laughed. "I don't want you to think I'm defending him or anything because believe me, he is one huge pain in the rear end most of the time."

"I hear a *but* in there," Teagan interjected suspiciously.

"But, he has a heart of gold underneath all that bling."

"From what I can tell, the only precious metal he has, is his tarnished man tackle," Teagan sighed in disappointment. Whether she was disappointed in *his* low moral standards or in *her* own for wanting to see him again so badly, she didn't know.

Teagan had barely slept a wink all night from fantasizing about him. She had tossed and turned restlessly, her mind kept going back to him. She couldn't get the memory of his spicy, masculine scent out of her nose. Nor could she forget how good his hard body felt against hers when he pulled her against him, or the zing of chemistry between them. When she did finally manage to drop off to sleep, she dreamt about him. Now she was tired, cranky, horny and more conflicted about him than she was yesterday when he kissed her.

"Tilly," Cassie called, but the mischievous dog didn't come. "Tilly!" she called again.

The bushes rustled behind them. The girls turned to see the energetic dog leap the shrub, carrying something in her mouth.

Tilly plopped the dead rat on the ground at Cassie's feet.

"I think she brought you a present, Cassie," Teagan said, taking a step away from the smelly carcass.

"Wow. Thank you," she said to the proud mutt, scratching her behind the ear. "And, it's been dead for at least a week by the smell of it."

So, so special. *Ew!*

Walking at a brisk pace, Teagan and Cassie were back at the manor in a matter of minutes, not wanting to dally and give Tilly more time to dig up any other *presents*.

They sat in the drawing room by the blazing open fire. The view from the windows on this side of the house overlooked an extensive garden of heirloom azaleas, camellias, gardenias, lilies and roses of all kinds. The garden was dotted with magnolias and crepe myrtles, all barren of their brilliant bloom, but still infinitely more beautiful than the garden on the other side of the manor.

Thanks to the thoughtful housekeeper, Mrs Philpot, tea and cake was already laid out on the coffee table. Cake wasn't normally on Teagan's diet, carrots and cottage cheese were more her style lately, but since it was nearly eleven in the morning and she only now realised she'd skipped breakfast, her growling stomach was very grateful for the calorie packed snack. Maybe she could jog back to Cadley later instead of walking.

The door to the drawing room creaked open just as she pushed the last of her banana cake into her mouth. Raising her hand to cover her bulging cheeks, she hurriedly tried to swallow as Alaric and Saladin entered. Instantly the room seemed to shrink under their domineering presence, both pairs of eyes firmly glued on her.

"Teagan. I believe I might owe you an apology for yesterday. I may have come on a little strong. Please let me start again," Saladin offered charmingly. "My name is…"

"Jerk," Teagan finished curtly.

Saladin chuckled. Touché.

He looked down at her for a long moment, he couldn't help himself. The way the firelight shimmered in her dark eyes, painting them with a mysterious glow, caught his breath. And, the way her raven hair fell in a heavy curtain past her shoulder blades, a stray lock draping over the back of her chair practically begged him to touch it, to stroke it.

She was fresh, pure and warmly tempting.

"Jerk is my middle name. No doubt you'd prefer my first name…Arsehole."

Her heavy scowl lightened into a suspicious smirk and she extended her hand tentatively to shake his already outstretched one.

As his hand enclosed hers, Teagan had to close her eyes and purse her lips tightly together, to stop the embarrassing release of a moan or gasp of pleasure, that were both lodged in her throat battling to escape.

Even after her reaction to him yesterday, she was still unprepared for the combustible heat that stole her breath and made her stomach clench with a surge of excitement that he induced.

Oh, and his scent. It was an olfactory delight. She wanted someone to bottle it and put it in her fabric softener so she could wear it every day.

"Well. Now we've got that over with, we can get on with business," Alaric encouraged, taking a seat beside Cassie.

Casually, Saladin took a seat directly opposite Teagan, his eyes never leaving her for a moment.

It was a little unnerving that he could stare for so long without blinking. It wasn't a threatening stare, it held more curiosity than anything. Nonetheless, she felt as though she had been cornered in the gaze of a hungry predator.

An hour later and the logistics of creating the new ward on the manor had been discussed and plans made, Alaric excused himself to take a phone call.

"Only one thing left to discuss," Saladin began.

"What's that?" Cassie asked.

"How long will you be staying with *us*?" he said, looking at Teagan.

"What? I'm not staying here. I *can't* stay here," she quickly defended, her heartbeat instantly doubling its pace.

"If I promise to behave and not make any inappropriate advances on you, would you stay then?"

His voice moved over her in an invisible caress.

Teagan tried desperately to tell herself she was not in the least bit curious about this man, or the raw sexual response he ignited in her. But in truth, all she could think about was this hard-bodied glorious man who'd permanently seared his image into the storage compartment of her female DNA. From this day forward, every man would have to survive a mental side-by-side comparison against him. They'd all lose.

She was so screwed.

And, the way he was looking at her, that thought may not be too far from the truth.

He was almost tempting enough to make her break her own rules.

Squinting her eyes, Teagan wrinkled her nose at him as she debated the consequences of being in such close proximity to him for an extended period of time.

He is dangerous to you. Just say no, she mentally scolded herself. She had practiced that word '*No*' over and over in her head. It wasn't that hard to say.

It would only be a week, she justified to the contrary.

"Must I appeal to your logic?" he asked, a grin playing on his lips. "You could get the job done much faster if you were staying here. The sooner the ward is complete, the sooner you can get on with your normal life again."

That part of her brain which was now marinating in a pool of whatever hormonal overload he'd triggered, was overriding every rational thought she had. His proposal was actually sounding good to her.

Teagan swallowed hard a couple of times before she could get her answer out with a husky rasp. "Alright."

Saladin lifted an eyebrow rakishly, but ruined the effect with a crooked grin. "You won't regret it,"

I already do.

"Tomorrow we can go over the list of things you need once you've had a chance to look around," he suggested. "Maybe over a coffee or a drink somewhere away from here."

"No. Absolutely not."

"I promise I won't bite," he answered smoothly, a seductive lilt to his tone implying, *"Unless you ask me to."*

"Sorry. I don't mean to be rude. It's just that…it's just…I can't explain it," she huffed.

"No need to try. If you change your mind, you know where to find me. Either way, we *will* be having a discussion tomorrow," he promised, giving her another one of his panty melting smiles which she was beginning to loathe, and love in equal portions.

Teagan watched him leave the room as silently and as graceful as a panther and sighed, her shoulders sagging in on themselves.

Regret was a bitter lump in her throat that no amount of swallowing was going to clear. But what did she regret? Not saying '*No*' to staying at the manor, or actually turning down the hottest man she had ever met, *again*, when he asked her out for coffee. She had reacted like he'd asked if he could pull out her teeth.

Saladin had promised to behave, and he had apologised for his presumptive proposition yesterday, sort of. He didn't actually use the word *sorry*, but she got the feeling that was about as close to the word as he would ever get. Would it really have been that bad to accept? To maybe meet him somewhere for just a coffee?

Yes. Yes, it would be that bad. He was a vampire, destined to live forever, and she was a druid, destined to grow old and die as any other regular human would. Besides, Saladin had a reputation for having a different woman every night. He had never been known to form an attachment to any female in the past, why would she be any different. If she let her guard down, she would only end up being another notch on his bed post.

Teagan on the other hand, she formed attachments far too easily, and she couldn't afford to fall for a man she could never have.

Teagan turned to Cassie. They had known each other for nearly a year, and in that time they'd come to know each other pretty well. "I was right to turn him down, wasn't I?"

"Not to split hairs or anything, but since you've just agreed to stay here at the manor, where Saladin is also staying," she pointed out. "Avoiding having coffee with him isn't going to be that easy."

"I didn't want to hear that."

"I thought you wanted my opinion?" Cassie asked.

"Well, not if you're going to bring reality into it," Teagan sniped irritably.

Oh, happy, happy, joy, joy. Wasn't life grand?

Damn.

8

Mortal and semi-mortal beings alike: Humans, vampires and lycans, were predictable. They were venal and selfish, something he promoted and preyed on. Being around them was like watching children squabbling and fighting over a broken toy. However, they never elevated his interest beyond the level of boredom. It had been a long time since he had felt even the smallest measure of curiosity for anything.

Until now.

Ahriman's thoughts drifted once again to Abby. This strange woman and her bond with Alex raised the first flicker of curiosity, and an alarming measure of uncertainty about himself which he hadn't felt in eons.

As he thought of the female, a rush of emotions flooded through him, so achingly familiar and yet at the same time, so foreign.

Ahriman's nerves felt raw, overloaded from the constant barrage of feelings and thoughts which filtered through to him from Alex. Not to mention Alex's cruel, bull-headed tenacity to pay him back for his treatment of Abby with a never-ending rendition of children's songs. Everything from Sesame Street, The Wiggles, Barney, every nursery rhyme he'd ever learned and even the theme songs from at least a dozen pre-schooler television shows…the list went on and on and on. Not content with providing only the lyrics to the most ridiculous and *extremely* annoying songs he had ever heard, Alex gave him a mental visual of all the actions that went with those songs.

Ahriman was ready to explode, his temper on a hair trigger.

Alex felt smugly satisfied. He had discovered Ahriman's weakness. He couldn't effect the evil fallen angel with a tirade of anger and verbal abuse, but as it turned out, he found children's songs as annoying as every other adult on the planet. If this didn't send him around the twist and want to purge himself from Alex's body, nothing would.

Children's songs weren't exactly high on Alex's most favourite list either, but he had become very familiar with them over the past eighteen months. One of his flat mates had a young son who stayed with them every other weekend. And, since everyone in the flat tended to work weekends, including the boy's father, everyone except Alex who tutored from home, he inadvertently became the three-year old's regular babysitter. Hence, the rather lengthy repertoire of children's songs. Thank you Nickelodeon.

It had been Ahriman's intention that Alex would be a usable tool in his hands just as Stedman had been, but as he was discovering he had a rather prickly grip.

Then again, Ahriman had expected no less from him. In fact, he was beginning to respect the son of a bitch, almost as much as he despised him. That didn't mean he didn't want to kill something.

Brutal savagery hid behind cold unforgiving eyes as he turned to the half finished portal device on his work bench. He had hit a stumbling block in the form of equipment failure which only increased his frustration levels. He had no more than one week left to complete the device. By then he figured, the Alliance would storm the compound. If they got their hands on the device, it was all over. That was something he couldn't afford to let happen.

He needed an outlet for his foul mood, and fast.

As Ahriman's anger simmered beneath the surface, something else seemed to come to life inside him. Something new and unexpected. It seemed that Alex's personality wasn't the only thing about him that prickled Ahriman. A tingling in his fingertips, subtle at first but as he concentrated on it he could feel it grow and mature into something....usable?

It was Alex's previously latent electromagnetic power, brought to life by Ahriman's higher soul vibration. Alex had always had a detrimental effect on watches and cell phones, and had a sensitivity to static electricity in the atmosphere around him. Now though, it pulsed through every cell in his body, stretching beneath his skin dangerously like a hungry bear waking from hibernation.

Ahriman's smile was cold and cruel. Since he had some 'down-time' there was no better opportunity to play with the energy he felt coursing through his veins, he thought with callous delight. Ahriman was a dark cloud of building power as he concentrated on feeling the ebb and flow of energy pulsing through him like a heartbeat. Learning the way it moved, the way it changed as his focus changed, examining and savouring the tiny sparks that licked the air from his fingertips.

Closing his eyes, he focussed on pulling more energy into himself, drawing on the electricity being fed into the compound. He played with it. Pulled it in and then released it. Drew it in again. Visible arcs of electricity darted at him like strikes of lightening as it arced, sizzled and sparked, clinging to him in a blinding white and blue aura, stretching around him, absorbing it until he glowed with power. Light globes exploded and power sockets smoked with the surge of power being forced through them until finally the compound's transformer blew, dumping the entire complex into darkness momentarily before the emergency back-up generators kicked in.

Oops. My bad, Ahriman thought with twisted satisfaction.

Still, he couldn't detach himself from Alex's bond to Abby. It had been twelve hours since she left his bed and his pecker was still a solid bar in his pants. With every passing hour a hollow feeling in his chest grew larger with a longing to see her again, to touch her.

It was maddeningly irritating. These were not his feelings, they were Alex's, and no matter how hard he tried, he couldn't block out the need which clawed at him. He should have realised instantly that their blood bond was not purely an emotional attachment, when his body began to grow stronger the nearer Abby had come to him. He should have backed away then. Found a new host. Instead, led by his arrogant belief in his own supremacy, he completed the bond and established the worst kind of self-flagellating torture imaginable. It was more devastating than anything Alex could ever do to him, far worse than those infuriating children's songs. The bond infused every physical cell of his usurped body, on every level clear to his soul, or more accurately, to Alex's soul. Fortunately, they were still separate at that level. Regrettably, they did share *all* the same physical sensations, and to the same degree.

That physical need had Ahriman's feet moving, out of the lab and toward the cell where Abby was being held.

Abby stood beneath the hot spray of the shower. No amount of soap or water could wash away the guilt in her soul.

Similarly, furious shame and agonised lust battled inside her for supremacy.

Even after she realised she had just made love to Ahriman, not Alex, she found herself torn. On one hand she wanted to beg him to let her go. On the other, she wanted to demand he fuck her into oblivion, again.

But this was Alex, she reminded herself sternly. Ahriman was only a parasite along for the ride. He said it himself, Alex was still inside his body, he just had no control over it. She hadn't cheated on Alex, not in the strict technical sense anyway.

There had to be more to Ahriman's possession of Alex. Two completely separate entities sharing the same body? She had to learn to decipher one from the other. Was Ahriman in complete control of Alex? She didn't want to believe that. Alex was strong, he was a fighter.

Abby could distinctly feel conflicting emotions, but whose emotions were who's? Alex's or Ahriman's?

Alaric and Cassie also shared a blood bond and they could feel each other's emotions. Surely it would be the same for her and Alex. She had to find out. She hated that she couldn't read his thoughts. For so many years of her life she had believed her gift to be a curse. Now, she would give her back teeth to be able to read Alex's mind, to communicate with him on some level.

She had no desire in having any kind of relationship with Ahriman, Alex was her *mate* and she would remain loyal to him, and him alone. But that was the conundrum she was faced with. How could she separate the two?

Right now, she had to stay close to Alex no matter the cost to her morals, and deal with the emotional fall-out later.

Her number one priority was to find a way to get them out of this compound and keep her blood in his system, just in case they needed to use the, *'If all else fails'* contingency plan. Besides that, Abby also needed to find a way to contact Sebastian who was waiting in the hunter's cabin for news. She'd stashed her smuggled phone inside the mattress of her bed, but being several floors below ground there was no signal in her cell. Not unless she could sweet talk her way out of her cell.

Turning off the taps Abby stepped from the shower and roughly dried herself.

Lost in her thoughts she was surprised to find Ahriman standing inside her room. His cold eyes heated, his hands fisted at his sides and the muscles in his jaw clenched tightly to hold in the hiss of desire as she stepped naked from the bathroom.

"What are you doing here? Have you come back for an encore performance?" she demanded curtly as she moved to grab the towel she'd dropped on the bathroom floor.

Ahriman blocked her path, his hungry eyes surveying her naked body, following the course of a droplet of water as it dripped from the end of her short hair, over her shoulder and bare chest, catching and hanging from the dusky bud of her nipple.

Memory of sucking that nipple had him licking his lips, his mouth watering for another taste.

Abby narrowed her eyes on him.

Testing her 'emotions' theory, Abby slapped Ahriman hard across the face. "That was for you impersonating Alex with me last night," she said.

His eyes blazed dangerously with anger, however, it was the emotional vibe coming from him that Abby focussed on.

She could feel him. She could feel Alex. She *could* differentiate between them.

Alex projected his emotions loud and clear. Even though she knew he felt the sting of her slap, she also felt his pride in her retaliation.

As harsh as it may be, she had found a way to communicate with him.

73

"And this," she said, "Is for Alex. A promise of things to come."

Abby's hands smoothed down his chest until she encountered the hard peaks of his male nipples beneath his shirt. She gripped their points, massaging them tightly as she stared into the darkness of his eyes.

He arched with a small involuntary convulsive move. His body shook, shuddered with pleasure as he cried out mutely at the caress. Yet, his hands moved with lightening fast speed, gripping her wrists and pulling her fingers away from him.

Abby stepped back, watching him breathing roughly. His expression was confused, conflicted. But, once again it was Alex's emotions she focussed on. Alex's arousal spiked under her touch and his body responded.

Ahriman had no control over the effect of their bond.

"You can't refuse me. You need me. As long as you and Alex are cohabiting, you need me." She tried to pull her hands out of his grasp, watching as he fought to catch his breath.

His face was flushed, his eyes glittering with some emotion that tugged at her heart. Vulnerability? Hunger? She watched him trying to hide his weakness. He swallowed tightly, his eyes closing for a moment.

"No. I can't do this," he told her firmly, releasing her wrists as though they burned him.

She could hear the confusion in his voice. A need to understand what to him was beyond understanding.

"Are you certain? Alex is my *mate*. You can't fight that bond, it's stronger than you," she told him softly, watching him with a sense of power and knowledge. Her fingers raked over his tight abdomen and reveled in his harsh, in-drawn breath.

"Leave me alone." His voice was raspy, desperate. His eyes raked over her with hatred and fear...and need.

Moisture filled her eyes, but she didn't break down. "You came to me, remember?"

"I made a mistake," he answered angrily grabbing her about her throat. He wanted to move away but couldn't, not yet.

"What do you want from me? Why did you come in here?" Abby asked. He still had his hand about her throat, but her voice was clear, unafraid.

He was there because he wanted her. And, it wasn't just Alex's bond to her. Abby intrigued him, called to him. She had aroused Ahriman's deepest needs, not the need for sex, but for something he couldn't articulate or give a name to the feeling.

Maybe it was her courage that excited him. Or maybe he wanted to dominate her as payback for her part in turning his world on its axis.

Both explanations were true, but neither defined the elusive feeling.

He watched her for a moment longer, her feminine body soft under his hands, her eyes moist with unshed tears of frustration, although equally as soft. She stared at him with affection, the earlier anger and hatred now gone.

"I don't want anything from you," he answered, his voice a husky whisper.

Ahriman made himself let her go. He stepped back, his gut clenching, his body shaking.

It would be so easy to give into his temptation, run his fingers along the length of her neck to trace the outline over her collarbone, then lower. His hooded gaze followed the line of his thoughts, skimming down her breasts to nipples that hardened with desire under his lusty gaze.

Instead, he smiled at her baffled expression. "Go," he said.

She stared at him. She was naked, damp from the shower, delectable.

"*Go!*" he said, the word jerking out of him.

Abby stood there, frozen. Hell, he couldn't blame her for looking at him like he had grown a second head.

Alex watched Abby. She was sexy as sin, beautiful innocence flowed from her with a new sensuality he loved. He wanted to show her how to revel in it, show her how to find the deepest pleasure imaginable.

Ahriman too watched her through the same eyes. He wanted to teach her, unwrap her layer by layer, until she was totally open to him begging to give him anything he wanted.

The power she wielded over the two men tweaked Abby's confidence.

She could feel Alex's love for her, his devotion. She could see the conflict in Ahriman's eyes, his desire to fulfil their bond's need for physical contact and his fear of the intense emotional deluge that came with it.

"Get dressed. You're free to walk about the compound."

"I'm not a prisoner?"

"Of course you are. But you're less of a threat to me than half the people who work for me."

That was true. Abby would never do anything to harm Alex. The same could not be said for Ahriman's own allies. They'd cut him down at the first sign of weakness. Mira had never endeared herself with anything that resembled loyalty or a conscience, and Morganna was beginning to assert her own power behind his back. Abby may be his enemy, but she was the only one he could trust right now.

"Walk where you please about the compound, just leave me the hell alone," he ordered gruffly.

"You can't run from the bond," she called after him as he almost ran from the room, slamming the door behind him.

At least she now had the opportunity she needed to get a message to Sebastian and the Alliance about what had happened to Alex. She could probably hear them cursing from here.

One hurdle down, about a million and one to go.

9

Something dark and frightening lurked behind his eyes, a secret as black as she knew his soul to be. A secret hidden and well guarded, but its presence was there nonetheless, just out of view. Threatening to make itself known.

The second Ahriman realised he was being watched, his face twitched and a moment later he was the poster boy of composure and control which he pretended to be.

Beneath the facade his memories tore a hole in his defences, their talons grasping and venomous, destroying any warmth left in his resentful soul. He was doomed, just as he had always been. Only now he was doomed in two worlds.

Lilith watched discretely from the doorway.

Compounding his own private pity party, Alex's cloying emotions wormed their way through Ahriman's pores and wrapped around his throat, choking, suffocating. Alex wanted to be with Abby so badly it was physically painful.

Ahriman tried his best to ignore him. Their bond was a painful open wound to him, a deep gash bleeding, burning every raw nerve ending he possessed, leaving a permanent stain on his soul.

If his body needed sex, there was an alternative, one he had used many times before to relieve his lustful desires.

"Come here," he called, his voice low, the tone petulant.

Lilith's body obeyed before her mind checked in with the command to move, as it always did when it came to Ahriman. Against her own better judgement, she was obsessed with him. She'd betrayed her friends and her beloved boss, for him. And she would do it all again if he asked her to. He was hers, and she was determined to keep it that way.

As she got close to him, he put one arm around her waist and pulled her against his hard body. His lips came down hot and hungry on hers as he buried his other hand in her hair. Through his woollen trousers she could feel his bulge of his manhood. She rubbed herself against it, teasing and stroking it with her hand. But it did not rise. It remained flaccid beneath her touch.

Lilith arched into him further, a delicious tightness coiled between her thighs building in anticipation of the rough sex he always demanded of her.

Nothing happened. His length remained unchanged.

Ahriman growled, a low dangerous, guttural sound that hitched the breath in her throat. He had no true interest in Lilith, he never did, but he refused to give into Alex's bond to Abby. *He* controlled this body, not Alex. If he wanted to have sex with someone other than Abby, then he would.

Then why couldn't he get a fucking hard-on? He'd never had this problem before.

Hell's hairy balls.

Ahriman shoved Lilith away in frustration. "No more, Lilith. Enough," he growled.

Lilith couldn't believe her ears. He was rejecting her?

This was Alex's doing, she surmised, infuriated by his interference once again. Alex had always hated her. The feeling was mutual.

Lilith had been willing to ignore the fact it was Alex's body she was going to have sex with. Instead, she preferred to focus on the consolation that it was Ahriman who controlled it. After all, she enjoyed the sex when he had possessed Stedman's body. In fact, it was the best sex she'd ever had. The giant blonde was hung like a horse. Disappointingly, it seemed she wasn't going to have the same pleasure this time. Not if the body's original owner refused to vacate it. *Why can't the arsehole just shrivel up and die like Stedman did and let Ahriman take over like he's supposed to*, she thought vehemently.

Alex's interference in her relationship with Ahriman was unacceptable, and she wasn't going to allow it. Not now, not ever.

Abby had just pressed 'send' on her cell phone, relaying her message to Sebastian about their current situation when she was struck with a feeling of overwhelming distress.

Alex.

What was that evil bastard doing to him now?

Quickly Abby followed her bond to Alex, down to the bowels of the complex. Deep inside a cavernous fissure in the mountainside she followed the dimly lit, musty corridors to the lab.

As the door opened, Lilith and Ahriman turned at the same moment and saw Abby approach. Her shocked expression, filled with hurt and betrayal tickled Lilith's warped sense of humour. Ahriman too, saw an opportunity to assert his power over Alex once again. He might not be able to have sex with Lilith, but Abby didn't know that. And, there was no better way to torment Alex than to hurt Abby, as he had already discovered.

Lilith took a step closer toward Ahriman, his hands gripped her hips, a smouldering grin replacing her petulant pout as she attempted to intimidate Abby. If she had half a brain she would have realised that defusing the situation was the wiser and safer course of action. After all, as a human she was far more breakable than Abby.

"Abby, what a pleasant surprise. Have you come to join us?" Lilith asked sweetly.

"What the hell do you think you're doing? Take your hands off him." All Abby could see was Lilith fawning over Alex. She may not have been able to hear his thoughts, but his emotions were projecting to her loud and clear, and he wanted nothing to do with Lilith.

"Why don't we talk like friends, since we have so much in common? My boyfriend occupies your boyfriend's body. It could be quite a bonding experience for all of us," Lilith said, stroking a finger down his abdomen seductively with brash self-assurance.

"What exactly do you mean by that? I'm not going to braid your hair if that's what you have in mind."

Lilith laughed, an arrogant, snooty chuckle. "Hardly. I mean, sex."

"I will not dignify that with a response," Abby bit back through grinding teeth.

"You just did," Lilith replied with a satisfied smirk.

"I'm trying really hard to understand what you're saying, but right now you're a few syllables away from seriously pissing me off."

Lilith let out a mock sigh. "You can give me some tips on what Alex likes in bed. I'm looking forward to a threesome. Oh, sorry, I forgot. You wouldn't know, you've never had sex with Alex have you, only my boyfriend, Ahriman," she bit out the snide remark, watching with satisfaction as Abby sucked in a harsh breath, her hands clenching into white knuckled fists at her sides. "And, just so we're clear," Lilith added smugly, "When I say threesome, I mean me, Ahriman and Alex. You're not invited."

What? Whatever. There was no way she was going to let this troll touch Alex for one second longer. The bitch was dead. "I don't think so. That's just wrong, in oh, so many ways."

Abby gripped Lilith by the throat. Her calm exterior belied her seething thoughts. As Lilith's face changed from pink, through to red and then to purple, she mentally pictured all the satisfying options of getting rid of the skanky bitch. Her fangs ached to rip out her throat, but the woman had been injected with enough Botox to paralyze an elephant. With all that Botulinum toxin flowing through her veins, Abby could only imagine what that poison would do to a vampire, it might be like silver is to a lycan.

As Abby debated Lilith's fate, a hand clamped on her shoulder. The firm but gentle grip effectively doused her murderous thoughts in cold water, pulling her back from the brink of killing the slutty shrew.

Dr Leon Greenville stood his ground. The man had balls of steel for stepping between an angry vampire and her prey, but he couldn't let Lilith be killed. He felt no compassion for the woman, but in the months he had been locked inside this compound, he had seen more killing than any one man should bear witness to. He didn't fear for his own life. On the contrary, secretly he dared to hope that Abby might retaliate for his intrusion and kill him instead. Even death would be preferable to being trapped in this hellhole for much longer.

Abby released her hold on Lilith's throat, dropping her semi-conscious body to the floor, gasping in ragged breaths of air. She could have killed her so easily and given it no more consideration than squashing a bug. Abby honestly doubted she would have dredged up even the slightest bit of Catholic guilt about it. She would have given a squashed bug more sympathy.

"Get her out of here," Abby said to the scientist, her voice cold and even.

Lilith scrambled away from Abby with the help of Dr Greenville, who practically carried her from the lab.

"Nobody touches you but me!" Abby decreed when the door closed behind them, her eyes burning with anger. Her approach was so volatile and aggressive that Ahriman wasn't sure what she would do, so he backed up from the path of her advance.

Until he hit the wall.

The minute she had him cornered, she reached to thrust insistent fingers into his hair, pulling his head forward to capture his mouth, thrusting her body hard up against his. His reciprocating kiss was hard and equally aggressive.

Abby broke away from him to place her fingers inside his shirt and raked her taloned nails down his bare skin with barely repressed anger. "Alex. Fight!" she yelled. "Damn you, fight him!"

Abby watched Ahriman's eyes widen. Saw the surprise that filled his expression.

"You're mine damn you, and I won't stand by and watch you be beaten. You're stronger than this. Fight him! Fight for me!" she yelled at Alex with furious determination.

Ahriman roared in outrage and pain and then found himself glued to her mouth once again.

Ahriman reeled. His world turned on its axis under her assault. She worked her kiss, hot and hard and with unbelievable aggression. He was assaulted by too much stimuli, hers, his and Alex's. Very quickly he found himself struggling to decipher the borders between them.

It was wild and intoxicating. For a minute all three were blended together.

Ahriman growled when she pulled away, something between regret at the sudden absence of her lips and fury for her assertive abuse.

She pushed him where she wanted him.

Too far.

Beyond thought, beyond pain, beyond reason, to pure instinct, naked emotions and reaction.

Alex watched, a helpless participant. He had never seen Abby's eyes glitter with such fury and arousal. Her body tense, primed for both battle and sex. How he wished he could soothe one and stoke the fires for the other.

But it wasn't just Abby who was feeling torn. Ahriman waged an internal battle for dominance and control that for once had nothing to do with Alex. Leaning forward he braced his hands on his knees, breathing hard.

Long moments passed as Abby held her breath, watching, waiting.

His head slowly lifted and for the first time in days she saw Alex staring back at her.

"Alex. Is it really you?" she gasped. The flaccid pole between his legs went impossibly hard at the breathy sound of his name coming from her perfect lips.

"Yeah. Yeah, it's me baby. Look at me, could I look any more like a dork?" he said, a dazzling smile lighting his face, his hands pointing to the dark woollen trousers, expensive silk shirt and the tacky white laboratory coat over top. Dr Evil's fashion sense wasn't even in the same ballpark as Alex's jeans and t-shirts.

Yep. That was definitely Alex.

"I love you baby. I'm sorry about what Ahriman did but I promise you, I was right there too. I felt your kisses and your touch," he said, his voice held a slight tremor in it. "That's not how I wanted your first time to be, baby. I wanted it to be long and slow and I wanted you to know without a doubt, just how much I love you. Please forgive me," his soulful eyes pleaded.

"There's nothing to forgive," she smiled reassuringly, stepping in to close the gap between them. "Maybe we can try for a re-do now?" she asked.

"I don't know how long I've got before Ahriman takes me over again."

"I'm willing to see how far we can get."

His lean body was taut with strong sinewy muscle. She licked her lips at the thought of running her fingers over all the peaks and valleys of his body. A slow, wet swipe of her tongue, the act deliberate, challenging.

Alex's hooded eyes narrowed on her tongue action.

She stared up at him, her lips parted, her breathing rough and hard.

Alex's arms wrapped around her of their own accord. A shivery sensation spread from every point of contact between them, electrifying her entire body.

Leaning down his lips met hers, parting them softly, gently. The kiss grew fiercer. His tongue forged into her mouth, the heated depths soothing the sudden ache of need as her lips melded with his.

Abby moaned as she arched into him further, a hand gliding over the curve of her hip, along the length of her waist and latched smoothly onto her breast, Alex's fingers gripping the hard, little nipple poking against the cloth of her shirt.

Another rich sound of longing and arousal escaped her lips as she met his kiss with equal force. His hands reached down to the firm globes of her backside and lifted her to him, pressing his steel hard erection against her heated core. She was a live flame in his arms, burning him, searing his body and soul as he fought to take his fill of her lips.

Tearing himself away from her was the hardest thing he had ever done, pulling her body from his, the absence of her lips on his, leaving an instant hole in his soul. "No, baby. You need to get away from here. Leave now and don't look back," he pleaded.

"I'm not leaving you," she promised, tightening her hold on his body.

"It's too dangerous for you here. *I'm* too dangerous."

"I'm not afraid of you," she whispered in reminder as she moved to kiss him soothingly. "And, I'm not afraid of Ahriman."

"Well, you should be. I have no control of my body. I am completely at Ahriman's mercy. I see what he sees, I feel what he feels but I can't control anything that he does. I'm useless to protect you from *myself* if he has a hissy-fit and decides to hurt you."

"Don'tt underestimate me or yourself."

"I don't think you understand. He has only allowed me freedom with you now because he knows that without physical contact with you and your blood, my body would wither and die, and he can't afford for that to happen."

"Then why isn't he the one in control now, holding me, kissing me?"

"Because…because…"

If he had even an ounce of blood flow to his brain he would have told her why. But as it was, all that blood seemed to be pooling agonisingly in his merciless erection pressing against her belly.

Arousal tested his resolve, and he found his will wasn't nearly strong enough to deny Abby what she craved, what he craved.

All Alex could think about was how much he wanted to drop to his knees and use his tongue to make her scream in pleasure, but he was going to do this right. He was going to worship her body and make it last.

Her breathy moans caressed his senses, her tongue tangling with his once more, her nails biting into his scalp as she fought to get closer.

He groaned in surprise as her legs lifted, her smooth thighs clamping at his hips as she moved against him, notching him higher, tighter against her heated core. And, it was hot. It seared him through his pants, the moist fire so tempting he had to grit his teeth to keep from releasing his thick length and pounding it into her furiously.

One hand slid south to the moist slit between her thighs, the other hand came up to cup her breast, and she shuddered at the dual sensations.

Her senses heightened with arousal, the scent of Alex's blood leached into her nose. A slow ooze trickled down his chest from where she'd scratched him.

She needed to taste him. She needed to heal him.

Dropping her feet back to the floor, she gripped his shirt and ripped it open. Her mouth watered at the sight. Abby ran her fingers lightly over his muscled chest, hairless, smooth, his olive complexion so dark against her pale skin.

Four shallow cuts marked his right pectoral where she'd scored him, the muscle bunched and flexed under her gaze. She met his hooded eyes, dark with hunger as she licked her lips.

"Baby, take what you need," he encouraged, guiding her face towards the wounds.

Alex moaned in ecstasy as her tongue swiped over him, the familiar tingle from her healing hormone, lifting his libido even higher.

Abby held her breath momentarily as hunger licked hotly through his irises, skimming over her, devouring her without so much as a touch. His dark pupils searched her face so thoroughly, she felt as though she couldn't possibly have a single secret left.

She was determined to explore more of him.

Her hands skimmed his taut abdomen to the clasp of his trousers, unfastening them and pushing them to the floor. He wore no underwear to hinder her view of his pulsing erection.

Tentatively she glided her fingers lower to the base of the thick shaft, hesitantly wrapping her hand around the iron hard length.

The heavy weight of his arousal rested in the palm of her hand. Her face lit up with wonder and excitement as she discovered what it was like to touch a man so intimately for the first time. The first thing she noticed was the contradiction of sensations, as hard as steel and yet that hardness was covered in velvety, hot skin. Soft and smooth with a delicate touch, rigid and powerful with a stronger touch. Her curious exploration went on and Alex broke out in a sweat as his entire frame shuddered. Her caress was pure ecstasy. And torture.

Lowering herself to her knees, she came eye level with his turgid masculinity. The tip glistened with a crystal bead, and without thinking, she licked it away.

Alex's body tensed and arched in sinewy lines. A riot of sensation attacked his overheated flesh. Her tongue flickered over the tip of his erection again, stroking and caressing. She met his heavy-lidded gaze as she closed her lips over the deeply flushed cap, and savoured his bold, spicy essence. Alex's hands came up to tangle in her hair, his fingers sliding over her scalp as she sucked him deep, and found a rhythm that soon had him pumping his hips. Abby's ministrations became more aggressive, applying powerful suction to the cap, then swirled her tongue in smaller circles, sweeping from the slit at its tip, stroking along its length to the heavy sac below, and back up again.

"Oh fuck!" he gasped, his abs and thighs visibly straining to hold himself in check.

Another pass of her tongue down his shaft, she licked and caressed, and when she sucked his left nut into her mouth, Alex shouted, grabbed his cock and squeezed at its base, a fine film of sweat glistening on his trembling body.

"Not. Yet," he panted hard, praying for self-control. He was ready to blow.

All the while Ahriman rested quietly in the back of Alex's mind, watching, experiencing their interaction. Curiously though, he did not attempt to take back control of Alex's body.

Abby looked up and it was her turn to gasp. No longer was his gaze heavy with a slow smoulder. Now it burned with raw hunger.

Sweeping her up in his arms, Alex laid her gently on the sofa behind them. With swift moves he relieved Abby of her shoes and tugged off her pants and top, discarding them haphazardly on the floor beside his own. Coming over her his heavy erection hung low, resting on her belly as he settled himself between her parted thighs.

Abby moaned as she took his weight. He was beautiful, perfect, and the way his hips flexed against her in the most primal of male responses, brought a purr of pure female appreciation rising from her chest.

She ground against him with an untamed urgency which he seemed to call forth from her with sinful ease, eager to seat his hard length where she desperately needed him.

"Not yet, baby. Let me show you what true pleasure is."

Alex's lips kissed a path down her neck, his large hand cupping her breast, gently kneading the swollen rosebud at its peak, the other hand skimmed lower, stroking the inside of her thighs softly. His drugging kisses ranged lower, his talented lips latching onto her breast as he suckled and groaned with pleasure simultaneously caressing it with fingers as much as he did with his tongue, swirling around the dark pink nub before suckling again. He loved the contrast between her silken skin, the cushion of her soft breast and the tight apex of her nipple. When he finished exploring one, he moved onto the other to thoroughly suck, taste and tease the other.

Abby gasped and writhed beneath him as his hungry mouth continued its path south. She felt so vulnerable and small as he eased her thighs a little farther apart, exposing her succulent core to his starving mouth and caressing fingertips. Her entrance lay before him like a delicate flower, its petals glistening, moist and inviting amongst the short dark curls. Her clit, a tender bud, pink and swollen, beckoning him closer. Alex closed his mouth over her and drank in her sweet nectar.

Alex's tongue was magic, a hot slippery wand of pleasure, stroking between the slick folds to the bundle of sensitive nerves in her clit, and delving deep into the recess of her core. Abby thought she might die from the pleasure. His tongue continued to move. The feeling was hot, wild, the friction nearly driving her insane with need for more. So much more.

Sweet honey filled Alex's mouth and clogged his brain. The taste of her was a drug, and he was instantly addicted.

Abby's body went rigid beneath him as her climax spun up like a storm, a whirlwind of ecstasy and taking her by surprise.

"I need you. Please, Alex I need you now," she cried.

Thank God, he thought desperately. He couldn't wait any longer himself. He'd wanted to show her the bliss of what making love was really about, but his self-control wasn't that good.

Covering her with his body once again, Alex rubbed the tip of his arousal through her slick heat, once, twice, pressing his hard length at her entrance on the third flex of his hips. On the fourth, Alex's mouth came down on hers hard, their tongues melding together in a heated dance as Abby jerked her hips upwards impatiently, sheathing the tip inside her heated channel.

Alex groaned and shuddered, unable to hold back any longer, rolling his hips forward and impaling his shaft further.

He was buried deep inside her, thrusting, pounding into her. His entire body trembled, nearing release, but still it wasn't enough. He wanted more, needed more. Flames of ecstasy burned through his brain, down his spine, pooling in his balls.

Abby cried out his name over and over, begging him for more. Her internal muscles clutching him tighter with every thrust, her nails digging deeply into his shoulders as he felt another orgasm building inside her.

Scraping a nail above her nipple, she twisted her fingers in his hair, guiding his hungry lips from her mouth to her breast, to take her blood once again.

A deep, dark wave so intense, so powerful that it swamped him, dragged him under as her sweet crimson nectar touched his tongue and trickled down his throat. Abby's climax ripped through her with the force of an atomic blast. The tight contractions of her heated channel milked him, sending him straight over the edge into the yawning abyss of immeasurable sensation with her. With one final hard thrust, he filled her with his seed. Alex cried out as wave after wave of pure ecstasy exploded within every cell, pumped through every vein and jetted from his hard cock with such force, it was almost painful.

Abby lay back on the sofa, her eyes hazy with pleasure.

Body and soul, they were joined so deeply they merged together, but it still wasn't complete. Their minds were still separated. Abby felt the absence of Alex's thoughts like a knife to her heart.

Alex eased away from her, laying on his back, pulling her with him until she lay on her side, one leg and arm draped over him. His heavy length lay glistening and spent on his stomach, his chest rose and fell in heavy breaths, gradually slowing.

His fingers were a light caress on her forehead, his ministrations deliberate, careful, as if he was afraid his touch would cause her physical pain.

Long, blissful moments passed with easy comfort, Abby curled up against Alex's body, lazy with contentment, it was easy to believe that everything was as it should be. And then Alex's caress changed.

Abby recoiled from his touch as her eyes met his. The person staring back at her was no longer Alex. His mouth tipped up in a cocky, sensual smile, although his eyes were devoid of emotion.

"Did you get your jollies from that too?" she asked curtly, raising her chin in that stubborn way Ahriman was beginning to admire. Especially because it bared the slender column of her throat and forced her to arch her back the way it did when he was driving between her legs. Correction...When Alex was driving between her legs.

Fuck. He didn't know what he meant. The lines between them were beginning to blur.

Ahriman didn't feel the emotion in the same way Alex did, but he was beginning to enjoy the sensations he felt through their bond. It was much easier to endure the bond when he took a backseat approach, it allowed him to dampen down the most intense sensations.

"Let's not pretend Abigail, that deep down you wished it was me in control, not Alex. You liked it rough, the way I gave it to you."

"Arrogant bastard. Dream on," she muttered as she quickly scrambled from the sofa and picked up her discarded clothes. The change in her expression was subtle, Abby schooled it hastily, but still too late Ahriman still saw it for what it was...fear.

His words hit a sensitive cord. There was power in his voice, seduction. And truth.

Abby held her head high as she glared at him. She was *not* going to give him the satisfaction of letting him see he had gotten under her skin, she did have some pride left. Even as she told herself this, her hand came up and flipped him her middle finger.

She loved Alex. She wanted Alex.

So why did her treasonous body ache for what Ahriman was boldly offering? Her heart and soul belonged to Alex, but her body didn't care that the evil angel occupied her *mate*'s skin.

Guilt, self-loathing and disgust seared her soul, threatening to grip her in its vice.

She wasn't betraying Alex.

Abby promised herself she would do whatever it took to get Alex out of there and deal with the emotional fallout later, and by God, that's exactly what she was going to do.

Ahriman watched Abby walk away. He was almost jealous of what she had with Alex.

That was an odd thought. Maybe it was a lingering side effect of such an incredible orgasm, he wondered. What other reason would he have for such worthless ponderings? None. He loved nothing. He feared nothing. He felt nothing. He was a part of this world...but apart. A shadow who could never become too involved.

Just the way he liked it.

10

Teagan sat quietly on the couch, staring into the flames of the open fire in what was once known as the great hall, but was now an enormous lounge room / entertainment room / man cave.

She'd spent the day exploring the manor, both the house and its grounds. The house was only a fraction larger above ground than it was below. Its hidden subterranean level comprised of an Olympic sized heated swimming pool, every man's dream home gym, decked out with more equipment than a special forces training camp. A weapons room, numerous guest rooms for the more photophobic guests i.e. vampires, and several underground tunnels that led from the house to various areas of the forest including the little village of Cadley, exiting only a hundred meters from the Drunken Duck pub.

As hard as Teagan had tried to focus on her task, she continuously found her mind wandering back to the annoying vampire lurking somewhere within the walls of the building she was traversing. With every new room she entered, and each new corridor she turned down, she secretly hoped to see him there, and at the same time hoped she didn't. Getting a mental map of the entire area she and her sisters had to protect with the ward they were supposed to create, just wasn't happening.

Once again Teagan's mind drifted back to Saladin. She'd managed to dodge a 'meeting' with him earlier in the day, but it seemed that the harder she tried to avoid him, the more of her head space he occupied.

He was an arse. No, he was an arrogant arse. No, that wasn't right either. He was an opinionated, arrogant arse. Yet, against her better judgement she couldn't help liking him. Saladin emanated erotic strength and fierce sensuality that curled her toes and sent her libido into high gear.

She'd been alone for so long, had felt so lonely she sometimes ached inside. And that loneliness made him all the more dangerous to her. It tainted her judgement and weakened her resolve.

"A penny for your thoughts," Hawke said, tilting her face up to his with a finger beneath her chin.

Teagan jumped, squeaking out a squeal of surprise. How the hell could he have seated himself next to her without her noticing? That was just creepy. Damn vampires.

Hawke watched her carefully, examined every line and contour of her face, his eyes fixing on her long dark hair. "Beautiful," Hawke said, his voice low, his gaze only for her, seductively compelling. "Like wavy black silk."

Teagan's breath hitched. "It's only hair."

Hawke stretched his arm across the back of the lounge behind her, stopping shy of touching her.

"It's beautiful, like you," he smiled. a little twitch to his lips that warmed his ice blue eyes and made her feel a little self-conscious.

Hawke reached out and wound his finger through a strand of her hair. "It feels as good as it looks," he said tugging it gently, smoothing it between his fingers.

"Stop that," she said, slapping his hand away.

"Yes, Hawke. Stop that," Saladin ordered from the doorway, his voice as harsh as a blunt razor, but infinitely more deadly.

Teagan and Hawke both jumped at the sound of the barely veiled murder in his voice.

Quickly removing herself from the couch, Teagan put several feet between each of the two men.

Saladin glared down at Hawke, his eyes and fangs flashing possessively. He was behaving like a jealous moron. He knew he was, but he couldn't seem to help himself. The sight of Hawke so intimately close to Teagan, touching her hair no less, just made his blood boil.

The need to touch her himself, wipe Hawke's scent from her body and replace it with his own was overwhelming.

Saladin approached Teagan slowly. His relaxed, graceful stride full of confidence, although an extraneous flare of confusion and insecurity coiled behind his indomitable exterior, intermingling with his anger.

Teagan froze as his fingers brushed her cheek. His touch was cool, but heat flowed through her. She found it hard to breathe, while at the same time her heart pounded fiercely. It would be so easy to turn her head and lick the side of his thumb, maybe take his fingertip into her mouth. The temptation to do just that surprised her.

Saladin brushed her cheek again, his gaze holding hers. Teagan's body was warm, pliant, the scent of her secret wanting gripped her more tightly as she tried to banish it, wrapping her feminine fragrance around his senses and drawing him even closer to her.

He was enthralled by the uniqueness of her scent, his head lowering slightly as he drew in a deep breath to bring the bouquet of her beauty deep into his lungs. Dipping his head to her throat he inhaled again. "Your scent," he breathed, "Is rich and drugging. I can't help but wonder what you taste like."

Saladin skimmed his hand down Teagan's arm and closed his strong fingers around hers, lifting them to his lips to kiss the back of her hand, the caress gentle, but heat burned in the depths of his blue eyes. "Walk with me."

It was not a command, not a suggestion, and he didn't plead. He simply said it.

Teagan twitched her hand free from his, staring into the most amazing eyes she had ever seen, flickering with luminescent flecks from his growing arousal.

"You're trying to compel me, aren't you?"

"I swear to you, my beautiful jewel, I'm keeping my 'vampire' charms to myself. You, on the other hand, are sending out signals like crazy."

"I am not."

"Yes, you are. You're thinking about something that involves me and its making you want me."

92

"Stop flattering yourself. I don't want you. You're an arrogant son of a…."

"Yes, you do." Saladin quickly cut her off before she could finish her sentence. "I know I'm right. I could smell your sweet scent of arousal from the next room, as could Hawke." He could have left that last part out, but he just loved how beautiful she looked when her cheeks blushed.

Shocked fury flashed through Teagan's veins. Saladin stood so tall and confident before her, as though his knowledge of things was supreme. Unfortunately, he was right. She did want him. She wanted him way too much, but she wasn't about to boost his already over inflated ego by acknowledging it.

Was it wrong to wish for him to spontaneously combust? What if it was only one area of his body, say, the zipper region of his pants?

Teagan pursed her lips and clenched her fists tightly, straining not to retaliate with the words ready to burst free. That, would just extend this embarrassing moment even longer.

She couldn't help herself. "You're a dick," she blurted. Glaring at him even as she turned on her heel, she marched haughtily from the room.

"And I thought I was a bastard," Alaric said from across the room with a chuckle.

"You are," Saladin growled.

"If I was you, I'd be careful. She is a druid," Hawke piped up.

"What's she going to do, cast a spell on me?" Saladin scoffed, as if the idea was ludicrous. Druid's have strict rules about using their magic, and payback on overbearing vampires wasn't within the allowed parameters. At least he didn't think so.

"All I'm saying is, don't push your luck," Hawke advised.

Alaric slapped a hand on Saladin's shoulder, his expression caught somewhere between amused and concerned. This young woman was affecting Saladin in a way he had never seen before. He just wasn't sure yet if it was a good thing or not.

Teagan's determination to ignore Saladin's advances drove him crazy. Her fierce will drew him, her fire fascinated him, and her sensuality held him in an iron grip that he couldn't break. His desire for her went well beyond mending his dented pride, it was a primitive reaction beyond logical reasoning.

He could neither stop himself from trying to seduce her any more than he could hold back the hurtful remarks that drove her away.

A few days ago, he wouldn't have cared if a female was upset by his crass manner. If one woman rejected him, there were ten more who eagerly begged for his attention. But, Teagan…He wished he could take back the carelessly spoken words the moment they left his lips.

Saladin groaned as his guilty conscience kicked in. Yet another new experience for him, and not one he was enjoying.

He had to make things right with her.

Teagan entered the darkened conservatory. She'd taken the wrong doorway in her desperation to flee Saladin and the room filled with conceited vampires. The conservatory wasn't as cold as she would have expected, given its domed ceiling and encompassing glass walls. The plants in the indoor tropical garden seemed to give off their own heat. A giant greenhouse of humidity.

She felt a strange sense of relief…until she realised she was no longer alone.

Saladin stalked toward her. The closer he got, the more her chin came up in that defiant way of hers. He cleared his throat. "Teagan, may I have a word?" he asked in an apologetic tone, his deep smoky voice, smooth enough to make any woman, living or undead, cream her pants.

"If you think being rude will get my attention, you'll be really bored before I care" she said, turning her back to him and crossing her arms defensively.

"About that…"

"I'm listening," she replied tersely.

"I'm…sorry". The word felt foreign on his tongue. It had been so long since he'd used it, he had to push the word out from around the moth balls.

Saladin waited with twitching impatience for her response as the seconds ticked by.

"Accepted," she answered warily.

Saladin sighed with relief. He hadn't even realised he'd been holding in a tense breath.

"Could we now please discuss business?" he asked smoothly, minus his customary overbearing, pompous manner.

Teagan shot him a look that clearly meant, *only if you keep your hands and comments to yourself.*

He lifted his hands in a sign of surrender.

"Walk with me," he said once again, gesturing for Teagan to walk beside him along the path that wound its way through the shadowed darkness of the conservatory. Somehow the darkness made her feel more relaxed in his presence, it was less confronting. The plant filled space, although quite large, seemed immense with her limited vision. It was an illusion of course, but one she could live with.

"Did you view the entire manor and the grounds today," he asked.

"Almost all of it. There was only one room I didn't have access to. It was a heavily protected room down a corridor with an enchantment on it."

It was a lead lined room with more security than Fort Knox, deep in the bowels of the lower levels of the manor. If she wasn't a druid and able to see through magical shrouds, she wouldn't have even noticed the corridor that led to the room.

"Ah, yes. That's the store room."

"Store room? What does Alaric keep in there that needs that much protection?" Whatever it was, it was obviously either very important or very deadly. Maybe even both. That was a pleasant thought, not.

"*I* don't even know everything that's in there. But it's best not to ask," he answered, hoping to dodge any further questions about its contents.

"If you want me to protect it with the new ward, I'll need to get in there so I can add it to my mental map of the place."

"What about the other preparations to perform the ward? Have you had a chance to start a list of things you'll need?"

"No, not yet. I need to see that room first. From what I'm guessing, that room will need something extra added to its protection and I won't know what that 'something extra' is, until I get in there."

"In that case, I'll take care of that for you. I have no pressing engagements tomorrow." Saladin turned to her and smiled, a dark, erotic smile that stole her breath.

"Thanks. I'd appreciate it."

He couldn't keep his eyes off her. "Please don't take this the wrong way," he said. "But I find you to be the most intriguing female I have ever met."

Teagan gave a tentative smile. Fragile, but it was honest. "That was almost a complement. You feeling okay?"

That was debatable.

"Saladin, is there any news about Abby and Alex yet?" Teagan asked, hoping to distract him into a safer direction.

Saladin's expression became suddenly grim. He related the latest message that had come from Abby. The news of Ahriman's possession of Alex was a serious blow, especially to Cassie.

Teagan had wondered why she hadn't seen her friend all evening. Now she knew. She must be taking it very hard.

"I need to go home to my flat sometime tomorrow," she told him. Instantly Saladin's eyes turned dark.

"Why?"

"I need to get a few things. I hadn't expected to be staying for so long when I packed." She'd only planned on being in Cadley for two, maybe three days at the most. She arrived the day before Brian Harlow's funeral, and she had planned on heading home the day afterwards. Instead, she had ended up here, at the manor.

"What do you need?

"Clothes and my grandfather's Book of Shadows."

"I'll see what I can do."

She knew she was pushing her luck with this one, but she had to ask. "I also need to do some shopping. It's nearly Christmas and I still need to get a few presents."

"We'll talk about that later. I can only give in so much, you know," he answered, his patience beginning to fray. He was Saladin, a leader among his kind, he wasn't used to being at anyone's beck and call. People normally did his bidding, not the other way around. Although, he had volunteered to oversee Teagan's work on the ward, he reminded himself, and it did give him an opportunity to keep her in his company. But, going shopping with a female? Well that just wasn't going to happen, not even with *this* female.

"I know," she said soothingly, patting him on the arm. "It's so hard being you."

"Yeah, well it is," he grinned as she laughed. "Meet me in the study in the morning and I'll take you to the storage room."

"And when will you take me home for my things?"

"I need to go into the club tomorrow night for a short while. If you don't mind waiting, I'll take you then."

"Sure."

Teagan was surprised. Saladin wasn't all that bad to talk to once he'd removed that enormous stick from his arse. This was a new side to him, and she liked it. It made him seem almost human.

Their eyes met and held for a long moment. "Well, good night then," she said.

Saladin's much larger frame filled the path leaving only enough space for Teagan to squeeze past. He gripped her arm lightly, steadying her as the warmth of her sensuous body brushed past him.

He made no effort to touch her again, but the temptation was strong. He wanted her softness under him, her full hips and breasts buffering the hard planes of his body as he pounded into her. He wanted her more than he had wanted any other female in history. Saladin didn't want to question the reason why, but he couldn't help reflecting on his past. He had only ever wanted women in a physical sense, to sate his physical needs. Their opinions of him had never been of consequence.

So why was it so damned important to make *her* like him? *Because she tests you. Because she's unpredictable and because she's a challenge.*

Yeah, she was a challenge that took away his boredom. That had to be it.

11

"Yes, my Lord."

As Mira silently left the ritual chamber, Morganna's deceptively soft voice echoed through the cavernous space.

Mira didn't know who Morganna was speaking to and she didn't particularly care. Morganna had an ally, someone other than Ahriman. Big deal. Clearly, she wasn't in the habit of putting all her eggs in one basket.

Mira followed a similar philosophy. Always keep your options open. As far as she was concerned, it's better to sit at the right hand of the devil than stand in his way. Mira had been accused many times of having no loyalties, but in truth she had been devoutly loyal to her progeny, Cain....Until recently. His death had come as a hard blow, one she had every intention of repaying in kind.

Narayan, Abby's vampire sibling had killed Cain a couple of months earlier and it had riled her that she'd had no opportunity to kill Narayan. However, now it seemed she had the next best thing...Abby.

Morganna's voice began to fade as Mira followed the underground corridor back to the compound. The normally abrupt woman spoke with sincere reverence and a hint of nervousness in her tone. It occurred to her that as powerful as she knew Morganna to be, if she was addressing someone as *'my Lord'*, it probably was in her own best interest to find out who *he* is.

She had always suspected that Morganna's loyalty to Ahriman was only temporary. Like Mira, Morganna had waited to see how Ahriman fared with his quest to become immortal. He'd failed at that attempt dismally, defeated by a Guardian. So, once again he was back in a human body with limitations and weaknesses, not the immortal demon she had signed up to follow.

Mira had watched him over the past few days and what she observed put new doubts in her mind about his ability to be a leader in their cause. He appeared more volatile, mentally unstable. Only yesterday she caught him singing the ABC song to himself, over and over, as if he couldn't remember where the letter J fit, then flew into a rage and electrocuted a guard with some sort of electromagnetic power he seemed to have acquired.

Right now, the only thing that was keeping Mira allied to him was the fact that he was making progress on the portal device. It was almost complete, or so he had told Morganna only an hour before. No doubt this was the news Morganna was relaying through her scrying pool back in the ritual chamber.

Mira put the issue with Ahriman aside as she moved her thoughts onto a more pressing problem. Every patrol they sent out over the past couple of days had disappeared, fifteen men in all. Nearly all of them were 'recruited' by Morganna and Ahriman. It begged the question, had the Alliance wised up to the Guild's recruiting methods? If so, had they killed the guards or merely captured them? Either way, the magical parameter alarms had not been tripped. Whoever was taking out their guards was a good hunter. Mira would admire the stealthy SOB, if it didn't place her own neck on the chopping block. She had to get answers, and fast, preferably without losing more men in the process. Between the ones that were disappearing, and the ones Ahriman had killed, they would need to do some more 'recruiting' soon, or they may not have enough men left to defend the compound.

Stepping from the elevator, Mira nearly bowled over Dr Greenville and Lilith.

"Do you mind? Watch where you're going," Mira snapped irritably.

Mira couldn't understand why Ahriman had kept the sniveling human female around. She had served her purpose, she got them the information they needed about Alaric, Alex and his sister Cassie, and she'd fulfilled her role in acquiring Alex from the manor. In her eyes,

Lilith no longer provided any worthwhile function, except maybe to become a healthy food source for the vampires in the compound.

Mira's mouth began to water as Dr Greenville's delectable scent reached her nose, rich, warm and inviting. It reminded her of the smell of a juicy roast dinner. Mmm…she was looking forward to the day when he too would no longer be useful. He was going to make a wonderful snack.

"Sorry," Lilith croaked.

Mira's eyes narrowed on Lilith's bruised throat. "Rough sex again?" she queried apathetically. There at least, Lilith served a purpose, she supposed.

"No. Thanks to that *bitch*!" Lilith rasped, still gasping in gulps of air. Only a millimetre more pressure and her larynx would have been crushed. As it was, there was a chance that she might have received some permanent damage. Lilith's throat burned and throbbed, and every swallow was like a knife being driven in. "I'm going to kill the bitch in her sleep."

"Not if I get to her first," Mira put in with a sneer. "Would you mind explaining what happened?"

Lilith opened her mouth to explain but the effort to speak again ended in a coughing fit that left her gasping for air. Propping her up against the wall, Leon Greenville related the story of what happened with Ahriman and Abby in the lab.

Mira listened with interest.

"I agree, Abby has to go," Mira concluded.

Abby was a liability to their cause. She was a distraction to Ahriman, stalling him from finishing the portal device and, Mira suspected she had something to do with the missing guards. Abby was trouble with a capital T.

"We need to be discrete. From what you've told me, Ahriman is becoming attached to her. We can't afford for him to interfere, at least not directly," Mira said.

Lilith snarled, her fists clenched, her body shook with rage at the thought of Ahriman having *feelings* for Abby. He was hers, and Abby was *not* going to take him away from her.

Mira dismissed Dr Greenville as though he had never been present and helped Lilith back to her room to continue their scheming.

The ageing scientist walked away as quickly as his legs would carry him without breaking into a run. Indecision warred with his conscience. Should he tell Abby what the two women were plotting, or should he keep his mouth shut? It was probably none of his business anyway. No doubt Abby could defend herself quite well against Mira. And Lilith...well, she was only human. Abby already nearly killed her once today, Lilith wasn't likely to survive a second run-in with her. If she had any sense, she wouldn't even try. But that was the conundrum. Neither Mira or Lilith seemed to have much common sense.

Dr Greenville was still debating what to do several hours later when he returned to the lab. His internal dispute elicited huffs, frustrated sighs and *tsking* noises as he clicked his tongue at regular intervals, as he worked alongside Ahriman. Lost in his thoughts, he was completely unaware of the distracting sounds he was making.

"Alright, out with it."

"What?"

"Obviously something is on your mind and your irritating noises are seriously pissing me off."

"Nothing's on my mind. Everything is fine," he answered quickly. Maybe too quickly he realised.

"I'm not going to ask again. You either tell me what's going on, or I loosen your tongue for you. It's your choice."

Dr Greenville gulped, his mouth suddenly dry, beads of sweat glistening on his forehead. What a choice. Rock, meet hard place. If he told him what Mira and Lilith were plotting, Ahriman would most likely kill him just for being the bearer of deceitful tidings. On the other hand, Mira and Lilith would do the job for him when they learned he'd betrayed their confidence.

On weighing the possible methods of his death, Ahriman was the one most likely to make it swift. There was no fury like a woman scorned, and that pair...he shuddered at the thought. They would delight in every painful minute they could drag out his torture.

Putting his options into perspective, the choice was easy. With one last heavy sigh, Leon Greenville braced his shoulders back and told Ahriman everything he knew.

"Please don't let them know I told you, they'll kill me," he begged after he realised Ahriman was letting him live.

101

In truth, Ahriman had thought about it, but unfortunately he still needed the man's insight and expertise in getting the device to work. Alex's knowledge was extensive, but he lacked the practical experience that Greenville had. After all, the older man had helped invent some of the equipment they were now using.

"Yes, they would," Ahriman answered simply, as though the man's life was no more significant than an animal in an abattoir. "Don't worry, your secret is safe with me," he replied. It was in both their favour not to say anything to Mira or Lilith. If the women didn't know they were under his scrutiny, he had the upper hand.

As much as he would love to break the blood bond, while he still needed Alex's body, he also needed Abby. Ahriman couldn't allow two obsessive psychopathic women to bring any harm to her. Well, actually, it was probably only one obsessive psychopath, Lilith. Mira was undoubtedly a cold-blooded sociopath, and infinitely more dangerous. She was the one to watch.

Over the past few days the blood bond between Abby and Alex had continued to grow, but so had Ahriman's tolerance to the intensity of it. Ahriman had been careful not to allow anyone any knowledge of their bond. He knew Morganna had her sights set on his position in the Guild, and Mira too had divided loyalties. If it was discovered that his hold over Alex wasn't as strong as he let on…

He could very well have a coup on his hands.

"We have to protect Abby," Alex appealed.

"I agree. But here is not the time or the place for this discussion," Ahriman replied. He checked the clock on the wall, it was much later than he'd thought, well past midnight. Where was Abby?

"Dr Greenville, I'll take care of it. Go and get some sleep, we need to test the device in the morning," Ahriman told him gruffly. With that, he swept past the relieved man and headed out of the lab. "You two," Ahriman addressed the guards by the door standing rigidly to attention. "Find Abby, discretely…and have her brought to my rooms. Now," he barked impatiently.

Instantly the pair scurried off. Their blank faces showing no emotion or even the slightest wariness to Ahriman's pissy mood. But that wasn't surprising since these were two of his *'recruited'* guards. Mindless drones willing to perform any act Ahriman asked of them with no fear, and no questions asked. They were the only ones he allowed near his private rooms and the lab. Bizarre really when you think about it. Ahriman surrounded himself with his enemy and trusted them more than he trusted those who willingly followed him.

The guards who joined the Guild voluntarily unfortunately still had their minds intact, along with their free will. Hence, they were less predictable and not trustworthy.

Abby was struck with a feeling of déjà vu as she opened the door to Ahriman's rooms.

"Abby, thanks for coming," Ahriman said. His T-shirt clung to his lean frame, his chest flexing as he fingered the glass of scotch in one hand and gestured with the other for her to join him.

"I didn't realise I had a choice."

"Of course you didn't, but Alex tells me that you respond better to polite requests." Request? A burly guard hefting her over his shoulder and carrying her here was a request? Someone forgot to explain to him the meaning of the word.

Abby eyed him closer. Ahriman doesn't wear T-shirts. Was Alex taking more control of his body, manipulating Ahriman? She desperately wanted to believe it was possible. "What do you want? I'm busy." *Yeah, busy counting dust bunnies.*

"We need to talk."

"About?" she asked. Crossing her arms defiantly, she made no effort to close the distance between them.

"You're to be restricted to my rooms until further notice…for your own protection," he added as an afterthought.

Well, that was vague. And weird. Just like everything else in this deranged situation.

"Way to go moron. What did I tell you about polite requests?"

"Why?" she asked suspiciously. Her previous indignation at being man-handled, quickly tipping her mood meter to resentful outrage.

"You need to tell her everything. Better still, let me tell her."

Ahriman snorted with pompous arrogance.

Abby was getting used to witnessing the animated internal discussions between them, even if she was cut-off from the dialogue. Although she knew that Alex was arguing in her favour, it still hurt to be left out of the conversation. She really missed her connection to Alex's mind.

"Fine," Ahriman gave in.

He poured himself another scotch and one for Abby, motioning for her to take it. Against her better judgement, she reluctantly approached. With every step closer, her resolve to stay strong diminished as the bond between them began to increase. As she took the glass from his hands, their fingers touched, a shock of electricity jolting through her veins, pooling in the moist folds between her thighs.

"Mira and Lilith are plotting against you. You need to stay where I can protect you."

"Is it because I nearly killed Lilith earlier?"

"No doubt that has something to do with it. So, you'll stay here in my rooms with guards at the door until further notice."

The pretentious tone of his delivery irritated her more than the domineering words he used.

"Ah, shitballs on fire!" Alex cursed.

"No," she said flatly. "I don't take orders, no doubt Alex told you that. Let him out to talk to me."

Protecting Abby was the first thing they actually agreed on, but of course they couldn't agree on how to get her to co-operate.

"Fucking craptastic! Your negotiation skills with women really suck, you know that? You're about as subtle as a sledge hammer." Alex huffed, pacing restlessly in the back of Ahriman's mind. How was he going to get her to see reason with this parasitic bastard screwing everything up.

"I'm not that bad," Ahriman protested.

"Compared to a chainsaw, probably not. But keep using your arse-cranking evil charm and you'll make things worse."

Abby put down her glass and took a step closer, knowing her close proximity to Alex had an effect on Ahriman too.

Ahriman scowled at her, his eyes narrowed with annoyance. She thoroughly tested his patience and sanity with her defiance.

Abby was pushing him again, trying to manipulate the bond to weaken him.

It wasn't going to work. Not this time.

"You," he growled, cupping her chin in his hand. "Will do what *I* say!"

Any other creature would have fainted in sheer terror. Ahriman was a demon who put the bad in badass.

But not Abby. Confident in her certainty that he would not harm her, she pushed even harder.

"They won't hurt me, I know how to kick arse. Would you like a demonstration?" she asked, her tone was friendly but the ice in her eyes could have snap frozen the Sahara desert.

"I don't doubt you can, *pumpkin*, but I'm not giving you the option to try. You *will* remain in these rooms until I say otherwise." His lips twitched as he fought the urge to smile.

Smile? Why would he want to smile at her tenacious insolence? He wouldn't. Alex would. Abby watched the conflict behind his eyes. Could she dare to hope that Alex might get the upper hand soon?

"Aw, it's not so bad. Stop your complaining" Alex gloated. *"I know you enjoy her defiance, I can feel it. You like the fact that she's not afraid of you, that she tells you exactly what's on her mind. You enjoy her honesty."*

"No. I. Don't," Ahriman bit out between clenched teeth.

"You're lying to yourself. You can't hide your thoughts from me any more than I can hide mine from you. Remember?"

Yeah, he remembered. All too well. "Suck my dick, motherfucker!" Ahriman sneered.

"Make up your mind shithead. Which is it, suck your dick or fuck your mother? Who is your mother by the way, Satan's skanky whore?" Alex bated.

"Sarcasm is the body's natural response to stupid," Ahriman retorted snippily.

"You think that's sarcastic? You should hear what I don't say."

"I really wish I *couldn't* hear what you have to say. Just for five fucking minutes."

The drawback from Ahriman's growing ability to tolerate the blood bond seemed to create a further blending between himself and

Alex. Their thoughts and feelings were beginning to merge. Alex's hunger for aggression had increased, while Ahriman's low tolerance threshold seemed to have shifted to a more mellow level, even the language he used was changing, becoming more….Alex-like.

He felt like a walking contradiction.

"Let Alex out." Abby asked demurely, changing tactics using a less confronting tone, her body making the demands instead as she stepped in closer, her hands gripping his hips as she pressed her own against him.

"Let me out. She'll listen to me."

Not going to happen.

A tight groan escaped him as her thigh moved against his, the firm planes of her abdomen cushioning the bulging length behind his zipper.

He was so hard he could drive spikes into railroad ties.

A growl, a rumbling purr, arose from his throat. Again, the response was a blend of Alex and Ahriman together, which only served to piss him off all the more.

Abby licked her lips.

The temptation was irresistible, Ahriman's brain short-circuited, leaving his body in control. Dipping his head, he slanted his mouth over hers. For a moment she stiffened, and then her hands reached for him, her body melting against him.

"Alex can't play today," he whispered hoarsely against her lips.

His voice was dark, his hands rough and aggressive. Blood surged through his veins as his heart pounded fiercely in his chest. Need roared inside him, threatening his tentative restraint.

Ahriman was determined. It was his way or no way at all.

He was in charge here, not Alex.

"Think again," Alex retorted in contradiction to Ahriman's mental thought, allowing his own response to Abby's touch to flair his body's response even further, driving Ahriman closer to the verge of his tolerance of their bond.

Abby could only melt against him, a prisoner to her own body's needs, held by unseen chains so strong, so hot, she could only tremble against him. She wanted nothing to do with the evil, parasitic bastard, but even as her mind rejected him, her body ached for more of his touch.

She couldn't let him do this to her again.

It was a battle of wills.

12

Abby struggled for release against the iron bands of his arms. This was insane. She was a vampire, he was human, she should have broken free easily, but she couldn't. Whether Ahriman's power made Alex's body stronger or her bond to Alex weakened her in his grasp, she didn't know. Regardless, the result was the same.

It was however a paradoxical situation. The harder she tried to pull away from him, the more she didn't want to leave.

She twisted away, his arms tightened about her waist, enveloping her in muscle-bound flesh and body heat.

Repressing her desire, she stomped on his toes. Ahriman swore, shaking the offended foot, but refused to release his grip.

Abby continued to struggle against him. His body a stone hard wall against her, slid across her hypersensitive skin as she fought his hold. Languorous need wound through her bloodstream like an insidious drug. His arousal, large and heavy, wedged against the small of her back.

Why not use his lust against him?

She was playing head games with an evil madman. Did that make her as crazy as him? Maybe. Probably.

His T-shirt had drifted up under their struggle, exposing his ribbed abs. Fighting back a shiver, she turned in his grip, bringing the angle between them closer. He towered over her, the bulging ridge of his erection pressing incessantly against her belly. *Oh, God.*

Danger and desire pelted her in an unforgiving rain.

The intense connection between them pulsated. She needed Alex's touch so badly the building desire within her core was almost painful.

Abby's fingers caressed his scalp, sending tingles from the base of his spine, sparking fiery bolts of pleasure straight to his balls.

Ahriman growled. A heated, tormented sound that spurred her on.

Get a grip, stay in control, she reprimanded, shoring up her faltering confidence.

Abby pressed her body hard up against him. Her aggressive behaviour had succeeded last time, forcing him to release Alex from his silent prison, temporarily. It would work again. It had to. However, without the impassioned anger and aggression Lilith had induced, she felt less assured.

Even with a sane man, she would fear to tempt this intense chemistry. And Ahriman was neither sane nor in possession of a conscience. His moral compass definitely didn't point north, and she had no way of knowing what he would do if he was pushed too far.

She had to try.

As Abby pressed against him, she found herself desperate to feel the effect of his touch on every inch of her body.

It was Alex she was touching not Ahriman, she affirmed to herself. *He needs you, as much as you need him.*

"Let Alex out," she asked demurely, attempting to appeal to his softer side. Wishful thinking, he didn't have a softer side.

"I have a better idea." Lightening charged through his blood at her touch. It was intoxicating, devastating. Ahriman wanted more even as he cringed against the thought. He knew what she was trying to do and it wasn't going to work, not this time.

Infuriated that Ahriman wasn't giving him a chance to talk to Abby, convince her she needed protection, Alex resumed singing the maddeningly irritating children's songs, only now he deliberately sang off-key to increase the annoyance factor.

Ahriman waged an internal conflict with himself, his anger bringing a minor reprieve, separating him from Alex's emotions and ramping up his natural savage response.

He had to prove to Alex who was stronger, who held the power. Abby was merely the most convenient method of achieving his goal, yet again. He needed a hard ride and an outlet for the pent-up rage building inside him.

At some point during their battle of wills, their goal had changed from: Who was going to convince Abby to accept protection, to who was going to fuck her.

Ahriman fisted his hand into her hair, forcefully pulling her even closer, urging her lips apart he swept into her mouth, the domineering kiss demanding obedience with its aggressive assault.

Need slammed into her and her world shifted on its axis. With every brush of his lips his unbearably male taste saturated her senses. Clutching his shoulders, she joined the untamed kiss, hungry for more.

The way she leaned into him, strained to be closer...fresh heat coiled and expanded inside him. Ahriman tried to absorb the overwhelming feelings washing through him as another dizzying surge of desire crashed over him.

It was too much.

Alex gloated, teased and tormented Ahriman in the back of his mind. Any moment now, Ahriman would give up and let him out. After all, Abby was his, not Ahriman's. Their blood bond was far too intense, too intimate for the demon to cope with.

Alex's arrogant conviction backfired, he realised all too late.

Ahriman pulled away from her and reached into a dresser drawer, determined to assert his control.

"Mother fucker. What the hell do you think you're doing?" Alex demanded heatedly. His mind-bending childish taunts forgotten momentarily as he reverted back to his futile, abusive retorts. Alex had seen what was in that drawer and he wanted no part of what Ahriman had in mind.

Ahriman ignored Alex. Gripping Abby's wrists behind her back he snapped on a pair of handcuffs, binding them together, quickly followed by a blindfold.

Much better. Much less personal, the reduced intimacy dimmed down the intensity of the bond. Ahriman snickered at Alex's anger as he ushered Abby up against the back of the recliner chair. Ahriman deftly removed her jeans, taking his time with her lace panties, indulging in their silky feel under his fingers, before unfastening the front of his own pants and releasing his turgid girth.

Ahriman pressed himself hard up against her, his hot, iron hard length pressed into the small of her back.

Pleasure rolled through Abby's body. She didn't fight it. He branded her neck with his lips, nuzzling her sensitive earlobe and breathing fire across her skin. In her mind she knew this wasn't Alex in control, but her tempestuous body didn't care.

Shifting his hips, he began to move against her, sliding the length of his steely hard rod between her thighs, through the heated silk of her intimate folds, drenching his shaft in her juices as he passed over the entrance to her core. Again and again he passed over it, sending shockwaves of pleasure to her clit, revelling in her breathy gasps and pleas for more, until the urgency of his own desire had his muscles trembling with the need to feel her inner walls wrapped tightly around him.

He slammed into her. Down, down deeper, through the tight squeeze of her moist, hot channel.

Abby writhed against him, pushing her hips back onto his, impaling herself on his stiff length, meeting his every thrust. Deeper. Deeper. He savoured the clasp of her inner muscles on him and the breathless moans he wrenched from her. Shafting inside her so powerfully, satisfaction surged through him as he felt her tighten around him.

Ahriman wanted her, far more than he should.

The truth was a knife to his soul. His own identity seemed to be merging with Alex more with every passing hour. They were still separate, but somehow more connected.

He was trying to work the frustration out of himself, and he was using his cock to do it. He was frustrated at being trapped in someone else's body, frustrated at the overwhelming bond between Abby and Alex, and he was frustrated that his own twisted soul was beginning to enjoy it. That *really* pissed him off.

Ahriman pistoned his hips, spearing her responsive depths in silent desperation. His face was set, his lips pressed together, his eyes were as hard as the steely flesh he was pounding into her with long, dominant strokes.

Abby arched her back a little further, her bound hands sliding between them, over her anal star and lower until she found the point where their two bodies met. Ahriman grunted, his body jolted a little harder against her as Abby wrapped her fingers around the base of his powerful erection as he forged deeper inside her.

This wasn't the pleasurable 'love making' she'd had with Alex. This was raw, hard *fucking*, so crazy hot, Abby wanted it to last forever.

Ahriman groaned, Alex's own pleasure rising alongside his. For once he wasn't fighting him for control of his body. He could feel Alex's curiosity and shared in it with covetous delight.

Alex had never been one for the rougher forms of sex, but he was beginning to see the attractive lure, as he felt Abby's excitement for it grow within himself.

The world ceased to exist, Abby knew nothing but the heat within her and around her, the three of them together, two bodies, three souls and one voracious hunger.

Sliding greedily through her silken channel, Ahriman buried himself to the hilt…but it wasn't enough.

Abby lost her grip on his throbbing length, the slick cream flowing from her body making the task more difficult as the friction between them continued to build. Her bound hands groped but failed to find purchase on the steely length as their bodies continued to slam together.

Ahriman watched as Abby's fingers glided over her tight little anal star in search for his cock. The sight sent a flood of heat through his blood, hardening him impossibly further.

He gripped her hip with one hand to hold her in place, the other he pressed to her back, bending her further forward over the chair.

Ahriman slapped her arse hard when she tried to regain their previous position. Abby gasped, the stinging sensation and shock tightening her inner muscles around him, enticing a desperate groan from his gritted teeth and a mewling cry of satisfaction from Abby as he thrust harder into her. She was so hot from the in-and-out friction of his shaft, and so tight, but Ahriman couldn't take his eyes off that other, tiny opening.

Smoothing his hand over the red mark he left on her butt cheek, he lifted his hand to slap the other.

Again, she cried out as she tightened around him, his cock throbbing with the need for more. Sweat drenched his body, dripping onto her like rain, making the slide of their bodies electrified.

Abby shivered as his hand slid between their bodies, first seeking her swollen clit, rubbing it, pinching it between his fingers. Abby arched her hips higher, giving him better access and exposing that tiny star more fully to his view.

Ahriman growled possessively as he slowed his thrusts inside her but did not stop altogether. Abby whimpered at the loss of sensation and pushed her hips back into him, desperate to regain their momentum, only to realise his fingers had found a new target for their exploration.

Abby gasped at the new sensation. A single finger circled the rear hole. It dipped between them into the moist slick at her core and back up to the anal fissure, drenching it in her juices, lubricating it until his finger parted its opening and breached the entrance.

Abby had never expected this. She heard a voice ring through the room, without any realisation that she had cried out. The noises were sharp, animal-like, and she couldn't stop them.

"Fuck, you're tight. I can't wait to get in there," Ahriman keened, his voice quivering with need.

Abby didn't comprehend his words any more than she realised the pleasure filled noises were coming from her own throat. Her mind, like her body, was focussed fully on his hard length filling one channel, and his finger filling the other. She was lost in a tidal wave of sensations swamping her.

A second finger joined the first, gently widening the opening, then a third. Three fingers fucked inside her in rhythm with the thrusting of his cock.

Ahriman pulled out of her all at once.

But he wasn't finished. Far from it.

Blindfolded and handcuffed, Abby was at his mercy, her other senses became heightened. She could smell his arousal, hot and musky and it drove her own even higher. His touch too was hot, a hand held her hips in place as the engorged tip of his cock, still coated in her juices, pressed against that tiny rear opening.

Abby jerked her hips forward at the unexpected intrusion, but bent over the chair she had nowhere to go. *No...* she couldn't take it. He was too big. He'd tear her apart. And why did that excite her so much?

But, he'd made her needy for him, and Abby welcomed him in, spreading her legs further to take him.

113

Ahriman gripped her hips tightly, holding her in place. Inch by slow inch, he worked his shaft inside her anal fissure, prying her open, stretching her wide. He lifted her higher to take more of him, until he was sheathed to the hilt.

Slowly, he began to move inside her, his fingers sliding between them to fill the empty void of her sex. The dual pleasures inside her added a new layer of torment to the pleasure.

Abby's inner walls gripped him with incredible strength as she teetered on the edge of climax, rippling over him, milking him as her orgasm exploded within her.

Ahriman was beginning to unravel. Another thrust, the sensations rapidly building, stacking up on one another, staggering him. His body began to tremble as he let the need build and build.

His breath came hard, ragged. He was so close...

Abby felt him come, his iron hard length thrust one last time, it throbbed inside her as he shot his scalding seed. They were both screaming, bodies slamming together, tears on her face. She seemed to be falling, but his strong arms were there to hold her.

He crashed over her, his weight hot and hard, and all the wildness went out of her. In its place a cold ice block formed in the pit of her stomach.

Ahriman pulled out of her, leaving her feeling hollow and confused once more.

"You're welcome," he said. She could hear the smirk in his voice as he uncuffed her.

Slowly Abby removed the blindfold. She didn't rush. Why would she? She could cover her shame with the blindfold, pretend nothing had happened. Without it, she was exposed. She would have to face herself in the mirror and she didn't want to see the sexually satisfied expression on the face looking back at her.

Had she betrayed Alex?

She loved Alex, her soul was bound to him, and she wanted his body no matter who was at the controls. But she couldn't ignore what just happened, no matter how she tried to justify it, and the truth terrified her. She'd wanted the hard, rough sex Ahriman offered her. It was thrilling and intoxicating.

Abby was confused and still horny.

What was she going to do?

Ahriman threw her underwear at her without meeting her eyes, and without a word he climbed into bed, leaving the covers open for her to climb in too.

Reluctantly she did, but lay as close to the edge of the bed as possible. The silence between them stretched until she couldn't take it any longer.

"Do you have nothing to say? Or are you so busy gloating because I want you, even as I hate you?"

Ahriman ignored her question. "You'll be staying in my rooms from now on and that's final." He'd gotten the upper hand on both Abby and Alex, and they both knew it.

"Won't your girlfriend have something to say about that?"

"I don't have a girlfriend."

"I don't think Lilith got that memo."

13

"What are you doing?" Teagan asked Cassie as she searched through the kitchen cupboards.

"Mrs P is out, and I have a craving for stewed apples and custard. Besides that, I feel like I'll go mad if I don't have something to do."

"Yeah, I heard about Alex. I'm really sorry. How are you doing?"

"Great. Just great. Where's the damn custard powder?" Cassie yelled at the cupboard. "I know it's here, Mrs P used it yesterday."

"Hey. It's okay, I'll help you look." It had been a long time since Teagan had seen Cassie so worked-up. She looked like she was holding it together by a hair. She and Alex were really close. Mix her stress with pregnancy hormones and, well, you got Cassie. A powder keg on two legs. "Where's Alaric?"

"He's outside with Saladin. They're having trouble with Lionel and Harold again." Teagan looked at her blankly. "The gardeners," Cassie told her.

"Oh." Teagan had heard everyone grumbling about them the night before. "Why does Alaric keep them on if they're so difficult to deal with?"

"Because..." Cassie huffed. "They're lycans and Alaric doesn't want human contractors here on the property. He thinks it would be too dangerous." Cassie disagreed but when it came to her safety and the baby's, he just wouldn't compromise.

"Cassie, I don't think you realise how lucky you are," Teagan challenged when Cassie grumbled about overbearing, domineering men.

Although she agreed wholeheartedly about the overbearing part, her friend was wallowing in her own private pity party and needed some perspective. "You have found your soul mate, the one person who will stick by you through eternity. He'll never leave you, never stop loving you and he'll never cheat on you. Do you know how rare that is? It's one in a million. One in ten billion. All the guys I know think monogamy is some kind of wood."

Cassie chuckled. "Yeah, I know. You're right. I just feel so useless. I can't do anything to help find Alex, or defend the manor. I don't even know how to defend myself," she sighed heavily. Her attempt at a smile came across more like a constipated grimace, but she tried.

"You're not alone in the way you feel. There are dozens of people out there right now trying to get Alex back and protect not just the manor, but their own families too, and every one of them is feeling just as frustrated as you."

Cassie nodded. The jolt of reality was a timely, although maybe not a welcome reminder that there were others suffering similarly to her. Other families, as they had discovered, had also lost loved ones recently too. Soldiers who had disappeared from their regiments and from their homes, both humans and lycans, seemingly vanished without a trace.

There was more at stake than just getting Alex back. The future of the whole world might well depend on them stopping Ahriman from creating some sort of portal device to the Underworld.

Keeping all that in mind didn't make her feel any better. In fact, she probably felt a little worse....or maybe that was just morning sickness.

"I have some good news for you," Teagan offered with an excited smile.

"I could really use some. Is it the ward, have you finished the preparations?"

"No. Far from it. I still haven't even made a list of things I'll need. I also need my grandfather's Book of Shadows...which brings me to my good news. I heard from him early this morning. My grandfather," she clarified. "I sent him an email explaining what's happened. He's promised to go to the Ukraine to help. He should arrive there some time today."

"Do you think he *can* help?"

"If anyone can, he can," Teagan assured.

The knot in Cassie's stomach loosened a fraction.

"Here we go. Custard powder," Teagan pronounced triumphantly. Getting to her feet she placed it on the bench.

Cassie read the packet's instructions, then read them again as she placed the ingredients in the saucepan.

"You've never made custard before, have you? Do you have any clue what you're doing?" Teagan asked.

"None," Cassie replied.

"It looks too...yellow. Are you sure this is going to work?"

"Not at all."

"So, this could turn out like that time you tried to reheat a pizza in the oven while it was still in the box?"

"Yep."

"Excellent. I'll just call the fire department now, shall I?" Teagan laughed.

"The recipe says to make thick custard. This is thick," Cassie defended.

"Are you sure it didn't say, a thick person to make custard?" Teagan quipped, making light of Cassie's terrible cooking skills. "It doesn't look fit for consumption by humans." Teagan made a face, screwing her nose up at the lumpy, gelatinous sludge.

"There's a few non-humans running about, we could test it on one of them," Cassie offered cheekily and then pouted dejectedly. She just wanted some damn custard. "It wasn't supposed to be this hard" she fumed. Whether she was meaning making custard or life in general, she didn't know. Probably both. She threw her hands out in front of her in the direction of the infuriating pot of goo on the stove as her emotional bank tipped past bursting point.

The explosion tore through the kitchen.

"Son of a beach ball," Teagan screeched, as Cassie shrieked her own version of the sentiment. "What the hell was that?" she gasped, almost hyperventilating on the adrenaline fuelled heart palpitations pounding hard enough to break a rib.

"You okay?" Cassie asked, her own heart pounding out a double-time rhythm in her chest. "Oh, boy. I really don't think making custard is my thing." The claggy mess was now pasted to the walls and ceiling.

"Hey, at least you found a use for it. It works well as poly filler," Teagan quipped to lighten things up.

The laws of physics were possessive of its greatest principle – gravity, as they worked to move the dead weight of the Yew tree, prying it free of the ground one accursed foot at a time. They'd been at it for days and even with chainsaws, an axe, vampire and lycan manpower, they had still made little headway.

"Lionel. Hold your tongue," Harold scolded.

"Yes, Lionel. Do what daddy says or I might hold your tongue for you," Saladin promised. Like everyone else at the manor, he was fed up to the eyeballs with the pair's *'delicate'* temperaments and whining.

Lionel swallowed hard, his face turning a paler shade. The pair may have been lycan but the intelligence and bravery gene, along with the usual attributes of speed and strength had somehow managed to skip them. They had however, managed to make whinging and bickering into an art form. Even Harold's wife couldn't stand him. The poor woman had endured what must have seemed like an eternity with the man before she passed away. Many believe he nagged her into an early grave. Harold's older son, Lionel, had unfortunately been tarred with the same brush as his father. His youngest son had thankfully taken after his mother. He joined the lycan military the day after his eighteenth birthday for his mandatory ten-year enlistment, and chose to make a career of it. He hadn't returned home since his mother died. Who could blame him?

Alaric was determined to have the garden cleared and repaired by spring, ready for his and Cassie's wedding. At the rate they were progressing however, it was more likely going to be spring of next year before they got the job finished. He even offered Harold and Lionel an incentive of half a million pounds to finish quickly. Most normal people would work twenty-four hours a day with that kind of carrot dangled in front of them. But, oh no, not this pair. In fact, somehow it made them work even slower.

Alaric gripped Saladin's shoulder tightly. The fact that his fangs had begun to descend and his eyes glittered fiercely, was a dead give away that Lionel was very close to having his body parts rearranged.

Alaric eyed Saladin carefully before removing his hand. His mood was as black as the clouds above. Something wasn't right with him. For days he had been edgy, his mood on a hair trigger. The reason he suspected, was Teagan.

Saladin had an impressive ego and wasn't accustomed to rejection. Alaric was a little surprised he hadn't resorted to compelling her to get his way. He had done that numerous times in the past without a twinge of conscience, so why not now? His attraction to her was eating away at him, that was plain for all to see. If he compelled her he could very easily have sex with her, then wipe her memory like windex. She would never be the wiser as to what happened, he would be in a better mood, and everyone's lives would be much easier for it.

The fact that Saladin hadn't compelled her, disturbed him. There was something else going on here that Alaric was obviously missing. Saladin clearly struggled with an inner turmoil he hadn't witnessed before.

Each man was lost in his own thoughts as they worked at removing the fallen tree.

The ground rumbled beneath their feet with the force of the explosion inside the house.

Adrenaline spiked. Alaric's warrior instincts flashed to the fore and he charged into the kitchen prepared to take out the threat, Saladin hot on his heels. What they found froze them instantly where they stood.

Cassie lifted her hands to look at them like they were foreign objects. "But I don't even know what I did," she said.

She looked caught between confusion, horror and the urgent need to giggle hysterically.

Teagan too, stood with her hands outstretched, holding suspended in midair the projectiles of shrapnel which had been hurtling towards the two women, jagged pieces of saucepan and stove, along with globs of yellow muck.

Teagan turned her head at the sound of dual ferocious growls. Her concentration was lost in an instant and the whole lot dropped to the floor in a clinking, clattering, splattering mess.

Well, at least they had an inkling into Teagan's power, Saladin thought with proud satisfaction.

Saladin walked towards Teagan, his gait purposeful but unhurried. Her body loosened in response as if anticipating his touch, needing his touch to ease her shaking limbs.

He turned to her more fully, fighting the need to reach out to her, to drag her to him. Every possessive instinct he had roared out in protest of his restraint.

"What happened?" his voice cracked like a bullwhip. He didn't intentionally mean to sound so harsh, but he was unaccustomed to feeling this, this....concern, and it was wreaking havoc on his mood. Softening his tone, he took her hand gently.

"Teagan?"

When she only stared at him in shocked astonishment, he smoothed his other hand over her back soothingly. Contrary to his intentions however, his caress created a longing inside her unlike anything before. His touch was firm, sure. His hands cherishing rather than possessive, though the dominance of his touch would never change, she knew. And, he was dominant. He held her close, despite the lightness of his touch.

Her heart hammered in her chest, it couldn't beat any faster if she was a hummingbird. *Just let it be*, she warned herself sternly. For all his easy charm the man was dangerous. A genuine bad boy. Only fools deliberately played with that kind of fire. Of course, when it came to men, she might as well have the words *'strike match here'*, tattooed on her forehead.

She couldn't risk falling for the wrong kind of man, a *non-human* kind of man, particularly this *non-human* man.

Saladin stared down at her covetously. He wanted to ravage her. Devour her. He wanted his lips on every part of her body at once, if only to reassure himself that she had not suffered any injury. The surge of sensation left him fighting for air. He could feel his muscles trembling as he fought to control himself.

Something was wrong with him.

121

He should walk away, leave her alone. But Saladin couldn't do that. Teagan was a fever in his blood he simply couldn't cure. Perhaps if he got her in his bed just once, he could purge his need for her, as he had with every other female. Why did she plague him so? It wasn't natural for him to be so intrigued by a woman, any woman.

There had to be a logical explanation, one that didn't involve his male hormones adopting female ovaries and becoming an emotional pot of sensitivity.

Saladin shot her a hooded look. Teagan decided she didn't care much for that look. The way his eyes glittered beneath those lowered lashes affected her way too much.

She meant nothing to him. She was barely even a distraction, she reminded herself.

"Are you hurt?" Alaric asked as he wrapped Cassie in his arms.

"No, I'm fine," she answered looking at the gaping hole in the kitchen where the stove used to be. "I think Mrs P is going to be really, really pissed when she sees this."

"No, she won't love, she's been asking me for ages to remodel the kitchen."

"Okay then, now might be a good time," Cassie said as she began to calm down, her mind slowly climbing out of the pit of shock.

"What did this? Saladin demanded heatedly. He needed an outlet for his foul mood and hoped there was a tangible culprit to blame. This irrational behaviour Teagan was precipitating in him, was driving him certifiably insane. He needed to relieve the tension building inside him, fight something. Or have sex. The wriggle room in the front of his pants became restricted instantly at the thought.

Saladin still held Teagan's hand, while his other drew soothing circles in the small of her back. She couldn't stop the sway of her body, as though she was a magnet and he was magnetic north, she found herself relaxing into the hard frame of his body.

"I think I did," Cassie replied, although acknowledging the fact felt ridiculous. Yes, she was immortal, but she had no special powers...or did she? Cassie looked at her hands again, turned them over and studied them. She'd felt a surge of energy that passed through her body and then...the explosion. "It was me," she said with more conviction, looking to Alaric for acceptance of her statement.

Alaric's face broke into a broad grin.

Holding Cassie close he turned to Saladin. "Well, old friend, I think we might have just found our answer to the problem in the garden."

"What? What are you talking about?" Cassie enquired suspiciously when Saladin also grinned. When this surly pair were happy it was usually a sure sign that at the very least, someone may be missing a limb or two very soon.

14

Cassie was right. There was to be a few missing limbs. Fortunately for Harold and Lionel, it was tree limbs they had in mind. In particular, the Yew tree.

With single-minded determination Cassie set her shoulders and furrowed her brow in concentration.

"Cassie, try and focus on the tree," Alaric urged.

"What? If I focus any harder I'll get a brain aneurysm," she responded defensively.

As much as she wanted to please everyone with another explosive spark from her fingers, she was clearly still rattled from what had happened in the kitchen.

Feeling his *mate*'s distress, Alaric decided a small distraction was in order to help calm her nerves down. Pulling her shaky body into the frame of his arms, his hand gently tilted her chin up to give her a short, but passionate kiss of encouragement.

Not content with his meagre offering, Cassie plunged her fingers into his blonde hair pulling his lips back to hers for more.

Alaric put the brakes on, pulling back from the scorching kiss. "That isn't why we're here," he forced himself to say. The heat in her eyes was nearly enough to throw decorum out the window, strip her naked and take her where she stood. Okay, so he hadn't intended to kick his own libido into high gear, but he had achieved his main objective, to help relieve Cassie's distress. Only now the pole in his pants had enough tensile strength to suspend a bridge.

Tilly loped around them, whimpering and whining almost as much as Lionel and Harold. Alaric threw a stick into the forest for her to chase, thankful for the distraction. It was just a pity he couldn't do the same for the exasperating gardeners.

Tilly returned with a different stick, one nearly as long as her own body. She walked proudly, if not slowly through the cratered garden, gingerly balancing her bounty as it teetered towards the ground one way, then the other.

Again, she loped off into the forest when Alaric threw the stick, much further this time, deep into the woods.

Cassie focussed all her will on recreating that tingling feeling she felt just before she exploded the kitchen, but it just didn't come, no matter how hard she willed it to. All the while Lionel and Harold continued their banter in that abrasively annoying tone that children use. Cassie concentrated harder, trying desperately to block out their droning noise and prayed that her own child, when it was born, would never sound like them.

The rest of the conversation between them sounded a bit like:

"Blah, blah, blah. I'm right and you're wrong."

"Blah, Blah. Am not. You're wrong."

"Oh yeah…blah, blah. Prove it, blah, blah."

Suddenly it became clear why no one wanted to deal with them. Male posturing was universal. Species was irrelevant. The only difference between Lionel and Harold and all other males on the planet? She didn't want to beat every other male to a pulp just to shut them up. The whinny tone and pitch of their voices was grating on her nerves like nails down a chalk board.

"Both of you…Can It!" Cassie hollered, her hands lifting automatically in frustration. As she'd listened to the aggravating gardeners, her frustration rising, the energy inside her had once again built up. A burst of energy detonated in the direction her hands were pointing, narrowly missing Lionel and Harold.

One large limb of the fallen tree exploded into a million pieces. A fine mist of sawdust fluttered down around them.

Reflexes kicked in. With his vampire speed Saladin placed his much larger body between Teagan and the wooden projectiles to shield her from the fall-out. Their bodies pressed against one another intimately, her arms reaching around his waist, but she didn't hold onto him, her hands were outstretched. Gripping her shoulders roughly, Saladin swiveled the two of them around on the spot in an awkward kind of dance.

Suspended in midair only inches from his chest in front of him, was a very thick, sharply pointed fragment of the branch. Saladin stood there for a moment in shock staring at it. Teagan had saved him. At least, she had saved him from a lot of pain and inconvenience. A wooden stake to the heart wouldn't have killed him, only removing his heart would do that, but it would have temporarily injured him.

He plucked the stick from the air and fingered the coarse, jagged edges of the wood.

The impetuous wood in his pants began to throb with renewed vitality. The need to have it touched, stroked and mounted was intensifying to point where it was becoming essential for his very survival. But somehow, he doubted even that would be enough to satisfy his craving for this strong-willed druid.

Teagan tilted her head in curiosity. They shared a look, both skeptical and intrigued. The touch of her eyes was akin to physical contact. The exquisite glitter in her dark eyes began with a light dance across his face, gliding gently over his shoulder and then slowly drifting along his broad muscled chest. Everywhere her gaze touched, Saladin felt his skin begin to burn, his muscles began to jump tensely to attention, his clothing seeming insignificant to her visual investigations. His abdomen tightened as his raging hard-on flexed under her gaze. Her examination branded him.

Saladin shot her another of those hooded looks, his blue eyes glittering with naked lust. Teagan felt her body responding with a surge of moisture, pulsing from her core and a hard ache in her nipples as they hardened.

He fixed his gaze on her throat, her pulse beating was eye candy to a hungry vampire. Suddenly he wished that the visual feast was also being enjoyed by his fingers, lips, tongue and fangs.

Saladin shifted his stance, grimacing at the tight fit at the crotch of his jeans.

If the way Teagan's face flamed red was any indication, she'd noticed his state of arousal. And the way her eyes darkened told him she liked it.

Teagan tried to look away but couldn't. With one steamy glance, he'd made her feel empty inside. Deprived. Hungry. And the look in his eyes promised salvation from the burning loneliness deep within her clenching stomach. Her mouth went dry, while every other nook and cranny of her body turned to a hot syrupy mess.

"I know you're curious, so what are you waiting for?" he asked her seductively, his smooth voice weakening her knees.

Teagan's cheeks flushed crimson with embarrassment, again. She would refute the claim, but she would probably choke on the lie. "I'm curious about tattoos too, but you don't see me lining up to get one of those either."

Cassie turned in defence of her friend. The two women glared at Saladin with daggers in their eyes before Teagan stormed off to another part of the garden in a huff. How was it that she managed to leave behind a lingering feeling of frosty disapproval and pulsing power, Saladin thought. He couldn't help wondering if there really were any spells to turn men into toads. God, he hoped not, or his next meal might consist of flies and crickets.

"You just can't help yourself, can you?" Cassie fumed.

Saladin held his hands out to his sides, palms up with his best innocent *'What did I do,'* expression.

Damn, Teagan's butt was cute as hell. He couldn't take his eyes off it as she marched away from him. Nice and round, but not too large. Just a perfect handful.

Saladin half sighed and half moaned. The idea of Teagan getting a tattoo tantalised his imagination. All the places she could put that tattoo…

"You're doing it again," Alaric whispered low at Saladin's ear.

"Doing what again, being an arsehole?"

"Mooning." The arsehole part went without saying. It was part of his DNA.

Saladin snorted. "Last time I checked, my arse was still in my pants."

Alaric arched his brows at the angry, exasperated tone he was using. "Not that kind of mooning, the sighing as you fantasise about Teagan, kind of mooning."

Oh.

Something was definitely wrong with him. He didn't moon.

No matter how much he tried to deny it, Saladin's desire for Teagan was more than mere appreciation. The need to possess her was rapidly becoming a necessity, an obsession consuming every waking moment. A madness threatening his very being.

Scrubbing his hands over his face, he pinched the bridge of his nose with his thumb and forefinger to relieve the pressure building behind his eyes. Clenching his eyes closed, he groaned. He was sure that if he could actually get headaches, right now he'd have a mother of a migraine.

His attention snapped back as Cassie let loose her power again, the explosion of timber showering down around them in a hail of splintered sticks, severing the tree trunk in half.

It looked like the key to Cassie's new power, was strong emotions. The angry kind was working a treat, Saladin thought as he pulled a baseball bat sized splinter from his thigh.

"That's your fault," she admonished. "You should have been paying attention. You could have easily dodged that."

Yeah, he could have.

As soon as the words left her lips she regretted her comments. The wound looked bad. Really deep, maybe to the bone. "Are you alright? It won't cause any lasting damage will it?"

"No." *Just to my pride.* "It'll be fine in a short while," he told her as he plucked it free and picked out a few stray chop stick sized splinters.

Lionel squealed and took several steps away from the group, his face suddenly pale. His eyes held a look of horror.

"What's your problem now?" Saladin bit out impatiently at the man.

Lionel didn't answer, just pointed behind them with a shaky hand.

Tilly stood as proudly as ever, tail wagging, dirt encrusted tongue hanging out the side of her mouth. She'd retrieved a new stick and dropped it at Cassie's feet. Yet again the mangy mutt had lost track of the original stick Alaric had thrown and brought back a new one. Only this one wasn't a stick. It was…was…something muddy?

"Ew. Another present Tilly? And, this one's been dead at least a week too. Oh crap, is that a hand?" she cringed, stepping back from the slightly decomposed present.

The missing mercenary's hand. This was the guy Alaric had torn apart when he found Cassie trapped inside that suffocating circle of poisonous mist. The mercenary had disappeared without a trace that same afternoon.

The light was beginning to fade, although that was of no consequence to the vampires, their vision was as good during the night as it was in daylight. Of course, very few vampires had the opportunity to test that theory though.

"Cassie?" Alaric asked calmly, but the concern in his eyes had her attention instantly. "Go and find Teagan and go inside the house. Don't come out until I tell you it's okay. Ring Oliver Harlow and see if he can bring some of his men out here and help us look for the rest of the body."

"Okay," Cassie answered, a wave of nausea clenching her stomach.

"That's my girl." He gave her quick peck on her lips. "You did really well with the tree," he praised, a cheeky glint sparkling his eyes. "I'll reward you *thoroughly* later."

"You promise?"

His lopsided grin answered that question for her. She had hours and hours of praise coming…just as soon as they found the rest of the mercenary's body…and the culprit who hid it. Cassie blew out a long sigh as she headed in search of Teagan. She could be waiting quite a while for that *praise* he promised. That was probably a good thing, the way she felt right now she just might throw up on him.

"Dad and I can get Oliver for you," Lionel stammered, his father nodding furiously in agreement.

"Yes, yes. Good idea. We'll go right now," Harold concurred. It was the first time all day they had agreed on something.

"Fine. Just hurry." Alaric was happy to let them go, if for no other reason than to get some peace and quiet for a while. He doubted they'd be back to help with the search.

Half an hour later the forest was swarming with lycans in their wolf form, along with the vampires from the manor, Hawke and Pan joining the search.

Hawke had been a Marine in his previous life as a human, and a damn good tracker. Pan was a spy, a skill not required on a search such as this, but his child sized stature gave him access to small spaces that the others couldn't reach. Along with the exceptional noses of the lycans, it didn't take too long to find the rest of the body in its decomposing state. The pieces had been scattered throughout the forest, buried in shallow graves. Foxes and ravens had feasted on some parts and cleaned the flesh from the bones. But, fortunately there was enough left of him to confirm he was the missing mercenary.

This was definitely a lycan's work. Although, he'd never seen such a sloppy disposal job. Lycan's had a particular flair for body disposal, it was how they'd stayed hidden from the world for so long. It was almost as if whoever did this wanted the body to be found.

Saladin's thoughts shifted to Teagan. He had promised her he would take her home this evening to collect a few possessions and her grandfather's Book of Shadows. That wasn't going to happen now. He let out a deep sigh of both relief and disappointment. A low growl rumbled in his chest.

There was definitely something wrong with him, he didn't know if he was coming or going when that woman was around.

15

Abby held back a whimper of longing as she rolled onto her back and stared up at the ceiling. She listened to him in the next room. Drawers opening and closing, a door, a shower. She imagined watching him stripping, his toned body firm and taut. Was he still hard for her? Maybe. Was it wrong to hope he was? She knew the sight of him erect was mouth wateringly impressive, although she was curious to know what he looked like limp and flaccid. But if he wasn't aroused by her, would that mean that Ahriman was winning their internal struggle?

No. That wasn't going to happen. Slamming closed the door to her anxious thoughts, Abby closed her eyes and once again focused on the sounds coming from the bathroom, letting her mind drift in a more appealing direction.

She listened as water flowed over his muscular frame, hot and steamy, slicking his thick dark hair to the chiseled features of his face. Were his dreamy, chocolate brown eyes closed as he washed? Did he imagine it was her hands skimming over his skin, caressing sensitive flesh with fondling strokes? Perhaps he did. The fresh scent of soap and male musk mixed together with the bathroom's moist heat, seeped through the cracks of the doorway, filling her senses and making her dazed from the need to taste him.

Abby whispered his name, "Alex." A desperate sound that made her chest ache.

The sound of the shower fell silent.

Ahriman entered the bedroom where she lay, eyes closed feigning sleep. Hunching down beside her, he stared into her delicate face. Her lips were parted, moist and tempting. Her auburn lashes lay thick and long against her cheeks. Her high cheek bones and delicately fine nose gave her a seductive appearance.

He allowed himself the pleasure of gently moving a stray strand of hair from her cheek, letting his fingers caress the silk of her skin. He marveled at the cream tone and flawless texture of her lukewarm vampire skin.

Why did he move her into his suite and not simply lock her in a cell? She'd be equally as safe there.

It was to keep an eye on her, he told himself. But another thought plucked a sour cord in the back of his mind.

Or, was it because she brought him a sense of warmth and peace, and maybe he wanted her for his own? No. Impossible.

Yet, she was an irresistible mixture of strength and vulnerability, kindness and combustion. She was beautiful. But, Ahriman was incapable of love. He had sacrificed that weakness from his nature long ago.

These were Alex's emotions, but he couldn't deny the warm feeling it left in his soul to have her around. Her presence filled a void he hadn't even been aware of.

It felt good.

How pathetic. The most evil creature on the planet, felt *good*.

Abby watched through concealing eyelashes as he dressed in front of her, his dark eyes brooding. He frowned as he pulled on Alex's faded, but well-loved ACDC T-shirt over his nicely defined abs.

She tried desperately to look away, to look anywhere but at the gaping opening of his jeans. She failed miserably. It was as though there was some sort of vision magnet embedded in the metal buttons. He was still semi-hard beneath she noted with relieved satisfaction, as he rearranged the bulge before fastening the top button. Abby swallowed the moan threatening to escape her throat, her fangs began to descend as her mouth watered.

Why had he touched her the way he did, so gently, almost affectionately. Was he trying to make her think he actually cared about her? Was this just a ploy to mess with her head, another tactic to intimidate her, weaken her resolve against him?

If so, it was working. She hadn't felt so hot and bothered since…since…well, ever.

Long minutes later she heard the door open and close. Alone. Always alone.

And, never had she felt more so.

Abby clenched her teeth and resigned herself to yet another day without her *mate* beside her.

She held onto the thought that Alex continued to fight for control of his body. It was obvious he was making some headway. Ahriman was wearing Alex's clothes, he was displaying some of Alex's mannerisms, and more and more of his colourful vocabulary was beginning to appear in Ahriman's speech. It was inconceivable to believe anything other than Alex being the one to come out the victor in this battle of wills.

Abby waited a while longer before climbing from the bed, unwilling to relinquish Alex's scent from the pillow on which she rested her head. Drawing in one last deep breath she let it out again on an equally long sigh, dropping her feet to the soft plush carpet.

Showering and dressing quickly, she considered her next move. She had to speak to Sebastian, find out what was happening outside the compound. She also needed to find out what Mira and Lilith were up to. If they really did want her dead, she was a much easier target for them if she remained in Ahriman's rooms, despite what Alex and Ahriman believed.

Memories flooded Abby's mind of her grandmother's home. Cast out by her parents when she was very young, embarrassed and afraid of their *'abnormal'* child with her mind reading abilities. Her grandmother's home became her palace.

It was her safe haven.

From the moment she stepped inside and closed the door she would block out the world that tormented her, and relax from the frustrating challenge to fit into a society that always seemed slightly out of focus to her.

That was until her grandmother died and her money hungry parents sold the house, institutionalising her in a home for the mentally unstable.

and criminally insane. They couldn't afford to let their embarrassing secret back out into society for their snobbish social circle to see, now could they.

Life in Dorland House wasn't so different from here she realised. There she'd had her share of enemies. Most were harmless, but others....not so much. She had to constantly watch her back. The biggest difference between Dorland House and here? While she was still a prisoner, her new enemies were free to come and go as they please.

After surviving Dorland House and having lived on the streets, Abby wasn't phased by the news that Lilith and Mira wanted her dead.

Abby didn't know much about Mira, hadn't had much to do with her since arriving in the compound. But, in the few brief times she had been around her, Abby had managed to pluck enough information from her brain to learn Narayan had killed her progeny, Cain. Abby had been there that night, she'd fought against them both, but it was Narayan who killed Cain. Unlike Mira, Abby felt no sorrow for the psychopathic vampire's demise. Unfortunately, it didn't seem that Mira was the type to let go of old grudges, quietly plotting her revenge.

Then there was Lilith. Well there was no need to read her mind to know her motive. The crazy shrew believed she had a claim on Alex because Ahriman shared his body. Fat chance that was ever going to happen.

Abby sucked in a breath, mentally fortifying her course of action. There was no point waiting around for trouble to come to her. She might as well go out and look for it herself. She was pretty certain her decision was likely to come back to bite her on the arse, but she decided to stand by it anyway. Besides, what was the point of being a kick-arse vampire if you're too afraid to act like one.

Abby grabbed her cell phone from under the mattress, placing it down the front of her jeans and headed for the door.

Outside waited two of Ahriman's personal guards, mindless lycans who had been 'recruited' to serve him. How they managed to re-program their minds she had no idea. The men never spoke unless requested to, they never ate or drank unless reminded to, and they rarely slept. They were the perfect soldiers, all brawn and no brains. They followed their orders to the letter.

The question was, what orders did the guards have regarding keeping Abby in Ahriman's rooms?

Opening the door, Abby stepped into the hallway, expecting to be halted the second she did so. But it wasn't the case at all. The two men remained unmoved, only their eyes followed her movements in a watchful, but unconcerned manner.

Well, this was interesting. Clearly Ahriman either couldn't conceive the notion that his orders to stay put could possibly be disobeyed, or more likely, he was too distracted in his thoughts to give the guards new orders. Either way, Abby appeared to be free to come and go.

As Abby made her way to the upper levels of the compound, she did so with a great deal more care and stealth than usual. Maybe Ahriman's personal guards didn't have orders to detain her, but maybe the guards who followed Mira's order, did.

One thing she had learnt when she lived on the streets, was how to blend into the shadows, a talent that was coming in very handy now.

Abby moved silently through the less used corridors, bypassing the main hallways. She had studied every inch of this place over the days she had been here, searched out every dark corner and every hidden staircase. The passage she now followed, only yesterday had shown no signs of having had traffic for many decades. Today however, dozens of footprints disturbed the dusty floor and the scent of aggressive males filled the musty air.

Abby didn't want to be a pessimist, but this wasn't good.

Reaching her destination, a small room only one level below ground, she pulled out her phone and began dialling Sebastian's number. The old storage room was damp and smelled of the rotting wooden shelves which lined the walls, but it was close enough to the surface to allow her satellite phone to work.

Even here Abby dared not make too much noise. She wasn't the only vampire in the compound with super sensitive hearing. In fact, the lycan's could hear almost as well as vampires and there were enough of those running about the place to rattle her nerves.

The phone rang once, twice. On the third ring a familiar voice answered.

"Prīvit!" The gruff voice answered in Ukrainian.

"Klaus? Where's Sebastian?"

"Liddle lady? Dat you?" he asked, his surprise plainly evident. "What you do calling now? Sebastian is sleeping."

"Sleeping? What time is it?"

"It's eleven in da morning. You should be sleeping too. What's wrong?" he asked concerned. Klaus didn't know her very well, but he liked her, and he damn well admired her courage for entering the enemy's subterranean headquarters without so much as a letter opener for protection.

Eleven in the morning? How was it possible *she* was still awake, particularly since she was still considered a baby vampire. She should be comatose at this time of the day. Abby thought about it for a moment. Her sleeping pattern had changed almost the moment she first took Alex's blood to save him from his leg wound. She had slept fitfully after that. But, since she had completed her blood bond with him, she had barely slept at all. His blood seemed to sustain her energy levels negating the need for sleep. She didn't even feel tired right now.

"I'm fine Klaus. How are you, how is your brother?" she asked.

"No change," he answered gruffly, his anger and frustration making his accent much stronger. "Wait, I get Seb."

A minute later Sebastian's sleepy voice croaked a 'hello' through a yawn. Abby smiled, she could practically see him stretching himself awake on the other end of the phone.

"Abby, finally. What news do you have for me?"

"It's only been two days, what are you complaining about? I've been busy." *Yeah, busy having sex with the enemy.* Her good mood at hearing a friendly voice for a change, took a dip south as her stomach twisted into knots with guilt. She wasn't cheating on Alex, she corrected herself. But no matter how hard she tried to justify her feelings, she couldn't ignore the simple fact that she had liked the rough sex with Ahriman, even if it was Alex's body she was bonded to.

"It's been three days. And, I was getting worried about you. Is everything okay?" Sebastian asked, his native Austrian accent coming through more strongly in his sleepy condition. He'd only spent his human years in his home country and had been a drifter for the past couple of hundred years, perfecting his English and adopting a few other languages. It's what any good spy would do.

"Ahriman has finished the portal device, he's testing it right now," she blurted out, choosing to forego the sugar coating on her news.

Sebastian's curses could have melted the circuitry in the satellites transmitting their conversation.

"Okay then, we'll need to step things up from our end. Can you get to it and disable it?"

"No. I can't get anywhere near the lab. I'll see what I can do though. I can't promise anything. I'm supposed to be under house arrest at the moment for my own protection."

Sebastian read between the lines of her comment and he didn't like what he heard. "Supposed to be? I'm assuming you've escaped. Do you need us to come and get you out now?"

"No. I'm fine, but I can't be gone long, not if I don't want my confinement to be made a little more permanent. Besides, I can't leave now. I think Alex is beginning to have an influence on Ahriman. He's not as much of a threat to us now as he once was. It's Mira and Morganna who are the bigger threat."

"Morganna? As in the new head of the Guild, Morganna?"

"Yes. And, she's not what she seems. She's some sort of witch, and a very powerful one. I think she is the one responsible for turning Klaus' brother Dieter and the others into their zombie-like state. She's also the one who put the parameter spell around the compound."

"Gustav informed me last night that there's an old druid heading for the L'Viv headquarters. Gustav's keeping the affected men we've captured from the compound in the cells there beneath the bunker. Hopefully he can help us return them to normal."

At least that was some good news.

"Is Morganna there now?" Sebastian enquired.

"I don't know. I've searched every inch of this place and I've found no sign of her, but whenever Ahriman calls her, she's there within minutes."

"She must have her own digs nearby, outside the compound walls. If she's a witch, and as powerful as you think, she could very easily conceal her location."

"That's my guess too."

"We'll send out a couple of scouts and take a closer look."

"Seb? Be careful. They've started moving some of their men. I don't know where to or exactly how many, but it makes me nervous."

"Yeah, me too." The whole situation made him nervous. "Don't worry, we won't take any unnecessary chances. And Abby, hold tight okay, we'll have the two of you out of their soon, maybe only another twenty-four hours, okay?"

One more day. One very long, long day where anything could happen.

She had to find Alex, get him and the portal device out before the raid.

The evil bastard had an ostentatious attitude with an agenda of desecration and annihilation of the world as he knew it.

Yet again, Alex's curses fell on deaf ears as Ahriman hooked up the portal device and switched it on. The lights in the compound flickered as it drained what little power its generators provided.

It wasn't nearly enough power.

Ahriman drew in the electromagnetic energy from the atmosphere around him, collected it within himself, releasing it in one powerful blast directly into the device. Slowly the box came to life with the whirring of gears and buzzing of power coursing through it.

His jaw set in a hard line of tension as he watched and waited as an energy vortex manifested a perceptible wave of luminosity, projected a couple of meters away. A small hole opened in its centre and a rush of bitterly cold air whistled through. With it came the familiar scent of home. The Underworld.

It worked. The damn thing actually worked.

As quickly as the euphoric endorphins flooded his system, they were replaced just as quickly by frustration and disappointment.

The vortex walls shimmered and swirled, and petered out only seconds after it opened.

Ahriman spit out a string of curses so toxic, it could have stripped paint off a wall. Yet another of Alex's attributes which Ahriman had adopted.

Despite the horror Alex felt that the device had worked, he couldn't help feeling elated too. This was his knowledge, his research, and his belief in the quantum universe that made it possible. Aristotle would have been pleased to know that his theory had been correct. There wasn't only four elements in the natural world, but five. Earth, air, water, fire and ether, the dimensional veil that allowed physical matter and the less tangible antimatter, or in this case, spirits, to coexist simultaneously but separately. They had successfully manipulated the tiniest particles in the universe apart, creating a breach in the dimensional wall between our world and the Underworld.

The question was, if the breach could be stabilised and opened wider, what manner of creature would come through? Would the evil beings remain insubstantial spirits, capable of tormenting the Earth like poltergeists, or would they take on a physical form as they cross the barrier into the physical world?

A shiver of dread shuddered through Alex as the reality of the situation took full form in his mind, or was that Ahriman's mind? Whatever, it didn't matter. What did matter was the devastation those creatures would leave in their wake if they were ever freed.

Hairy Hell's balls. What kind of fucking shitfest had they created, and how the fuck was he going to fix this? Alex thought miserably.

Fortunately for now at least, the Earth may still be safe. The compound's generator didn't have nearly enough power, not even combined with his own electromagnetic energy, to keep the portal open. In fact, putting it into perspective, it would take the energy of a thousand nuclear weapons on a sustained basis to open a stable portal.

The device they had built was useless without the necessary voltage and sustainable power source.

Ahriman grumbled and growled out curses as he paced the room. He needed a better outlet for his irritation, and he knew just where to get relief.

"Dr Greenville, take a break. We'll try again later. We need more Iridium to increase the number of anti-protons. It might give us a more stable portal."

"Yes sir. Would you like me to call you when it's ready to test?"

"You do that." Ahriman didn't give the man another thought as he stormed from the lab, eager to get to Abby in his rooms.

16

Saladin had searched throughout the manor for Teagan. He hadn't seen her since his latest attack of foot in mouth disease in the garden which had sent her running from him, yet again.

He needed to apologise, not only for his inexcusable behaviour but also for breaking his promise to her. After finding the mercenary's remains, he had become preoccupied with finding the culprit who scattered the body parts about the forest. There was no time to take her back to town to get her things from her apartment, as she'd requested the night before.

So, now here he was once again, standing before her in the conservatory with his proverbial tail between his legs begging for her forgiveness. Teagan sat in the wicker chair scowling her indignation at him, her arms crossed and foot tapping impatiently.

"I'm sorry about earlier," he told her. "I'm a bad-tempered bastard at the best of times. What can I say, it was your scent and the excitement of Cassie's new power…I just couldn't help myself. Will you forgive me?"

What? Forgive him? At every opportunity he had deliberately embarrassed her, very publicly. She felt like a yoyo, being drawn to him one minute, then cast away the next. Why should she forgive him?

"That was the biggest crock of……"

Out of the blue he bent down and kissed her, hard. His kiss gentled, his lips becoming soft and velvety as he delivered an unspoken apology before releasing her once again.

He was an arse, but she couldn't help melting into a puddle of drool every time he came near, and when he kissed her....*Oh, this is bad, really, really bad.*

"Back off and stop harassing me," she ordered indignantly. But her flushed skin, the breathless pitch of her voice, and the sweet spiced honeyed scent that rolled off her betrayed her true feelings.

It also engaged the predator in him.

"I can see your desire. I can smell your desire. You want me, I want you. Therefore it's not harassment. So, why don't we bring this to its natural conclusion sooner rather than later."

Teagan's outraged gasp made him laugh.

He needed a lobotomy. He just did it again. He came to apologise, and he just did the same thing again. He couldn't seem to stop himself. What was his problem? His cock was the problem. It had somehow managed to become the control centre of every thought that came out of his belligerent mouth.

"You are so... so..."

"Sexy?"

"Arrogant!"

The more determined she was to deny him, the more he wanted her.

"True enough, but admit it, you also think I'm sexy."

With an irate huff Teagan stood from her chair and tried to push past him. "Let me pass," she bit out between clenched teeth.

"Make me," he answered with cocky smugness.

She tried to push him back away from her. His rock-hard pecs rippled beneath her hands, sending a surge of blood to that command centre between his legs.

Her sinful, wicked mouth pursed. Saladin raked his gaze from her head to her toes, lingering on all the sweet spots. Maybe he was being obnoxious. No, he conceded, he was definitely being obnoxious, but the temptation to stir this prissy woman was irresistible and her sweet spots were definitely worth the ogling.

"You've got a screw loose, you know that? Leave me alone," she growled furiously.

Saladin seriously pissed her off. He did other things to her too, things she wished she could ignore, but it seemed that when it came to this particular obnoxious vampire, her body and brain were divorced.

"I...can't."

The pained tone in his voice halted her impending verbal tirade in its tracks.

What the hell was wrong with him, he wondered. He never behaved like this, like some sort of crazed, love sick puppy. It was unnatural.

Saladin's mind ticked over with possible causes. He refused to believe he was suffering a chronic case of male PMS.

His scowl deepened, his eyes narrowed with annoyance as he came to a new conclusion. She was a druid...

"Whatever your game is, I'm not playing any more. Take it off me this instant!"

"I have no idea what the hell you're talking about," Teagan confessed with as much patience in her tone as was in his.

"Yes, you do. The spell. Take it off me. Now!"

Teagan shook her head in exasperation. "I haven't got a clue what you're on about. What spell?"

"You put an infatuation spell on me. Now, take it off."

"I've done no such thing," she proclaimed her rebuttal contritely. "I assure you, there is no spell of any kind on you, Yusuf Saladin. Whatever's wrong with you has nothing to do with me. I'm pretty sure you were always this screwed up." Teagan suspected that an over abundance of arrogance might have unhealthy consequences. Now she had proof, it resulted in insanity.

"Yes, you did. There's no other explanation. You did this, I know you did," Saladin's voice began to rise in a concoction of arousal, suspicion and anger.

Teagan let out a frustrated sigh. Butting heads was going to get them nowhere fast. As much as she was sure she would regret it later, it was probably better to get to the bottom of his accusations now rather than later. Especially since she was doomed to stay under the same roof as him for at least another week.

"Calm down and tell me what's happening to you," she asked, her soft, slow words urging him down from the precipice of panic he was perched on.

"You're in my head every minute of every day. I can't think straight, and my dick…" he grabbed his crotch to emphasise his distress. "Has been as hard as rock for the past week. It's not natural. You did something to me," he accused again angrily.

He burned. He ached. He needed in a way he had never needed before. It was insane the way he wanted her, the way his body craved her scent, her touch.

Saladin flashed her a brooding look. He looked sulky and sexy all at once, irritated and put-out, and just a little aroused. Or a lot aroused if the bulge she had glimpsed in his trousers meant anything. Her pulse suddenly spiked.

"Fine. Come with me. I'll prove to you there's no spell on you."

Teagan marched into the kitchen and began rummaging through the cupboards removing a variety of ingredients. Mixing together cod liver oil, a raw egg, a bitter breakfast spread called vegemite, anchovies for saltiness and a dash of orange juice to make it all more palatable, she handed him the concoction. "Drink it," she ordered.

"Drink it?"

"Isn't that what I just said?"

Saladin screwed up his nose at the revolting looking, and smelling brew. Was he really that desperate to be rid of his unnatural crush on Teagan? Umm, yes, actually he was.

Swallowing the God awful brew that threatened to trigger his gag reflex and vomit, Saladin bit off a violent curse.

"How do you feel?" Teagan asked sweetly after waiting a moment for the brew to take full effect.

"Queasy." His face scrunched, fighting to quell the belch rising that may very well be followed by a technicolour yawn of the projectile kind.

"Good. That'll teach you for accusing me of putting a hex on you," she crowed with a satisfaction.

Saladin's temper flipped from frustration to fury at her trickery. His eyes lifted, their sapphire colour unbelievably beautiful, radiated his anger effectively killing her buzz.

"There's your proof," she informed him haughtily. "If you were under a love spell you would have still found that cute," she said, backing up towards the bench with Saladin in slow pursuit.

This woman before him was an enigma. He tilted his head, watching her, seeing irritation and impatience reflecting in her face.

"Sweetheart," he drawled, his predatory eyes fixed onto her. "I still find that arse of yours cute. Only now I might just have to spank it."

Teagan turned to make a dash from the kitchen but never made it a single step.

She could barely breathe for the agony of suspense. Overriding emotional and physical needs coursed through her as Saladin's hands first gripped her shoulders, then slid down her arms in a slow caress. His grip was possessive but not so firm that she couldn't get away if she tried. She should run, she knew she should, but she couldn't dredge up the willpower. She wanted his touch more.

Teagan drew in a hard, shuddering breath as his fingers moved further, dropping to cup her hips, pulling her against his body until the hard ridge of his erection pressed into her lower back.

Saladin's breath was doing wicked things to her neck, sending shivers of pleasure throughout her body. Heat seared through her veins like an explosion of wildfire.

Teagan gasped.

"You want me, as much as I want you." His voice dripped with erotic promise.

His extended fangs raked sensually over the pulsing vein in her throat, his tongue snaked out past his hungry lips to taste her.

"No." She wasn't sure if she was protesting the accusation or their present location.

"Yes," he whispered, sweeping her hair aside. His mouth watered.

Teagan cried out with a tortured moan, her neck bending further to grant him greater access to his delicate kisses as his hands roamed further, touching her, stroking her. One hand cupped her swollen breast, the other travelled further to the throbbing space aching between her thighs.

The feel of her hot skin, the fullness of her breast pressing into his hand, penetrated the haze of his hunger with a sharp, spearing intensity. It combined with the erotic narcotic of her chemistry sweeping over his tongue, wrenching his body into a new awareness and a brutal form of arousal, starting from the inside and exploding outward. Saladin's hands flowed over her flesh boldly, searching, exploring. His anger was dissolving beneath the onslaught of a fury of lust.

Teagan groaned on a hitching breath. She was shaking so badly with the desperate need tearing through her, she didn't know if she could survive it.

Saladin kissed her neck, tasting her, nipping at her with his sharp fangs, grazing just enough to draw tiny droplets of blood.

"God, Teagan, you feel so good, you taste so good," he whispered, his breathing rough, heavy, barely audible from the intensity of his raging need.

"Please. It's too much," she cried out, barely able to breathe, her body no longer her own, uncontrolled, riding the crest of pleasure which terrified her.

She could feel her inner walls of her heated core spasm, her juices leaking from her entrance, soaking her panties and coating his fingers as they began to slide through the thick honey. She needed relief from the hunger overwhelming and attacking her body.

Saladin's fingers caressed the silken folds, sliding them back even further. Teagan lost her breath as she felt one circling her entrance, spreading the thick cream of her arousal, teasing, taunting her.

"I can't..." her whispered entreaty became an agonised gasp of pure sensation as he penetrated the entrance to her burning centre.

Saladin groaned in her ear. She felt his finger fill her, pushing inside her, hard and hot. She was trembling, her knees weakening, her breath loud and rough in the silence of the room. Oh God, she wanted him so badly.

Oh Hell, control. Where was her control?

"Mine," he growled at her ear, his tongue laving the lobe with a slow, sensual sweep. "You're my woman."

The words penetrated her dazed senses slowly as his hand moved from her soaking flesh to push at the stretchy rim of her yoga pants.

"No." She shook her head in dazed rejection, denying his claim. If she gave into him this once, she knew there would be no going back for her. It would destroy her when he moved onto his next conquest with no further thought to her.

"Yes," he snarled at her ear, ignoring her weak attempts to keep him from lowering the elasticised pants over her hips. Despite her protests, Teagan's body shuddered with delighted anticipation.

Ready to give in to his seductive demands and her lusty need, she turned in his arms to face him.

Her breathy moans caressed his senses as he took her lips in a ravenous kiss, her tongue tangling with his. Her hands delved into his hair, her nails biting into his scalp as she fought to get closer.

Saladin groaned in surprise as her legs lifted, her smooth thighs clamping at his hips as she moved against him, notching him higher, tighter against her heated core. And, it was hot, an inferno of explosive heat seared him through his jeans.

The kitchen's back door opened, shocking them back to reality.

"Oh, my. I'm terribly sorry." Mrs Philpot covered her eyes and turned to back out of the kitchen once again. Although for her, this was a common sight since Alaric and Cassie had become mated. They regularly forgot that other people also lived in this enormous house.

Teagan jerked out of Saladin's grip, her cheeks burning with embarrassment.

"No, Mrs Philpot. I apologise. Excuse me," Teagan implored as she stumbled to her feet and ran from him.

"This isn't over Teagan," he growled behind her. Far from it.

The erotic promise etched in his tone burned a hole in her heart and seared her brain as they warred against one another for supremacy. She couldn't help wondering if she had just made a close escape or if she had sealed her own fate.

17

"I thought I told you to stay put," Ahriman growled as Abby crept back into his rooms. The air crackled and sizzled about him, his furious cold eyes blazing with anger and something else...concern?

Crap.

Abby hadn't expected him back so soon. She'd hoped she could sneak out and get back without him ever being the wiser as to her little outing. The guards wouldn't have dobbed on her. At least, not unless Ahriman asked them specifically about her movements and that wasn't likely to happen. He never spoke a word to them unless he was giving an order.

"Last time I checked, you weren't my boss, and you certainly don't own me," she answered haughtily. Abby's heartbeat pounded in her ears. Caught off guard, her anxiety and guilt kicked in. She needed a plausible excuse for having left the room.

Think fast. Her mind raced, but the only thing she came up with was: *'Think fast!'* Her brain drew a total blank.

Ahriman watched as she marched toward the bathroom, her head held high in total disregard for his angry outburst. Ignoring too his pulsing power, despite the flickering lights and the fact that every hair on her body stood on end from the static electricity he was throwing off.

"We can rectify that problem."

Abby wrenched her neck around to peg him with a glare, which might have had more effect if he didn't look so damn hot in his body hugging T-shirt and muscle loving jeans. The same pair he wore earlier with those mesmerising buttons, and the same spellbinding bulge beneath. Abby's remaining functional brain cells fuzzed over as desire took hold. His natural scent, infused with potent male pheromones was like candy for her brain. She couldn't seem to raise her eyes to meet his, they were glued to the twitching outline of his thick erection beneath those shiny buttons. She wanted to rip them off with her teeth and lick his candy cane from base to tip.

"Don't even think about it," she snapped, more irritated by her own reaction than what he had implied.

"When are you going to learn, dip shit? You attract more bees with honey than with vinegar," Alex chastised Ahriman, giving him a mental smack in the head.

Ahriman growled. He didn't know what was more irritating, the fact that Alex was right, or the fact that Abby wasn't intimidated by him, not even when every other creature on the planet would be cowering away from him right about now.

She was sexy and spirited. An admirable combination, yet annoying.

"Abby, we were worried about you. We thought that Mira and Lilith had taken you," he reasoned. His milder, less chastising tone however, did little to appease her.

We? Where did this *we* business come from? Alex and Ahriman were separate entities. They did however have one thing in common, she capitulated. Her. They both wanted to keep her safe, for their own reasons of course, but their end goal was the same. As such, Abby dismissed the thought as being trivial.

Abby snorted out a very unladylike derisive laugh. "Do you think your rooms would still look so pristine if they tried to take me?"

True, they hadn't considered that. Instead, they had allowed their distress at finding her missing to conjure all manner of foul play that may have befallen her. Abby may be female, but she was no push over. She would never give up without a fight.

Keeping that in mind, Ahriman considered the other possibilities of her whereabouts, his eyes narrowing on her. Suspicion flickered in their depths.

Abby saw his expression change and swallowed hard. If she thought he looked dangerous before,...Now he looked downright terrifying. His eyes hardened to glittering chips of ice, the power behind them glowed. His jaw clenched and set into hard lines of anger as small blue sparks of electricity arced between his fingers.

Abby stopped dead in her tracks. Maybe she'd pushed him too far. He'd wanted her alive, but she was still only a pawn in his game. No doubt he would see it as no more than collateral damage if she was to meet with an untimely demise, especially now that he had completed his portal device. He didn't need her blood to keep him strong. Not any more. Ahriman really didn't need to keep her alive. Alex however, did.

"Abby, what have you been up to?" he asked with forced calm, the static in the air prickling her skin.

What should she tell him? Should she lie? Should she tell the truth? *Think fast.*

Crap, crap, crap.

She could feel Alex's fear. Even he wasn't sure what Ahriman would do right now if he didn't like her answer.

Crap, crap, crap.

Think fast!

Abby tested and discarded several excuses in her mind in an effort to find one that sounded conceivable. She came up with nothing, nada, nil, zilch, zip.

Except for one.

Ahriman fumed. His jaw couldn't look any harder if it had been set in stone. He was angry that she had disobeyed him and left his room, but it was the idea that she had gone behind his back and possibly betrayed him, that really stung. He felt…something, but he couldn't quite define what it was. Feeling anything was foreign to him and his inability to control it, flipped his mood from mildly pissed off to homicidal.

"I, I, um…." Abby couldn't think straight under the pressure.

"You're scaring her, arsehole. Let me talk to her."

"No chance," Ahriman bit back at Alex. "She is mine to deal with." His eyes bored into her with the intensity of a laser. "Well? I'm waiting." His acid tone transforming her mere reluctance to speak into involuntary mutism.

"I, I couldn't stay in here," she stammered.

She was going to tell the truth, minus a few important details.

"Why not? You're safe here," Ahriman said, waving his hand around him to indicate the room he'd designated for her confinement.

"No, I'm not," she answered quietly, pausing for a few seconds to see if his temper had levelled out. When she felt it was safe, she continued. "When you left earlier, you gave the guards no orders to keep me in here. I suspect you also forgot to give them any orders to keep Mira or Lilith out," she told him.

"Fuck a duck," "Fuck a duck," Alex and Ahriman both said at the same time. Abby was right. He had stuffed up. If the two crazy bitches had come looking for her here, she would have been a sitting goose.

"Where did you go?"

She couldn't very well tell him what she was doing, but she could tell him where she went, right? Telling him what she was up to would put the neck of every man in the woods waiting to rescue them, in a noose. She couldn't afford to jeopardise their lives or whatever they were planning. The element of surprise was essential, she understood that well and Ahriman couldn't be trusted. He was still the enemy after all, even if it was getting harder to tell Alex and Ahriman apart.

Ahriman's temper had eased off considerably, her hair no longer stood on end like a crazy Einstein doll, but his anger still simmered at a dangerous level.

Abby told him where she went. She described the tunnels she followed to the old store room where she had sat for the past couple of hours. She also described the fresh footprints in the dusty floors of troops having been moved. It had come as no surprise to her that he had known nothing about it.

"Mira has some explaining to do," he growled. And Morganna, he thought to himself. Alex shuddered. Even the name, Morganna, creeped him out after what she did to him in the ritual chamber. Such dark, dangerous power he could feel flowing from her, filling the room. If he had control of his own body right now, he would probably start dry retching.

Ahriman's anger may have subsided, but his frustration had not. He had come to his rooms earlier looking to relieve his tension within the depths of Abby's delectable body, his goal had not changed.

"Come here my little pet, you disobeyed me, you need to be punished." A smile twitched across his lips, anticipating her reluctance, eager for the chase. The more she fought to deny him, the harder he would fuck her and the more he would enjoy it.

He crooked his finger beckoning her to him.

She refused to move, no matter how badly she wanted to. She was *not* going to be Ahriman's play toy today.

There was however a glitch in her conviction, a very big glitch. It had been more than a day since Alex had taken her blood.

She knew that sometime in the next twenty-four hours the Alliance was going to storm the compound. The risk of Alex getting hurt or even killed, terrified her. He needed her blood in his veins if he had any chance of surviving what was likely to come.

Abby stood her ground.

His eyes flared with rapacious hunger. Ahriman wanted her, she could see it. But Alex needed her, she could feel it, and he was willing to drive Ahriman to the point of his sanity to get to her.

Ahriman closed the distance between them, reaching for her with a tight grip on her upper arms, holding her in place as he leaned down close, his cheek brushing hers sending a bolt of electricity through her body.

"You will give me what *we* want, Abby. You can't refuse."

Hot breath feathered over the skin of her bare neck as he spoke, his voice dripping with erotic demand.

Had he used the word *we,* again? Had that been a Freudian slip or a sign that the two were actually becoming one?

Abby nipped his shoulder in retaliation, her breathing was ragged. Alex opened his senses to her, showering her with his love, drawing her closer to him. He could feel her turmoil of confusion, need, fear and desire. He felt it all within himself like a mirror image of hers.

Ahriman almost pulled back and let Alex out, the emotions coursing through him threatening to overwhelm him again. Abby arched into him with a shudder of anticipation, holding him firmly rooted in place as her soul reached out for Alex, touching him with her light and brushing over Ahriman's soul in the process, sending a convulsive shiver throughout his body.

Ahriman reeled at the contact. What was happening to him? He didn't understand it, but he craved more. Needed more. That caressing touch against his soul, no matter how unintentional it had been, had opened a void that needed to be filled, but with what, he had no idea. He just needed…more.

Abby moaned. She couldn't help it. Desperation wracked her body as it never had before. Arousal was like a ravenous beast lurking just beneath the surface, crying out to be free.

She thrust her fingers into his hair, twining them in the thick ebony waves.

Confusion and need filled Ahriman's hungry eyes. Alex hovered just beneath the surface, pounding Ahriman with his own desires. His body hummed with the urgency of both men's dual demands, coalescing and fusing.

His fingers lifted to touch the outline of Abby's trembling lips. A mouth that was as ripe and delicious as cherries. Her lips instantly parted at his searing touch.

He caressed her cheek with the backs of his fingers. "Look at me, Abby, don't be afraid." The soft sensual overtone in his voice was so much like Alex she almost believed it was him. How ridiculous. She'd finally lost her mind. She was so desperate to have her *mate*, she was beginning to believe her own lies, the ones she told herself to justify cheating on the man she loved.

Could she dare meet his gaze and be forced to acknowledge once again that she was lusting after her enemy?

His fingers continued their path, along the length of her neck to trace the low neckline of her figure hugging top.

Abby slowly turned her head, her eyes reaching up to meet his. The sight took her breath away. Two hypnotic jewels of seduction drew her in like sexual gravity, urging her to leap across the wide-open stretch of insanity and fulfil every one of her secret carnal pleasures.

With exaggerated care, Ahriman reached out and stroked her cheek again, gently, lovingly. She leaned into his hand and basked in his touch.

"You are so beautiful," Alex's whisper was barely audible, even to her sensitive hearing.

He was so close to breaking free of his captors hold.

Lust, thick and hot, swirled in the air around him. The scent of her sweet feminine need was like an aphrodisiac, driving him mad. Ahriman's lips covered hers, his tongue pushing into her mouth to claim the velvety depths demandingly. She moaned against him. A whimpering, needy sound that made his body flame. Abby's lips were as hungry as his own. When he pulled back to catch his breath, she sought him again, desperate to remain in the oblivion of the kiss.

"Ahriman, please," she pleaded, her body straining against his as she tried to align her mouth with his once again. The second her lips met his, he exploded, imploded, caught fire in the most desperate, painful way.

Abby's lips nibbled at his as her tongue stroked inside his mouth, and he knew she was going to burn him alive if he didn't do something to stop her, to slow down the meltdown he was speeding towards.

"It's me, Alex," he corrected her through a breathy moan.

Abby pulled away from him, her shock at seeing Alex staring back at her quickly morphed into a blend of relief and dismay.

"Don't go there, baby," he told her gently when she opened her mouth to apologise for everything that she had done with Ahriman. "It is what it is. We're bound together, all of us. None of us can control what's happening," Alex professed. "I've told you before, you're not doing anything wrong. Even though Ahriman is a part of me, it's you and me who are bonded, not him. When you think Ahriman is controlling the sex, I'm the one driving his need to be with you. Do you understand?"

"Yes, but..." He hushed her with a finger to her lips.

"I love you, baby, more than I could ever express, and one day, hopefully very soon I will have you all to myself. We will have a life together, hopefully a very long and happy life. Just you wait and see," he promised.

"But..." Abby tried to argue again. She'd been raised by her good Christian grandmother who believed that there should be only one man and one woman in a relationship. She would turn over in her grave if she could see her now. "I need to tell you something, Alex....I'm scared. I enjoy the sex too much with Ahriman," she confessed.

Alex's hooded gaze darkened with the memory of just how much she had liked Ahriman's form of sex, his hardened middle leg twitched uncomfortably in his jeans. "I know exactly how he effects you, baby, and I'm doing my best to learn everything I can from him to please you too," he chuckled.

"You're not annoyed with me?"

153

"How could I possibly be annoyed? You are inexperienced in sex, I am skilled in the more sensual forms. We could have spent months, maybe even years practicing the missionary position before we discovered we both enjoy a bit of BDSM. I could actually thank Ahriman for that."

"But…" Abby just couldn't get her head around the fact that Alex was okay with her carnal enjoyment, especially when she wasn't okay with it herself. The relief she felt however, was immeasurable.

"We could argue about this all day, or we could occupy our time more pleasurably." Alex's husky voice petitioned for an end to the conversation since his ability to form coherent sentences was failing at an alarming rate, a consequence of all his blood draining from one head to fill his other head further south.

Breathing heavily, he drilled her with a combustible stare. Without words, Abby knew he wanted to be inside her. That look siphoned off her fear and inhibitions. In that moment she forgot everything as he pulled her close and pressed passionate kisses to her neck, his hands cupping and caressing her breasts. Alex gripped the twin globes of her backside, lifting her higher against him until the throbbing length inside his jeans pressed between her thighs, as if begging for entry.

She burned. She itched, and she lusted after something only he could give her.

Abby opened herself to him, gave him her kiss, her need, her heart and her soul. He took them. He took them all, melding them with his own in a hungry and unrelenting passion.

Abby ripped at her clothes. Their tattered remains falling to the floor in a ménage of fabric confetti all about them in her rush to feel skin against skin.

Alex nipped at her bare breast with his teeth, then licked softly. As he repeated the process on her other side, he released the clasps on his jeans and kicked them off. His T-shirt was barely over his head when Abby grabbed him with lightening speed and pushed him against the wall, pinning him with her hot little body and holding him there with her sensuality.

Ahriman's eyes flashed at her, her aggressive move stirring him to the fore once again, but only for a moment.

Alex reversed their positions, covering her with his tightly wound body and took her mouth in a dominant kiss, driving her higher and higher with his hungry demands, pushing her legs apart, rubbing his aching erection over the sensitive bundle of nerves at the apex at the V of her thighs.

His lips traced her jaw, down her slender neck, licking the soft skin of her cleavage and tasted the spice of her desire before dusting her breasts with kisses. He could barely think beyond his desperate need.

Trailing his fingers across her stomach and down into her damp, dark curls, his fingers became wet in her slick heat. Touching her pouting flesh, caressing her swelling clit, bringing her to the brink...his mouth watered.

Against him, Abby moaned. The long, pleading sound went straight to his balls, as if she held him in her fist. The power she held over him. God, it was incredible. Never had he known anything like it. He never wanted to lose it.

"I need you inside me. Now!" She whimpered and groaned at once.

Alex closed his eyes and clenched his jaw tight. That was the wrong thing for her to say if he had any hope of maintaining control over his body. But it was too late, those desperate words stirred Ahriman's own lustful desires and he pushed to assert his dominance once again.

They were on a collision course as they battled to enforce the other's submission, blending their needs into one staggering combustible passion.

He fisted his hand deeper into her hair, pulling her even closer. Abby tried to absorb the surreal moment as another dizzying surge of desire crashed over her.

The dominant way he leaned into her, strained to be closer, flushed fresh heat, coiled and expanded all the way from her belly to her toes.

The need to feel him deep within her rose hard and fast. He willingly complied.

Up against the wall, he lifted her, wrapped her thighs around his hips, and thrust deep. Abby cried out at the sudden intrusion, pleasure washing over her as their bodies aligned.

His expression raged from determined to possessive as the internal war continued. Impaling himself within her heated confines in one long, controlled thrust, his never-ending kiss claimed her, swallowing her cries of ecstasy as he plunged deep into her tight channel, as if he refused to share the sound with anyone.

Abby's body eagerly devoured every inch of his hard length, squeezing it tightly between her inner walls as he pistoned inside her, craving more.

He withdrew almost to the tip before plunging forward, filling her again. As he thrust, his groin glided over her clit and Abby's breath caught. So perfect. He pushed in once more, the tip of his hard shaft nudging the entrance to her womb. She gasped and gripped him tighter.

The world around him vanished in a haze. Everything except Abby. He had become a willing prisoner in her body and his own pleasure, ecstasy spiralling through his gut to his balls and...straight to his cock. The ache inside skyrocketed through every cell, burning him, threatening to ignite his blood with her searing passion.

Abby too, was catapulted into the blinding world of pleasure as it expanded and magnified, sending her into a tail spin of sensation that nearly drowned her.

Blood rushed to her swollen clit, the friction of his thrusts brushing over it sent sparks of euphoric bliss straight to her brain. Alex exploded inside her with the force of an atomic bomb. Abby convulsed as pleasure spiked and overtook her. Her inner walls gripping him tighter as her own climax hit, sending them both into a free fall of mindless ecstasy.

Abby plunged her fangs deep within his vein shattering the world around them, shattering the universe as their climax multiplied tenfold.

Alex wanted to stay there forever, buried deep inside her. He shuddered with an aftershock of his orgasm. Slowly, he lowered her shaking legs to the ground. How could something feel so perfect and be so screwed up?

Abby's legs felt like boneless rubber, incapable of holding her weight. Without releasing her, Alex shifted his grip, lifting her into his arms. In long strides he crossed the room to the bed effortlessly, laying her down and covering her.

"Sleep, Abby. You need to rest. I promise you will be safe here now." Abby looked up, his voice calm and soothing. Her breath hitched as she looked into his eyes. Ahriman stared back at her minus the aggressive dominance. "I have a few things to deal with, but I will come back and check on you soon, okay?" he said, gently stroking her cheek with the back of his hand.

For the first time she didn't cringe away from his touch to wallow in a pit of self-loathing.

"You're going to see Mira, aren't you?" she asked him, her brow furrowing with concern.

"Yes, she is one of the people I need to deal with."

"Be careful. She can't be trusted," Abby heard herself say.

Ahriman chuckled, a wry almost bitter sound. He knew that when he hired her, but back then his judgement was determined by his goals. He saw things from a very different perspective now. "I will. Rest."

Abby's eyes drifted closed. She really was tired. For the first time in days she felt sleep creeping up on her.

He kissed her forehead and silently slipped from the room. This time he gave specific orders to his guards that no one but him was to enter. Her final thought as sleep took hold: *Alex hadn't taken her blood.*

"She wasn't telling us the whole truth about where she went earlier," Ahriman stated to Alex as they marched along the long corridor.

"No. I don't think she was. But that's not to say you can't trust her. I think she's still the only one in this Godforsaken place you can trust."

"I don't doubt you're right, but I can't help feeling she's betraying me."

"Her loyalty was never to you Ahriman, but she would never deliberately put you in danger either."

"Don't you mean, she would never put *you* in danger?"

"Isn't it the same thing? You are me and vice versa. You have to trust her and I'm sure when she's ready, she'll tell us what's she's been up to. Face it, who else has your best interests in mind?"

Good point.

18

Richard rounded the corner onto the cobblestone street. The sun was high in the sky, but it did little to alleviate the chill from the icy, winter wind as it whipped at his face, making his ears and teeth ache.

So, this is the place, he thought with a flutter of uneasiness in the pit of his stomach. He'd heard about the Northern European Alliance headquarters, hidden within the underground Bunker Restaurant, but he hadn't thought he would ever see it.

Until a year ago there had never been a reason to become involved with anything remotely Alliance related.

Until a year ago he'd lived a relatively ordinary life, raising his four granddaughters, teaching them the traditions of their ancestors. Admittedly, it hadn't always been an easy task raising them by himself, especially when all four girls had inherited their mother's stubborn streak. His own dear wife had died many years ago, his daughter, the girl's mother, died in childbirth with the youngest, and their spineless father fled his responsibility before she was even cold in her grave. Yet, Richard wouldn't trade one moment. He had no regrets, save one.

He had abandoned the girls a year ago with no warning, no explanation. The older three were already living independently, creating lives for themselves, so fortunately his disappearance had not caused them any great upheaval. But not so for Elise. Guilt weighed heavily on his heart for abandoning the thirteen-year old to the care of Oliver Harlow and his family. He had no doubt the family would care for her as their own child, he wouldn't have left her otherwise. Regardless, it did nothing to remove the stain on his soul for surrendering her. He had spent twelve years despising the girl's father for deserting them, and he had now committed the same sin against them.

How the girl's must hate him for it. God knew, he did.

What other choice did he have though?

None.

Like Merlin, the first druid in his ancestry to carry the legacy of protecting a very powerful spell, or as Teagan preferred to call it, the family curse, Richard had shouldered the responsibility for many decades and had come to terms with his obligations. Although, for him it had never been a true burden, he didn't have the options available to him that Teagan and the other girl's now did, or the temptations. Their futures were filled with potential and hope. If he could spare them his burden he would in a heartbeat, but to do that he would need to live for all eternity. An unattainable impossibility. As protector, he was destined to live a normal human life, no exceptions. At the time of his death, the curse will be passed to the next living relative, Teagan. And there wasn't a damn thing he could do to spare her from it.

He could however, try to spare all the girls from the threat that was no doubt hunting him this very minute.

Richard had felt a ripple of warning in the atmosphere of a malevolent presence as it re-entered the world almost a year ago to the day. It should have been impossible, nonetheless it had happened.

Down through the ages Richard's ancestors had protected the spell, all the way back to Merlin. Before that, the spell had been used on a man. For the past year Richard had searched Europe for the amulet which contained the essence of that man. Deemed too dangerous to be kept by its owner, the amulet was confiscated and the man was banished from Earth, his amulet given to another clan of druids for protection.

Fifteen hundred years passed without incident.

Until now.

Several artefacts had been hidden throughout history. The whereabouts of each was a well guarded secret. So well guarded in fact, that over the centuries druids had become complacent, traditions lost as the centuries past. Little attention was paid to the whereabouts of those artefacts of power which had been entrusted to them, and many of them had become lost, forgotten or discarded. As was the case with the amulet that Richard was searching for.

It was his hope that if he could find it, he could learn some clue about the artefact that would not only help protect himself from the owner of the spell, but also free his descendants from the burden of carrying the curse when he died.

If the spell's owner was truly back in this world, the lives of anyone from Merlin's druid bloodline was in danger, not just Richard.

That was a prospect he was not willing to accept.

So far, unfortunately, his search had turned up very little. The trail had run cold in St Petersburg, Russia, where he had just left.

Richard shook off the powdery flakes of snow from his heavy coat and hat, and stomped his muddy boots on the mat as he entered the cozy ambience of the Bunker Restaurant with its blazing open fires and the smell of hearty food cooking. His mouth watered. It had been some days since he had eaten a decent meal.

"Would you like a table?" the young girl politely asked him in Ukrainian.

"Thank you. Yes."

"Will you be eating alone or are you expecting company?" Nadia asked again, switching to English, sparing him the effort to speak in her native language. She loved every chance to show off her fluent English, and fortunately the Bunker Restaurant attracted a number of English speaking tourists, enough for her to make regular use of her linguistic skills.

"Alone," he answered. "Could you please let Gustav know that Richard Caddock is here to see him. I believe he is expecting me."

Nadia examined the older man, the druid her father had been expecting. Fine wrinkles bracketed his thin lips and fanned out from the corners of his eyes. White and grey intermingled through his black hair contrasting strikingly against his short pure-white beard. The laugh lines once so prominent on his ageing face, had been replaced by heavy creases of worry and stress, evident in his furrowed brow.

It was hard to believe that this frail looking man was the most powerful druid in the world. She stared for a moment debating whether or not to ask for his autograph and quickly discarded the thought. Powerful he may be, but he was no celebrity, and in her mind, only a celebrity like Abby, the progeny of Sammael, the first vampire, or Alaric as he preferred to be known, she mentally corrected herself, was worthy of an autograph.

"Sure. I'll let him know right away. Is there anything else I can get you? Coffee maybe?"

"That would be wonderful. Thank you." Richard rubbed his icy hands together, willing the feeling back into his fingers. Nadia hurried away in search of her father. Richard closed his eyes and soaked up the warmth of the cosy room. It was early afternoon and the restaurant had virtually emptied of its lunchtime crowd, the only sounds came from the crackling of sap in the dry wood in the open fire nearby, and the clinking of cutlery as tables were being set for the dinner crowd later.

Heavy boots and the scraping of a chair startled Richard awake. He hadn't even realised he had dozed off. He cleared his throat to speak but was beaten to the punch.

"The name's Gustav, Mr Caddock. Thank you for coming all this way to help us. What do you know about our situation?" he said, setting down the steaming cup of freshly brewed coffee in front of Richard. His matter-of-fact introduction, straight to the point. Gustav didn't believe in wasting time, and right now they didn't have a minute to spare. They were planning on moving out to the Guild's compound that evening and there was still too much to do to prepare.

"Not a lot I'm afraid. I believe you have some men who are under some sort of spell?"

"We think so, although I've never seen anything quite like it. Their minds seem to be almost completely gone. Some of them are my own missing men, mainly lycans, but there are others from various other military and mercenary groups around the globe. They're all highly trained combat specialists and all have gone missing under mysterious circumstances over the past six months. We're in over our heads here and we'd be very grateful for your help."

"I'll see what I can do, I'll need to examine them. Are you keeping them nearby?"

"Yes, in the holding cells beneath the bunker." Gustav stood again and waited for Richard to follow his lead. He almost groaned at the thought of getting up again. His weary bones had just gotten comfortable in the padded wooden chair.

"No time like the present, I suppose," he muttered and pulled himself upright once more. He was not however about to leave behind his coffee, grabbing it from the table he followed behind Gustav's towering figure through a hidden panel at the back of the storage room, down two flights of stairs to a fortified basement.

Dim light and a musty odour filled the air, but the pungent stench of dark magic overpowered everything else, causing Richard to cough and shudder against the sense of evil that surrounded the men inside the metal cages before him. Fifteen men in all stood or sat, staring vacantly like inanimate robots.

Carefully, methodically, Richard examined each man, none of whom made any attempt to move or gave the vaguest indication of being aware of his surroundings. Richard *tsked*, shook his head and sighed loudly as he worked through the line of men. When he looked into these men's vacant eyes he had to agree with Gustav. The lights were on but there was no one home.

"Well? Can you fix them?" Gustav asked impatiently.

"It's not as simple as that, I'm afraid," Richard offered sombrely, his furrowed brow pulled together tighter than ever. "There is a binding spell on them, a very powerful one. This isn't the work of just any magic user, this is very dark and very old magic."

"But, can you fix them?" Gustav asked again.

"There's a way around every curse, spell and charm, if you know how."

"And, you know how?"

"I believe there are three options," Richard began, keeping his answer vague and stretching Gustav's normally lengthy patience to their limits. "The spellcaster would need to release them voluntarily, or they could be freed if the caster dies, or whomever the caster has bonded them to...."

"And, the third option?"

"They could stay like this until *they* die."

Gustav fisted his hands at his sides in frustration. "How do we catch the spellcaster and kill her?" he growled.

"Her?" Richard asked, a slight quiver of surprise in his voice. "How do you know it's a *her*?"

"We had word a few hours ago. The new head of the Guild, Morganna is the witch who put the magical parameter alarm around the compound. We suspect she's also the one most likely to have put the spell on these men."

Richard cleared his throat to cover his distress.

"Indeed. I have no doubt she is," he answered absently. "May I ask, how long has this Morganna woman been head of the Guild?"

"At least six months that we know of, possibly nine. Why?"

"Just curious. Are you're sure it couldn't be longer. Maybe a year?"

"No. Rudolf Stein ran the Guild before Morganna. We actually believed her to be male until today. What do you know about her?"

"Not enough I'm afraid. Having said that, I do believe she's extremely dangerous and she will be nearby wherever you found these men."

Trepidation clutched Richard's heart as it skipped an accelerated beat.

The pieces of the puzzle were beginning to fit together. But for now, he would keep his suspicions to himself.

"The compound." Gustav's eyes glowed with golden fury, his wolf hovering just beneath the surface, itching for retaliation for his damaged men. "If we kill Morganna, it will free all the men?"

"Yes, I believe so."

"Will there be any side effects from the spell, memory loss, personality changes? Anything?"

"I'm a druid, not a fortune teller, I'm sorry to say. My best guess is they should all return to normal, but you need to be prepared for the worst. You may never get back the men you once knew."

Gustav fell silent as he paced the basement, stopping in front of Dieter, Klaus' catatonic brother. "The way I see it, we have one option, to kill Morganna. Can you put a protection spell on my men so we can get close enough to kill her?" Gustav's heavy gaze fell on Richard expectantly for a favourable answer.

"No, I'm afraid not. Someone this powerful would no doubt sense the presence of another magic regardless of the cloaking effect. I doubt any of your men would get within a hundred metres of her. They're more likely to wind up becoming victims to the spell themselves or worse…You need someone who has defences against her spells."

"Are you volunteering?"

"I guess I am," Richard sighed, mentally kicking himself for the idea. If this woman was who he suspected, being in such close proximity to her was a very, very bad idea. "However, I must tell you, it goes against everything I believe in. I am a peaceful man, not a fighter. Moreover, I have no combat skills."

"If you seek peace, you must prepare for war." Gustav gave Richard a consolatory slap on the shoulder, accompanied by a sympathetic look of agreement. "With any luck you won't have to be anywhere near the fighting. We only need you to neutralise her spells, we will take care of the rest."

Richard appreciated Gustav's optimism and confidence, but he was more of a realist.

Gustav explained their plans for that evening and their strategy for their siege on the compound. Just after sundown, they would leave for the six hour trek to the hunter's cottage a couple of miles from the Guild compound. There they would meet up with the men currently stationed there and the reinforcements coming in from England.

The afternoon quickly passed as Richard silently examined their preparations and watched the men sparring. Beating the crap out of each other apparently had soothing qualities that the old druid couldn't understand, although he wished he could find some form of release for his own nervous tension.

As the time grew closer to leave, Richard's agitation grew. Instinct screamed at him to run, far, far away, to leave the Alliance to fight their own battle and go back into seclusion.

Regrettably, he couldn't do that. Without his help they had no chance against Morganna. None of them.

Besides, eventually she would bring the fight to him and his family whether he liked it or not. He couldn't hide forever. It was *his* duty to face this evil creature, not his granddaughters.

Nonetheless, he remained torn between logic and hope. It was a huge gamble he was taking to be that close to Morganna. He could be risking so much more than just his own life or those of his family.

Rock, meet hard place, a voice mocked in the back of his mind.

"What am I, your house elf?" Mira snarled, handing Lilith the bag of flour.

"Thank you Dobbie," Lilith bit back with a contentious smile.

There was no love lost between the two women, but for now they had a common goal. Get rid of Abby. To do that, they needed to get Ahriman out of the way temporarily. Mira couldn't give a shit if he *'accidentally'* died in the process. Unfortunately, since Lilith was the only one who knew how to bake the biscuits laced with the paralysing drug to accomplish that goal, Mira was forced to remain relatively amicable with her and had been coerced into promising not to harm him...too much.

Lilith still clung to the delusional belief that Alex's influence had caused Ahriman to abandon her, and once Abby was out of the way he would come running back to her. Ridiculous fool. The woman lived in a fantasy world as far as Mira was concerned, and was slipping further and further away from reality into her own personal paranoid utopia daily. She was obsessed with Ahriman and couldn't see that he didn't give a flying fat rat's shit about her.

Not that Mira cared one way or the other. Lilith was merely a stepping stone to achieve her own goals.

The fact that Lilith was human and considered *'no threat'* to Ahriman was an essential part of their plan. She could get closer to him than Mira ever could. Once they had him secured away, it would be only a matter of time before they cornered Abby. The savage pleasure of the upcoming fight would be rewarding, although it wouldn't bring back Cain. That was one void that no amount of revenge could fill. It was that loss that drove Mira's hatred. She didn't care how dirty she had to fight, Abby was going to be a pile of dust by the time she was finished with her.

19

Cassie and Teagan followed Mrs Philpot and her tray of tea and cake to the room filled with male laughter, a sound that had been sadly lacking in the house in recent weeks.

Entering the enormous lounge room, they both stopped dead in their tracks.

Great. More dangerous men, Teagan thought.

Gwynn ap Nudd. The high lord of the nephilim stood regally with the pool cue resting loosely in his hand. The ancient being carried a graceful, shining, ageless light within him, tempered with a stern, elegant power.

To his left, Raif leaned over the pool table lining up his shot. Leader of his wyvern clan, the dragon came accessorised with a lethal vibe. Opposite him stood Alaric and Hawke heckling him as he shot the white ball into the pocket without so much as grazing another ball.

Saladin stood silently by the bar, brooding over his latest run-in with Teagan the night before. He could have chased after her. He should have made things right between them. Despite what he wished he had done, he suspected he would have ended up trying to finish what they started in the kitchen, which in the end would only have made things worse, he feared. He couldn't seem to do anything right with her.

Coulda. Shoulda. Woulda. The three stooges of regret. All he needed now was a smack in the back of the head.

What could he do to fix things? He seemed to have a terminal case of foot in mouth disease, everything he said seemed to offend her. If only she had the same effect on him. The way she made him feel whenever she was near confused the hell out of him, setting off another bout of verbal Tourette's, and sinking him deeper into the pit of emotional quicksand that was rapidly sucking him under.

On top of that, he still hadn't managed to get her into his bed, which was an irritation driving him to the point of madness. His cock was a permanent rod in his pants which ached to the point of pain. Saladin considered relieving his need with another female, but the fanciful notion left him feeling ill. Even the friction of his own hand failed to relieve the tension within him, he'd practically built up calluses on his palm trying.

But, what bothered him the most, was the realisation that his obsession for her was not lessening, but increasing. It had been wrong of him to accuse her of hexing him with a love spell. He knew deep in his soul she wasn't capable of something so despicable. Frustratingly, knowing that didn't change the fact that she occupied every waking moment in his thoughts.

Saladin followed Teagan's scent through the house and spied on her when she thought she was alone. Without any conscious intention, he had even found himself in her bedroom in the early hours of this morning. He'd sat on her bed next to her and stroked the silky waves of her ebony hair as he watched her sleep. Much to his surprise he discovered he was content just to be by her side. He simply relished the sight of her stretched across the sheets.

Now, here she was once again standing only metres from him, her vanilla-orchid scent heightening his senses. Awareness coiled within him like a cobra ready to strike as a fiercely possessive emotion clawed at him. The need to touch her, taste her, and wrap her in his own scent seized hold of his entire being, banishing his rational thinking brain to no-man's land. It was an oddity he couldn't fathom, and it scared the crap out of him.

After eliminating all the nefarious possibilities for his current condition, Saladin was slowly coming to the inevitable conclusion. Short of having lost his mind entirely, Teagan may well be the one person who could fill the perpetual emptiness in his soul.

His *Mate*.

"I'll just set this tray down over on the sideboard for you boys," Mrs Philpot chirped cheerily. She was always happiest when she had people to fuss over. The more the merrier. "There's plenty more where that came from so eat up, I can't have you going hungry."

"Mrs P, you're a gem, but you're going to *over* feed us," Raif told her.

"Never. You all look like you could use a bit of fattening up, you're all too skinny," she chuckled, looking at the group of men whose body mass consisted almost purely of leanly chiselled muscles. Although to be fair, everyone looked too skinny to Mrs Philpot. She might have been short on stature, but her personality was larger than life, and she had the hips to carry it.

Despite Raif's protests, it wouldn't matter how much food this group consumed, not one of them would ever put on an ounce of weight. Cassie and Teagan just looked at the platter before them and groaned. Cassie may not gain any extra weight, but for the baby's sake she was willing to forgo her chocolate and sugar fix for a healthier diet. Teagan on the other hand, only needed to look at the decadent chocolate fudge cake, slathered with glossy calorie packed ganache frosting, and she put on five pounds. It was so depressing. She was still trying to work off the last piece of cake she ate...a week ago.

Cassie looked to Alaric with a questioning gaze. "You're all leaving for the compound tonight, aren't you?"

"Yes, love," he answered a little warily. Cassie had a fiery temper and he knew she'd make him pay for not telling her about it first. "We received word a couple of hours ago that Ahriman has finished his portal device and the Guild may be planning to move out soon," he said, his gaze quickly shifting to Teagan. "Oh, I believe your grandfather has arrived in L'viv."

Teagan wasn't quite sure how to feel about that. Relieved he was okay? Annoyed that he would take the time to visit strangers but not his own family? Whatever. She didn't have the emotional capacity to worry about that right now. She was too busy dealing with her overactive libido and a sulky vampire who seemed to ruin her day just by showing up. Her issues with her grandfather could wait.

Alaric explained in more detail the news they had received and the plans that had been made. More vampires would be arriving just after

168

night fall. They would meet them in Cadley with the lycan clan. From there they would enter Savernake Forest where Gwynn would sift them through the dimensional rift, directly to the forest in the Ukraine where other Alliance men were already camped out.

"I'm coming too," Cassie decreed.

"Now Cassie, love…" Alaric began.

"Don't you Cassie me." *Poke, poke, poke.* Her finger nearly drilled a hole through his chest. "I'm coming and that's that," she protested belligerently.

"Now love, be reasonable," Alaric appealed, his lips twitching with amusement as he fought the urge to smile. He loved her fire and determination, it also stoked his internal fire, the one that almost burned a hole through the crotch of his pants. "I know you could kick arse with your new power…if you knew how to harness it properly, which you don't," he pointed out. "And I know that you're indestructible, but you're pregnant, so you're not coming. End of discussion," he instructed, replicating her obstinate tone.

Cassie pouted and crossed her arms in protest but said no more about it. This wasn't an argument she was going to win no matter how much she wanted to help rescue Alex and Abby.

"At least I can go. You haven't seen half of what I can do," Teagan challenged with stubborn determination.

Saladin growled, his dominant presence suddenly filling the space between them with stifling ease. "I won't have you endangering your life. You and Cassie will stay here, is that clear?"

"You can't stop me," Teagan blurted out defiantly, and wasn't that mature. Maybe she should stomp her foot too and be completely immature, she thought.

Breathing deeply, she calmed herself. "If I wanted to endanger my life, I could think of better ways of doing it, skydiving with a moth-eaten parachute, swimming in Piranha infested water, or eating Cassie's cooking. I would be a valuable asset on your team and you know it," she huffed, plonking her hands on her hips in frustration. "No offence intended about your cooking," she quickly apologised to Cassie.

"Non taken," Cassie replied, amiably waving off the comment. She was a lousy cook and was the first to admit it.

"This is not negotiable. You will stay here with Cassie and that's final." Saladin's ebony brows slammed down over eyes that darkened dangerously.

Teagan looked from Saladin to Alaric, her eyes pleading for support. Unfortunately, Alaric's face was equally as stern as Saladin's. None of the other men in the room were willing to wager into the conversation, conveniently stepping back out of the firing line.

Teagan's indignation turned to outright anger. "Really?" she answered, crossing her arms over her breasts. "And, exactly when did I give permission for you to become my keeper, Yusuf Saladin?"

What right did he have to dictate what she could and couldn't do? He had no claim on her. She was an adult, an independent woman capable of making her own decisions and she told him so, in no uncertain terms.

A groan escaped his lips as his gaze lowered to all the curves that emphatically declared her womanhood.

Teagan held her breath momentarily, entranced as hunger licked hotly through his irises, skimming over her, devouring her without so much as a touch. She was acutely aware of his power, his strength, and all the things he could bend to his will. It was not lost on her that she was very quickly becoming one of those things. Whenever he was near, she inevitably bowed to him like a flower seeking the sun.

The scent of lust rippled off her in subtle undercurrents, the sweet spice made more sweetly poignant in the throws of despising him. The pressure behind the zipper of Saladin's pants tightened uncomfortably. All she had to do was think about opposing him and that stubborn flesh rose to rigid life.

He stalked toward her. The closer he got, the more her chin came up in that defiant way of hers, inciting his fickle man tackle to twitch with zealous demand.

Saladin rubbed his chest to ease the ache there and took a deep breath to steady himself. Taking her hands in his, he calmly waited until she looked him squarely in the eyes before speaking. "I know how much you want to come with us, and I agree you would be a very valuable asset, but…" he paused, looking at the floor for a moment to build up the courage to confess his fears.

Heavy silence hung between them. "If you were there, I wouldn't be able to concentrate on what was necessary. I would be too worried about what was happening to you, and if I'm not fully focussed it could compromise the mission, or even jeopardise other people's lives," he said with sincerity. His voice lilted in its complexity, his gentle tone took the wind right out of her sails, her breath hitched on his heartfelt words.

Teagan conceded. She'd lost the debate and caved under the pressure of his will once again. She wanted to help, but not if it meant she would become a hindrance, and she had no intention of putting more lives at risk. "Oh, fine, put it into perspective why don't you," she grumped irritably.

Wait a minute. Did he just acknowledge he had feelings for her other than wanting to nail her knickers to his bed post as a trophy?

Teagan's fiery zest might have fizzled out, but it was replaced by another kind of flame.

She rolled her bottom lip between her teeth and worried it in a way that stirred him in an extremely inappropriate manner considering how serious he was trying to be at the moment.

"Better still, you can both go and stay at the Drunken Duck pub in Cadley until we get back," Alaric stated firmly. "Take Tilly."

Take Tilly? That went without saying, Cassie thought. The dog never left her side.

The remark induced simultaneous grumbles from both women as they huffed out their indignation at his inference that they required babysitting.

"Fine," Cassie grouched. "But you're going to make this up to me later."

Alaric's lips turned up into a lopsided grin, his eyes sparkling with mischief. "It will be my pleasure, love," he answered, wrapping her in his arms for a passionate kiss which held the promise of so much more.

Teagan turned away, not from embarrassment, but envy. "I'm going for a walk," she informed them. A painful knot twisted in her stomach. It really sucked knowing she would probably never have the kind of contentment and happiness her friend did. That didn't stop her from taking a final look back in their direction as she opened the door to leave, her eyes falling not to the happy couple, but to Saladin, his brooding eyes watching her intently.

"I'll be out in a minute," Cassie called after her.

Teagan quietly walked along the long hallway to the stately entrance hall. Filtered sunlight cast a kaleidoscope of colour over the tiled floors from the stain glass windows beside the beautifully carved double wooden doors. Slipping outside she took a deep breath to relieve the heaviness in her chest.

The air was crisp with winter's chill and the clouds above were wispy and thin. It was only a week until Christmas, but for the first time in her life she really didn't care. She felt none of the excitement she usually did. Her grandfather was not likely to be with them this year and her sisters were spread out across England. She had never felt more alone or lonely.

Teagan walked across the gravel driveway, the semi-frozen ground crunching beneath her feet. She noted that the Porsche which Alaric had given Alex the night he was injured at the Drunken Duck Pub, still sat in the same spot where it was left the following day, just before he was kidnapped. He hadn't even had a chance to drive it yet, and no one had the heart to put it away in the garage.

Some time later tonight, Alex and Abby should be home, reunited with the rest of their family. At least they would all have a good Christmas, Teagan thought.

"Teagan, is everything okay?" Cassie called out to her.

Teagan turned, forcing a relaxed smile on her face. "Everything's fine. Why?"

"You left without your jacket. You'll freeze before we get half-way through the forest," Cassie said, handing her a thick woollen coat.

"Oh. Thanks. I guess I was a little distracted."

"Say no more. Vampires! They're infuriating…but lovable."

Yeah, and sinfully tempting, Teagan thought.

"I also brought my purse. If we go to the Drunken Duck now, you can get a head start sinking a few shots of tequila."

"Why would I need to do that?" Teagan asked suspiciously.

"To help you forget how much Saladin wants to get into your pants, and how close you are to giving in to him, of course. I'm restricted to juice," she griped with a pout. "Accept it, you're hooked on him."

"It's that obvious?"

"If you were any more transparent, you'd be invisible," Cassie sympathised.

Teagan didn't want to accept it. She was too smart to give her heart away to someone like him. But maybe she wanted to think that because a little white lie tasted less bitter going down than swallowing the truth.

It's just sexual attraction, Teagan lied to herself again.

Arghh, she had to pull herself out of this vat of hormone-induced fog she seemed to be floating in. *Bad hormones.* Even if he wasn't off limits to her, he'd trample her heart in a second.

Saladin was a complication she didn't need.

Cassie and Teagan had walked no more than a hundred metres into the forest, Tilly loping along ahead of them, when the ground beneath them shook with an explosion that came from the manor's direction. They both turned at once to see a huge fireball rising from the driveway.

Alex's car.

"What the...?" Cassie screeched, ready to run back to the house.

Tilly growled as Teagan gave a squeal of shock, the wind knocked out of her lungs as she flew backwards through the air, coming to land heavily on a fallen tree trunk. Cassie turned her head in the direction of their distress.

Oh, crap!

20

The explosion had the men's attention immediately and they raced from the house to see what had happened, fully expecting to discover Cassie had accidentally blown something else up.

Within seconds they all stood around the remnants of Alex's new car, the explosion which had torn it apart was definitely not Cassie's handiwork. A symphony of furious growls and expletive curses echoed through the car park.

Panic seized Alaric. He sent out his senses to search out Cassie's location. The earth rumbled beneath them and a blast of arctic wind almost knocked the men from their feet as his icy power detonated.

Not again.

The terrified scream did not come from either Cassie or Teagan, neither did the unearthly roar that followed, but it was enough to make the men forget about the car as they tore across the property and into the forest with supernatural speed.

Saladin and Alaric both saw red, fifty shades of it, as they raced toward the sound of screams and unearthly howls, with Hawke, Pan, Raif and Gwynn hot on their heels.

"Holy hell. What the fuck is that?" Hawke shouted as they all came to an abrupt halt.

Hawke pulled out his SIG semi-automatic from the holster at his side, taking aim at the monstrous hellhound tearing at the lycan half his size, which was saying something since the lycan was the size of a small horse in his wolf form.

"Wait. Stop," Cassie screeched. "That's Tilly. Don't shoot."

A wave of disbelief coupled with relief flooded through Alaric. Cassie stood unharmed off to one side, away from the fighting canines.

He gave a frigid nod to Hawke to lower his weapon after closer inspection of the hound whose razor-sharp teeth clamped around the lycan's throat, effectively quelling his ability to fight her off.

Alaric carefully pushed the rhinoceros sized hound aside, she growled and snapped at him but stepped away from her prey. His fingers closed firmly around the lycan's throat squeezing tightly. Nostrils flared and fangs flashed, as the wolf began to thrash in his hold.

The lycan's body shimmered for a moment in a haze, before returning to his human form.

Lionel.

As Alaric leaned closer, his eyes glowing and fangs fully extended threateningly, Lionel's whimpering fell silent, his face closing up.

Ahhh. Guilt. It was so strong, he could smell it. Acrid. Annoying.

Menace rolled off Alaric in icy waves. Only someone on a suicide mission would cross him, especially now, so soon after Cassie had been attacked and Alex kidnapped. He wasn't in the mood to play nice. There had been a time when he would have killed first and asked questions later. Right now, he was seriously tempted to follow his old ways.

No one threatened his family and expected to live.

Gwynn's hand replaced Alaric's, his need to see to his *mate* trumping his need to kill the snivelling lycan. He tucked those thoughts away and focussed on Cassie, pulling her close and stroking the small of her back in circular, caressing motions, offering her comfort with a gentle brush of his lips against hers. Nothing mattered more.

Saladin ignored the furry commotion, his thoughts too were focussed elsewhere. Teagan lay on the ground, silent and still.

"You've got two seconds to start talking before I rip your heart out," Gwynn promised Lionel. "This forest is under my protection. How dare you break our treaty," he snarled out his anger.

"I'm sorry, I had no choice," Lionel whimpered, his words no more than a raspy whisper.

"Not my problem," Alaric growled as he pulled Cassie closer, shielding her from the traitorous lycan. Irritation snaked through his veins, his tone as arctic as the sub-zero freeze which settled on the vegetation around them as his power continued to leach into the air.

"Just rip the fucking band-aid off already and explain yourself," Hawke growled impatiently, his finger itching to pull the trigger on his revolver and put a bullet in Lionel's brain.

"I had no choice," Lionel repeated more frantically. His voice raw and rabid as terror pounded a path through his torn and bloodied body. Tilly's alter ego it appeared, came accessorised with some deadly assets. Along with her impenetrable hide and razor sharp teeth, the nails on her paws were hooked and as sharp as knives. She paced back and forth behind them, warily vigilant. Gone was the silly, playful puppy. In her place stood a fearsome predator, alert and intelligent.

"We've already heard that excuse, dip shit. Now, unless you want your pelt to become my next coat, start talking," Raif told him, letting his eyes flash with the power of his own alter ego. A very hungry dragon.

Pan crouched down to where Lionel lay on the ground, the pint-sized vampire ready to provide some facial remodelling to his already battered face, guaranteed to give the lycan a serious canine tooth ache if he didn't co-operate.

However, it was Tilly's low growl close by his ear, her acidic drool dripping on his face painfully, that finally loosened his tongue...and his bladder.

Leaving Lionel to the others to deal with, Saladin rushed over to squat beside Teagan. "It's okay, you're safe," he told her in a gentle tone.

Teagan could only nod in response as she struggled to raise herself, blinking back the tears that filled her eyes.

Saladin wrapped Teagan's shaky body in his arms and held her tight, lifting her carefully until she was standing on her own two feet. Closing his eyes, he rested his face in her hair, releasing a tensely held breath that rumbled free from his chest. The deep, rough cadence reverberating against her cheek.

Teagan was safe.

Relief washed over Saladin's frayed nerves. His agitated breath fanning across her neck sent shivers down her spine, intensifying the tingles in her blood, which he generated just by being so near. Shifting in his possessive hold, Teagan tilted her face up to his, reaching her hand up to stroke his cheek with her fingertips in an attempt to reassure him that she was fine.

Slowly Saladin opened his eyes. His gaze was hard, iridescent, rapacious. Those two orbs sizzled with all the emotions flooding him, threatening Teagan's sense of stability and claiming her soul in one look.

"Thank you," she managed with a faint whisper.

Saladin couldn't speak, his voice locked in his constricted throat. Instead, he traced his hand compulsively down her back. She was exquisite, nature's violin, plucking at invisible strings which undeniably tugged on his spirit at its fundamental level.

Hearing the terrified scream and fearing it was hers, seeing a hellhound and lycan tearing at each other only meters away as she lay on the ground....

The thought of harm coming to her almost destroyed him. Saladin felt a wild, violent upsurge of emotion, a combination of fury and a desperate need to keep her near and safe, driving him to the brink of insanity.

He couldn't put into words what he felt.

Instead, he showed her.

Without warning, Saladin tilted his head toward her upturned face, claiming her lips with his possessive kiss, gently nudging them apart with his own.

Teagan's lips parted on a gasp of surprise and Saladin barged in. Long languorous slides of his tongue, soft brushes of his lips, a melding of breaths and mouths and needs. Her eyes fluttered downward as desire flowed through her, as heady and intoxicating as the finest wine.

Saladin groaned, enchanted by her taste, her scent. Encouraged by her eager response. It wasn't enough. It would never be enough.

Putting the brakes on the scorching kiss, Saladin pulled back gently.

He was breathing hard, and that, as well as the burn in her dark eyes as they slowly opened, was nearly enough to throw decorum out the window, race her back to his room and finish what they'd started the night before.

Teagan knew there was something she should say, retaliate against his presumptuous kiss, it was right on the tip of her tongue. It

177

was…gone. Her mind was blank. All she could think about was how good his lips felt against her own and wondered if the rest of him tasted as sinfully good as his mouth.

"This is why you need to stay behind," he muttered, burying his face in the dark silk of her hair once again, her vanilla orchid scent soothing to his raw nerves. "I can't think straight if you're in danger."

Saladin continued to hold her, wrapped her in the shelter of his hard body.

As his panic subsided, the scent of her blood filled his nose, tripping his homicidal switch to 'on', once again. Saladin stepped back from her, holding her at arms length, scanning her from head to toe for the site of her injury. Sapphire blue eyes glittered with fury when his gaze came to rest on a long cut on the back of her arm. Her heavy coat torn, a stain of blood leaching into the fabric at alarming speed.

A wild, violent upsurge of fury erupted from deep within his chest in a vicious growl, lethal fangs in full view beneath his snarling lips.

Saladin turned towards Lionel. The murder in his eyes sizing him up for a body bag, but Teagan's shaky hands still clutched at his waist, held him firmly in place.

He warred with himself. Tenderness and aggression fought for supremacy and somehow against his own will, tenderness won.

"Let me fix that for you," Saladin purred, swallowing back the raging storm inside, fully aware that his own aggressive behaviour was likely to frighten her far more than the snivelling lycan cowering on the ground. That didn't stop his body from trembling with the effort not to rip Lionel's head from his shoulders.

Lionel hurt my…his what?

Lionel had hurt Teagan! Saladin quickly amended his internal dialogue to something more generic, lacking any kind of obsessive overture.

"It's only a scratch."

"A very deep scratch which needs attention." Teagan didn't argue with him, instead she reluctantly shrugged off her jacket as he slid it from her arm with gentle care.

"See, it's not that bad," Teagan said, but couldn't hold back a wince of pain as she tried to stretch her neck around to see the cut.

"I've seen worse," Saladin reassured her with a forced smile. Teagan didn't doubt his statement. He had been a warlord once upon a time, fighting against the Crusaders in the holy land. Her wound was probably no worse than a paper cut in comparison to what he would have seen over the years.

"It's nothing a couple of band-aids won't fix."

Saladin's concerned scowl held Teagan's attention. "No. I'm afraid it will take more than a few band-aids to fix this cut, it's quite deep. I can heal it for you, but you'll need to trust me."

Trust him?

Did he deserve her trust? Maybe. Did she want to trust him? No. Did she have any other options other than Saladin? Probably. There were several other vampires there who were capable of healing her cut as easily as Saladin. So why did she hear the word, "Yes," leave her lips.

"This won't hurt a bit, I promise," Saladin told her as he pulled her closer.

Teagan shivered, half from the frigid wind which suddenly attacked her body, and half from her heated reaction to how well his hard body fit against hers.

Clutching her against his larger frame, Saladin sheltered her from the worst of the wind. One hand wrapped tightly around her waist, the other he held her injured arm out for closer inspection. "Hold tight, okay?"

All she could do was nod and watch, mesmerised as his mouth, fully fanged, lowered to her raised arm.

His eyes never left her face, expecting to see fear and uncertainty reflecting back at him. Instead, he saw only curiosity and trust. He hadn't expected that, considering how loudly she protested against everything else he did. Saladin barely stifled a sigh of relief.

His tongue flicked out making a pass over her wound. Bolts of ecstasy shot straight to his balls. He had tasted a few drops of her blood as he'd grazed her neck the night before, but the rich elixir that coated his tongue now was more decadent, more intoxicating than anything he had ever tasted. It was liquid gold and completely addictive, like her.

A possessive growl rumbled deep in his chest. Turning his body, Saladin sheltered Teagan from the other men's view. He knew what was coming, how the healing hormone in his saliva was going to affect

179

her...and affect him. The last thing he wanted was to share the sight of her rapture with anyone else. His possessive nature wouldn't allow it.

Mine.

That thought reverberated through his mind as his tongue made a second pass over the deep laceration. On the third, his lips latched onto the wound as he poured more of the healing hormone into her.

Teagan shuddered in his arms, her knees grew weak as euphoric exhilaration flooded through her veins. It was as though she had just been infused with the most powerful aphrodisiac ever created, magnified by one hundred.

Saladin held her tighter against him and braced his leg between her thighs to steady her. As the hormone connected them he felt every sensation that rushed through her, his eyes remained firmly fixed on her face, mesmerised. Watching her expression of rapture sent his heart racing and his breathing became rough. He was fast losing his grip on his restraint as their combined desires intensified.

But, here was not the time or the place to make his claim on her.

Must...not...! He could barely hold a single coherent thought.

No longer aware of her surroundings, Teagan began to ride his muscular thigh between her legs. She needed more, so much more. Her swollen clit rubbed against him, driving her crazy with need. The hand about her waist dropped to grip her backside, lifting her higher, grinding her harder against him.

Oh God! Now she knew why he told her to hold on to him. So many gloriously dangerous sensations.

All she could think about was wrapping herself so tightly around him he could never escape. Her body ached so badly for him she wasn't sure she could survive it.

"I need you, so...bad...it hurts," she groaned and whimpered at once.

Saladin closed his eyes and clenched his jaw tight, reluctantly pulling away from her. Those were the wrong words for her to say if he had any hope of maintaining his control. His body shook with the effort of restraint.

Fate had shitty timing.

"Soon," he promised, caressing her bare, newly healed arm, letting his fingers glide further down until her fingers tangled with his and her body relaxed against him once again.

On a groan, he leaned down to claim her mouth, his lips soft, his tongue stroking an easy glide against hers as he eased her down from the precipice of passion he had brought her to.

"More. I want more," she slurred drunkenly.

Voices filtered through the haze of desire. Gruff, angry voices, bringing her back to reality with a sharp nudge, but still she clutched to him, her body still humming from the healing hormone.

"I will give you anything you want, my beautiful jewel. Later," he promised, a smile twitching across his lips. His smoky voice was gentle against her ear, sending a new ripple of longing through her body, not of lust, but a soul felt need to belong to this dangerous, infuriating man.

Saladin continued to hold her close, but she could feel his attention being drawn to the confrontation only metres away. They had Lionel unsteadily on his feet as Oliver Harlow and his brother Damon, along with several other lycans, arrived to deal with their traitor.

Teagan actually pitied the man, although she noted that Alaric didn't look quite as homicidal as he had earlier.

What had she missed?

Teagan shivered against Saladin's hard body, this time from the cold as he helped her on with her jacket. As tepid as his vampire temperature was, she'd preferred the warmth of his body to her tattered coat. Looking down, his groin displayed the unmistakable outline of his rather large and very firm erection. She practically purred with satisfaction, reassured that she hadn't been the only one affected by the hormone.

"I'm fine now. Go and deal with Lionel."

"I'm not leaving you alone," he growled.

"Yes, you are. You need to go and deal with Lionel. Cassie and I are fine. Besides, who'd be crazy enough to come near us with Tilly on guard?" she slurred.

Teagan looked past him to see the hellhound had once again returned to her normal form of an overactive, playful Irish Wolfhound, who for once, was sitting calmly at Cassie's feet.

"We're going to continue this, soon. Do you hear me?" Saladin promised.

Teagan nodded drunkenly.

"You go straight home," he ordered.

She attempted a salute, unsuccessfully, as she stared at the finger waving in front of her face. "Yes, Sir. Go straight home, do not pass Go, do not collect two hundred dollars," she giggled, which only made him more reluctant to leave her. She was as high as a kite on the healing hormone.

"I'll take care of her," Cassie assured him. "You need to go with the others."

Saladin kissed her again, swiftly and hard, and then with another protesting growl he released her and strode off after the group of alpha males, and the lycan who he still contemplated practicing his filleting skills on.

Without his support, Teagan's rubber legs buckled. What was that feeling? Astonishment? Relief? Euphoria?

Whatever it was, she wanted more.

Cassie caught Teagan about the waist, supporting her weight as she led them back toward the manor, Hawke and Pan in tow. The blonde vampire with the itchy trigger finger and his pint-sized sidekick radiated enough protective power to make an angry mamma bear proud, as they followed silently a few paces behind.

"So, how do you feel?" Cassie asked, a sly grin on her face.

"That healing hormone really packs a punch, doesn't it?" Teagan drawled and swayed on her feet.

"Yeah, it does. Just wait until you take *his* blood," she chuckled.

"Never," Teagan gasped, astonished and horrified at the thought. However shocked she may have appeared, the idea sent a flutter of excitement through her. She was oddly tempted. If the healing hormone in his saliva could almost bring her to orgasm, how much more intense would it be with his blood in her veins?

Don't go there, she warned herself. *He can never be yours.*

That didn't mean she couldn't dabble a little with him, have a bit of fun, keep it light and uncomplicated?

Light and uncomplicated...with a man like Yusuf Saladin? What was she thinking? There was no such thing.

The need to relieve her hormonal overload, sexual tension, or whatever you wanted to call it, was beginning to cloud her judgement. Saladin's kiss, his scent, his touch, everything about him was addictive. Saladin was the kind of man who could make smart women do stupid things. Teagan had enough sense to realise she was heading into dangerous territory. So why did she feel like her IQ had just dropped by half?

Teagan sighed as she turned to Cassie. "I think I need a drink. Got any Tequila? I could go a Calibre right about now."

"How about we make that a Virgin Calibre."

"Yeah, right," she snorted. "With Saladin around, it won't be a virgin for long," she mumbled.

Cassie chuckled. She sympathised with her friend. Saladin had his sights set firmly on her, and despite her protests to the contrary, the cracks in her wall of resolve were so deep it would only take a minor push for that wall to completely crumble.

"What did I miss back there when I was getting…um…healed?" Teagan asked. She wanted to say *tended to*, but that seemed to imply more than just innocent *tending to* some torn skin, it had more sexual connotations. Although, she had to concede, the extra meaning may just be construed in her own brain and no one else's. Saladin seemed to have that effect on her. Damn annoying vampire.

As they staggered their way back to the manor, Cassie filled Teagan in on what Lionel had told them.

"It would appear that Lionel's younger brother was one of the men captured by the Guild. They used him to blackmail Lionel and Harold to dispose of the body so the man couldn't be traced to the "Missing in Action" list. Then they forced Lionel to blow up the car to keep everyone distracted, delay them from heading to the Guild's compound in the Ukraine."

Lionel had known the moment Raif and Gwynn had stepped from the forest that time had run out. He'd soaked some rope in petrol, dropping one end in the petrol tank and lit the other. He had been in the process of trying to escape when he accidentally ran into Teagan and Cassie…and Tilly.

"He didn't mean to hurt you," Cassie reassured her. "He wasn't expecting anyone to be out walking today."

Well, that was good to know.

"So, they were deliberately causing trouble in the garden and procrastinating, to stall Alaric from going after Alex and Abby?"

"No. Unfortunately that's how they always are."

Teagan's foggy mind tripped over another important question. "What exactly is Tilly?"

"Tilly was a normal dog until recently. I think she must have gone through some sort of metamorphosis after she drank my blood from the Cup."

A couple of weeks earlier Ahriman had filled the Cup with Cassie's blood and drank from it. It had been the boisterous mutt who was responsible for finding it under the couch later that day. There had been some blood still left in the bottom which Tilly drank before anyone could take it away from her.

"Maybe my brain is still a bit hazy, but I don't understand the importance of the Cup in changing Tilly. I know it's the Holy Grail, and drinking your blood turned Ahriman into a monster, but why would it effect a dog?"

Cassie explained the history of the Cup. How blood containing the immortality gene she carried transformed mortals into immortals when drunk from that Cup. It had not only transformed Ahriman into a monster, but it was also what transformed Alaric into the first vampire.

"The Cup brings out the alter ego, the dark side of someone's soul and makes it the dominant part of who they are. For Alaric, whose soul is that of an angel, he became a vampire. Ahriman on the other hand is a demon, rotten to the core already, which made his dark side unimaginably evil." Cassie told her.

"Oh. I see. And Tilly is just another breed of mortal," Teagan said, swaying slightly on shaky legs, watching Tilly lope ahead of them as though nothing had changed. "So, now you have a hellhound for a bodyguard. Cool."

"She's not my bodyguard," Cassie insisted.

"I was there. She transformed into that hellhound when she saw you were in danger. She is very much your bodyguard. Plus, she never leaves your side."

Cassie couldn't argue with Teagan's logic, the dog was practically super glued to her. Not that it made her feel any more comfortable about the situation. Bringing a baby into the world with a pet hellhound? They were going to have to set some hefty ground rules for the mutt.

"What will they do with him?" Teagan asked, changing the subject back to Lionel.

"I don't know. Alaric's handed him over to Oliver to deal with."

The two women shared a concerned look.

"I don't think Oliver will have him executed, but I do think at the very least Lionel and Harold will be looking for new jobs. There's no way in the world Alaric is going to let either of them set foot on our property again."

"Hey, that would mean he has to hire outside contractors, right? The garden might actually be finished in time for you to have your spring wedding after all."

"That would be nice. I'd really like to get married before I'm the size of a beached whale," Cassie chuckled, rubbing her stomach thoughtfully.

21

"Good job on the upgrade, Dr Greenville," Ahriman praised.

Dr Greenville lifted his head and stared at him over his glasses, not quite sure if he had actually heard a compliment, or if it was some sort of back handed reproach. He was inclined to believe the latter, but the smile on Ahriman's face suggested the former. Either way it made him nervous. He'd watched Ahriman kill a guard for nothing more than accidentally bumping into him. Considering he was no longer an asset but now a liability, having finished building the portal device, he was sure his evil boss would sooner eliminate him than pay him a compliment for a job well done.

It didn't make sense.

Unless...Alex really was having a greater influence over Ahriman than he'd believed. If that was the case, he may actually get out of this hellhole alive.

He'd been a gullible old fool to take this job, seduced by the idea of fame amongst his scientific peers and a pay packet he'd only ever dreamt of. That alone should have set off warning bells, but instead he indulged in all the ego inflating hogwash that Ahriman fed him, preferring the view of reality through his rose-coloured glasses only to discover far too late that he was nothing more than a pawn in the evil man's ambitious plan, and a prisoner with a very limited life span. Hindsight was a wonderful thing, he thought. Unfortunately, it never changed the consequences.

"Thank you," he answered. "I think," he added, mumbling beneath his breath. Covering the awkwardness he felt, he reached for one of the biscuits just delivered from the kitchen. Freshly baked and still warm, the biscuits smelled delicious and irresistible. Ahriman too grabbed a couple and between them they managed to devour the entire plate in under five minutes.

Dr Greenville began to notice an odd after-taste in the back of his throat, a bitter/sweet herbal flavour. Soon after he noticed a slight tingling in his limbs. He began to sway on his feet only a moment before his knees gave out from beneath him, hitting the floor with a thud.

A heartbeat later Ahriman too began to feel strange. His arms and legs felt heavy and tingly, as if they belonged to someone else. He stumbled from his work bench and almost managed to reach the door to the lab where his guards waited outside, before he too collapsed limply to the floor in a boneless heap.

"That bitch Lilith, poisoned us. She put the same stuff in those damned biscuits as she put in the tea when you kidnapped me. I'm going to kill her," Alex promised.

"Not if I get to her first." Ahriman was equally as incensed as Alex. "But, you're forgetting something my friend."

"What?" Alex bit out.

"Lilith isn't working alone. She's working with Mira, and if Mira is willing to cross me, then I'm betting she now has a new boss. One whose been operating her own agenda behind my back from the beginning."

"Morganna? Who exactly is she?"

Ahriman didn't get the opportunity to explain. At that moment Mira entered the lab at blinding speed, quickly covering Ahriman's mouth, cutting off his call for help to his guards. They would obey only him and would fight to the death to protect him, *if* he gave them an order. Unfortunately they weren't going to lift a finger unless they were given direct, verbal instruction to do so. It was part of their programming. In the beginning Ahriman had seen this as an asset. Now?...It was a serious flaw that was looking like complicating their current predicament.

Ahriman's eyes glittered with hatred. Power coursed through his body tinging the air around him with static.

He willed his arms to move, but nothing happened. A vicious growl rumbled in his chest, stifled by Mira's hand over his mouth.

He was paralysed, and worse, the drug had also suppressed his power, it pulsed through his body but had no outlet. He could no sooner give off enough charge to spark a light bulb into life than he could fry the flesh off the traitorous vampire restraining him.

Pulling a wad of material and a separate slip of cloth from her back pocket, Mira quickly stuffed the wad in his mouth before he could speak, binding it in place tightly.

Ahriman's glare could have stripped paint from a wall, but was as ineffectual in retaliation as his string of muffled curses.

Mira simply ignored him.

Grabbing his arms, she hefted his weight over her shoulder and stood, the movement barely dredging an ounce of effort from her.

Ahriman's muted curses continued, although they posed little threat to her getting him past his guards. Even if their feeble minds did register Ahriman was in danger, which she doubted, the guards had the brains of a dead jelly fish in their near catatonic state, she could easily take on two lycans.

Mira smiled at herself with satisfaction. As the lab door swung open, she pivoted around in such a way that Ahriman's head 'accidentally on purpose' collected the door frame. Momentarily stunned by the blow, his muffled noises silenced. It was better to make certain his guards didn't get involved, she thought.

"Stand aside, oaf," she ordered the nearest guard. "Ahriman's unwell, he needs to be taken to his rooms."

As the guards both began to follow, Mira quickly reprimanded them. "I don't believe he gave you an order to leave your post." Both guards halted with quizzical frowns as their brains sluggishly processed the information, returning to where they previously stood.

With his guards out of the way, Mira quickly made her way to the cell where Alex had originally been held. No one would look for him there.

Her plan was coming together perfectly.

Alex and Ahriman watched as corridor after corridor disappeared behind them until they finally reached the cell's open door.

Mira marched into the white washed room and dumped him heavily on the small bed, not caring that his head connected with something hard and inflexible, i.e. the wall. She untied the gag about his mouth and stood back with a satisfied smirk.

Immediately Ahriman rattled off a string of caustic curses. "Mira, I order you to give me the antidote. Now!"

"Just in case you haven't worked it out yet, you're no longer in charge," she sneered haughtily. "Although, I believe my *new* boss is very grateful for the portal device."

"Betraying my trust and lying to me, I can forgive. But, you've gone behind my back and aligned yourself with Morganna. Am I right?"

"You're not just a pretty face, are you. I'm just surprised it took you this long to work it out. But then again, you have been rather preoccupied with Ivana Humpalot," she commented. "And, I haven't lied *exactly*, but I might have told a teeny tiny fib or two," she offered with false innocence. "I only went behind your back when I could see you were weakening, losing focus on the objective. It was all very innocent, I assure you," Mira quipped.

Alex listened to her explanation, but his mind got stuck on one comment. Did she just call Abby a slut? That would be like saying triple fudge chocolate cake was the basis of a staple diet.

Ahriman *t'sked* condescendingly. "Harmless lies, innocent betrayals. They don't exist. I should know, I wrote the book on it."

"True, but your pot is much blacker than mine," Mira defended.

"Not in deed, only in the number performed. In that, I've had more time to perfect the art. But Mira, let me reassure you, your soul is every bit as black as mine and *one day*," he emphasised carefully, "You will become a minion at the Master's feet like every other delusional wannabe before you," he sneered.

"Conceited, puffed-up toad," Mira snarled, even as his words struck a cord of uncertainty within her.

"She's obviously spawned from the shallow end of the gene pool," Alex sniped.

Ahriman chuckled, answering his remark silently.

Their silent banter infuriated Mira.

She looked at Ahriman with such evil amusement, it sent chills up Alex's spine. It was like watching a sword being drawn. "I know just what you need."

Mira opened her Comm-link. "You can come in now."

Less than a minute later the door opened. He couldn't see past Mira to view the newcomer, but he only needed one guess. Lilith.

As she approached him, Mira stepped aside. Ahriman noted her agitated eye movements and dishevelled appearance. The Lilith he knew prided herself in her perfect hair and crinkle free, immaculate clothes. This Lilith was not dealing a full pack of cards, which made her unpredictable.

He needed to tread carefully.

"Why are you doing this, Lilith?" Ahriman appealed with an air of confused disbelief in his tone, keeping his anger and his hatred of the woman carefully controlled. "I thought you loved me."

"I do love you," she simpered. "We're not going to hurt you, we just need you out of the way for a while. That's all, Bunnikins."

Alex almost puked at her term of endearment. It was even worse than Ahriman's pet name for her.

"You don't want to do anything to upset me, now, do you pumpkin? So, why would you drug me?" he asked, maintaining the temperance in his voice to appear genuinely perplexed and upset by her betrayal.

He was a master of deceit and manipulation, but he feared he was on an uneven playing field. They had him at a significant disadvantage. His smooth words were likely to have little effect on women mentally unhinged and hell-bent on revenge.

"I would never hurt you," she assured him. "This is for your own good. Alex has had too much influence over you. He's getting in our way," she defended, stroking her fingers over his cheeks lightly, laying a soft kiss to his lips.

Ahriman froze. The little movement he retained in his body held rigidly still, not willing to upset her. At this point she was his best hope of getting out of there. But, the effort not to turn his head away from her kiss was more torturous than walking barefoot across a bed of hot coals. Her touch churned the bile in his gut as Alex's body rejected the woman's touch.

190

"You need to let me go, Pumpkin. We can't be together if you keep me locked up in this room, now can we?" he appealed, forcing a bashful smile on his face. "I have Alex well controlled, he can never come between us."

"But Abby *is* getting between us and I can't have that. We belong together, you and me. I need you," she whispered, staring down at him with love struck stars in her eyes. "I love you, Ahriman. I have from the moment I laid eyes on you, and I know you love me too."

Lilith watched his jaw tighten. His friendly, caring façade was much harder to maintain than it should have been, given his expertise at lying.

"There's no need to be afraid, I'll look after you," she crooned, laying more soft kisses on his face. She had interpreted his tenseness for nerves or maybe even remorse?

Lilith began unbuttoning her blouse exposing the creamy complexion of her bare breasts. Her nimble fingers flicked over their hardened nipples, pinching them and moulding them as she leaned down, dipping them towards his face.

"Don't you fucking let that crazy cow touch me with those flabby udders. There's not enough disinfectant in the world to....Oh, fuck, fuck, fuck!"

Alex's curses blistered Ahriman's mind.

"You could've at least turned your head this time, fucking fucker. I'll never get that vial smell of her swamp troll stench out of my nostrils. I can't believe you've actually fucked her. Besides the flabby tits, she's got a face like the arse end of a baboon. Fuck!"

Ahriman's cold, unnerving gaze slid over Lilith's skinny features, his top lip curling with contempt and disgust as his façade shattered. He stared at her as if she was demented. A legitimate hypothesis he wryly concluded. "You're fooling yourself. I never cared for you. I could *never* care for you."

Lilith pulled back in shock. She wanted to believe it was Alex who had spoken, but it was Ahriman's eyes who glared so coldly at her. Her face creased into a frown of such bitterness and pain, she wanted to scream, and then rip out his heart.

"Don't lie!" she screeched, flipping from calm to hysterical in an instant. "You're just afraid of commitment. You need me," she whispered huskily.

Lilith took a deep breath to compose herself once again and leaned down and planted another delicately soft kiss on his lips. "I forgive you. I know you care about me, you're in denial because of Alex."

Ahriman gasped in a ragged breath, the touch of the woman made his skin crawl. Alex was right, how could he have ever had sex with her? Lilith saw his shudder and smiled, a simpering, needy, hopeful expression and moved to give him another. Yet another wrongful interpretation of his reaction to her.

"Don't confuse indigestion with affection," he sneered at Lilith as he tilted his head away from her, his tone turning arctic.

"You want me, I know you do. Only me!" she screeched at him again, tugging at her hair in hysterics. "Alex is controlling you, I know, but it's going to be okay. As soon as I find you a new host we can kill Alex and be together again. I promise."

"The woman's crazy! Delusional and crazy," Alex accused.

"You think?" Ahriman answered.

Crazy was too kind a word to describe Lilith. She was bat-shit crazy. Actually, that still didn't give her insanity justice. Alex just couldn't think of anything that fit, which was saying something, he could define terms for crazy in seven languages, but she fell into a whole new category of crazy all her own.

Heaven forbid they single out Lilith for being crazy. The only thing missing was the banner saying 'welcome to the Crazy-Shrew Olympiad'. Mira and Lilith together were like some elite women's movement, only evil.

Lilith jumped up and away from him, as though his indignant words had slapped her in the face. On some level she had understood he had spoken truthfully, but her unhinged mind refused to accept it. She began pacing the room, frantically muttering to herself, arguing a point only she could understand.

Ahriman refocussed his attention on Mira.

"What the hell is your game?" Ahriman demanded heatedly.

"I have no game."

"Don't insult me by pissing on me and calling it rain," Ahriman snapped. His voice could have frozen mercury.

"Where are your manners?" Mira drawled, pulling a switch blade from her pocket and flicked it beneath his nose dangerously.

"Ahriman doesn't speak like that, Alex does," Lilith sniped from across the room. She couldn't grasp the concept that Ahriman, the man she has sacrificed everything in her life for, could possibly discard her without a second thought. It was inconceivable. And yet another reason to hate Alex.

"You were right Lilith, Alex seems to have had quite an influence on Ahriman," she said in a patronising tone, although Mira wasn't hampered by any idealistic delusion regarding Ahriman's true countenance.

Ahriman snarled. The air sizzled with static as he tried to focus his energy to burn away the toxin in his veins, but it was to no avail. The paralysis remained with infuriating persistence. "I tell you what," he snarled, the calm evenness of his voice sending a chill down Lilith's spine. "We'll play a little game of hide and seek. I'll give you a head start but I promise you this…"

"Stop your blathering," Mira cut in. "You are no more dangerous right now than a wet kitten," her eyes glittering with menace. "I could kill you now and you'd be helpless to stop me." To prove her point, she ran the edge of the razor-sharp knife lightly across his throat from one side to the other, drawing a thin line of blood from the shallow wound. "You're lucky that it's not *you* that I want dead."

"*We* want dead," Lilith protested, just as eager to inflict her own revenge.

The bitter hatred in her voice eclipsed Ahriman's ubiquitous hostile retribution.

Abby!

Despite the drug paralysing his limbs, Ahriman's eyes were clear and alert, his sardonic smile taunting, intimidating them with his petulant superiority.

"I promise you this…" Ahriman resumed once the two women finished their ineffectual rant, "When this drug wears off, I'm coming for you, both of you, and if you so much as harm one hair on Abby's head, I'll make your deaths painful and slow. That I promise."

"Not in this life, lover boy," Mira chuckled, patting him on the cheek with a little more vigor than necessary, leaving her palm print as a reminder. "It's been nice working with you though. But, as they say, all good things must come to an end," she said, turning away from him to leave. With her head turned she missed the lethal chill that momentarily tightened his handsome features. If there was one thing he did better than anyone, it was hold a grudge. He was also a master at retribution. He wrote the book on it.

"I don't like this," Ahriman complained as the door shut behind the two women, the lock clicking into place.

"Yeah, and I'm having a party here too," the *'mother fucker!'* expletive went unspoken, but they were both thinking it.

"We have to find a way out of here," Ahriman said.

"No shit Sherlock. But take it from someone who's been in this room before. You need someone to open the door from the other side." Besides that, they had an even more obvious problem. Alex's body was still suffering the influence of the paralysis drug.

They weren't going anywhere anytime soon.

"By the way, in case you're unaware, you have the worst taste in women"

"In my own defence, I wasn't interested in Lilith for her mind, I was only using her as my way in the back door to Alaric, to get the Cup and Spear. And Mira, well, she's a good assassin. She came in handy."

The problem with having hired mercenaries as allies is that very few of them had an original thought and even fewer could be trusted. He had anticipated Mira switching loyalties, but not so soon.

"We need a plan of attack," Ahriman said.

"I have a plan. Attack!"

"You're the brains here, can't you think of something?" Ahriman asked, only marginally calmer than Alex. Accessing Alex's eidetic memory was no help. The careful mental notes of the door's locking mechanism which Alex had filed away in his memory banks, only proved it to be infallible. Yet again Ahriman wished he had left a few loop holes in the complex's security...now that he was the prisoner and not the captor.

Despite Ahriman's confidence in him, Alex was lost for a solution to their plight. Maybe he had missed some crucial detail that could help them, he wondered. He hadn't always been the most observant person. He recalled his mother's resigned complaint that he could recite the periodic table when he was barely five, but he didn't know the name of even one classmate. She didn't understand that there was no need to know, that not a single one of his classmates ever spoke to him without a taunting slur for the nerdy geek.

Alex hastily squashed the old memory before Ahriman had a chance to dissect it. They needed to focus on getting out of this confounded room and find Abby. Then, find those two-faced bitches.

Déjà vu. He'd been through this scenario before. Poisoned by the immobilising drug and helpless to save the one he loved. Only last time it was Cassie whose life was on the line. Now it was Abby.

Alex felt as though he was on the verge of breaking, trapped inside a nightmare that wouldn't end.

"Focus," Ahriman growled.

"Easy for you to say," Alex growled back, his distress increasing exponentially as he thought about Abby being in danger and his inability to protect her.

He couldn't lose his *mate*, even the pain just thinking about it was unbearable.

"That's it. Keep that up," Ahriman encouraged.

"What the fuck are you talking about? Keep what up?"

"Abby can feel when you're distressed. If she thinks you're in danger hopefully she'll come and find us and get us out of here."

"You're as crazy as those two shrews. For all we know Mira and Lilith are waiting outside that door, expecting Abby to come rescue us. That would be like handing her to them on a platter. No way. It's not an option."

"It's our *only* option. No one knows we're down here. And, think about it. No one but you and I know about the blood bond. They're not going to be expecting Abby to know where to look for us, they'll be expecting her to be wandering around near the lab or in our room, not here."

That had Alex thinking. His panic subsided a notch, although not his fear of danger to Abby.

"Okay, fine. I agree you have a valid point."

195

Abby came awake with a start, her heart pounding hard as a flush of adrenaline hit her blood stream. She had her legs swinging out of bed before she could even get her bearings.

Alex was in trouble again, she could feel it, but unlike last time he wasn't in pain. It was fear, but fear of what?

Dressing quickly, she checked the clock. Damn 6:00 pm. She'd slept all day. This wasn't good. Could Alex's fear be because the Alliance had already started invading the compound?

No.

She'd hear fighting in the hallways if they had.

Maybe Mira and Lilith had done something to him as a way of getting to her.

More likely.

Or, something happened to him in the lab.

Either way she needed to find him, fast.

Pulling her top over her head she reached open the door to find the two lycan guards had placed themselves directly in front of the doorway.

Abby tapped them on the shoulder. When neither responded, she used a clenched fist.

"Hey you. I'm talking to you. Move out of the way."

Still, nothing.

Pushing and shoving these two bruits was getting her nowhere, she needed a new tactic. Living on the streets had taught her many things, one of them was how to deal with difficult men. Kneeling down behind them, Abby reached a hand between each of their legs, grabbed hold of their male pride, and squeezed. Hard.

Regardless of their inability for individual thought, the pair were still male. They doubled over and dropped like stones to the floor the moment she released them.

Abby leapt over the top of them and hurried along the corridor, following her bond to Alex. Acutely aware that if he and Ahriman were in danger, then Lilith and Mira were probably behind it, and they, or the other guards may be waiting for her.

Following the unused corridors, taking a couple of detours to avoid the main thoroughfares, she finally came to a heavy steel door a couple of floors down.

Alex was inside and there were no guards nearby, which was unusual. Ahriman never went anywhere without his personal guards.

Opening the door silently, only a crack, Abby slipped inside.

"Alex, are you okay?" she called out when she noted his prostrate body lying on the small bed.

"Don't let the door close," he yelled.

Too late. By the time Abby turned around the sound of the locking mechanism clicked back into place.

"Now we're really screwed."

"Ahriman, what's happened?" she asked ignoring his grouchy tone. It seemed to be something she was becoming very good at lately, ignoring behaviour she found disagreeable. That included her own intimate behaviour with Ahriman. Since her last conversation with Alex though, she'd started to feel better about having sex when Ahriman was in control. She was even willing to admit she enjoyed it. Especially since Alex had admitted her response excited him too.

"Did anyone see you come down here? Does anyone know where we are?" he asked.

"No. Why? Who put you in here, and why aren't you moving?" she asked, worry colouring the tone of her voice.

"Lilith poisoned me with the same paralytic drug I had her use on Alex and Cassie, so she and Mira could keep me out of the way while they dealt with you."

"When you say *deal with me*, you mean kill me, right?"

"Is there any other way to deal with someone?" Ahriman asked.

Abby huffed in frustration. They needed to get out of there. The Alliance were coming to rescue them sometime in the next few hours....which she supposed, was something she should tell Alex and Ahriman about. Probably before the sound of guns and explosions brought it to their attention.

Hmmm...Thinking about it, now was probably the best time to break the news of what she had been up to. Ahriman couldn't exactly strangle her for betraying him if he couldn't move his arms, could he?

Abby also had another problem to deal with. Alex still needed to take her blood before the rescue. Just in case something went wrong.

"So, does any part of your body move?" she asked with a seductively smooth voice, dripping with erotic promise.

"My head," he growled.

"How long until the drug wears off?"

"Probably another hour, I ate quite a few of those damned biscuits."

"Gluttony is a sin, don't you know," she purred, leaning down to his ear, her tongue snaking out to trace its outer ridge.

"It's one of the minor ones I'm guilty of, so sue me."

"Oh, no. I have no intention of chastising you for it. In fact, I plan on encouraging you to do more of the same. Only I have a different forbidden fruit in mind."

Ahriman's eyes heated with dark desire as Abby's gaze followed the length of his body slowly.

"You lied to me, Ahriman. Your head isn't the only part of your body that still functions," she smiled, stroking her fingers over the hard length of his erection beneath his pants.

"How about I instruct you on sucking cock properly?"

"I don't think so. But, don't be too disappointed, I intend to play with you, Ahriman. Only, this time I'm in control."

Her smile widened, revealing a sexy hint of fang.

22

Abby's gaze scanned his body once more, coming to rest on the thin stream of blood as it trickled down Alex's throat. Only a shallow cut, but oh, so enticing to a vampire with an agenda to make Ahriman squirm.

Payback is a bitch, she thought with a thrill of excitement.

"We have to get out of here. Now!" he commanded tersely. Ahriman cursed in several languages, but no amount of colourful or inventive words changed the fact that they were up shit creek without a paddle. At least, until someone else opened that door. Until then....

"Now, now. I think you need to learn some patience," she said, her glittering eyes still fixated on that thin red line around his throat, licking her lips. Instantly his aggressive speech ceased as her head dipped down toward him.

She couldn't resist the temptation, swiping her tongue over the long shallow cut on his throat.

Ahriman hissed.

"Hurts?" she asked with mild amusement.

"Like a wet dream," he answered roguishly. "Since you seem to like me so much, you'll let me lick you too," he uttered with dark hunger. "It's only fair."

"What if I don't want to play fair?"

Ahriman looked at her like he was starved for her, but she wasn't about to give into his demands.

Abby gently stroked the back of her fingers over his cheek. The word, 'gentle', seemed odd when paired with Ahriman, he radiated power. For now at least, it seemed to be contained. The hard angles of his face and even the unforgiving set of his mouth had become less severe, almost kind. Maybe it was only her perception or maybe Alex was just below the surface asserting his influence over him again. She couldn't tell. It was getting harder to tell them apart.

Abby glided her mouth over his cut throat one more time, flooding him with her healing hormone, spiking his desire. She smiled to herself. Who knew she could be so deviously mischievous. If she had known how much fun it was to hold this much power over a man she would have tried it long ago. However, this was still all very new to her. Did she have the courage to take control, become the dominatrix, even if she desperately wanted to?

Yes. Yes, she did.

Abby kissed a path from his newly healed throat, along his jaw until her lips met his. Her lips were satin fire, her tongue a jolt of electricity as she closed her lips around his and speared her tongue into his mouth possessively. Alex almost came in his pants. His hardened length pulsed and throbbed. He wished he could grip her hips, lift her onto his lap and wedge his heavy arousal against her heated mound. But, his arms wouldn't move, not even an inch. This time it wasn't because Ahriman wouldn't allow him control. There was none to be had by either of them. They were both at Abby's mercy.

Abby explored the valley's and ridges of his muscled torso, skimming over his bulging pecs, lightly caressing his ribbed abdomen, and still lower, until her fingers curled around his impressive bulge. Even through the thick material of his jeans she could feel the pulsing heat and straining urgency of his need.

It was intoxicating.

Just being next to him was like being plugged into an electrical storm. The heat, the sizzle in the air, and the prickles of anticipation that warned her she was about to be struck by lightening. And that didn't include his electromagnetic discharge that pulsed through her whenever he touched her. That, was a whole other sensation that only added to the chemistry between them.

Ahriman watched her with growing hunger. He wanted to rip off her clothes and take her in a glorious storm of passion. He wanted to kiss her with a hunger that would drown out the voice of insecurity he knew whispered in the back of her mind.

He wanted to demand her willing submission.

Not this time though. She was in charge, she reminded herself. She made the rules and Ahriman was going to obey. Both men were.

"It's time for you to thank me for healing your cut."

Ahriman looked at her blankly, as though she spoke another language.

"How would you like me to thank you?"

"You can kiss me….," she purred into his ear, the short strands of her hair tickling his face.

"Will there be more tongue involved?" he asked, his voice little more than a hoarse whisper.

"To start with," she grinned.

Ahriman growled and enclosed his mouth over hers as she brought her lips to his once more. His hot male taste filled her as he forced her lips open and thrust his slick tongue in and out. His limbs may have been paralysed but he still managed to gift her with a grinding kiss, stealing her breath and fogging her senses. He sucked her tongue, followed it up with erotic little bites of her lips. Then he retreated, making her chase his tongue back into his greedy mouth.

His kiss softened, sweetened as Abby complied with his demands.

Abby pulled back, annoyed for giving her power over to him so easily. Her eyes flared with annoyance as she looked into his handsome face, only to meet with Alex's gaze.

It took only a second to realise the two men were playing with her too.

Her resolve crumbled momentarily as she eagerly resumed their kiss. Alex explored her reactions, licking and stroking the inside of her mouth, sliding the wet velvet of his tongue against hers. He pulled back to tease her further as he nibbled on her bottom lip, brushing soft, yet insistent kisses on the corners of her trembling mouth.

Abby whimpered. Never in her life had she been kissed like that. Her panties flooded with cream, her nipples were as hard as pebbles, her head spun like a tornado and he hadn't touched more than her mouth.

"Is that thanks enough?" Ahriman asked darkly, a look of pure male satisfaction smirking on his face as Alex retreated once again.

"I will tell you when it's enough," she purred. Ahriman wasn't going to win this game. It was time to turn up the heat.

Abby shifted her weight on the bed to straddle his thighs, sitting directly over the pulsing bulge beneath the zipper, eliciting a groan of frustration from deep within his chest when his hips refused to flex into the silken heat above him.

Pulling her stretchy top over her head, Abby discarded it to the floor before reaching behind her back to unhook the clasps of her bra. The white lacy straps slithered down her arms. She held the cups in place for a few more seconds and then let it drop to the floor.

Silence filled the room, except for the sounds of heavy male breathing.

"You're so perfect," he growled with primal lust.

Unused to compliments regarding her body, Abby blushed.

It was hard to tell if this was Alex or Ahriman. The definition between them now seemed flawlessly non-existent. Alex's emotions rolled off him, filling her with love and devotion, and not a small amount of searing lust. Ahriman's eyes skimmed the length of her body with the same heat flowing from Alex. Where did one finish and the other begin? How could she tell them apart?

His gaze slid down her perfect ivory form, with the rose-crested breasts and softly flaring hips.

"Stunningly beautiful," Ahriman praised.

"Mine," Alex added proudly.

All mine. Well, mostly his, he corrected silently. He didn't plan on sharing her forever, although he felt strangely unperturbed by Ahriman's affection toward her.

Abby closed her eyes for courage. She'd never been an exhibitionist and never had any desire to flaunt herself in front of a man, but the dark hungry look he was giving her spurred her on, and she was Hell-bent on taking back some of the control Ahriman had taken from her.

Her palms skimmed over her smooth belly, along her ribs and around her breasts, stopping to trace tiny circles around her nipples. She arched her back, lifting her breasts high, squeezing the soft flesh between her fingers, plucking at her nipples. Hard.

Locking her gaze with his, Abby leaned down until her nipple was barely a millimetre from his lips. He stretched his neck, straining until his parted lips reached their target and hungrily sucked her puckered nipple into the wet confines of his mouth, his teeth nipping at the peak in retaliation for her teasing.

Pulling back, she asked, "If I gave you the opportunity, what would you do with these?"

Ahriman chuckled. "Suck on them. Bite them. Make *you* squirm a bit. Then I'd wrap that creamy flesh around my cock and thrust high and hard until the tip reached those pouty lips of yours."

Moisture gushed from her core, as though a dam had burst between her thighs. She'd never been so hot, so ready to be touched in her life.

"If you're a very good boy, I might let you do just that…later."

"What do you want me to do instead? I know you've got something else in mind, I can see the cogs turning in your mind and Alex is getting all worked up from the sexy vibe you're giving off." He didn't mention he could feel everything Alex did, or that he too was equally as turned on by her dominant antics. Their emotions were becoming so intermingled. At times even they had trouble differentiating the boundaries between themselves.

"Do you really want to know what I want?" she asked. She looked pointedly at his erection pressing hard against the material of his jeans with as much petulant demand as the man who it belonged to.

She looked down on him curiously. She loved his strong masculine jaw line and the way he considered her from beneath his ridiculously long eyelashes. She loved how his nostrils flared when he was aroused, and the determined set to his mouth just before he kissed her. Everything about this complex, sexy man…correction men, drew her closer.

Leaning down over him once again, Abby scraped her fangs sensuously along the line of his pulsing vein at his neck, and licked its length in one long stroke. Ahriman groaned as he turned his head, giving her better access, his body humming with his growing need for more of her touch.

203

In between nibbling bites on his neck, she whispered the words every man wanted to hear, just not when their limbs were paralysed. "I want you, Alex. I want to run my hands over your skin as your body rubs against mine."

Abby had never talked dirty before and surprisingly, she found she enjoyed this too. The power her words had on him were an aphrodisiac, making her feel fearless, bold and sexy. "I want to wrap my legs around your hips as you drive that huge hunk of man flesh inside me."

He groaned once again. She could feel his cock twitch beneath her. "Baby, you're cruel," Alex protested sulkily, as Ahriman let him out once again in the hope he could manipulate her through her *mate*.

Abby ignored them both, continuing her seductive assault. "I want to look into your gorgeous brown eyes as we're barely a breath apart. Taste your kisses," she teased, placing a gentle kiss on his lips. "I want to see those cute dimples wink at me when I do something that turns you on." Abby held eye contact with him as she spoke, sliding one hand down his body slowly, drawing a growl of pure longing as she shuffled down his thighs just enough to release the clasp and zipper of his jeans and fingered the weeping tip of his heavy erection.

Lifting her finger to her mouth she licked the bead of moisture from the tip, savouring the salty masculine flavour. "I want your sweat mingling with mine, our bodies sliding perfectly together…"

"Enough," he pleaded hoarsely. "Jesus, you're killing me here. Baby, please do something, anything. Touch me or throw a bucket of cold water on me. I can't take it anymore."

Abby smiled, a sweet demure, butter wouldn't melt in her mouth, smile.

She dismounted from his body and moved to the end of the bed, pulling off his shoes, followed by his jeans. His hard length sprang free from its confinement, standing proud along his belly, its tip almost touching his navel.

He sighed with relief when Abby nudged apart his legs to kneel between them.

This was a side to her Alex had never seen before. Adventurous, curious, confident. She had something to prove to Ahriman and to herself, and he'd be damned if he was going to spoil it for her, no matter how desperate he was to be inside her. And, he definitely wasn't about to let his alter ego, Ahriman, steal her thunder either.

Abby reached for his hard length. It filled her hand, hot and heavy, as she wrapped her fingers around the thick stalk. It was as beautiful as the rest of him, large and velvety smooth. His testicles, voluptuous twin globes beneath, were drawn up tight ready to spill their full load at their earliest provocation. He was so hard she could feel his pulse slamming against her palm. Her thumb flicked over another drop of liquid beading at the tip, spreading the moisture over the smooth head.

Gripping his hard length beneath the flushed head, she parted her lips, opening her mouth as she lifted the tip to her lips and sucked him in. The broad tip passed between her lips, over her tongue. Abby kept taking him deeper into her mouth until he hit the back of her throat.

His head slammed back against the pillow, sucking in a sharp breath before mouthing a silent prayer. Abby's hunger grew at the sight of his erotic pleasure. A moment later that wet rock hard pole slid back out, almost to the tip.

She was so fucking sexy, he found it hard to breathe. "Suck me. Wrap those talented lips around my cock and suck."

And she did. Abby sucked him to the root again, burying her nose in the short dark curls of hair above, inhaling his musky scent. She deep-throated him several more times. Then her hand circled the thick base of his shaft, stroking him along its heavy length, flicking the tip of her tongue around the sensitive head on every sucking stroke.

Ahriman grunted in pleasure. "Oh, yeah baby, that's it. Fuck my cock with your greedy little mouth."

Abby sucked and pumped his shaft with her palm.

"Faster," he panted. "Harder. Like that. Fuck, more!" he pleaded. His hips flexed marginally as he fought the paralysis in his limbs.

Moist sucking sounds and stuttered male breathing clouded her brain and filled the small room.

As the two men melded into one under Abby's onslaught, he whispered to her ancient words of endearment, heightening the intimacy between them. The language spoken was as foreign to Alex as the affection Ahriman felt was to him, but in that moment their minds were as tightly joined together as their souls were bound to his body.

Abby grinned and licked a path from the base of his balls to the tip of his pulsing shaft. Finally, she had the control over him she desired. Now, he was the submissive and she was the dominatrix. His inability to move, to touch her in any way other than when she allowed it, sent her heart racing with excitement. He was trapped by the chemical bondage of Lilith's poison, and was all hers to play with.

Abby chuckled and pulled away, drawing from him whimpering pleas not to stop. He'd promise her the world at this point and would agree to anything she wanted, if he thought it would get her to finish off the blow job and bring him to the climax he was teetering on.

Now would be a good time to tell him her 'good news'.

"Alex, Ahriman. I have something to tell you," she said as she removed the rest of her clothes slowly and methodically in front of him, her fingers tracing the outline of her full breasts, pinching their rosy red peaks in her thumb and forefinger, before sliding her hands over her flat belly, down to the dark curls and beyond.

Ahriman groaned and licked his lips as her finger disappeared into the cleft between her moist folds.

His hard erection laying along his washboard stomach, jerked with need.

"I want to taste you," he pleaded, seemingly oblivious to the fact she was trying to tell him something important.

Climbing onto the bed she moved the dead weight of his arms aside before straddling her legs over his shoulders.

He groaned in anticipation, licking his lips.

The sweet scent of her arousal was a drug all of its own, making both Alex and Ahriman light-headed. The sweet nectar weeping from her core glistened in view, but just out of reach of his greedy mouth.

"Lower, baby, please come lower."

"Alex? I really need to tell you something."

"Yeah, baby." Alex felt her distress, her confusion. "It's okay baby, you can tell me anything. Just come lower, please," he pleaded desperately.

Abby gripped her hands on the bed head, slowly lowering herself closer, his hot breath feathering over her cool skin, stroking her intimately without so much as a physical touch.

"Yes," she gasped as she tilted her pelvis over him and his tongue made a pass over the slick petals of her sex. A shivery gasp of pleasure escaped her as he made a second pass. He licked and nibbled, and at last sucked on the tiny jewel which hid the source of her pleasure.

Abby moaned, gripping the bed head even tighter as he continued to tease her with his talented mouth, stroking over her sweet spot. She was falling into a bottomless whirlpool of sensation that was threatening to overwhelm her. She was close, so close to her climax, but she needed to hold off, just a bit longer.

"Oh, God!" she cried, arching her hips closer to the warm puffs of breath that caressed the sensitive flesh.

"So sweet. You taste like honey." His straining tongue stroked her sensitive clit. Her hips jerked under his onslaught, the movement driving her aching slit closer to his torturously slow caresses.

Abby could barely breathe, agonised whimpers of her nearing orgasm escaped her as she pumped her hips against his hungry mouth.

His tongue stroked her with feathery lust, sensual, insatiable lapping at the thick cream of her passionate need, groaning his appreciation as he ate at her like a delicate treat.

She had to tell them that the Alliance were storming the compound sometime tonight to rescue them. There was also something else important she had to do, what was it…?

Her head was filled with fairy floss, she couldn't think straight.

A moment of clarity pulled her into action. With quick reflexes Abby hooked a taloned nail through the delicate tissue of her slick folds, so close to her clit the small cut sent a ripple of excitement through her body.

Alex jerked beneath her as the first drop of blood touched his lips. Instantly he latched onto both the delicate bundle of nerves along with the gash and began to suckle from her. He began to shake with pure unadulterated need as her blood hit his tongue and slid down his throat.

"The Alliance is coming tonight to rescue us," she blurted between gasps and groans of pleasure.

Abby wasn't sure he had heard her, but she was incapable of repeating it as his tongue's demanding strokes through her sex suddenly intensified. The added pressure of his teeth nipping and his sucking action on the gash, heightened the tactile pleasure rushing through her.

As the wound closed over, he once again began to roll her weeping folds between his lips, sucking delicately, tugging on the delicate bundle of nerves between them. Back and forth he stroked his tongue, giving it more direct stimulation, sucking hard as he flicked his tongue.

Abby's clit throbbed beneath his assault, sending tingles to her toes as the sensations built. He continued to use his mouth on her, devouring her greedily.

She came with a gasp, her back arched, her legs clenched tight on either side of his face as she screamed out, "Oh God. Oh God. Oh God!"

Ahriman chuckled. The intimate vibration against her sensitive flesh made her cry out again.

He licked at the juices trickling down his cheeks. His cock twitched, ready for more action.

"Did I hear you correctly? The Alliance are storming my compound, tonight?" Ahriman enquired his tone deceptively calm.

"Yes," she answered breathlessly.

"And, how by chance, do you know this?"

The poison's effect was wearing off thanks to the healing hormone in her blood. He flexed his toes, then his fingers.

Movement had returned.

Abby's blood pulsed through his veins, burning away the effects of the paralytic drug with every second that passed.

As Abby shifted her weight over him, Ahriman grabbed her waist while she was off balance, reversing their positions, pinning her face down beneath him. His hard length pressed between her thighs, twitching and pulsing as the head slid between those slick folds to press intimately against her entrance.

Caught off guard Abby lay still beneath him and held her breath. Her post orgasmic addled brain unable to process his question, but his tone sure as hell registered.

Strong hands gripped her ankles and jerked her body down to the end of the bed.

A warning growl sounded next to her ear as he leaned over her.

Before she could contemplate how to differentiate one man from the other, a solid smack landed on her right buttock.

Ahriman eyed the woman before him disapprovingly. "How do you know the Alliance is storming the compound?" he asked again.

"I've been keeping in touch with the men in the forest."

"The ones kidnapping my men?"

"Yes, those ones." Another hard smack landed on her left buttock. Abby squealed at the sting.

"And, just how have you been keeping in touch with them?"

"Satellite phone," she rasped. "I've kept it hidden."

"You've been a bad girl, Abby. You betrayed me. It's time to take your punishment," he berated.

Ahriman knew Abby was only trying to protect her *mate*, yet there was a part of him that had hoped, maybe even believed, she would also be loyal to him. How this could ever be possible was irrelevant. In the real world, Alex and Ahriman were enemy's. Although to him it didn't feel that way anymore. He shared a connection with Alex which continued to grow, and that connection included Abby.

Through eons of his existence, Ahriman had believed himself immune to mundane human emotions and attachments. To him, any softness or kindness was a personality flaw to be trampled or manipulated and used against his enemy.

That was before he became part of Alex and Abby's blood bond.

He was beginning to feel like a hypocrite. Several times recently he had caught himself enjoying their connection, the sense of peace the blood bond brought and the intimacy that entailed. Initially, at the height of sex when their bond felt so overwhelming, he had needed to retreat within himself. Now he lingered closer to the surface, sharing the love making with Alex.

It came somewhat of a surprise to actually *feel* the sting of hurt in the pit of his stomach at Abby's admission that she had plotted behind his back.

He didn't know what to do with that feeling, but he knew how to get recompense.

His hip bones brushed her arse as he spread her wide, the thick head of his cock poised at her entrance. He didn't ease in. He thrust to the hilt in one swift move, sinking deep. His hands curled over her hips as he slammed into her like the demon man he was.

Dual needs, dual desires, one combustible force of nature.

"You're a bad, bad, bad girl," he growled thrusting harder every time he said the word *bad*. Her hot, tight channel was driving him crazy. He shifted his angle, delving deeper inside her.

Abby gasped. She felt every vein, every ridge of his hard shaft. The friction of every thrust inflamed her even more. Perverse pleasure bordering on pain filling her as he hammered her from behind. His heavy balls slapped her clit, his pubic hair tickled her arse and she lost her mind in the heady reaction of his absolute desperation to dominate her.

Long, thorough stroke after long stroke of his rigid pole had her breathing raggedly.

The hard penetrations were followed by slow, exquisitely sensual withdrawals. Each one pushed her closer to the merciless storm building inside her. Each inward thrust stroked against slick, inner flesh. Each withdrawal was accompanied by the shift of his weight and a gliding pressure over her G-spot.

It was so good.

It was addictive.

The pleasure so intense, she knew she would beg for it again later.

Abby teetered on the brink of another climax, craving the rush at that elusive point dangling within reach.

His right hand left her hip. She felt his eager fingers swept over her rear hole only a moment before he breached that puckered opening.

"Oh God."

His slick finger pumped in and out of her arse in time with his pounding cock in her pussy.

A few more deft strokes, then his finger slipped from that tight hole and she whimpered at the loss of fullness, until he returned with two fingers, stretching deep inside, making her muscles clamp down even harder around his marauding fingers and iron hard shaft.

"Do you want me to fuck your arse?" he asked.

"Yes. More. I want more. Oh God, please don't stop."

"Not today, *baby*," he growled. "You can't have what you want, you need to be punished."

Abby groaned. The pressure inside her increased sending ripples of electricity shooting through her body, tightening her inner walls around him further.

210

It seemed however, that despite his determined words to withhold any further pleasure from her, his own body was beyond his control. "Fuck. I can't hold on. So fucking...tight," he grunted, a hoarse cry echoing through the room.

She felt the pulse of his cock as he came, coupled with the rhythmic stroking of his fingers in her arse, sent her rocketing over the edge, her orgasm so intense, spots formed in her vision as the blood vacated her upper body, pooling in her quivering womb.

His fingers slipped from her anal star as he collapsed over her back, pushing them both flat to the mattress, leaving his spent shaft still sheathed to the hilt inside her.

Abby lay beneath him, the feel of his solid weight over her a comfort, despite the knowledge that this passionate, intimate moment would only last as long as it took Ahriman to recover from the blood bond's effects.

He panted and shuddered with post orgasmic bliss. Eventually he found the strength to move. Tracking tender kisses along her cheek, down her neck to the delicate curve of her shoulder, he slipped his semi hard length from her body.

Abby groaned in protest and raised her hips to stave off the moment of separation, and the more severe reprimand he was no doubt dying to give her.

"I'm sorry. I didn't want to go behind your back, but I had no choice," she defended contritely, her voice tight with emotion. The combination of an incredible orgasm and Alex's feeling of relief and pride washed over her, cancelling out her ability for emotional self-control, her eyes welled to the brim. "I couldn't be sure you wouldn't do something to jeopardise things. For all I knew you would have sent out a team to ambush and kill all the men waiting out there."

Instead of chastising her, Ahriman rolled to one side and gathered her body against his. Tears wet his shoulder. Silent sobs shook her body as he stroked her hair in silence, bathing her face in his soothing, adoring kisses.

"A week ago I would have done just that, maybe even a couple of days ago."

"Not now?" she asked, not hiding the surprise in her voice.

"No. Not now."

211

"Why? What's changed?"

"I have," Ahriman admitted with a hint of disbelief in his voice. Abby raised herself onto an elbow and stared into his intense brown eyes.

Not willing to take the conversation any further, Ahriman quickly jumped from the bed and started dressing. "Come on. We're not getting out of this compound until we find a way out of this room."

"We can draw the power in this room and channel it into the locking mechanism to override it," Alex suggested.

"Would that work?" Ahriman asked sceptically. He could feel his electromagnetic abilities had returned along with movement in his limbs, but would a bolt of lightening open a door?

"It should."

"What have we got to lose, I'll give it a go," he acquiesced, raising his hands and concentrating on the electricity flowing through the power points in the room. The lights began to flicker.

"No. You're not doing it. You're too gung-ho with everything. You'd more likely fry the circuits completely and we'll be stuck in here forever," Alex chastised. *"Let me do it."*

Without so much as a second of hesitation, Ahriman moved into the background and allowed Alex the freedom he needed to circumvent the lock and escape their current prison.

The air in the room crackled with electricity, building until blue sparks arced between his fingers. A moment later a bolt of power charged into the locking mechanism. It smoked and sizzled, a soft pop inside the circuits and the door's lock clicked open.

They did it.

Alex whipped around and wrapped his arms about Abby's waist, lifting her up in a huge hug, his broad, jubilant smile beaming.

"I love you, baby."

She grinned shyly and smooched the end of his nose for a moment before he unceremoniously plonked her back on her feet and pulled back away from her.

"I'm still going to punish you, just not now." The sensual overtone in his voice implied a more erotic form of play, than any true punishment, but with the suddenly stern look in his eyes, she wasn't so sure.

"Who wants to punish me, Alex or Ahriman? I can't tell who I'm talking to any more."

"I'll leave it to you to work that one out by yourself."

Abby huffed in frustration and crossed her arms over her breasts. She was getting whiplash trying to deal with these two men.

As the door opened, Ahriman took back full control of Alex's body. Casually, he straightened to stand at his full height, tall, imposing. His dark eyes turned cold and calculating. He appeared as cruel and emotionless as he ever had. No weakness, was his motto. When your back is against the wall, that's when you show no fear at all.

The depravities he was capable of were unimaginable, and right now he was gearing up to unleash them all on Lilith and Mira.

Ahriman was once again filled with his own self-importance, his utter confidence in his own abilities. It had been his downfall more than once he realised, but this time however, he had Alex to balance his impetuous zeal for revenge, with the common sense of a mortal with morals.

"Stay close behind me," he ordered Abby. With Mira and Lilith hunting for her throughout the compound, he wasn't about to let her out of his sight, not until he knew she was safe.

For a moment he thought she'd argue, since, as he had learned, her back bone wasn't the only stubborn bone in her body. But for once she appeared to listen to him. He almost sighed with relief.

23

Whispered murmurs and aggressive growls rumbled through the small group gathered near the heart of Savernake Forest in close proximity to the Elder tree. Several lycans waited, pacing impatiently, their eyes gleaming golden with their wolves itching to be released for the fight. The new Alpha, Oliver, stood beside his brother Damon. His older brother was a seasoned soldier, but he had not yet fully recovered from the wounds he had suffered in their last battle against the Guild, and Oliver worried for his safety. He had only just buried his father, he didn't want to bury his brother too. But it seemed Oliver's fears fell on deaf ears. Damon was determined to go.

In the darkness, more eyes glittered. A small group of hand picked vampires silently approached the assembled band of elite warriors. Saladin, Dray, Hawke, Pan and his brother Nicolas. In all, there were roughly twenty men, but three in particular stood out, their power flowed from them menacingly. Alaric, Raif and Gwynn were a force unto themselves. Each one more than capable of decimating an army single-handed.

Gwynn raised an arm and drew a symbol in the air. The air vibrated and hummed with energy as the portal opened between dimensions.

One by one they stepped through the shimmering opening.

The world around faded into a whirlwind of nothingness. For a moment there wasn't anything solid or stable anywhere as the maelstrom of energy engulfed them.

When the world re-formed, they stood in a frozen forest only metres from a heavily armed group of men readying for battle.

As Gustav and his men waited for the last of the reinforcements to arrive, the silvery half-moon crossed the horizon, showering them with dappled, dim light. A gentle breeze rustled bare branches on nearby trees, but the heavy covering of snow muted the forest sounds.

A heavy weight of uneasiness settled over them as they waited by the hunter's cottage.

While time seemed to have lengthened, in reality it had been no more than half an hour from the time they had arrived at the small clearing, to when the portal opened with the group from England.

Alaric stepped from the rippling rift. His leather pants and calf-length leather duster were as black as his mood.

Payback and death weren't his only companions on this trip. He was on intimate terms with chaos and strife too, and he intended to abuse their friendship today. If the Ukrainian wilderness wasn't already in the height of winter, Alaric's icy power could have very likely plunged them into an instant ice age with his impressively foul mood. Leaving behind his *mate* so soon after another attack on his home and family, even though the culprit was caught, really set his crackerjacks on edge.

However, Alaric gained satisfaction from knowing Saladin felt as badly as he did. Misery loved company.

It was a relief that neither Cassie nor Teagan argued their temporary relocation to the Drunken Duck pub, to the care of Oliver Harlow's lycan clan. Not that he actually expected a refusal, not after what happened in the forest earlier that day with Lionel.

Lionel, the snivelling arse wipe, hadn't had time to warn the Guild of their plans, fortunately. That didn't mean Alaric was prepared to believe that Lionel was their only spy, he had dealt with the Guild too many times over the years to be that gullible. And with the ward on the manor still sub-optimal, he wasn't about to leave anyone on the estate to become another bargaining tool for the nefarious cult. He had already learned that lesson. The hard way.

Hawke stepped up alongside Saladin. He was a killer. Cold. Clean. Efficient. And in as much of a foul mood as his companions.

One by one they filed through the portal, Raif and Gwynn following at the rear to close the dimensional doorway behind them.

Sebastian stepped aside as the father of the vampire race passed him by, his progeny Saladin in tow. Danger followed in their wake. Seb too followed, because only a fool would stand in their way, and he was no fool.

"Alaric, I'm Gustav," he said, extending his hand in greeting.

"It's good to finally meet you," Alaric replied. "Is this the druid?"

All eyes turned to Richard. "Yes I am. Richard Caddock," he answered, dipping his head for a respectful bow.

Saladin's eyes narrowed on the older man. "You're Teagan's grandfather." It was a statement, not a question.

"Yes. How do you know my granddaughter?" Richard's voice tightened with suspicion, his eyes hardening with mistrust.

"Teagan is a delightful woman and is a great credit to you, sir," Saladin replied courteously, tactfully avoiding his personal involvement and feelings toward her.

Saladin's use of the word *woman*, put Richard's teeth on edge. "How do you know her?" Richard repeated, straining to maintain his polite tone. It rankled that his granddaughter had become friends with a vampire. One, he suspected, had his sights on her for a tumble between the sheets, if the sparkle in his eye was anything to go by.

"She is a good friend of my *mate*," Alaric quickly put in, as the tension between the two men began to build. "Until recently, Cassie worked with Teagan at Meg's Café, waitressing. Plus, Teagan and her sisters have agreed to perform a new ward on my property, Havenswood Manor."

"You don't say," Richard said, his brow lifting questioningly. "It would seem I have missed quite a bit recently with my *girls*," he added, shooting Saladin a reproving look.

At his side, Sebastian merely raised a blonde eyebrow.

Alaric cleared his throat as the men gathered around. "Gustav, what sort of situation are we looking at here? Has Mr Caddock..." he nodded in Richard's direction, "Removed the parameter spell yet? What can you tell me about Ahriman?" Even saying his name stirred Alaric's

216

anger. He hated the evil demon with almost as much passion as he loved Cassie.

"He's manipulative, ruthless and evil," Sebastian piped up humorously. He knew very well that wasn't what Alaric was asking. But, with so many Alphas in one place and nerves running thin, things were likely to degenerate if tempers flared, until they were fighting each other instead of their enemy. That was of course, if someone didn't lighten things up a bit.

"You left out back stabbing, blood thirsty, maniacal and power hungry. What he's not, is stupid," Dray added, sending Sebastian a wink of acknowledgement. The two spies both experts in their diplomatic manipulation of others.

They all nodded in agreement.

"The compound has been silent for the past day."

"How much of a threat is Ahriman likely to be? Do you have any idea if he has retained any of his demonic powers?" Alaric asked, clarifying his previous question. He remembered all too well what the demon spawn had been capable of when they last met, and he wasn't too keen on any more surprises from him.

"You're forgetting that he has taken Alex for his host. From what information Abby has passed on, he is having a strong influence over the evil bastard. And, you also have Abby in there. She's smart. She's our best hope to pull this off without too many casualties," Sebastian reminded them.

Alaric growled with frustration. Abby was his progeny, his youngest vampire child and Alex's *mate*. Alex was also Cassie's brother and soon to be his brother-in-law. Regardless, he couldn't promise he wouldn't kill him, if it meant killing Ahriman.

If you want to leave the zoo cages unlocked, best to have a monkey pose as a zookeeper. Richard surmised thoughtfully as he listened to the discussion, rubbing the white stubble on his chin. "I don't think Ahriman is our problem. I think this witch Morganna, is a much greater threat," he piped up.

"Abby had the same opinion," Sebastian informed them.

They hashed out their plan of attack. Richard would disable the compound's parameter spell and would follow them near the rear, staying well clear of any fighting. Once inside, Alaric could follow his bond to Abby. Hopefully both she and Alex would be together. Richard would seek out Morganna with Raif, and Gwynn would search for the portal device. The rest of the men would try to disable as many of the guards inside the compound as possible, preferably without killing them since many of them were no more than prisoners themselves, hexed by Morganna's binding spell.

That left one dilemma. Without knowing how many men the Guild's army comprised, those hidden away beneath the compound's fortress exterior, they would have much less chance of completing a successful mission.

Fortunately for them, Abby had come through with the information they needed, Sebastian informed them.

Attached to the inside of a flack jacket worn by one of the guards they had captured, Abby had managed to pin a hand written, detailed map of the corridors and main rooms in the compound including the guard's sleeping quarters. Counting the number of bunks drawn, they surmised they were looking at a contingency of around one hundred and fifty men, most likely all carrying guns with silver nitrate filled, hollow tipped bullets.

None of the lycan's needed reminding of the damage those could do.

As their debriefing wrapped up and they prepared to move out, a single crack from a sniper rifle echoed through the trees and one of their men dropped to the ground blistering the air with fierce curses.

A bullet to the back.

However, an injury such as this to the vampire it struck, only succeed in pissing him off and put everyone on instant guard.

"Where the fuck did that come from?" Hawke cursed.

"Where the fuck is the shooter?" Saladin growled.

Men ducked for cover but held their fire.

Why couldn't they see anyone?

"It's a cloaking spell." Richard confirmed what they were all thinking.

"Morganna," Gwynn snarled. The ageing druid turned his hard eyes on him and nodded silently in affirmation, his nephilim perception noting an instant of fear flashing through the old man's eyes. He needed to speak with the druid, but now might not be the best time he thought, as he ducked the machete aimed for his head.

That was too close for comfort.

Richard incanted a spell, revealing the guards closing in on them.

Silent shadows darted about in the moonlit darkness, blending, merging with the surrounding vegetation, moving quickly, but not fast enough to avoid their retaliation as they returned the gunfire.

Voices were raised furiously, curses tainting the air blue with their virulence.

Several figures dropped. Gustav prayed they had enough tranquilisers. Killing the guards was not the objective today, at least not until they could delineate the hexed men from those aligned with the Guild willingly. There would be no mercy for the willing.

The hail of gunfire ceased.

"Good news for you, druid. I don't think you need to worry about breaking the parameter spell," Raif remarked. "But since they know we're here, I think you might want to crank up your magic. We're going in, now!"

Not giving Richard any time to think about it, Raif pitched him over his shoulder and ran for the compound before any more guards could make an appearance.

Alaric rounded the doorway into the compound boldly. There was no need for stealth now that their surprise attack was busted and he, in particular, had no need to use cover from enemy fire. He was a true immortal, nothing they could do to him would kill him. They would be lucky if they could even slow him down.

Alaric sent out his senses, searching for Abby. With his blood flowing through her veins, she would be easy to track.

Beyond the next doorway guards filled the corridors, rushing toward them in silent formation.

Alaric rounded the next corner, directly into the path of one of the guards.

The guard spun away, bringing his foot up between Alaric's legs. Alaric yelped, more from surprise than from any true pain, hiking up his foul mood further. Unfurling his silvery wings, he slammed a heavy wing down on the top of his head with an explosion of pain, dropping the man in an unconscious heap.

Close by, Pan was twice as fast and more agile than his opponents, and less than half their size.

A knee to the groin, and the flat of his palm to the man's nose. He figured that if their enemy was going to fight dirty, then so would he. It was only fair.

Alaric watched as the two hundred plus pounds of male crumpled to the ground and stayed there. "One more down, how many to go?" Pan asked with a cheeky grin.

Alaric liked Pan. Now he understood why Saladin had sent him to the manor as extra protection. Despite his size and appearance of a thirteen-year old boy, he was a cunning spy and assassin, one of Dray's finest.

His brother, Nicholas, fought beside him, equally as talented, but the gleam in his eye smacked of sadistic enjoyment. If it wasn't for the direct order not to kill, Alaric suspected Nicholas would do just that. His victims most likely dying a slow, agonising death at his hands.

The group split up.

Alaric went in search of Abby and Alex. Raif and Richard took another corridor with Hawke and Saladin in tow, while the remaining men dealt with the guards.

Down one level, then another. They followed the map Abby had drawn them as they searched for Morganna. She had to be close by since she'd only recently cast a cloaking spell on the guards. It was only a matter of time until they found her.

The very idea of confronting Morganna made Richard's stomach churn. He swallowed hard to steel his courage. He had to do this. He had to face her.

What he couldn't do, was let her kill him. That would result in a fate worse than death, for the whole world. If she was who he suspected her to be.

Corridor after corridor they searched, leaving a trail of unconscious bodies behind them.

Tempers frayed as frustration mounted. They appeared to be searching for a ghost. They were several levels below ground and had not come across any sign of Morganna. "Enough of this crap. I'm sure one of these sons-of-bitches would be willing to tell us where to find her," Saladin growled.

"I agree, vampire," Raif said dispassionately. He wasn't one for passive interrogation. He was more of an action man. Removing body parts usually loosened a man's tongue.

Three more guards stormed towards them. Saladin and Hawke dropped two with their tranquilisers, leaving one standing.

"I've got this," Richard offered.

With a quick spell, Richard whipped invisible bonds around the man's ankles and wrists. The man fell to the ground with a heavy thud, his eyes growing wide with shock. He searched around, trying to find his attackers only to find a grey haired old man.

"You've been holding out on us, old man," Raif smiled and gave him a friendly pat on the back. The seven-foot tall baseball mitt, sized hand sent Richard stumbling a couple of steps.

What was it with these men, always slapping each other about, Richard thought to himself, disgruntled.

Stepping up beside the man, Hawke grinned and pulled a very long and lethal looking knife, the kind that would give Rambo wet dreams. Kneeling down beside the guard, Hawke grabbed hold of his most vulnerable asset and squeezed.

The man let out a high-pitched scream of pain.

"You'll pay for this. Release me." The man thrashed fruitlessly in an attempt to escape.

"I'll keep that in mind. Answer my questions and I'll let you keep your stones attached."

Under the flickering light in the dank and musty corridor, the mercenary steeled himself. "Eat shit."

"No thanks." Hawke knew he could make the man not only confess everything he knew, but sing it in a three-part harmony. "Let's start again, shall we? I don't want to hurt you, but I'm likely to change my mind," he said, his cold voice alluding to promises of pain and suffering he was itching to inflict. Slowly Hawke squeezed his hand a little tighter. "Tell us what we want to know and I'll let you go, got it?"

"Where is Morganna?" Richard asked.

Another minute passed. Sweat covered the man's brow and his face turned a dark shade of red from the pain in his balls, but he hadn't uttered a single helpful word.

221

"I don't think you're doing that right," Raif commented analytically. "He's not talking, maybe you should put more pressure on his tackle?"

"It hasn't worked so far," Saladin argued.

"I think I should give it a try. Give me that knife," Richard offered.

"Are you any good with one of these?" Hawke enquired, surprised and amused by the druid's enthusiasm to help *interrogate* their prisoner.

"Terrible. I can't promise any neat cuts. I could probably manage a few jagged gouges though," Richard told them with just the right amount of enthusiasm.

"Perfect." Hawke handed over his knife, the shiny blade with its serrated top edge glinting in the light.

"No. Please, no," the man pleaded as the tip of the blade pierced his trousers, its point alarmingly close to the base of his pride and joy. The man tensed, swallowed. His frenetic gaze bounced from Richard to Hawke, then back again. "I can't tell you. Please, don't make me."

At his side Hawke merely raised a blonde eyebrow.

"I think we're finally getting somewhere. Talk," Richard snarled, gripping the wicked blade only millimetres from his family jewels. The man whimpered, flinching under Hawke's grip and reluctantly gave them the information they were seeking.

"Who do you take your orders from?" Saladin asked, getting up close in the man's flushed face.

"Mira," he answered.

"Who does Mira take her orders from?" Sebastian asked, not at all surprised by his answer.

"Morganna."

"Why don't you take your orders from Ahriman? I thought he was your boss," Saladin growled.

"I don't know. We were told not to follow Ahriman's orders any more. I don't ask questions."

"Where is Ahriman now?" The four men surrounding him exchanged curious glances with varying degrees of concern.

"I don't know what Mira did with Ahriman. She put him somewhere. I swear, that's all I know," he grovelled.

"What about Morganna, where is she? Has she left the compound?" Richard asked.

"I don't know. I don't think she's left. If she's here, she'd probably be in the ritual chamber."

They talked amongst themselves in hushed voices, intermingled with huffs and angry sighs.

One thing they all agreed on, they had gotten as much information from the guard that they were going to.

Richard removed his spell, freeing the man. Hawke retrieved his knife from Richard and moved to sheath it back at his belt.

With quick reflexes, the man grabbed the knife from his grip.

He made a high-pitched, ear shattering sound as he shrieked in pain, his belly laid open like an unzipped coat. The man slowly slid back to the floor, his eyes wide with disbelief and horror. He had no clue why he had just performed such a gruesome act upon himself.

"Good God!" Richard gasped, his top lip turning up in revulsion. "Morganna has a compulsion spell on her men to commit suicide if they betray her."

"Wow, that sucks," Hawke remarked dryly.

It seemed that even those who followed her willingly paid a hefty price for the privilege.

Not that they really cared. The man had forfeited his right for compassion the day he promised his allegiance to the Guild.

24

Alex carried Dr Greenville's limp body from the Lab, the partial paralysis from Lilith's herbal biscuits unremittingly persistent.

Ahriman opted to leave the old man there to rot, preferably in his own filth, for *allowing* Morganna to take the portal device. As if the poor man had a choice. That point of course was irrelevant to Ahriman, who didn't believe in helping others regardless of their situation. That was one weakness removed from his genetic code long ago. Although, when it came to helping himself...Well, that was a different matter altogether. You could say he wrote the book on self-preservation.

He needed to find Morganna and get that portal device back. The old man was only going to slow them down.

Abby pleaded to help him, but it was Alex's off-key singing of those infernal children's songs again that finally persuaded him to compromise. He allowed Alex control of their body, so *he* could carry Dr Greenville, while Ahriman blistered Alex's mind with curses so foul, even a hard-arsed biker would have blushed.

It was supposed to be payback, but Alex could only smile. Ahriman may be some sort of deity in the Underworld, but Alex was the uber king of cussing. Instead of being offended by Ahriman's foul speech, he took mental notes for future reference.

"How many of those biscuits did you eat?" Abby asked the scientist, easily keeping pace with Alex's long stride.

"Too many," he groaned, sluggishly flexing his fingers open and closed.

"Don't worry, we're going to get out of here," she promised him.

Dr Greenville closed his eyes. He prayed she was right, but he was an old man whose belief in hope had become jaded long ago. Even if he did make it out of this Godforsaken place, he doubted he could live with his conscience for what he had done. He had helped to create a device capable of literally unleashing Hell on Earth.

As unintentional as it had been, and by no means was he justifying his actions since ignorance was no excuse, he'd sold his soul to the Devil in pursuit of professional notoriety and wealth. He was a gullible and stupid old fool.

If he got out, he was determined to do everything in his power to set things right.

They stopped abruptly as heavy footsteps approached.

Guards.

Abby quickly slipped past the men.

"Abby, get back here," Ahriman growled, taking possession of Alex's body once again and continuing his licentious curses out loud when she ignored him. Carrying the weight of Dr Greenville, he was no match for Abby's vampire speed and agility. Silently she crept forward into the path of the guard as he stepped into the corridor.

A shattered male scream followed. Alex grimaced at the white knuckle grip she had on the man's crotch. She twisted. The bastard paled and went to his knees as she released him, crumpling over as he began to vomit disgustingly. She didn't want to kill the guard, but no doubt he wished she had. Despite the phantom pain he felt in his own crutch in response, Alex's concern was limited. After all, the guy was a lycan, so he would recover…in a day or two.

However, Abby had been roaming these halls long enough to know which were the recruited guards and which weren't, and clearly her next victim was one of the Guild's loyalists. Pride filled Alex as he watched her slender leg kick out to connect with his chest. The sound of the man's sternum and ribs shattering echoed through the passage. Alex had a feeling, seeing the power behind the blow, that the ole boy just might not survive that one.

Ahriman too, watched Abby with cold, hard satisfaction. In the face of Morganna's challenge against him, and Mira and Lilith's betrayal, his dark soul seethed, eager for retribution. Seeing her dole out a beating to Morganna's guards filled him with a sense of justification for what he planned on doing to the sorceress and the other two evil bitches when he found them.

He wasn't sure when or how it had happened, but he had begun to see Abby as an extension of himself, an integral part of how he gauged his changing thoughts and feelings. It was her opinions and actions he was using as a measuring stick to decipher right from wrong. How odd was it, that he actually wanted to differentiate the two. At the same time, it made him incredibly irritable.

Morganna was close, he could feel it. Her soul, equally as dark as his own, and in some ways more so, was like a homing beacon to him.

"Come on, keep moving," Ahriman ordered testily, stepping around the immobile guards before withdrawing into the background of Alex's mind. He and Alex and been swapping control so frequently recently that they could now perform the *change-of-guard* flawlessly. No twitches or jerks as either one resumed command of their body.

"Alex?" Abby's brow furrowed quizzically, not asking who was speaking to her, but rather she was asking where they were headed. She'd passed the point of trying to guess who was in control, she'd only end up with a migraine. A hypothetical migraine of course, since becoming a vampire headaches had become a thing of the past, thankfully, but she could still feel a throbbing pressure in her temples. There was no pain with the feeling, but it was annoying and distracting. Something she didn't need right now.

"She's in the ritual chamber," Ahriman answered.

They were getting close.

Rounding the last bend in the corridor, the open doorway into the chamber came into view.

Black tapers burned in the cast iron candelabra arranged around the chamber, their pulsing flames glowing an insidious red hue around the walls. The illumination alone was enough to give Abby the heebie jeebies, however, it was the pernicious evil that permeated the air so thickly which kept her senses on high alert. She rubbed at her arms to alleviate the feel of ants crawling over her skin as she opened her mind to scan the enormous room for the thoughts of anyone who may be lurking inside.

Nothing.

They entered the chamber. Ahriman surveyed the room looking for Morganna, every muscle and tendon in his body was wound tighter than piano wire.

Damn it. Where was she?

"Abby can you hear anyone?" he asked, hoping her sensitive hearing picked up the minute noises inaudible to his human ears. She shook her head. "Anyone's thoughts?"

"No. I hear nothing," she told him apprehensively.

Morganna was here, Ahriman could feel her presence. She may be able to cloak her physical form, but not the foul stench of her soul.

Placing Dr Greenville down on shaky legs, he propped him against the stone wall to help steady him. Releasing his hold on the older man he moved to scout out the witch's whereabouts.

Fighting could be heard further down the corridor beyond the chamber.

"The Alliance are in the compound," Abby blurted out quickly, a rush of relief lifting her spirits.

Alex too, felt a surge of excitement, but his thoughts of rescue only fuelled Ahriman's frustration and anger.

Ahriman had to get the portal device back. He knew the Alliance wouldn't let him keep it, but he would rather see it destroyed by them than let Morganna have it.

Where the fuck was the bitch?

Fighting spilled into the chamber behind them.

Distracted by the commotion, Morganna dropped her cloaking spell around her retinue of bodyguards who filled the chamber.

"Holy crap, where did they come from?" Abby yelled and jumped out of the way of a fist targeted at her, and narrowly missing her mid section, as the first of Morganna's guards reached them. Exchanging punches and kicks, the man was equally her match. Beside her, Alex fought as Ahriman mentally plotted a course through the wall of guards protecting Morganna.

Alex tried to spark his electrical power to life, but the best he could do was give his opponent a new Einstein hair-do from the static he threw off. Cursing, he tried again. The problem wasn't his power, it was his ability to focus on it. With Ahriman's mind on Morganna and his own engaged in his battle against a mindless Neanderthal hell-bent on beating

227

the crap out of him, he couldn't concentrate on his power long enough to activate it.

Though he could ill afford it, Alex diverted his eyes in Abby's direction for a moment as another guard moved to ambush her. She leapt clear of another massive fist, darting around behind the man she king hit him, dropping him like a sack of potatoes.

Distracted by yet more guards entering the chamber, Abby didn't notice she now had a new foe stalking her.

One who had broken away from Morganna's side.

One much more deadly.

Mira.

Alex's distress pulled Ahriman's attention back.

Fuck, fuck, fuck!

With a smirk that made Ahriman want to punch the woman into the next century, Mira approached Abby with twisted savagery in her fixed gaze, fingers clawed into lethal talons ready to rip out her heart. She didn't rush, Abby was cornered, there was nowhere for her to run. More distressingly, she still hadn't seen Mira coming for her.

But Alex and Ahriman had.

Fuck, fuck, fuck!

Alex landed another punch to the side of the guard's head, dazing him long enough to follow through with an upper cut to the jaw, knocking him out cold.

"Abby, run!" Alex yelled.

Abby looked up into his frantic eyes. Shock crossed her face as she turned her head, following the direction of his pointing finger and cry of warning.

He raced toward her using every ounce of speed he could muster from his legs. Mira remained focussed on Abby, only spotting Alex when he was within a few strides of her. Growling she vamped up her speed to beat Alex to her.

Mira had waited months to kill Abby, she wasn't going to fail now. She could taste victory.

Every protective instinct rumbled to the surface as Alex tore across the room in long strides. His eyes roiled like the coastline waters with an impending storm approaching.

228

In one last leap, Alex wrapped his arm around Abby, swinging her around to cover her body with his own, holding her tightly in his arms.

A furious roar erupted behind him.

Alaric reached the chamber shortly after Raif and Richard.

Instantly his fangs descended to their full length, his eyes glittering fiercely. Silvery, angelic wings extended to their full width. The ground rumbled with his fury. But he could only watch in disbelief at the scene unfolding before him, shock chilling him to his bones.

To his left, Mira and Alex both ran for Abby, murder on Mira's face and fear and determination on Alex's.

To his right, the sorceress dropped her cloaking spell, her glare fully focussed on Richard. Eyes glowing red with power, her face twisted in bitter hatred. Between her hands she conjured a ball of dark energy, aimed and ready to unleash on the druid.

Alaric roared out his fury. Even with his speed, he was too far away to save either Abby or the druid. It was like watching a horror movie playing out around him.

Morganna looked at Richard with such evil amusement it sent chills up his spine, like a cat cornering a mouse.

Richard threw up a barrier spell to protect himself and Raif who fought the guards behind him.

Morganna merely passed her hand through the air and his spell collapsed.

Holy Hell! A cold shiver ran down his spine. Morganna was far more powerful than he had imagined.

"I know who you are druid, I can sense my spell on you. I've waited a long time for this," she sneered.

"You will never have it back," Richard promised defiantly.

Beneath his jacket Richard drew out a small dagger, just long enough to pierce his own heart. If he couldn't save his granddaughter from the curse, he would at least save the world from the curse of Morganna.

She was not getting her spell back today.

Richard placed the dagger against his chest and closed his eyes, whispering words of apology and a prayer for forgiveness.

It was needless to say that so far nothing about this trip had worked out the way he expected, so why should his planned exit from this world be any different.

Morganna screeched out her fury. The evil witch waved her hand once again. A moment later, Richard stiffened and dropped to his knees, releasing the dagger to claw at his throat, mouth open, his face turning red as he gasped for air.

Morganna seethed with rage. How dare he try to take his own life and cheat her out of her prize. She eased up on her invisible grip about his throat, she didn't want to choke him to death, she was merely getting his attention, making a point.

She wanted something much more dramatic to finish off this druid. His ancestors had banished her to Fey's equivalent of purgatory more than fifteen hundred years ago and stole her most precious spell.

Now, she intended to make this druid pay for every minute of her suffering.

Killing him was a necessity in reclaiming her spell, but a simple execution wasn't enough. She'd had centuries to plan how to maximise Merlin's descendant's suffering. Now it was time for pay-back.

The druid's soul would be hers forever to taunt and torture.

Morganna began to chant. A small ball of dark energy began to grow in her palms, sucking in and suffocating all light around it, a black void suspended between her hands. Its evil mass grew, intensifying in power until it was the size of a basketball.

Raif stood only meters away from the stricken druid, his attention split between Morganna and the horde of guards who continued to swarm the chamber. He'd take one man down and two more would take his place. It was damn frustrating. He could put an end to all this fighting in under a minute if he let his alter ego out to play. Sadly though, while the chamber was large, it wasn't quite large enough for his dragon.

Nearby, Richard watched in horror, unable to move a muscle as the sorceress thrust her hands out, releasing the ball of energy across the cavernous room toward him.

He'd failed. He'd taken a gamble, and failed.

Closing his eyes, Richard waited for the inevitable impact he knew would kill him.

From the corner of his eye Raif spied the dark ball of energy bearing down on the druid. Not one to consider the consequences of acting first and thinking later, he let out a battle cry and leapt between Richard and Morganna's evil spell. The impact knocked the air from his lungs. For a moment his momentum halted, seemingly caught in midair, his eyes widening in surprise as the spell struck him squarely between the shoulders. Lurching forward unsteadily another step, Raif collapsed, unmoving on the floor at Richard's feet.

Morganna screeched out a savage howl of fury, her red eyes darkening to only a shade above black, and conjured another ball of dark power between her fingers. But this one had less substance and petered out to nothingness.

She didn't have enough energy left to create another spell equally as powerful.

Morganna had performed too many powerful spells too closely together and it had left her drained. The cloaking spell on the guards in the forest, then one on herself and her companions, and now her *pièce de résistance* spell had just failed to kill her intended target. Not to mention maintaining the binding spell on all the guards.

Across the room, Alex covered Abby's body and waited for Mira's killing blow…that didn't come.

Mira howled in rage behind him but there was no attack.

Alex turned his head to peer over his shoulder.

Mira staggered back a step, trying to reach something behind her. As she turned aside, Alex saw the blade imbedded deeply in her back with Dr Greenville holding the hilt, eliciting a cry from her hateful lips as he twisted it more deeply.

"You'll pay for that," she promised, more pissed off than ever. Mira's eyes glittered with fury, her top lip peeled back revealing pearly white points of hostile malice. "You didn't really think you were ever getting out of here alive, did you?" she taunted, her voice seductive and mesmerising, holding him enthralled.

With lightening speed, Mira gripped him by the back of the neck, tilted his head to the side and plunged her fangs deeply into the soft flesh. A sneer of satisfaction twisted her lips up into a snarl as she ripped into his jugular vein, then released her grip to watch his rapidly dying body drop to the floor with a thud.

Alex stood his ground in front of Abby who pushed unsuccessfully to get past to help the old man. She watched a single tear escape the corner of his eye as the light behind them drained away. It wasn't a tear of regret, but relief, she realised as his final thought filtered through her mind. He may not have lived long enough to reverse all the damage his research had caused, but his sacrifice had saved Abby and that at least, had restored a small part of his soul.

With Mira within his grasp, Ahriman rose to the fore with a tidal wave of rage. Blue sparks of electricity began leaping from the tips of his fingers as he built up the power within him.

Mira was going to die.

Alaric watched the scene through glittering eyes of cold hard rage. He was torn. Before him stood two of his greatest enemies.

Ahriman and Morganna le Fey.

Which one did he kill first?

Abby pushed again to get past Ahriman.

Alaric's decision was made for him. He needed to get Abby to safety, then deal with the others. In a flash he was across the room knocking Mira out of the way, sending her skidding face first across the stony floor.

This was the second surprise attack on her in less than a minute. Her anger bubbled to boiling point….until she raised her head and saw her new assailant. Alaric.

Mira stood and began pacing back and forth, her right arm hanging limply by her side. While she was not willing to go any closer, she refused to relinquish her prey, her eyes following Abby with a fixated gaze, determined she would not leave the chamber alive.

Regardless, Mira could do little to effect her revenge until she got the dagger out of her back and healed, she thought with frustration. It had severed the tendons in her shoulder, making her arm useless.

Ahriman and Alaric faced off. A deathly silence filled the air around them, even more shocking than the violence they had inflected upon each other when they last met.

Abby didn't dare breathe as the two powerful men glared at one another.

Curling back his lips to display his enormous fangs, Alaric spoke in low commanding tones.

"Release Abby now and I'll make your death quick. I'll even personally send your soul back to the Underworld." His words were firm, clipped with anger.

Alex's jaw clenched as he fought to hold Ahriman back, but he was too strong.

Ahriman began building the electricity within his body, sparks licked from his splayed fingers by his sides, only to be halted when Abby laid a restraining hand on his forearm. He could feel every one of her fingers tightening in a silent plea. "No. There's no need to fight," she said calmly, her glittering eyes still watching her *mate*'s face as Ahriman's hatred boiled behind his eyes. "Is there, Ahriman?" she emphasised sternly, gripping her nails into his flesh until she held his attention.

Alaric's eyes never wavered from Ahriman's fierce gaze. He too looked just as eager for a fight. The razor sharp tips of his wings fanned out extending threateningly as he flexed his wings and clenched his fists.

Ahriman wanted to shake off her hand and fry the man to crispy bones. But, he quickly quashed the impulsive thought. Abby was right. There would be no fighting between them today. There were other, more important things to worry about, like getting the portal device from Morganna.

"I'm not his prisoner, and if you both don't put your ego's back in your pants, I'll give you both a smack-down you won't forget. This is not the time or the place for your pissing competition," Abby fumed. "In case you haven't noticed, the real enemy is over there," she said, pointing to Morganna who had now refocussed her attention on their little group.

Alaric grappled with his emotions. He had a score to settle with Ahriman. He had killed Cassie. As temporary as it turned out to be, Ahriman had killed her with the belief that her death would be final. That, he couldn't overlook and required serious retaliation in kind. Death. Slow and painfully.

On the other hand, he had just witnessed him stand down at Abby's demand and, he *did* put his own life on the line to protect her from Mira. That had to have been Alex, he thought. The Ahriman he knew was an evil prick devoid of a single kindness in his whole sorry-arsed soul. The question was, how much influence did Alex really have?

Goddammit! Rock meet hard place. He had to give Alex a chance for Cassie and Abby's sake, or he'd never hear the end of it…from either of them.

He still planned to send Ahriman's demonic arse back to the Underworld, but he would choose the timing more carefully. He had no intention of becoming the bad guy in Cassie or Abby's eyes for killing their brother and *mate*. But that didn't mean he wouldn't do it, he just needed the right opportunity.

Behind the fighting, a shadowed form lurked along the back wall, creeping slowly toward the chamber's only exit, and as usual, managing to avoid attention.

Lilith.

Morganna cursed. More Alliance fighters were arriving by the second, and her own guards were becoming overwhelmed.

Turning her attention to Ahriman and Alaric, Morganna casually approached, leaving Richard kneeling, breathless on floor beside Raif's unconscious body. Somehow, he had managed to restore his protection spell around himself, thwarting her third attempt at killing him.

For now.

There would be another day. Morganna knew who he was now. She had touched his magic, imprinted the essence of his soul into her memory. There was nowhere he could hide where she would not find him. It was only a matter of time.

Very soon she would have her spell back and then no one would be able to stop her. Ever.

Morganna stopped beside Mira. "Stop your blustering," she chastised curtly. "You'll get another chance to kill her. That I promise you," she said as she plucked the blade from Mira's back with no more emotion that plucking lint from her angora sweater.

"Not good enough. I want that bitch dead today, right now!"

Morganna turned her head in Mira's direction, her expression calm but the anger in her glowing red eyes silenced Mira from further verbal ranting. Morganna's temper was hanging by a thread and Mira didn't want to be on the receiving end of it when it snapped.

"Follow me," she ordered, handing Mira the portal device.

Dutifully, Mira followed in her wake, her injured arm already regaining some strength as her wound healed.

Abby grabbed at both Alex and Alaric's arms at once. "Morganna." The word left her lips as barely a whisper, her eyes focussed squarely on the two women heading their way.

Instantly, both men were standing protectively in front of Abby.

"Morganna," Alaric spat. Just saying her name left a sour taste in his mouth.

Before Alaric could reach out for her, Morganna incanted a spell. Three ancient words of power immobilised his limbs and held him rigidly in place. She lifted a finger in warning at Ahriman when he too shifted his stance to make a move against her.

He stilled. He needed to keep his head on straight if he wanted to get the device back.

"Sammael. Or, what is it you go by now…Oh, yes. Alaric." She smiled at him. The expression was a remarkably nasty one, a mere widening of lips on a very cold face.

"How and when did you escape your prison?"

"Where there's a will, there's a way," she responded.

"What do you want?"

"I have what I want," she answered, patting the box which Mira now held. She couldn't help a sideways glance at Richard. He was her ultimate prize.

"Give me the portal device," Ahriman demanded, his voice as deadly as a coiled cobra ready to strike.

Morganna was weakening. Her hands began to visibly shake.

"I can't do that. It's not mine to give you," Morganna answered haughtily.

"Then you'd have no problem giving it to me, its rightful owner."

235

Morganna laughed. "It was never yours. It belongs to the one who commissioned it, in case you have forgotten," she scoffed with satire tones of mockery.

"And I suppose you expect to claim the reward by presenting it to him?"

"Of course. That was the deal we made."

Ahriman's top lip peeled back as he growled out his anger.

Morganna had made a deal with Mephistopheles, no doubt the Lord of the Underworld was hedging his bets. He had no care who delivered him the device, so long as he got it.

Mira chuckled. A malevolent sound, lethal and cunning. "Send my regards to your master," she laughed. "I have no doubt that Alaric will send you back to him the moment he unfreezes."

Morganna wrapped her fingers around a amulet about her neck and snapped her other hand around Mira's wrist.

With quick reflexes, Ahriman lunged forward. But as fast as he was, he was a fraction of a second too slow. The two women dissipated in a swirl of black smoke and vanished.

Alaric and Ahriman roared in unison.

The instant they disappeared more than half the guards dropped to the floor unconscious, leaving only the Guild loyalist guards still standing.

Not for long.

On Morganna's departure, the spell on Alaric was also broken, lurching him forward suddenly as his effort to move his limbs was no longer hindered.

More Alliance men entered the chamber.

"What did we miss?" Saladin asked as he reached Alaric's side. Sighting the fierce glare he and Alex shared, he took a step back to take in the scene more carefully. "Anyone want to share what happened here?"

Sensing Alaric's hair-trigger mood, Ahriman decided to once again take a back seat and let Alex run the show. Self-preservation really should have been his middle name.

Alex wrapped Abby in his arms protectively and kissed her possessively. His gentle kiss, feather-light brushes of his lips against hers deepened with every stroke, his tongue traced her bottom lip, his teeth nipping at it until she opened for him. He ate at her mouth hungrily, desperately.

Her hands slid over his chest, the light caress sending lightening bolts of pleasure through his tense body. Relief bubbled in his veins, even as the furious arousal she caused, heated his blood to boiling point.

Abby had come so close to being taken from him at Mira's hand. The thought of losing her nearly ripped out his heart and drove him into a frenzy of need.

He needed to keep her safe.

He needed to have her delectable body beneath him as he filled her with every ounce of passion and pride he felt for her.

He needed to have her all to himself.

Acutely aware of everyone watching them, Abby pulled back from his burning kiss. Her cheeks flushed a brilliant pink as she thought of the way Alex possessed her so completely. She craved the sense of belonging she found in his arms. She closed her eyes against the dizzying rush.

Slowly, the guards began waking up, returning to their former selves.

Except Raif.

Richard examined the wyvern leader. His breathing was steady, there were no visible wounds, but he was unresponsive.

"What's wrong with him?" Gwynn asked, his concern growing more acute with every passing minute.

"He was hit with a spell that was meant to kill me. Obviously, being a wyvern it has affected him differently."

"You're a druid. Magic is your specialty, isn't it? Can't you fix him?"

"I don't know, maybe. The spell should have been broken when Morganna left the Earth plane, just like all the others were."

Gwynn's brow furrowed, his lips pressed in a thin line of worry. "I'll take him home to Fey. His sister is a healer. Hopefully she can fix whatever Morganna did to him."

"That would be for the best, I'm sure," Richard replied sombrely.

Picking up Raif's still form, Gwynn called out to the others. "We're leaving."

As the crowd began to thin out, Alex spied a familiar figure from the corner of his eye as she attempted to escape the chamber.

Not going to happen.

"We're not going anywhere yet. Not until I finish something," Alex growled, watching Lilith slinking along the back wall.

Mira got away with Morganna's help. There was no way Lilith was leaving alive too. There was a price to pay for her treachery and payment was overdue.

Shrugging off Abby's restraining hand, all eyes watched as he stalked after Lilith. Alaric followed close behind, not willing to believe Ahriman wasn't up to something. However, he didn't make a move to stop him. He too had a score to settle with the traitorous bitch.

"She's mine," he growled at Alaric.

Heading Lilith off at the doorway, Alex gripped her about the throat as she attempted to run. Leaning in close to her ear, his hot breath feathered against her skin.

"I told you what I'd do to you when I caught you, didn't I *pumpkin*" he snarled.

"Ahriman?" she squeaked.

"Guess again." His anger raged and boiled in his veins, sizzling the air around him. An electric blue glow illuminated her terrified face beneath his hand a second before she convulsed in his grasp. The smell of barbequed flesh and burning hair left an acrid scent in the air. Releasing her, Lilith dropped to the floor in a lifeless, smoking heap.

"Now, we can go," Alex sneered with satisfaction.

Alaric narrowed his gaze on Alex, his ruthless suspicion easing back to an uneasy mistrust. That had been Alex using that power? No doubt Ahriman had use of it too, he had seen him building the energy earlier. But, he didn't use it on him.

In fact, so far Ahriman hadn't been aggressive toward anyone in the Alliance. He'd reserved his wrath for the she-devils whom he wanted dead equally as much as the rest of them. To his credit, Ahriman had even allowed Alex to take his revenge on the psychopathic shrew who had started this whole nightmare. Okay, so technically Ahriman had been the one to start this whole debacle, but Alaric was in favour of splitting hairs. At least in this instance.

Maybe Alex really did have more control over Ahriman than they dared believe possible. Whether that was a good thing, Alaric wasn't sure. His future brother-in-law pissed him off on a daily basis, and now he came tag-teamed with a demon who brought out his homicidal rage just by breathing. Maybe small mercies came in annoying packages, Alaric thought. Only one of them could piss him off at a time. However, not acting on the antagonism that the two men provoked in him was going to be tough.

Alaric growled out his frustration. Just because he had decided not to kill the bastard....yet, didn't mean he would let him roam free.

Far from it.

"Cassie is going to be so happy to see you," Abby said. Her excited grin quickly turning into a scowl of disapproval when Alaric growled.

Alaric didn't want Ahriman anywhere near his *mate* and their unborn child.

"We discussed this, remember?" Saladin reminded Alaric, leaning in close.

Yeah, he remembered. He remembered Cassie threatening to castrate him if he didn't bring her brother home in one piece.

"It's not you I don't trust, Alex, it's your other half," he growled.

"Hey. Watch what you say, I don't appreciate you offending Abby like that," Alex objected with mock indignation.

"I see your sense of humour hasn't improved any," Alaric huffed.

"So, what are you going to do with me? I know you don't want Ahriman anywhere near the manor and I don't blame you," he said, setting aside his sarcastic attitude for a moment.

It really grated Alaric's goolies that he had to take Ahriman back to his home, but there really wasn't anywhere else to put him until they figured out some way to separate him from Alex's body. The lycan clans already had their hands full with all the recruited guards and if he was really honest, only Havenswood Manor had the security to hold someone like Ahriman.

There was also nowhere else he could keep a close eye on him 24/7.

"You'll be locked up until we can figure something out."

"One of those dingy rooms in the lower level of the manor?" Alex asked.

"Yeah."

"Will there be chains and shackles involved?" he asked, a hopeful lilt to his voice.

Alaric stopped and stared at him suspiciously, not sure who he was talking to. That didn't sound like something Alex would ask. "It could be arranged if you misbehave. Why?"

"You see, we've been experimenting with a bit of BDSM since we've been here and…"

"Too much information," Saladin grumbled as he stepped up behind Alex and slapped some cuffs on him.

"Do I get to keep these later?"

"Alex. Shut it, would you," Abby growled, her cheeks a lovely shade of beetroot.

"Sorry, baby. I can't help myself. There's something about Alaric that makes me want to push his buttons….Okay, shutting up now." Alex pursed his lips together under the combined glares of Abby and Alaric.

"You were an annoying little shit before. You really don't want to push your luck now."

Fair call.

25

Gwynn ap Nudd, the high lord of the nephilim opened the portal to take the Alliance warriors back to Savernake Forest in England. From there he intended to sift back through the dimensional veil to Fey with Raif and return him to his family.

Unfortunately things didn't go quite as he planned.

Gwynn took a step into the portal with Raif's limp body in his arms and waited for the familiar feeling of weightlessness to come. Instead, the weight in his arms began to convulse. Quickly, Gwynn stepped back out of the portal and Raif stilled.

"What the hell was that?" Alaric asked with alarm.

"I haven't the first idea," Gwynn answered perplexed.

Once again Gwynn stepped into the portal, and again Raif began to convulse.

"This isn't good my friend," Alaric's concerned frown mirrored Gwynn's.

"Druid, what's happening to him?" Gwynn demanded, his concern making his tone harsher than he had intended.

Richard shrugged his shoulders. What could he tell them, he had no answers either. He'd never seen this before. Whatever spell Morganna had used was dark magic beyond his understanding. In the fifteen hundred years since she had been banished, her power could have grown well beyond anyone's predictions. He doubted that even Merlin's Book of Shadows would hold any clue on how to cure Raif.

"I have no knowledge of how her dark magic works," he confessed. "Druid's use earth magic. It can be equally as powerful, but our power is drawn from nature. Morganna's magic is corrupted and twisted. It doesn't conform to the natural laws."

"What if Raif's sister can't heal him, what do we do then?" Gwynn asked, looking to Richard for answers as he shifted Raif's heavy weight in his arms.

"We'll need to find someone who understands dark magic, although I don't like our chances of finding anyone with *this* kind of knowledge," he replied.

"Morganna was banished to the Valley of Vardin with the other rephaim. Surely there's at least one other among their kind who would know how to reverse the spell?" Alaric speculated.

"Maybe," Gwynn admitted. "But I can't send anyone in there to find out. No nephilim can venture into their land and return again. It's a prison made to hold any nephilim who crosses its borders, the containment ward can't differentiate between who belongs in there and who doesn't."

"If only we had Morganna's Grimoire," Richard muttered beneath his breath to himself. It was a fanciful, wishful comment to say the least. He hadn't even realised he'd voiced his ridiculous thought out loud. Like so many other items of power from so long ago, the evil book of spells hadn't been seen in a millennium.

"We do," Alaric spoke up. "We do have it. Before the Professor ascended, he left me details of a security deposit box. Inside we found a grimoire sealed inside a lead lined box. I'm almost certain it belonged to Morganna le Fey."

Richard suddenly became animated, a mixture of excitement and fear. Stories of this book and its power was used to frighten young druid children into focussing on their studies. He was surprised to discover that even as an old man, just the mention of that book could still cause a flutter of fear within him. "Where is it now?" he asked hesitantly, his voice wavering with anticipation.

"It's in my storage room at the manor."

"I need to see it."

"Sure," Alaric answered, mindfully assessing the man's pensive reaction.

The portal's shimmer began to wane as Gwynn's focus was drawn towards their conversation. "That doesn't fix our immediate problem," he said. "How do we get Raif back to Fey?"

"I guess we don't," Alaric declared. "At least, not for now. I'll take him back to the manor." Unfurling his wings, he took Raif from Gwynn's arms. "You get his sister and I'll meet you back at my home in a few hours."

"That sounds like a plan," Saladin seconded the idea.

Alaric watched as everyone from England returned through the portal, leaving behind Gustav, Sebastian, Klaus and the rest of the Northern European Alliance.

Gustav slapped Alaric on the shoulder and took a step back. "Keep me posted on Raif?"

Alaric nodded, taking a step away from the group before spreading his powerful wings to their full width amid shocked stares and amazed gasps. With a hard angle he thrust his wings downward, lifting him from the ground with a rush of arctic wind swirling the powdery snow about the men's feet. With another flap of his wings, he was gone.

"Honestly, I have no idea how Callum can be so oblivious to Elise's crush on him. I mean, look at her. She follows him around like a lost puppy everywhere he goes and he's completely clueless," Kaitlyn said, looking to her sisters for agreement. Paige and Teagan both nodded as they watched their youngest sister batting her long eyelashes seductively at Callum Harlow, to no effect.

"He's only eighteen. Most guys at that age are pretty clueless, aren't they" Teagan remarked thoughtfully.

"I guess. But she's been living under the Harlow's roof for a year, maybe Callum is just used to Elise's doting attention toward him," Paige surmised.

"Probably," Cassie agreed. "He's an only child, isn't he?" Cassie asked, each nodding in agreement. "He's probably been doted on his whole life from his parents. For him, Elise's attentions probably don't even register on his radar as anything out of the ordinary. Except that now he has a little sister he can tease or ignore as he chooses," she

243

chuckled, remembering how it was growing up with Alex. Cassie's happy mood dimmed at that thought. Where were they? Surely, they would have rescued Alex and Abby by now.

The girls tossed around a few ideas to help Elise get Callum's attention. Not that it would do much good in the end, he and Mrs Philpot's grandson, Marcus, would be leaving just after New Year, in about three weeks time, to start their military training. A compulsory passage to manhood amongst the lycan clans. A minimum of ten years in the armed forces was mandatory. Many, like Damon Harlow, choose to stay in service much longer, but for the majority they choose to only do their allotted time. Just long enough to gain the necessary skills to defend their homes and clan if necessary.

"Men," Teagan grumbled under her breath as she stared into her empty wine glass. "I don't want to talk about them anymore. They're annoying and confusing and more trouble than they're worth."

"They're not all bad," Cassie defended.

"Yeah, you can say that. You're the only one of us in a stable relationship with a man who loves you more than life itself."

"I can't deny it. Alaric is wonderful," she sighed adoringly. "I love my life. Well, most of it anyway. I hadn't expected my life to turn out to be quite this complicated." Cassie's whimsical smile began to slide into a frown, thinking about the reason why they, and nearly half the lycan clan were still huddled together in the Drunken Duck Pub at two o'clock in the morning. They'd all tried to keep their spirits up, but no one really succeeded in taking their mind off the men who were out there somewhere in the Ukraine trying to rescue Alex and Abby, and hopefully taking down the Guild's stronghold. With every hour that passed, the agitation in the room increased.

"What I wouldn't give to be as happy as you," Kaitlyn sighed, Paige nodded in agreement as she absently finished the last of her drink.

"So, if we're not going to talk about men," Paige pouted, "What are we going to talk about? Careers? How about your power to blow things up, Cassie?" she asked excitedly.

"You heard about that?"

"Who hasn't. All the lycans in Cadley are talking about it. You blew up your kitchen!" Kaitlyn chuckled.

"Yeah, well, Mrs Philpot is happy that she's getting a new kitchen, but she's not too happy that it happened so close to Christmas. Apparently, she'd planned to cook a really big Christmas lunch and all the contractors have closed for the holidays." Cassie scrunched her nose and hunched her shoulders like a young child in trouble, instinctively trying to make herself smaller as her eyes glanced in Mrs P's direction.

"I thought you'd become some sort of Seer," Teagan suggested. "You've always gotten these funny vibes when something bad is about to happen."

"That makes sense," Kaitlyn added. "You'd think that a natural gift would automatically develop into an awesome power when you became a Supernatural. So, maybe you have two gifts?"

"I wouldn't call blowing things up a gift, more like a curse," she grumbled, "And my *funny vibes* seem to be more of a dodgy sixth sense. They're more like an excuse to seek medication. I honestly can't tell them apart from an anxiety attack. It's only with hindsight that I've recognised the signs," Cassie answered uncomfortably as her knee began jiggling incessantly beneath the table. This conversation was just a little too personal for her liking, she was beginning to feel like a bug under a microscope. It seemed everyone knew more about her than she did these days.

"I think everyone has heard quite enough about me. What about you?" Cassie asked, eager to divert the attention away from herself. "I know Teagan can freeze things in midair," as demonstrated when she suspended the flying shrapnel of the exploding kitchen from reaching them, and when she blew apart the Yew tree. "But, what can you do?"

Paige and Kaitlyn looked to Teagan as though looking for permission to tell Cassie.

"I can become invisible," Kaitlyn said.

"And, I can astral project myself," Paige replied.

"But Paige doesn't just project an image of herself," Kaitlyn clarified, "She can project an image you can touch. If you didn't know what signs to look for, you'd actually believe her projection was the original, not a copy."

"Wow. I'd love to see that sometime," Cassie gushed, in awe. "What about Elise? What's her gift?" Their heads turned in unison to watch their sister, stacking glasses behind the bar, right next to Callum who was pouring drinks.

"Elise can pass through solid objects."

"You girls are amazing. Growing up in your house must have been really interesting," Cassie grinned, a hint of mischief in her eye. No doubt, if it had been her and Alex with such incredible gifts, they would have gotten themselves into all manner of strife, repeatedly and often.

"Yeah, interesting," Paige grumbled. "Growing up when our mother was still alive, was fun. She let us explore our gifts, but after she died and we went to live with Gramps, well..." Paige's shoulders slumped as she remembered her time with her grandfather. She loved him dearly, they all did, but he was strict. Very strict. He was like a Sergeant Major drilling them daily about proper conduct for the descendants of Merlin and hours of practice with their magic every day.

Since their grandfather had left a year ago, all four sisters had begun to actually enjoy their lives again.

"Teagan tells me you two share a flat in London? Are you both working?"

"I'm a hairdresser in the East End and Kaitlyn is a nurse at the Royal London Hospital," Paige offered cheerily.

"And are you staying in Cadley long?"

"Only a few days. Once we've finished the ward on the manor we have to get back. You know, back to the real world. Or at least the world that everyone else thinks is real," Paige chuckled.

Their conversation lapsed into weary silence as they continued to wait well into the early hours of the morning. Cassie stared into the dying embers of the open fire near where they sat, watching the logs shimmer with a red glow as they rested in the hot coals, while small licks of flame ate slowly at the sides of the remaining wood. Her eyes were fixated on the hearth, but her mind was miles away. Surely they would be back soon? The wait was starting to make her stir crazy.

It seemed she wasn't the only one.

Nerves were beginning to fray as the time stretched. Worried women waited for husbands and sons to return. Over-tired children bickered and concerned friends paced the length of the pub.

Suddenly a cry went out as the pub's door silently opened and the first of the men walked through.

Despite their obvious exhaustion, they were a walking wall of strength and testosterone.

Cassie was on her feet in an instant, her eyes immediately latching onto Alex as he was escorted through the door....handcuffed. Abby walked close at his side while Hawke followed close behind, his eyes flicking between Alex's relaxed frame and the agitated crowd gathering around them. His fingers lightly caressed the handle of his gun at his side, his body still wired from their recent battle.

Cassie's heart sank into the pit of her stomach. Handcuffed. That could only mean one thing....

Regardless. Alex was her brother. They hadn't even had a chance to talk about that unexpected discovery before he was kidnapped. Until this moment she hadn't fully realised just how much she'd needed to. They had lived their whole lives believing they were cousins, and not even blood related, when in reality they shared the same father and never knew it.

Crossing the room, Cassie rushed towards him.

"Cassie?" Alex's broad grin greeted her.

"Don't get any closer," Damon growled, blocking her path with his much larger body. "That isn't Alex, *it's* Ahriman," he bit out, his anger curling his top lip into a snarl. "Don't get any closer," he warned again in a gravelly tone.

Caught off guard, Cassie took a sharp step back, her breath catching in her throat, taking another second to assess the situation more carefully.

"Let me pass. *He* is my brother." She moved to push past, but Damon was a wall of immovable muscle. "Let me pass, arsehole," she bit out impatiently.

"Cassie, it's okay. We'll talk later," Alex said as he and Abby were shunted toward the back of the room, away from the door, and away from her. Anger and frustration seemed to be a constant companion these days. Her calming force, and often the antagonist for her aggravated outbursts, was Alaric, her *mate*....who wasn't anywhere to be seen. Her mood switch suddenly, flipping from annoyed to anxious again.

Walking through the crowd, she singled out the first familiar face and seized hold of him for answers.

"Pan, where's Alaric?" she begged, squeezing his thin arm tightly in her grip.

"Raif was injured and Gwynn couldn't take him back to Fey with him, so Alaric is flying him back to the manor."

"What? What happened? Is Alaric okay?" Panic set in. All she heard were the words *injured* and *Alaric,* in the same sentence.

Pan snorted out a laugh. Alaric hurt? Even the idea was ludicrous. Alaric was Sammael, the *immortal* vampire. He couldn't be killed. In fact, he doubted Alaric could be injured for more than a minute.

"Raif's hurt, not Alaric. Don't fret," he said patting her on the arm for reassurance. A thirteen-year old boy comforting her? The gesture seemed so out of place, even though she knew he was actually born sometime in the 1800's. Her brain was still conditioned to living in the regular world where people looked their age and life followed conventional rules. "He said he'd be home in a few hours."

Saladin's eyes scanned the room for Teagan, zeroing in on her in seconds.

Moving toward her, his ground-eating stride rippled in a symphony of muscle as graceful and calculated as a tiger on the prowl. The need to touch her and hold her in his arms, outweighed every other thought at that moment.

Stopping in front of her, he reached for her hand, lifting it to his lips to kiss the back with flirtatious charm.

"Forgive me?" he asked with a rueful grin.

"For what?" Teagan asked, her brow furrowed quizzically at his odd question.

"For this." Saladin curled one hand around the nape of her neck and pulled Teagan into him, the other anchored about her waist, pressing her firmly against his hard body as he urged her lips apart. He swept into her mouth, his possessive kiss shifting from persuasive to demanding. Need slammed into her as her world tilted off kilter. With every brush of his lips, his unbearably male taste saturated her senses. Clutching his shoulders, she abandoned herself to the untamed kiss, hungry for more.

"Your mouth... Your taste..." He breathed hard against her lips before he sampled them again. "I can't get enough." He inched back and looked at her, framing her face in his hands. "Beautiful."

In seconds, he nearly overwhelmed her with his fevered kiss and the burning need seeping from his touch.

Teagan moaned and arched into him further before she remembered all the reasons why she shouldn't. Pressing her palms against his chest, she pushed back from him, not an easy task in his vice-like hold.

"I did apologise in advance," he chuckled, leaning down to take her silky lips once again. Teagan's scent teased his nose, more intoxicating and potent than the most powerful aphrodisiac.

Only inches from her glistening lips, he froze.

His eyes grew wide with shock. He couldn't move, not a muscle. Even his growl had seized in his throat.

"That's enough vampire. My granddaughter is not for your pleasure," Richard warned. A flare of irritation swirled through the air.

The room fell silent in an instant. All eyes being drawn to the elderly druid and Saladin.

"Gramps. What do you think you're doing?" Teagan protested, separating herself from Saladin's immobilised body to confront her grandfather.

"I'm saving you, my dear. What does it look like?" his irritable glare fixated on the vampire caught in his spell, but his ire was not directed at Saladin, that he laid squarely on Teagan. He had raised the girls the same way he had raised his own daughter, their mother. They knew how dangerous it was to form an attachment to supernaturals, no matter whether they were a vampire, lycan, nephilim or wyvern. They were off limits to *his* girls.

"Gramps. Stop this right now. Release him. He's done nothing wrong. In fact, he's..."

"My dear, I'm not interested in what he has done. I'm more interested in what he plans on doing in the future." Teagan flinched at his abrupt tone, but she pushed her case again, stepping up nose to nose with him.

"Let. Him. Go."

Richard's raw power filled the air around her making her wince.

"On one condition...You stay away from him. Do you here me, young lady?"

"Whatever. Just unfreeze him."

249

Richard waved his hand and Saladin became a blur as he moved to grab Richard by the throat, his eyes ablaze with fury, his fangs fully extended. He wanted nothing less than to rip the man's head from his shoulders and shove it up his arse…sideways.

"No. Saladin." Teagan reached for his hand and gripped it tight, threading her fingers through his as she attempted to pull him further away from her grandfather. The effect was like having a bucket of cold water dropped on him, bringing him back to his senses. Killing Richard would only hurt Teagan and most likely drive her away from him. That, he could not bear.

"Don't even think about it," Richard warned. His vision lowered to their joined hands. "My granddaughter is off limits to you, vampire."

"Teagan is a grown woman, capable of choosing who she associates with, old man, and I…."

"Her associates, yes. Her lovers, no," Richard spat angrily.

Teagan fumed and paced between them, humiliation burning her cheeks. "Saladin, just leave it, okay? Please," she pleaded. Exasperated, she cupped his cheek in her hand to draw his wrathful gaze away from her grandfather's vengeful stare. She couldn't let this get out of hand. Saladin may be stronger and faster, but he was still no match for the old druid. "Please," she pleaded again more softly.

Saladin's body relaxed under her touch, his eyes dropped to study her with a searching gaze, but his fury hadn't lessened. It simmered just beneath the surface of his control. "I'll not have you dictated to," he ground out between clenched teeth.

You're mine.

"Saladin, go home. I'll talk to you later. I promise."

Mine!

"Yes, you will. We have business to finish." By the hint of fang poking beneath his top lip and brooding eyes, Teagan knew the business he wanted to *'discuss'* would be conducted between satin sheets, wearing nothing but their birthday suits. The enticing thought sent a flare of heat through her blood.

"Just so we understand each other," Richard said, his eyes narrowing once again on Saladin. "*I* will be helping the girls with the final preparations for the protection ward on the manor, and *I'll* be overseeing the spell. Teagan in particular, since she's the principal

250

caster, will require *constant* supervision over the next couple of days," he said, not so subtly informing Saladin that he wasn't letting Teagan out of his sight for a moment.

Saladin grumbled under his breath, blistering those with more sensitive ears with his foul curses.

Reining in his aggressive instincts, Saladin kept his focus on Teagan. He tried to pretend a nonchalance he was far from feeling, his lips twisting up into a wry smile. "I guess we'll be seeing each other again very soon then, since Alaric put me in charge of overseeing the ward."

There was a long pause. Teagan could physically feel the weight of silence as the two men stared each other down.

Saladin bent down and placed a kiss on the tip of her proud, delicate nose before turning on his heel to leave. Grabbing Alex about his upper arm, he dragged him along behind.

Saladin was infuriating, illogical, stubborn and so typically male, that most of the time Teagan wanted to scream. He was also wickedly charming, highly intelligent and intensely lovable, especially when he was standing up for her against her grandfather. No one had ever stood up to her grandfather before. He may be old, but he was scary.

Teagan's eyes were glued to the vision of Saladin's proud back walking out the door with an entourage of vampires in tow as they disappeared into the fading darkness of night.

Hushed voices murmured throughout the crowd as the tension in the room scaled back.

Cassie tentatively sidled up next to Teagan, a look of sympathy on her face.

"That was embarrassing," Teagan muttered.

"Yeah. You okay?"

"I'll be fine," she said shooting a sideways glance to her grandfather who had moved on to talk to Oliver Harlow. "I take it that I'll be staying here now until we're done with the ward on the manor," she grumbled, meaning the Harlow's private residence at the back of the Drunken Duck. How she wished she was in her own apartment back in town, well away from all the prying eyes and knowing snickers.

"It looks like it," Cassie answered, noting the body language coming off Richard and the serious discussion taking place. "But you still have to come back to the manor tomorrow to make preparations for the spell. Right?"

"Don't you mean today? The sun's coming up."

Cassie peered out the pub's window. The first hint of light was just beginning to filter through the barren trees with a dull red glow. So close to sunrise there wasn't enough time for any of the vampires to return to town. It looked like the manor would be overflowing with testosterone today. She didn't feel tired, one of the perks of being newly immortal was not needing as much sleep. But looking at Teagan, her friend was showing signs of fatigue, not all of which was physical. The strain of her emotional tug-of-war over her feelings for Saladin, and now her grandfather's public hissy-fit episode, was beginning to take its toll.

"I'll call you a bit later," Teagan smiled wearily.

Damon watched from behind the bar as he downed his scotch in one long gulp. He watched the scene between Saladin and Richard with impassive interest. It made no difference to him if the two men ripped each other apart, nor why.

His focus was on Ahriman and his brother, Oliver. His *younger* brother who was now Alpha of his clan. It should have been him. He was older, stronger, a better tactician in war. And, there was no question in his mind, they were at war. The Guild had declared it the day they attacked his clan and murdered his father.

Pouring another glass of scotch, Damon downed that one too in a single mouthful as he shifted his weight to his good leg.

His good leg!

Yet another reason to hate Ahriman.

He was a lycan, capable of healing quickly from any wound. Except for wounds caused by silver. Those healed much more slowly, and it would appear that wounds caused by silver nitrate filled, hollow tipped bullets, didn't heal well at all. He had taken a bullet in his calf the night his father was shot in the chest. His father's wounds had been fatal. His...? Well, his had maimed him. His wound had healed but it had scarred the calf muscle leaving him with a distinct limp. If he had been anyone else, the injury would be considered minor, but he was an elite soldier. He commanded a team of black ops lycan soldiers, and his fitness and ability to withstand any situation equally as well as his men was essential.

Because of Ahriman, he had not only been overlooked as the new Alpha in favour of his younger brother, but he may also end up relegated to a desk job.

Pulling his cell phone from behind the counter of the bar, it flashed indicating a new message waiting to be read.

26

The birds chirped their early morning calls, unperturbed by the fearsome predators marching below, along the forest floor.

The first rays of sun crossed the horizon just as the group reached the border to Havenswood Manor. Frost blanketed the expansive lawns before them, tiny icicles glistened in the sunlight and crunched softly beneath their feet as they moved quickly toward the manor and its protection against the sun's effects on the more photophobic vampires in the group.

Saladin stomped more heavily than normal, unaware that he continued to mutter and growl beneath his breath as he fumed over his encounter with Richard. If it hadn't been for the *minor* fact that the old man was Teagan's grandfather, the lycans would have had one more body to dispose of.

However, if there was one thing that Saladin did exceedingly well, it was hold a grudge. Teagan was a grown woman, more than capable of knowing her own mind, she certainly had no problem speaking it. He was *so* close to winning her over, he had no intention of letting her grandfather persuade her against him, especially not now. Just the thought of a forced separation from her caused a feeling of desperation inside him such as he had never experienced before. It wasn't a feeling he enjoyed, and since he was unaccustomed to forfeiting the things he desired, he intended to do everything he could to avoid it e.g. get rid of Richard and make Teagan his. That shouldn't be too hard, should it?

Alex too, walked pensively onward. As they broke from the tree line, his eyes latched onto the immense stone building looming before them with mixed emotions. On one hand he was glad to be back, this place had come to feel like home to him.

But he also felt Ahriman's emotions, his trepidation at being back here again, where he'd only recently caused so much pain and destruction. Ahriman could honestly say he had never in his wildest imagination thought he would ever wind up at Havenswood Manor again, especially not as a prisoner.

Had it really been just over two weeks ago? It seemed like an eternity.

He'd had the delusional belief he was invincible, that his status in the Underworld ranked him above all others here on Earth in both power and importance. How wrong he had been on so many levels.

Dray moved ahead of Saladin, halting him in his tracks, his keen eyes falling on a shadowed figure in the doorway of the manor. "Saladin, you have a visitor," he announced.

Saladin's body immediately tensed. Following Dray's line of sight, his eyes widened in surprise. "Well, I'll be buggered," he declared.

Alex looked to Abby, her eyes too were focussed on the curious figure, but the corners of her mouth turned up into a cheerful smile. "Who is it?" he asked.

"Narayan," she answered happily.

"Are you sure? I may not have your eyesight, but even I can see that he's wearing jeans and sweatshirt, not monk's robes."

"Yes, I'm sure," but her brow furrowed in thought at the puzzling question.

Narayan watched them approach, his interest focussing on Saladin's bewildered reaction, shielding his eyes from the glare of the early morning sun.

He was only twenty-six years old when he had first met Saladin, five centuries ago. At the time he had already been a monk for more than half his life. His family had sent him to the monastery at the age of ten, it was the highest honour his poor family could give him. For Narayan, it was to be the beginning of a long life free of poverty, but his life took a turn his parents hadn't planned for him.

255

It had been a particularly cold and harsh winter that year, and whilst in the mountains for solitary meditation, he was unaware that he was being stalked. A hungry wolf and her pups, starved beyond the point of their natural fear of humans, attacked him.

Alaric and Saladin had been travelling through the mountains and the smell of a large amount of blood attracted their attention. Following the scent led them to Narayan.

Laid in a craggy knoll, bloodied and torn, Narayan's body was injured beyond its ability to heal. The cold, frigid air of the Tibetan mountain range was the only thing that had kept him alive in the hours since his attack, slowing his heart rate, constricting blood flow in his semi-frozen limbs...what was left of them. He was reaching his last breaths when he was found.

Saladin and Alaric debated what they should do with him. After long minutes Alaric gave Narayan a choice, to live or to die. He chose life, even though at the time he believed he would live out the remainder of his life, crippled and disfigured from his injuries. He clung to his belief that he could still contribute to his monastery in a meaningful way despite his disabilities.

He didn't realise the incredible gift that Alaric was actually offering him.

Alaric offered him blood from his wrist. Shortly afterwards the world around him went dark. When he awoke he was sheltered in a cave, Alaric and Saladin were still watching over him....Two days later.

He felt great. He felt better than great. He felt amazing. He was stronger than he had been before. Faster. His senses were immeasurably more sensitive. But the biggest changes, the ones he couldn't have prepared himself for...his mauled limbs had regenerated. What a fantastic surprise that was.

He had also developed an insatiable need for blood. That surprise took some getting used to, since Buddhist monks were generally vegetarian.

His new diet wasn't the only new thing he had to get used to. He also discovered he could no longer walk in sunlight.

Narayan was not like Alaric who was immortal. Nor was he like Saladin, his vampire sibling who could tolerate almost a full day of sunlight before succumbing to its effects. It seemed the injuries he'd suffered had been so severe that even though becoming a vampire had restored his body and made him infinitely stronger than he had been as a human, he had still been left a weakness.

Generally, vampires could tolerate at least an hour or two of direct sunlight. Narayan could tolerate no more than a few minutes. Not that he was complaining. If it had been any other vampire who had found him and tried to transform him, Narayan most likely wouldn't have survived at all. Only Alaric's blood, as the first vampire and an Angel of Death, was potent enough to have saved him.

Narayan continued to watch Saladin's perplexed expression as the group drew closer, his mind digressing back in time once more. He remembered the gratitude he had felt toward both Saladin and Alaric, for what they had done for him.

Unbeknownst to him, Alaric and Saladin had been travelling to see the Dalai Lama with the legendary Cup, the Holy Grail, as it had become known. It was to be given to the Buddhist leader for safe keeping.

As a monk in the Dalai Lama's temple, Narayan knew the way to the monastery well and it was on that day he made a vow to watch over the Cup along with the Dalai Lama. For five hundred years he had performed his duty and kept that promise, never wavering from his task. Not even when the Guild had stolen the Cup. He did everything in his power to retrieve it and return it to its rightful guardian.

Nor had he ever considered leaving the monastery.

Not until recently when he was given a better offer.

"You're back. Where's the robes?" Saladin asked, shock evident in his voice.

"As they say, life is a journey, not an idle station. It was time for a change," Narayan said, as way of an explanation. His eyes scanned the group, stopping on Alex and the restraining handcuffs, and then on Abby who hovered protectively next to him.

Narayan may have been away in India for a couple of weeks, but he had kept in close contact with Alaric and was well versed in their current situation. He assessed Alex warily for a moment before resuming his customary jovial manner.

"So, you're the prick who taught Alex all those infuriating quotes...," Ahriman blurted. He couldn't help himself.

"You remembered them?" Narayan asked, addressing his question to Alex with sudden enthusiasm.

Alex nodded his head even as Ahriman continued his incensed rant.

"I'm impressed," Narayan grinned, walking down the front porch steps to where they all stood and gave Alex a jubilant slap on the shoulder and ushered them all inside. "I have some new ones for you. I can see we're going to have hours of philosophy to catch up on."

"Ahh, fuck no. Now there's two of you," Ahriman whined. "All I need now is for someone to play Wiggles and Sesame Street songs on a repeating track to complete the torture. Just kill me now," he mumbled as they led him away to the lower level of the manor.

All eyes stared at him as if the evil demon was a few fries short of a happy meal. Abby however, understood his predicament perfectly and had to cover her mouth to hide the snickers of laughter from escaping.

Cassie hovered around the end of the corridor and waited for all the vampires *not* on guard, to tuck themselves away for the day to sleep. She was lost in her thoughts, debating how she could best slip past Dray outside Alex's door, to get in there to see him, and nearly jumped six feet when Mrs Philpot appeared beside her with a tray of coffee and cake.

"I thought you might like to take this into Alex and Abby," she said. Her impassive tone may not have revealed her feelings, but her delight bubbled in her eyes. She was just as happy to have Alex and Abby home as Cassie was.

"I owe you one Mrs P," she grinned.

"Yes, you do," she chuckled. "We have lots of mouths to feed today which means there will be at least...," she squinted one eye as she counted for a moment, "At least ten kilos of potatoes to peel this afternoon."

"But, I blew up the kitchen!" How was Mrs P going to cook without a kitchen?

"Ever heard of a spit roast? We have plenty of firewood lying about the gardens, perfect for a barbeque," she replied happily at Cassie's pouting bottom lip.

"Ten kilos?" she asked dejectedly.

Mrs Philpot's grin widened. "Don't worry love, it will only take an hour or two," she told her. Handing Cassie the tray of refreshments as she walked away.

Cassie turned back towards the corridor only to find another obstacle in her way. Narayan.

"And, just where do you think you're going?" he asked, putting on his best authoritative tone. If that wasn't enough, his raised eyebrows, pursed lips and hands on his hips made her feel like a small child trying to sneak a peak at an adult's party she'd been banned from.

"I'm taking Alex and Abby this tray," she answered, adding a stubborn edge to her tone.

"You're not going in there right now Cassie, Alaric would have my hide."

"I'm going and that's that, Narayan. Not you nor Alaric can stop me."

"You do realise that Alex isn't just Alex anymore, don't you?"

"Of course I do, but he's also still...my brother," she huffed out an exasperated breath. Even as she told herself that her brother wouldn't hurt her, she remembered all too well what Ahriman had done to her and a flutter of nerves tightened in her belly. "But, Tilly will be with me, and...so will you?" she answered.

"Fine, but if Alaric strips my hide, you owe me."

"Join the queue."

Abby looked around the small room. It was the same as all the other guest rooms in the lower level of the manor, except this room was missing anything that could be even vaguely construed as a weapon, which left a fairly sparsely decorated room. A double bed with a few cushions scattered on it, an arm chair in the corner and empty dresser by the door. Its mirror had been detached and removed for safe keeping, leaving the outline on the wall where it had been leaning. The pale grey carpets had recently been cleaned leaving behind a faint smell of citrus which tickled her nose.

Abby had her own room in the manor, much more comfortable than this one, as did Alex, but if Alex was going to be kept in this room, then this was where she would stay too.

"Come here," Alex beckoned enticingly. The huskiness in his voice and the musky scent of his arousal sent shivers of desire through Abby's body. Her nipples hardened, her clit began to throb, and her insides liquefied and coalesced between her silky folds in preparation for the promise of unbridled pleasure blazing in his eyes.

They were home, they were alone, and he wanted to celebrate.

"Alex, we can't do this now, someone could come in here any minute," she protested weakly as his arm slipped about her waist, anchoring her to him. Despite her prudent words of practicality, he felt her still. He licked at the tender flesh of her neck. His body tightened, and her body heated and shivered as his hands roughly skimmed down, cupping her backside, pulling her higher against him. He kissed and nipped and licked a path up her neck to her jaw, and finally to her lips.

"We'll make it quick."

"You're impossible," she chastised breathlessly, as his teeth nipped at her lips before his tongue soothed the small pain. The sensuality of the caress had the breath halting for long seconds in her chest.

Alex looked down into her beautiful face with her narrow sculptured nose, high cheekbones and sensually curved lips. Anticipation and vulnerability backlit her dark eyes as a rush of emotions flooded through her. Abby moaned with a low, soft sound of hunger. He loved that sound, and loved what it did to his own excitement when he heard it.

"Agreed," he chuckled against her neck, the vibration rippling over her skin.

His heart raced in his chest, making breathing a chore as he stepped back to unbutton his shirt, leaving it to gape open. Abby watched, greedily eyeing his broad chest, almost hairless over sinewy muscles with only a light arrowing of dark hair beneath the waistband of his tight jeans, which he was quickly releasing. Abby licked her lips as he toed off his boots and began to push down his pants. She wanted that job to be hers. To peel away those pants with her teeth as her lips and tongue tracked every inch of flesh she revealed.

A sharp rap on the door sounded loudly in the small room.

"Shit!" Alex growled under his breath. "Fuck off, were busy."

Abby began buttoning Alex's shirt quickly with lightening speed, as he refastened his jeans, a mixture of disappointment and anger blazing in his eyes. Closing his pants was made painfully harder by the bulge of his heavy erection, protesting against its confinement, the material barely stretching around it, straining the zipper to its limits.

"Alex, it's me, Cassie."

Suddenly all his frustration melted away. He wanted to see his sister almost as much as he wanted some *alone* time with Abby.

Dray opened the door and stepped aside to allow Narayan to enter with Cassie and Tilly following closely behind, his sharp senses noting every detail about Alex/Ahriman's posture and disposition. Closing the door behind them he listened intently to every word being spoken, prepared to burst in at the first sign of trouble. His neck too was on the line if anything happened to Cassie. Besides that, he was an intelligence expert and gathering information was his life. Why else would he volunteer to babysit Alex/Ahriman's room?

Well, he did have a sideline, working for Saladin at the Phoenix Nightclub. That job served multiple purposes: Obtaining intelligence, no drunk can hold their tongue; It filled in what would otherwise be an endless existence of tediously long nights and even longer days; And of course it was his favourite smorgasbord restaurant, a nightly parade of females offering themselves for sex and to feed from.

Tilly bounded past Narayan and Cassie, and leapt at Alex. His eyes widened with the shock as the huge hound crashed into him, tail wagging and tongue lapping at his face amid playful growls and pawing of excited feet on his chest.

Instantly Narayan relaxed, reassured by the protective dog's enthusiastic response to Alex. If there had been any threat of aggression from Ahriman, he suspected the mutt would have reacted very differently.

"Cassie? What's Tilly doing here?" he asked laughing, batting away her wet greeting.

"Hello to you too, *brother*," she grinned happily, handing the tray to Narayan.

Pushing Tilly aside, he opened his arms for his sister, his eyes welling with emotion as she buried her face in his chest and cried.

261

Ahriman lurked in the background restlessly. He too felt something from Cassie's embrace, but he couldn't determine if it was a good feeling or a bad feeling. It was however, one he had no experience with. What a shocker. That practically described every emotion he'd experienced since he'd taken up residency in Alex's body.

"I've missed you," she blubbered, hiccupping as she tried to control her sobs.

"I've missed you too, kid." His familiar use of his annoying term of endearment had her sobbing a fresh flood of tears with relief. It really was Alex holding her.

But that didn't mean that Ahriman had suddenly vanished. Cassie pushed back from him and wiped her eyes on a wad of tissues Narayan handed her, turning her attention to Abby to give her a huge hug too.

"We've been so worried. What did that bastard do to you," she asked Abby, referring to Ahriman with a sideways glance.

"It wasn't as bad as you think. Ahriman..." she looked toward Alex, "was very...accommodating," she said with an uncomfortable smile.

"I find that hard to believe," Cassie replied more tersely as she rubbed at her wrist where he had slashed her with a knife and drained the blood from her vein.

Alex's eyes changed. His warm emotion filling them suddenly became colder, more distant. Cassie took a step back towards Narayan who instantly became tense, as he too recognised the presence of Ahriman becoming the dominant personality. Tilly however, remained her happy, carefree self, unconcerned by Ahriman's commanding presence.

Ahriman covered his heart with his fist and bowed slightly to Cassie. "Please accept my apology for the distress I have caused you and your family."

What could she say? Thank you, apology accepted? What she wanted to say was a spiel of vindictive diatribe, potent enough to make even this demon wince. But what came out of her mouth instead surprised even her. "No harm done in the end. Thanks to you I'm now immortal." Although it was still to be determined whether her unborn baby was too, which is why Alaric was being so protective of her.

Ahriman watched as Cassie covered her belly protectively. "I believe congratulations are in order. I hope what I did to you hasn't harmed your young one," he said. Abby placed a hand on his arm, a wistful smile on her lips. She knew how hard it was for him to make any sort of apology, and for some reason he was making a greater effort than she would have believed possible to gain Cassie's forgiveness.

Tilly paced between Cassie and Alex, as if confused who she wanted to be with.

"What's with the dog?" Ahriman asked perplexed. Only one animal had ever been attracted to him before. When he incarnated as Adolf Hitler, his German Shepherd, Goldie, had been very attached to him. Although, Ahriman could never understand why. He hadn't even tried to hide his dark soul back then. Most animals seemed to have a natural aversion to him, even when he was the police detective. Sure, he had still been an evil son of a bitch for the most part, but he had tried to bury his darker tendencies, so he could blend in more efficiently. He'd fooled the people, but not the animals.

Cassie called Tilly back to her where the mutt sat on Cassie's feet. Rubbing behind her ears, Tilly's eyes closed and she growled happily. Taking a deep breath Cassie began to explain what had happened after Alex was kidnapped. Abby was familiar with the fact that Tilly had drunk the remainder of her blood from the Cup which Ahriman had used to try to make himself immortal. The repercussions of Tilly's new alter ego, being a rhinoceros sized hellhound, was a new development Cassie was happy to share with them.

"Now I understand why you let Cassie come in here," Ahriman said to Narayan. "If the mutt is as protective of Cassie as you say, any sign of threat from me and she'd be picking her teeth with my bones," he correctly surmised, or more precisely, Alex's bones.

Narayan only nodded in response, his alert eyes following every tiny movement that Ahriman made, not willing to rely solely on Tilly's judgement of the evil bastard.

"Can I ask you..." Cassie began, "Why did you need to kidnap Alex. I get the fact that you needed my blood, but why did you need to take Alex?"

"To make the portal device," he answered.

"That's what I don't get. I mean, the nephilim can open the portal to Fey, why did you need to build a machine to open the veil between dimensions, and why did you need Alex to build it?"

"Alex is an expert in the technology required to build the portal. His genetics also turned out to be rather…useful, to me personally," Ahriman said with a lopsided, grimaced smile. "And, the device is needed to open the veil to the Underworld. Unlike Fey where the Elders left the veil thin between there and Earth, the Underworld is a prison for some of the darkest souls imaginable…"

"Like you?" Cassie quickly put in with a snarky tone.

"Yes. Just like me," he chuckled. "There is a hierarchy in the Underworld, just like everywhere else. All new souls that arrive are automatically relegated to the bottom of the ladder. They are tormented and tortured by those ranked above them. The strongest souls rise through the ranks, if they choose to."

"What do you mean, *if they choose*?"

"The Underworld is a prison, but they do have a natural way out. They can choose to reincarnate back into the world."

"Like you did, coming back as Adolf Hitler and then as Detective Renkin?" She shuddered involuntarily, goose bumps appearing along her arms.

"Yes. Incarnating gives a soul the chance to redeem itself and maybe ascend to the higher realms. More often than not though, they repeat their prior mistakes and fall back to the Underworld. Only, when they return they become one of the lowest ranking souls, regardless of how highly placed in the hierarchy they were before incarnating." *Normally.*

"I still don't get it. So, why did you need to build the portal device?"

"Because my dear, there is more chance of Hell freezing over than an upper level demon becoming *'good'* and ascending, which means…"

"Which means that the only way they can come to Earth and retain their power status, is to enter this world in their current forms, not incarnate as human," Narayan finished for him.

"Exactly."

"Oh, that doesn't sound good," Cassie said.

"No, it wouldn't be. The device is functional, but short of charging it up with a nuclear reactor, there isn't enough power to open a stable or large enough portal to be of any concern," Ahriman told them.

"Why are you being so forthcoming with this information now when only a few weeks ago you couldn't give a damn about the consequences of anything you've done. Why have you changed your tune?" Cassie asked suspiciously.

"Because...." That was an interesting question. Because he had changed? That was true to a degree, he supposed, but that wasn't the reason. Because he had grown a conscience? Not likely. The truth was, he didn't really know why. "Because, I don't want Morganna to have it. There's no telling what kind a deal she's made with Mephistopheles to free him from the Underworld. She is an evil and vile creature who should have been disposed of at birth, an abomination who is quite possibly as great a threat to this world as Mephistopheles himself."

Maybe Ahriman was right, but Narayan had difficulty agreeing with the demon. Just because he wasn't wearing his Buddhist robes any longer, it didn't mean he didn't still follow their teachings.

"All creatures were created for a purpose," Narayan answered philosophically.

"Yes, but don't be fooled, humans aren't the only ones who believe they have the right to choose which ones were mistakes," Ahriman told him.

Cassie became suddenly distracted. "I have to go, Alaric's back," happiness lit her eyes, even though her expression and voice remained stoic.

"I have to go too. Alaric wants to speak to me," Abby told them, laying a soft kiss on Alex's cheek before she escorted Cassie from the room, Tilly in tow as usual.

Dray smiled and dipped his head politely as they passed him in the doorway, but his attention never faltered from the informative conversation taking place on the other side of the door.

"This world has enough problems as it is, without letting a horde of demons loose in it," Narayan said as the door quietly closed behind the women.

"Too true. There is more conflict in this world than there is kindness, which is why it was so simple for me to dominate humans. They are easily persuaded, greedy and self-centred."

"I disagree. There is a lot of good in this world. Despite your attempts, and every other nefarious dictator who has ever tried to assert their dominance. The good people in the world have always managed to conquer them in the end. What's to say we won't do the same again now?"

Seeing he wasn't getting through to Narayan, Ahriman decided to speak to him on his own level. It was something that seemed to flow easily from him now, after suffering so many hours listening to Alex spewing philosophy at him. "Harmony is balance wouldn't you agree. Life and death. Poverty and abundance. Love and hate."

"Yes, it is…"

"But think about what would happen if any of those were to dominate or disappear. Even a lack of sufficient evil might be detrimental. Humankind would grow complacent and lazy. They would cease to quest for enlightenment. Morals and spirituality would become obsolete."

Narayan's head nodded solemnly in agreement catching onto his meaning. Although religion itself is of minimal importance in the greater scheme of things, it is spirituality which causes the soul to grow and mature, to evolve. In order for that to happen, balance is the key. Humans evolve through spiritual growth. If they were denied that spiritual yin/yang balance, their evolution would be stunted.

Never would Narayan have believed he would sit down to a philosophical conversation with Ahriman. He had watched him tear apart Alaric in the gardens, had watched him slowly suffocate Cassie to death in the toxic mist he had created. He had sworn to kill the son of a bitch the moment he laid eyes on him. His homicidal tendencies may have been in opposition with his Buddhist teachings, but he was also a vampire who was very protective towards his family.

But now? Now he was sharing coffee with him and *enjoying* their conversation.

"And you're saying that if Mephistopheles breaks free of the Underworld, that balance will be tipped in favour of evil."

"Yes. Humans and every other creature here on Earth and in Fey, will become nothing better than slaves. Human history has shown that it has often taken several armies banded together to defeat individual dictators. Human dictators who had no special...talents," he said. "But Mephistopheles is no ordinary dictator, he has the power of a God. And..." he added, "He won't be coming alone. He will send his generals, others like me, to prepare the way for him."

"But we defeated you...twice. We can do it again."

"Maybe. If these generals come here like me, in human form, weak and vulnerable. But if Morganna opens the portal, they will come through in their true forms as immortals with their power intact. Most of Mephistopheles' generals are fallen angels who want revenge against the Elders."

"And what better way to get back at them than to mess with their pet project, all their Earthly creations."

"You're catching on."

They talked for several more minutes before Narayan too had to excuse himself.

"Do me a favour?" Ahriman asked as he was leaving. Narayan turned in the doorway and viewed him with a questioning glance. "Could you send down a TV?" With only these four walls to stare at, for who knew how long, he would go stir crazy, especially if Abby was detained by Alaric for too long.

"I can't do that. Besides, you're not lacking for company. I'm sure Alex could share a few more philosophical quotations with you to keep you entertained," he chuckled at Ahriman's stricken look of horror. "Or, maybe you could share your feelings with one another. Either way, I'll leave you to meditate on it."

"You're a cruel man, monk." Even if Ahriman wasn't devoid of emotion, he was still male, and males don't share their feelings, right?

"Cruel maybe, a monk...not any longer," he said has he turned and left.

Alex stared after his mentor as the door closed behind him. Narayan may not have been wearing his robes, but until this moment he didn't believe it could be possible that he would ever leave the monastery. His list of questions about what had happened while he was gone was growing steadily longer, but first he had to deal with Ahriman's *issue* that was beginning to bug him.

"You're wrong you know," Alex said to him after Narayan had left.

"What are you talking about?"

"You are capable of feelings. In case you've forgotten, I feel everything you do. You felt something when Cassie embraced me."

"That was indigestion."

"Bullshit. Stop lying to yourself!"

"I'm not lying. It's not possible for me to feel happy or think kind thoughts, and it's definitely not possible for me to feel love."

"You honestly believe that, don't you?"

"It's the truth. Why would I lie to you? You'd only start singing those irritating children's songs again and honestly, I don't think I can take another rendition of the ABC song."

"You've got a point. I don't think I could sing it one more time without becoming as insane as you."

"If you're so sure I can feel good things, explain to me what I felt when Cassie hugged you."

"I'm not exactly sure, it was pretty complex, but there was definitely guilt in there. That's a positive emotion, it means you have a conscience."

Ahriman grumbled and huffed and paced the room restlessly as their conversation progressed. He refused to grasp the concept he may have a latent soft side that had begun to emerge.

"What is it I feel for Abby then?" he asked, flustered. He felt something for Abby, although couldn't identify the feeling either, she tugged at something deep inside him. He liked being near her. Her bright smile hit him in the gut like a welcome burst of sunlight after eons of darkness.

Alex's mind went to his *mate*, and he immediately felt their bond flair brighter between them.

"It's love. That feeling you have, is love."

"I've already told you, that's impossible. I'm incapable of love!" Ahriman growled angrily.

Ahriman shuddered at the thoughts rolling through Alex's mind. Love terrified him. He wasn't afraid to admit it. The very thought of it threw him into a panic, even when that love was not his, but Alex's. He was susceptible to the potent lure of their bond and that deeply troubled him.

He was cursed. Cursed for all eternity.

"You may not be familiar with the feeling, but I am. There is more than one kind of love. Love for a mate, love for a parent or child and a love for a friend. Each kind of love is different but equally as powerful," Alex explained.

"What kind do I have?" he asked.

"It's not a disease you've contracted, moron," Alex snorted in amusement at his panicky tone. *"What you feel is something akin to a close friendship."*

Ahriman was pathetically clueless, which tempted Alex to use it against him, but after a moment of deliberation, he decided against it.

"How do you know what I feel, when I don't?" he asked in a pained tone.

Alex was silent as he gave the question some thought.

"You only truly know yourself through the eyes of others. It wasn't until I met Abby that I realised that I was an arsehole. I saw myself through her eyes and I didn't like what I saw. When you find that one person who connects you to the world, you become a different person, a better person."

"I envy you, Alex. I can never have what you and Abby share. I was cursed many millennia ago and forfeited my heart along with my soul," Ahriman divulged tentatively.

"What happened?" Alex asked, minus his customary snarky tone.

"It was a long time ago, before the Elders sent the Watchers to Earth to oversee human evolution. I was a high ranking angel in the order of Seraphim. I took my role very seriously and took pride in my achievements. At that time humans were still very young and unfortunately were not progressing in their evolution as expected. They were not the peaceful race the Elders had wanted. They fought amongst themselves violently. I challenged the Elders and their decision to allow them so much freedom to cause chaos. I warned them what they would become if they were left unchecked, unguided. Needless to say, they didn't like my thoughts and banished me to the Underworld."

Alex listened intently.

Ahriman knew Alex had seen fractured glimpses of his memories. As hard as he'd tried to hide them, he hadn't been able to block them out entirely.

"I explained to you earlier about the hierarchy in the Underworld. It was no different for me. When I arrived, I was one of the lowest ranking beings there. Except, I was a fallen angel of the order of Seraphim, one of the highest level of angels, which made me one of the most powerful beings in the Underworld regardless of my rank. Naturally Mephistopheles saw me as a threat."

"So, if Mephistopheles is the head honcho of the Underworld, what about Lucifer?"

Ahriman snorted out a bitter laugh at the ludicrous idea that Lucifer might hold any significant rank higher than a court jester, and chose to ignore the question. Instead of distracting him, Alex decided to file that question away to follow-up another time.

"I was angry at the Elders, disillusioned by the beliefs I had so faithfully followed for hundreds of thousands of years and was looking for retribution. Mephistopheles promised to give me special privileges, become one of his generals and offered to help me enact my revenge on the Elders. All for the small price of my soul. It didn't matter to me at the time, I was blinded by my anger. By the time I realised my mistake, it was far too late."

Mephistopheles branded him with his mark, binding Ahriman's soul to his. The process was long and painful, designed to remove any lingering goodness that may have survived his fall to the Underworld.

"Is there any way you can break free of his hold on you?"

"None I'm afraid," he answered sombrely. If Alex was right, and he was starting to *feel* again, that meant he had developed a weakness, one Mephistopheles would love to exploit. Ahriman was no fool. He knew that his time in this world, sharing Alex's body was nearly at an end. They would find a way to remove him and send him back to the Underworld.

For the first time since he fell from grace in the upper realms, Ahriman regretted his choice to side with Mephistopheles.

27

"Your face is going to set like that when the wind changes, you know?" Cassie informed Saladin, interrupting his pacing in the enormous entry hall.

"What? What are you talking about?"

"You've been scowling like that for the past two days. And you've been even more of an arsehole than usual."

"Oh, sorry."

Saladin apologising, voluntarily? He really wasn't himself.

"Don't get yourself worked up over it. Richard will be gone by tomorrow and if recent history is anything to go by, he won't be back for some time. So, I doubt he'll be able to stop you from seeing Teagan."

Saladin turned to meet Cassie's optimistic gaze. He'd tried to get Teagan alone since his run-in with Richard at the pub, but the old codger had blocked him at every opportunity. "That doesn't mean she wants to see me. She's done her best to avoid me so far," he answered her with pessimism.

"Do you blame her? Every time she's seen you, you've acted like a complete knob, not to mention your womanising reputation. That's not exactly a turn-on for a girl with morals. She's not the sort who wants a one night stand you know."

"Yeah, I know. Believe it or not, I don't want that either." Funny enough, that wasn't just a throw away line to get Cassie to butter Teagan up for him. He meant it. It shocked him far more than it shocked her.

Cassie smiled inwardly. "Then wait until Richard leaves and tell her how you feel. I doubt she'll take much convincing."

Saladin's eyebrow raised questioningly. What had the two women been talking about, he wondered. Ordinarily, girl talk bored the crap out of him, but for once he wouldn't mind being clued in.

"So, what exactly can we expect with this ward they're going to perform," Narayan asked as he joined them.

Saladin explained the preparations that had been made and what was left to be done. Several hundred small, thumbnail sized hematite stones had been placed around the boundary of Havenswood Manor, both inside and outside the house, as well as throughout the sub level tunnel system. Each stone had a protection spell placed on it. The type of spell depended on what and where it was going to be protecting.

With all the preparations now complete, it just left the binding spell to be performed to connect each stone to every other stone and seal the ward, which the sisters would commence as the sun begins to cross the eastern horizon.

"What about the stones? Do they have to remain in place permanently, and if so, what if they get moved accidentally?" Narayan asked, spying one of the tiny silvery stones only meters away by the front door. Hematite was a fascinating stone with spiritually grounding properties, shiny silver on the outside but when crushed to powder, it became red dust giving it its alternate name, blood stone. Quite appropriate he thought, considering they were going to be protecting a vampire's home.

"From what Teagan has told me, once the spell has been cast the stones will dissolve into their surroundings. They will remain permanently, unseen and immovable," Saladin answered.

"Good to know."

The old grandfather clock down the hallway near the study chimed 6:00am. They were nearly ready.

"I'm not comfortable about Alex and Abby being sent away while the new ward is performed," Cassie grumbled unhappily. None of them were, but Alaric was adamant that Ahriman was not to be within a hundred meters of the perimeter, just in case...

"They'll be fine. Damon and several other lycans will be watching them. Besides, the Drunken Duck Pub is only a couple of hundred meters from the forest. At the first sign of trouble, they know to make a run for it there. Although, I seriously doubt the Guild have enough fighting men left to attack a flea, let alone a lycan stronghold. The only men we didn't kill were the mercenaries under Morganna's spell, and they've now all had their minds and free wills restored." Saladin told her.

"If it makes you feel any better, I'll keep an eye on things from a discrete distance," Narayan told her. He too was uncomfortable with the idea of letting Ahriman out of their sight, even though he was pretty sure he wouldn't try to run, he couldn't rule it out. Ahriman was still an evil bastard at heart. He had proven time and again he always had something unexpected up his sleeve, a Plan B. Narayan fingered the handcuffs in his coat pocket. He doubted he'd need them, but it was better to be safe than sorry.

"You're going out there?" Cassie pointed toward the forest. "But...the sun's coming up in an hour," she told him incredulously.

Narayan smiled. "Yes, about that." His grin broadened. "What are my favourite TV shows?" he asked her.

"Um, I don't know. The next top model or those make-over shows... Why? What's that got to do with anything?"

"I've had a make-over too," he answered in his jovial manner.

"And?"

"And, nothing."

"You're going to make me guess?"

"If you want to."

"No, I don't want to." Cassie let out a disgruntled huff. Obviously, he still wasn't prepared to talk about what had happened to him in India. The suspense was driving her nuts. Whatever his reason for being so damned cryptic, he couldn't deny that something fundamental about him had changed. "Can't you at least give me a hint?"

Narayan chuckled, ignoring her question, choosing instead to continue inspecting the druid sister's placement of each of the tiny stones.

One by one, the occupants of the house gathered in the entrance hall, nervous anticipation keeping the conversation buzzing with anxious excitement.

273

Once everyone had gathered together, they exited the house to watch the spectacle from just inside the forest line, leaving Teagan and her sisters inside with Richard to oversee things.

One other person remained behind. Raif. The wyvern leader had not regained consciousness despite everything they tried. Richard used every spell he knew and Raif's sister Brin, attempted tirelessly for two days to heal him with her gift. But nothing had worked, he remained in a comatose state. Now, as the house emptied out, he lay alone in one of the guest rooms, unaware of the magical feat about to take place around him. His brother Wade, was the last to leave. It had taken a great deal of reassurance that Raif wouldn't be harmed in any way by the spell, before he reluctantly left his brother's side.

The forest was full of curious onlookers. Even Gwynn and Oliver joined the group to watch the once in a lifetime magic show.

Then the spell began.

Abby and Alex/Ahriman stood near the rear of the car park at the Drunken Duck Pub. The rise of land gave them a reasonable view over the top of the trees where the forest dipped into a hollow. They watched and waited with eager anticipation with Damon and another four lycan's, their designated guards for the next couple of hours. Not that Ahriman planned on doing anything stupid at this point.

He knew his time was almost up. Richard had located a spell in his Book of Shadows which would effectively remove him without harming his host body, Alex. He only had a few more hours, he assumed. In the meantime, he waited eagerly, just like everybody else for the spectacle that was about to be performed. There were very few beings throughout history who could achieve such a complex spell with such a degree of competency. The last one he knew of was Merlin. His druid descendants were certainly worthy of his name. Ahriman only hoped they would be strong enough to survive what Morganna had planned for them.

They hadn't waited long when the pre-dawn sky began to shimmer. A mist began to emerge over Havenswood Manor and over the entrances to the hidden exterior tunnels, with a kaleidoscope of shifting

274

and swirling colour. The shimmering veil lifted as the sun broke across the horizon, the swimming colours condensing into spectacular beams that domed the borders of the property and tunnel entrances like lasers that criss-crossed, joining together forming an intricate web.

From the corner of his eye, Ahriman watched as Damon sent his men to the far corners of the car park, while he himself moved a little too close to Abby for his liking.

Alex narrowed his gaze on the man, his vague unease solidifying into ruthless suspicion. The hair on his body stood to rigid attention in warning. The odd thought barely had time to form when a familiar presence seemingly appeared from nowhere behind him.

"Ahhh hmm."

Pivoting on the spot, Ahriman growled as Mira deigned to greet him. She sneered with pleasure at his shock and the scent of fear which suddenly filled the air. Her lips stretched into a smile, the gesture about as reassuring as a hyena's deadly grin. "Did you miss me?"

Mother fucking fucker!

Quickly he put his body between Mira and Abby and gestured for her to move back. Damon had the same idea and grabbed her wrist, pulling her away. His grip was strong and unyielding, way too strong for Abby's comfort and she tried to pry herself loose, to no avail. Looking into his hard eyes she saw it then, the hatred and contempt staring back at her.

Confusion warred inside her. Damon was a lycan, he was a protector, not the enemy. But the resentment in his eyes told a whole different story. Her eyes darted quickly about to the other lycans, each man was frozen in place.

Oh, crap. This was bad. Not only was Mira here, Morganna was somewhere nearby too.

"You've got some fucking nerve coming here, bitch. You're a bigger dumb fuck than you look if you think I'll let you get anywhere near Abby, ever. You fucking whore-bitch piece of shit." Alex told her.

"Did anyone ever tell you, you have a foul mouth?" Mira chastised.

That foul mouth in question curled into a derisive smile. "All the time. It's one of my more endearing qualities."

"You think you're so smart, don't you? You act like arrogance is your greatest virtue…"

"You act like stupidity is yours, I'd stop boasting about it if I were you," he retaliated, earning himself a back hand to the cheek. All the while he watched as Abby fought against Damon's hold as he too came to the conclusion that Damon wasn't working on their side. Alex knew he had to buy her time to get away. He doubted he could fight them both off, but he could at least give Abby a chance.

"I'm not here for your female…this time," she hissed contemptuously. "Killing her is personal. I'm here on a professional job today."

"What the fuck are you on about now, dick splash?"

"You, half wit. I'm here for you," she chuckled. "It appears there is more than one person who wants you and Ahriman dead," she said sliding a sideways glance to Damon. "Morganna in particular doesn't want either of you around. It isn't in her best interests to have anyone living who could possibly build another device. So, you see…" she paused. "It's time for you to go back to your *Master*," she addressed Ahriman. "Maybe if you're lucky Alex will join you in the Underworld and you can keep your debauched male bonding thing going for eternity," she said with pretentious exaggeration.

"No!" Abby screamed. There was panic in her voice. Alex could sense her fear increasing. Her body tightened with it, her fists clenching at her sides as she doubled her efforts to free herself from Damon, who held her in an immobilising lock, with a gun to her temple.

Mira shot her a conceited grin. Hatred rolled off her in sizzling lashes. It was clear that she had no intention to making him her only target today. Then just as quickly the look was gone. Her gaze became shuttered, considering.

It was different when he thought she was afraid of him or repulsed by him. Now that he knew she wasn't, he had a serious problem.

Damon hadn't counted on Abby's martial arts training. She wasn't the helpless female he took her for. As quick as lightening she twisted out of his hold and used both hands in a slapping motion toward each other knocking the gun from his grip, then followed through with a punch to his surprised face.

"Guess you misjudged me, arsehole." Abby swung again, but he blocked, landing a hit to her solar plexus.

"Not so much," he replied and reached for her, locking her in a vice grip once again, his lips twisting into a bitter grin.

Abby may have been a vampire with superior speed, but he was a lycan which gave him the superior strength, not to mention his combat skills were that of an elite soldier. He was more than prepared for anything she could throw at him.

While Alex's attention was diverted towards Abby for a moment, Mira delivered a punch to his ribs with an audible crack.

"You're going to pay for that bitch," he promised, sucking in a painful breath.

As his fist raised to hit her with a bolt of electricity, she smashed hers up into his nose throwing him off balance to land in the semi-frozen mud, but he was up again in a flash.

Crouching low on one leg, Mira spun a complete circle swinging her other leg out, hitting him in the knee, shattering his knee cap and dropping him like a stone with a sickening crunch. Alex howled in pain.

"Mother fucking cock sucker! You broke my fucking leg, bitch," he snarled.

Alex stumbled to his feet.

Blow after blow Mira laid into Alex until every square centimetre of his body blazed in agony. She was too strong and too fast for him. His only defence was his electrical power, which she was all too wary of, dodging each bolt he aimed at her.

He feigned a left hook and when she moved to dodge it, he followed through with the right, landing a sickening thud to her face, dazing her for a second.

Blood trickled into Mira's eyes from the cut to her brow, clouding her vision.

Alex tried to block the pain. "I hate to tell you, but you'll always have the face like the arse end of a baboon, although a beating does make some improvement," he taunted. His own face was rapidly swelling making it hard to talk. He knew he couldn't defeat her, but it felt good to piss her off.

His smashed jaw and crushed eye socket was the least of his problems though. He had multiple fractures to every limb, broken ribs

277

and a punctured lung. His spleen and kidneys had been ruptured and a depressed fracture to his skull, and still he fought to remain conscious even if he was virtually immobilised.

Looking in Abby's direction Ahriman and Alex watched with pride as she fought against her captor and drew strength from her determination.

Damon loosened his grip to reach behind him for another weapon.

Seeing an opportunity, calm determination spread through her body.

Abby spun in his grip, turning to face him. Breaking free, she stumbled and fell.

"Get back here, demon whore," he snarled and gripped her foot, pulling her back toward him. She kicked out but couldn't shake his hold. Scrambling she fought to free herself and get to her feet. The click of a gun stopped her cold.

This was it, she thought. With a clean shot, the .50 calibre semi-automatic revolver would blow a hole in her chest large enough to effectively remove her heart. Game over.

All she could think about was Alex. She had so many regrets. They would never get that chance to have a life together she thought sadly.

Biting back her emotions, she turned to face him. She was not a coward.

"You can kill me, but you'll never leave here alive. Alaric will hunt you down."

"See you in Hell then," Damon growled as he pulled the trigger.

Abby was thrown off her feet with a burst of pain as the bullet punched through her shoulder.

Alex turned at the sound of the gun shot to see Abby knocked through the air with a spray of blood and tissue explode from her shoulder.

"Abby!" his voice strangled as his body stiffened suddenly, his eyes wide with shock, pain detonated in his mind and the sound of crunching bones filled his ears. It was his spine shattering as Mira stomped on his back with all the force she could put behind her boot.

Morganna remained out of sight but watched intently with excitement as Mira beat into Ahriman and Alex, watching as the life was slowly drained from their body.

Ahriman and Alex pooled their strength for one last retaliation. There would only be one person walking away from here alive today, and that would be Abby. With unified determination they willed their power to life once more, focussing every last remaining ounce of their energy into one last blast.

"Hey, Mira," she turned to stare at him as he smiled through toothless, bloody lips. "Fuck you." A bolt of lightening left his hands and blasted into Mira's chest, sending her sailing through the air, her dark skin a new shade of black from her charred and smoking flesh.

Narayan burst free of the tree line, running at top speed in time to see Abby take a bullet. Fear and determination drove him even faster toward the male who was once again raising his gun for another shot.

Narayan had Damon face down in the dirt with a knife to his throat so fast the others were barely aware of his movement. Pulling the cuffs from his pocket he'd originally thought he might need to use on Alex/Ahriman, he quickly bound his hands and flipped him over. Nose to nose with Damon, Narayan's eyes flashed instantly with homicidal rage. His curses blistered the air around them.

Narayan had remained in one of the hidden tunnels just out of sight inside Savernake Forest, thinking he was close enough to help Alex or Abby if anything happened.

Of course, something did happen. What he hadn't anticipated was that as the new ward was being activated, it would block him from exiting the tunnel until the spell was complete. For the second time in just over as many weeks, he had been forced to watch his family being slaughtered at the hands of their enemy. His rage and no doubt Abby's distress, would have triggered their bond with Alaric. Heaven help the man he held in his grip when he arrived.

Mira's limp form landed twenty meters from the edge of the car park, close enough for Morganna to easily reach her. Gripping Mira's arm, she waited for just a moment longer to watch Abby's anguish as she reached her *mate's* side. Satisfied that she had accomplished her goal, she wrapped her other hand around her amulet. In a flash, both Morganna and Mira were gone once again.

279

Alex would be dead within minutes and Ahriman would no longer be a threat to her plans. He would be returned to the Underworld where he belonged.

The lycan guards were freed from her immobilising spell the instant Morganna disappeared and they rushed to assist Narayan contain Damon, leaving him free to tend to Abby and Alex.

Abby wanted to scream at the unfairness of it all, but self pity wasn't going to save her *mate*. It had been more than two days since he had taken her blood. With everything happening since they returned from the Ukraine, they hadn't been given any time alone.

"I won't lose you, Alex. Do you hear me? You are not going to die. I'm not going to let you, do you understand me?"

Time seemed to stand still as Abby cradled Alex's broken body in her arms. Blood gushed from her shoulder wound in a continuous stream down her arm. She trickled it into his open mouth and willed him to swallow.

Ahriman's eyes looked up at her, a softness in his gaze she hadn't seen before.

"I'm sorry, Abby. If I could save Alex for you I would."

"I know," she sobbed.

Her face flushed even as his turned a shade of grey, his gaze flickered with something...regret. Abby's chest bloomed with pain.

Tears prickled her eyes as she grabbed the hard line of his jaw and looked deep into the depths of his fading gaze.

"No. You can't die. If you die, so does Alex. I won't let this happen."

"When you've lived for thousands of years, death becomes an old friend. It's my time to go," he told her.

Ahriman's attitude shouldn't have shocked her. But it did. He almost sighed with relief. Sharing Alex's body had left a stain on his soul. Like a watermark, barely there but indelibly imprinted on him. Thoughts and emotions once so foreign to him, he now almost longed to feel again.

Almost.

There is no place for soft sentiment in the Underworld. Besides, his soul belonged to Mephistopheles. His every thought and desire was monitored, dictated and controlled.

Releasing control of his body for the last time, Alex rose to the fore.

"How am I supposed to live without you? Alex, please don't leave me," she pleaded, her voice hitching on a sob. She had no idea if he had taken in any of her blood, there seemed to be more of his own blood flowing from his mouth than what she was trying to give him of hers.

A heavy, burning pain seared his thoughts, but it had nothing to do with his broken body. His pain was for Abby. A thousand regrets at how little time they'd had together. He really wished things could have been different.

"I...love...you...Abby," he managed to choke out as his eyes fixed on her face and glazed over, his final breath sighing free of his lifeless body.

As everything went dark, his pain dissolved. Only one thing tangible remained. Ahriman.

"We will meet again, my friend," Ahriman told him.

"Maybe. But under better circumstances I hope. You know, every saint has been a sinner and every sinner can become a saint," Alex whispered to Ahriman with his last conscious thought as Ahriman's soul left his body.

"Please, Narayan. Please tell me he's going to be alright," she begged through broken sobs, rocking back and forth with his still body cradled to her chest.

What could he say? He didn't know. Even if he had taken in enough of Abby's blood to transform him into a vampire, his body was so damaged, her blood may not be enough to revive him. If he did wake as a vampire, there was no guarantee that he wouldn't retain weaknesses, like he had done, with his ultra-sensitivity to sunlight. Narayan couldn't lie to her, she had to know the truth, and he told her so.

Abby refused to give up hope. "How long before we know?"

"Maybe a few hours," he replied sombrely. "Maybe less. If he is going to be transformed, we should start to see his wounds beginning to mend by then." Secretly however, Narayan didn't hold as much hope for him as Abby wanted him to. He had seen this situation before and it didn't end well.

Alaric approached the pub with a determined stride, Oliver, Gwynn and Saladin in tow.

No one said a word. By the look of Narayan's profile as he paced the car park, they could see something was seriously wrong. It took only another second for the scent of blood to reach them.

Oliver rounded the corner of the pub and saw him. The traitor. His broad back faced him as he knelt on his haunches, hands cuffed and guarded by his own clan members. Oliver hoped, wished, it could have been anyone else but who it appeared to be.

"Shit!" The word broke from Oliver's lips as barely a whisper, shock locking the air inside his lungs.

Oliver reluctantly walked over to Damon, grabbing him by the shirt front, a mixture of regret, disappointment and anger tormenting his eyes. "How could you do it?" he asked hoarsely through clenched teeth, shaking his head in disbelief. "You've really fucked up, brother," he told him sadly.

"What would you care, *brother*," he spat back, his top lip curling in contempt. Resentment and hatred clouding his eyes as he glared back at him.

How had this happened? Oliver wondered. Why hadn't he seen this coming?

"Why did you do it?" Oliver asked, trying hard to keep the pain of betrayal from his voice. He had been alpha of their clan for not quite three weeks and already he'd had a shit storm to contend with. Multiple shit storms.

First Harold and Lionel for their part in what had happened at Havenswood Manor. Fortunately for Lionel, he had done nothing more than hide a body and blow up a car, which he'd been blackmailed into believing it would help save his brother who had been *recruited* by the Guild. For his actions, he had been sentenced to another mandatory ten-year period of active duty in the lycan's military. His father, Harold, had not actively partaken in anything Lionel did, although had known about it but nonetheless never reported it. His sentence was twelve months community service.

Damon on the other hand, was another matter altogether. He was a true traitor to the clan and the Alliance, and it fell to him as alpha to deal out the punishment.

When Damon didn't answer his question, only continued to glare at him, Oliver turned away from his brother, the heaviness in his heart seemingly no match for gravity as his shoulders slumped on a heavy sigh.

He was going to have to kill his own brother.

"You know the punishment, why did you do it?" he asked again, keeping his back to Damon. "Was it because I was chosen as alpha over you? Do you hate me so much that you would sabotage our whole clan for your pride?" Oliver spun around, anger rising in his voice.

"*I* was supposed to be alpha. I'm better and stronger than you in every way."

"Except in judgement," Oliver bit back, eliciting a vicious snarl from Damon, his eyes turning gold as his wolf neared the surface under the influence of his rage.

"*I*, was supposed to be alpha," Damon repeated through clenched teeth. "And, I would have been too, except for him," he growled, looking at Alex's lifeless form wrapped in Abby's grieving arms on the ground in a pool of blood. "Ahriman! He ruined everything. Ahriman murdered our father. Ahriman caused the troubles that swayed our father toward you on his death bed. And Ahriman was responsible for me being shot and crippled. I know my punishment, and I welcome it. What do I have left to live for? I'm not alpha and my career is over. At least I will die knowing the evil bastard, Ahriman, is dead and gone too."

Unspoken words filled the bitter silence between them.

"Do you have anything else to say before I carry out your sentence?" Oliver asked, his sadness seeping into his voice.

"Yeah. Hurry the fuck up. I'm sick of looking at your face."

"Fine."

Oliver left his brother and marched inside the pub, away from the growing crowd. Pacing back and forth behind the bar he downed a scotch for Dutch courage.

"I know Oliver has dibs on the son of a bitch, but I swear, I will kill the bastard a second time," Hawke growled, his eyes flaring with anger. He was a soldier through and through, and soldiers had a code of honour, which Damon had just broken.

"Take a number," Saladin said.

"Make the prick suffer first, I say," Gwynn added.

Alaric entered the pub silently and waited patiently as Oliver attempted to make his peace with himself before fulfilling his duty as alpha.

"My brother's death is on my hands and my conscience. I will have to live with that for the rest of my life. I don't know if I can do it."

"He made his own choices knowing well what the consequences are. He wears the full responsibility, not you," Alaric reminded him.

"If…when, I kill him, can you send his soul on, like you did for my father?"

Alaric's expression was grim. "I can't do that," he said. "The choices Damon has made have corrupted his soul. I'm afraid your brother is headed for the Underworld."

Oliver stilled as the reality of the statement sank in. "Fucking bastard," he muttered under his breath, pitching his glass into the open fire place in rage, and running his fingers through his hair in frustration. "Fucking, stupid bastard."

The irony of Damon's situation was that he hated Ahriman so much that he had forfeited his own life and his soul to send the demon back to the Underworld, only to find he will be spending eternity with him.

"Let's get this over with," Oliver said, stripping off his clothes he laid them carefully over the bar before shifting into his wolf form. An enormous grey wolf the size of a small horse on steroids. His eyes shone gold, but they held the sadness of the man within.

Oliver emerged from the pub and entered the car park once again to face his brother.

Steely silence filled the air. Even the birds seemed to hold their breath and wait.

Oliver's eyes roamed the crowd of witnesses. Lycans mostly, but also the high lord of the nephilim, Gwynn and Alaric's family of vampires. His heart sank when his eyes fell on his youngest son, Callum and his best friend, Marcus. The two boys would be joining the military for their mandatory service in only a few short weeks, and no doubt will see all manner of atrocities during their service. But, he never wanted to be the one to introduce his son to the harsher side of their life.

There was nothing he could do about it though. It is what it is. Damon had forced this upon them.

Fortunately, none of the druid girls were present. He was especially grateful that Elise was absent. She had become the daughter he never had, and it would have destroyed his soul for her to witness this.

Finally, his gaze came back to his brother. Oliver's wolf pawed the half frozen ground, gouging out long divots with his razor-sharp claws. His ears went back, baring his enormous canine fangs as he crouched ready for attack.

Damon lifted his head high and sucked in a tight breath. A flicker of fear crossed his eyes a moment before Oliver lunged for him.

A sickening crack of his neck reverberated through the silence as Oliver wrenched his head with his powerful jaws. Damon was dead, painlessly and quickly before he ripped out his throat.

Oliver's head dipped low, shutting his eyes he battled back his misery, his body trembling from the effort.

It was done.

Leaving the crowd behind him, Oliver ran deep into the forest where his pitiful howls of anguish echoed throughout the region.

Leaving Damon's body to the lycan clan to deal with, Alaric turned his attention to Abby and Alex. Alex's torn and battered body lay so still, Abby's inconsolable pain of loss tore at his own heart. Only a few short weeks ago he had been in her position, cradling Cassie's lifeless form.

"Please, Alaric. Can't you do something for him?" she pleaded.

"Why don't we take him home. We'll get him cleaned up." He wasn't willing to tell her more than that. They could be cleaning him up for his funeral.

What the hell?

Alaric looked down to see Alex's wounds closing, a curious zipping, followed by a heavy thud in his chest as his heart began beating once again.

Abby sat perfectly still, too afraid to look at him in case she had just imagined the slight movement she felt in his limbs. She didn't think she could survive the disappointment if there had been no change, if it had only been her imagination.

"Abby?" Alaric said slowly as if not wanting to spook her. "It's going to be okay. Look at him."

Those words alone had her breath catching in her throat and her eyes welling with hope. Slowly she dropped her eyes to Alex's face, his long dark lashes raised to reveal glittering chocolate eyes.

"Baby. I'm back. Don't cry. I'm here and I'm never going to leave you again. I promise."

As Alex sat up, Abby leapt into his lap, wrapping herself around him so tightly he couldn't breathe. Fortunately for him, he no longer *needed* to breathe, except to speak. Her tears of joy were so heart felt, she had every tough-arsed man around her discretely sniffling back a tear.

Climbing to his feet, Abby reluctantly loosened her grip and slid to the ground, refusing to relinquish her hold on him altogether, snuggling against him as he wrapped his arms around her.

"It's good to have you back. I'm glad I don't have to go home and tell Cassie you're dead," Alaric stated blandly.

"That makes two of us," Alex grinned. "It looks like you're stuck with my ugly mug around the place for a while longer."

"Yes, I believe so." A lopsided mischievous grin lit Alaric's face. "I have a theory I'd like to test. Give me your hand," he ordered Alex.

True to form, Alex lifted his hand but only offered him his middle finger.

With lightening speed Alaric reached out and snapped off his finger.

"What the fuck do you think you're doing?" Alex screeched, continuing his colourful selection of curses at his future brother-in-law.

"I've always wanted to do that," he grinned.

"That was my favourite finger. What's your problem?" Alex demanded as he stared at the gaping hole on his hand.

"We know you're a vampire now, so the finger will grow back either way. The question is..."

Holy fuck. He wasn't just a vampire.

Alex's finger began to dissolve in the palm of Alaric's hand and reform back in its rightful place.

Like Alaric, he was an *immortal* vampire.

"What the....?"

Alaric gave him the answer before Alex could finish the question. "You transformed far too quickly to be a regular vampire, and you were born with the same immortality gene as your sister. I assumed, since Ahriman was once an upper level angel, his soul might have retained its high level of vibration even though he is now Fallen..."

"Which means, his presence inside my body was all that was needed to activate the gene?"

"That's my theory," Alaric agreed.

"You feeling alright?" Abby asked him as he began to sway on the spot in shock.

"I feel better than I have in a very long time, ever, in fact. Just a little surprised," he replied, his mildly perplexed grin quickly shifting to take on a sly lilt. He wasn't just talking about the movement returning to his limbs, but also the warmth that was flooding his body and soul.

"Well mate, what do you say we go home and get cleaned up. It looks like you might need to feed to get that shoulder completely healed," he told her, waggling his brows suggestively. After all, sex and feeding *did* go hand in hand with vampires. And he was very keen to find out what it would be like, now that they were *both* vampires.

"I can hear your thoughts again. Oh my God! I can hear you in my mind again," Abby proclaimed, jumping into his arms once more and bathing him in kisses as fresh tears streamed down her face.

Alex gripped the nape of her neck, to bring her feverish kisses to his lips and holding her there for the longest moment until she stilled. Slowly he kissed her back, short soft, gentle kisses that quickly deepened into long sensuous strokes of their tongues against one another.

A sharp sting to his lower lip had him pulling back in surprise. His fangs had descended in his excitement and nicked his lip. Abby licked the droplet of his blood from her lips. Her eyes glittering with anticipation and his manhood throbbed with as much excitement as his new fangs.

"I *really* think we should be going home," he encouraged suggestively. Abby wrapped her legs about his hips even tighter, grinding his growing erection harder against her weeping core. "Now, would be good," he almost begged.

"Listen to your *mate*," Saladin advised her with a congratulatory slap to Alex's back. "Welcome to the family. You're officially one of us now," he told him.

"Don't remind me," Alaric groaned. Alex was annoying as a human, but how much more so would he be now that he was not just a vampire, but an immortal.

He thought about that for another moment, a sly smile crossing his face.

Immortal…Every time Alex pissed him off he could remove one of his body parts, i.e, his head, to shut him up, he'd revive, Cassie would get pissed off with him and then they'd have make-up sex.

It was a win/win situation as far as he could see.

This might actually work out.

28

Relief combined with a dark, intoxicating need threading through him. Abby was safe, if not a little worse for wear, and he was alive. The scent of Abby's blood teased at his nose, the warm silk of her lips as potent as the finest aphrodisiac.

Alex's lips touched hers, his tongue swiped over her lips, flicked past them to tangle with her own, deepening the kiss with devastating effect.

His hands pulled her against him tighter. His erection pressing against her stomach had her tilting her hips and arching to meet him.

Breathing was a chore. Her chest was so tight with the need to hold back the moan rising inside it. She felt light-headed from the effort. Driving her fingers through his hair, Abby's body shook in his arms, her shudders vibrated through his body, heating it further.

"Baby, please, let's go home," he begged as he attempted to peel her legs from about his hips.

Alex stared at her. His eyes eating up the frantic, sexy look on her face as she clung to him tighter, pressing her pelvis up against the hard length of his cock, grinding the gears in his mind to a halt momentarily with a tortured groan.

Why did he want to go home?

So he could fuck her.

Senselessly.

Mindlessly.

Alex grinned and hefted her over his shoulder, mindful of her injury. But she didn't seem to care, or even seem aware she was still bleeding from her gunshot wound as it slowly closed over.

"See you at home," he told Alaric, cheekily giving him the middle finger again as he took off, leaving a vacuum of wind and a group of amused vampires in his wake.

His new agile speed and strength was exhilarating, and the ease with which he navigated the obstacles in the forest was invigorating.

Wasting no time, he reached the manor and raced upstairs for his bedroom, setting Abby's feet on the floor and clamping his mouth over hers. Without conscious thought, Alex ripped away the tattered, muddy remains of her top, leaving her satiny bra in place. It's soft padding pushing her breasts higher into a pair of pouty cushions. Alex moaned with mouth watering anticipation as he pushed her back toward his bed, giving his full attention to her wound.

The scent of her blood tormented his senses triggering a hunger so deep it was painful, as his desire for more than her body gnawed at his control. His tongue flicked out to lick away a rivulet of blood as it trickled from her shoulder, along the valley between her rounded breasts, as his fingers traced the swell of their upper curves. Alex watched, transfixed by the colour of her alabaster skin tone, mesmerised by the way her delicate muscles moved beneath, and marvelled at the smooth texture. Everything seemed new and wondrous with his heightened senses.

"You need to feed for that to heal faster," he growled. His tongue made another pass, this time over the wound itself. Alex shuddered from the euphoria of tasting Abby's blood. He had consumed her blood before, but now the flavour seemed to have changed into something inconceivably addictive. The sweet nectar on his tongue was the most incredible thing he had ever tasted. It was decadently rich, sweet as honey and as heady as the finest red wine. His body shook with unbearable need, his cock and fangs pulsed in unison, each desperate to sink as deeply into his *mate* as possible. The need was actually painful.

"No, I'm fine. Look."

Alex stared down at the ragged hole in her shoulder which was now almost closed. Her quick reflexes had saved her, but it could have ended so differently, he knew.

Alex captured her lips once again, consuming them as their limbs tangled and teased. Flames scorched her with every touch. The pulse of Abby's blood thrummed through his ears, its quick cadence beat in time to her ragged breaths, deep and fast.

"I want to lick every spot where I can see your pulse pounding, and I know where my favourite spot to feel that throbbing against my tongue is," he told her in a barely audible whisper as he lowered himself down her body, kissing a trail over her stomach, grinning with satisfaction at her reaction.

Abby gripped his hair and yanked his head back to meet the fire flashing in her eyes. "Not just yet," she told him as she flipped him over and reversed their positions. Alex hissed in a breath as she squeezed and stroked his heavy erection, inciting a riot within him even as he did the same to her. His satisfaction turned to frustration as Abby climbed off him and headed for the bathroom. "Shower first."

They were both covered from head to toe in mud and blood.

Alex conceded.

He watched Abby march lithely toward the bathroom. He loved the way her arse cheeks rolled and her hips swayed from side to side when she walked, like a panther on the prowl. A very sexy panther.

Taking his time following her, he listened as her remaining clothes hit the floor and the shower turned on. How he had waited for this. He'd dreamt of what it would be like to have Abby all to himself, to not compete with Ahriman for her affection and attention. To be the one to initiate and enjoy the blood bond with her without Ahriman freaking out in the background.

He was going to savour this. Draw it out and make it last. This was after all, their first time together having sex, alone....officially.

Abby watched Alex as he entered the bathroom. His body in movement was mesmerising, full of grace and power, and so effortless, he seemed to float. Watching him for those few seconds had taken her breath away.

He had taken to his new condition of an immortal vampire so naturally, it would be easy to believe he had been so for an eternity already.

Abby kept her back to him as he unfastened the clasp on his jeans and lowered the zipper, watching intently over her shoulder as he kicked away his pants. Her eyes widened at the sight of his powerful erection. The darkened head was engorged, the stalk thick and hard. Her mischievous smile had him hardening further with every second. It was the look of a woman with a plan, or a seductive secret. Either one was fine with him so long as he was included.

As much as Abby wanted to face him, to see him in his full glory, she refused to turn around as he entered the shower. Instead, she crossed her arms to cover her breasts protectively.

Stepping up behind her Alex groaned as he filled his hands with her bare arse. Her slender hips. Her silken thighs. "I've been waiting for this, baby," he whispered in her ear as his roaming hands explored her lower body thoroughly. "To have you all to myself. No more sharing you with Ahriman. You're *mine*, all *mine.*" One hand slid around to her stomach, his fingers brushing through the short curls at the apex of her thighs, gliding into the nectar laden slit in search of her throbbing clit. The other teased her tight little anal star. Abby moaned and pushed back against him until his hard, heavy erection rested firmly against her lower back, pulsing and twitching with lusty need.

Her wound had stopped bleeding and had virtually closed over but that didn't stop him from laving his tongue over it. The slow, sensual strokes combining with a light scraping of his fangs and heated breath, had Abby's blood almost to boiling point.

Wrapping an arm about her waist, he held her firmly against him as he continued his tactile exploration of her body, only to be restricted by the barrier of her crossed arms.

"Baby, what's wrong?"

His concern was met with silence.

They'd been over the situation about Ahriman before. Was she still worried that he would hold it against her? Did she still feel some sense of misplaced guilt?

"I liked what Ahriman did with me," she said sheepishly. "A lot."

A slow radiant smile lit his face as he shared with her his mental thoughts of how he had experienced it. He'd grown used to having Ahriman in his head every minute of every day. It was a relief to him now to have Abby filling his mind instead. Somehow, after sharing his body so completely with the evil bastard, he didn't think he would feel whole again without his blood bond to his *mate*. Where Ahriman had occupied his mind and body, Abby now filled his mind and soul. Oddly though, he had this nagging feeling that a part of him was missing, he just couldn't quite put his finger on what it was.

"If it wasn't for Ahriman controlling my body, it may have taken months, maybe even years before we discovered we both like our sex a little rougher."

"Don't get me wrong, I love the slow gentle sex too, but I..." she tried to cut in.

"No buts. I liked it every bit as much as you."

Relief seemed to unravel the pent-up tension inside her, her eyes glistening with moisture. "I'm so glad you said that because..."

Turning her in his arms, his iridescent eyes filled with confusion as he met her strangely shy but mischievous gaze. Slowly he peeled her arms away from her breasts, her nervousness increasing with every inch of revealed flesh beneath. Alex's eyes dropped to the cause of her tentative behaviour, his breath hitching in his throat.

"Fuck me dead!" he exclaimed.

Now he knew why he hadn't seen her the day before.

Abby giggled a nervous laugh at his shocked expression, his eyes practically bugging out of his head, glued to the shiny metal rings piercing her nipples.

Alex suddenly gripped the base of his cock, pinching it at the stem, clamping down hard on his balls. A sudden injection of blood to his already hard erection had his balls drawing up and contracting, catching him off guard in painful need. He was only a breath away from an explosive orgasm just from the sight of Abby's body piercings.

"When?....Where?....Oh, fuck that. Just let me at 'em."

Her mind swam with a million questions.

"You're not allowed to think right now, sweetheart," he growled gently. *"Turn off that enquiring mind of yours,"* he whispered into her thoughts.

A gratified smiled lit her flushed face, though her breath caught at the sensation of his tongue as it licked out, hooking the metal ring, tugging at it as his lips encompassed it, sucking it deep into his mouth. Alex wrapped his arms firmly around her, holding her close. His body was heated, hard, corded with strength and tense with demand against hers.

Hot water streamed over them, the steam mingling with their fevered breaths. Abby arched into him further with a groan of pleasure as his teeth bit down on her pierced nipple, trapping his thick stalk between their bodies making its presence known as it pulsed. She moaned and wriggled against him, desperate to feel his heavy erection pressing as firmly between her moist folds, as it was against her belly.

The sweet ache had her clenching, her body tightening against his as he bent his knees and angled his hips lower to grind his cock against her sensitive mound. Her clit swelled in response as she felt the moisture flowing from her heated channel.

"Please don't tease me," she begged.

Not willing to take his mouth from her delectable body for a second he answered her. *"What do you need, baby? Tell me what you want."*

"I want you inside me now," she whimpered, lifting her leg to hook it over his hip to angle his cock to where she desperately needed it to be.

He smiled, a wicked flash of brilliant white teeth and fangs, as he ran a finger through the luscious slit of her soft intimate folds. Abby's breath hitched, and her hips jerked into his touch further. Her gaze flicked to the heavy length of his cock, so close to where she needed him, and yet too far away.

"Please, now. I need you inside me, now," she pleaded breathlessly.

"I'm not going to last long, baby. You've got me so fucking horned up."

"I don't care. Just get that cock inside me now before I rip it off and use it as a dildo."

"Oh, baby. Such sweet words," he grinned, lifting her other leg up around his hips. Their eyes locked as he slid into her welcoming heat, impaling his heavy length deep inside her tight channel in one hard thrust. Alex froze as ecstasy combined with a sense of...rightness, bladed through him.

"Mine. You're my Mate," he told her, pacing his words in time with his thrusts.

"Always. There will never be anyone else but you," she promised.

With her back against the wall, water flowed between them, their bodies sliding freely against one another, cooling their skin even as the friction boiled their blood. Abby watched as Alex's eyes glittered more fiercely the closer he came to his climax, his fangs fully extended.

At the last moment, when she could feel his thrusts changing, becoming more desperate, intense, she gripped his face, pulling him down to the pulsing vein at her throat.

Instinct took over.

With one last powerful thrust, Alex buried his thick length deep to the hilt and his fangs buried themselves in her neck. His orgasm hit with such force, he imploded, exploded and drowned in a sea of ecstasy as a tidal wave of release washed over him with the violence of a riptide. Abby's inner flesh gripped and spasmed around his shuttling hard shaft. Abby screamed out his name as she felt herself suddenly hurtling through a blaze of rapture. Her tight channel clamping down on him as her own climax hit, milking him of the powerful jets of his seed as his mouth clamped onto her pulsing vein, drawing her crimson nectar down his throat.

Their climax seemed to have no end as time stood still. Locked together, body, mind and soul. There was no end to one or a beginning for the other. They were One.

Gently, Alex lowered Abby to the floor as his body convulsed with violent aftershocks of orgasm. As satiated as he was, his erection was unrelenting. He was going to love being a vampire. No limp dick after sex for him. Not any more. He could go another round right now, he thought to himself as Abby reached down to palm the heavy length.

"I can't get enough of you."

"I'm so glad you feel that way because now that we've got the hot, frantic sex out of the way, I want to give you your Christmas present," she told him.

"Christmas present? It's Christmas?" he asked perplexed. He had no idea.

"Nearly. It's Christmas day, the day after tomorrow, but I want to give you your present early." Anticipation mixed with a vulnerability she hadn't expected, backlighting his dark eyes. "Wait in here for five minutes, then come out," she ordered.

Abby quickly towelled off and left the room. Alex waited patiently, one-cat-and-dog, two-cat-and-dog....for five minutes. The suspense was killing him. What could she be planning to give him that took five minutes preparation?

"You can come out now," she called.

Alex opened the bathroom door. The light was dim, only small slivers of sunlight peeking through the tops of the curtains to radiate streaks of pale gold across the ceiling.

Once again he was grateful for his new eyesight.

Standing before him, Abby was decked out in a skin tight, candy apple red, leather lace up corset, its bustier so low her breasts perched high above, her nipples jutting forward. A leather collar fitted firmly about her slender neck with chains attaching to her nipple rings, matching crotchless knickers, fishnet stockings and a pair of patent leather, red high heel shoes finished off her ensemble. All in all, Abby looked like a Christmas tree. A very, very naughty Christmas tree that he wanted to do very naughty things to.

Alex shaft rose once again to full tensile strength, tenting the towel about his waist, and his fangs descended at the sight of his Christmas present standing before him.

"Merry Christmas," her voice was low and husky.

In two long strides he was in front of her, his eyes never leaving her incredible body, circling her, he feasted on every visual inch of her.

"You like?"

He could only growl in response, leaning down to kiss her lips possessively, greedily.

"I'll take that as a yes," she giggled, feeling empowered. "I also got you these," she grinned, spinning a pair of spiked handcuffs around on the end of her finger. In the other hand she held a butt plug. His eyes lit up and all she could think about was licking this very sexy vampire's candy cane as it stood rigidly to attention under her hungry gaze.

Mine! All mine!

Alex couldn't keep his hands off her for one more second. Once again, his hands, lips, teeth and tongue explored the textures and contours of her body in her scrumptious outfit.

"I feel so unprepared. I have no idea what to get you," he stuttered, so star struck by the ravishing beauty before him, he could barely dredge up the mental capacity to speak.

Abby's face turned bashful once more, swallowing hard on the knot in her throat. Butterflies fluttered in her stomach, but she was determined to tell him what she wanted. "There is one thing I'd like for Christmas," she told him sheepishly.

"Anything baby, just name it. I'd collect the moon and stars for you if you asked me."

"It's nothing that dramatic," she chuckled wistfully.

Alex waited in suspense wondering what it was that made her suddenly shy again. Maybe she wanted a spreader bar or maybe arm binding restraints to go with that outfit, or maybe a suspension sex swing, he thought with a shiver of delight. He'd definitely be in for that.

"Marry me?" she asked.

"What?"

"Say you'll marry me. That would be the best present you could ever give me."

"Yes."

It took almost as long for Abby to process the fact he'd just said yes, as it did for Alex to realise that her asking him to marry her wasn't an auditory hallucination.

"Yes," he repeated. "Just name the date, today if you want. Yes, yes, yes!"

The elated smile that lit her face, captured and enchanted him. He was going to spend eternity with this magnificent woman.

He couldn't wait.

Abby rushed to lavish him with hugs and kisses, giggling all the while with happiness. When she reached to remove his towel, to render him completely naked, Alex pulled away with a mock scowl. "If you don't mind, I'd like to unwrap my present first."

And he did. He took his time unwrapping Abby from her very naughty outfit, removing everything but the collar and chains attached to her nipple rings. He found they came in very handy, along with the handcuffs.

Once again, he explored her body, only this time much more slowly and thoroughly.

297

The butt plug, as he discovered, gave his own sexual experience a new layer of enjoyment as he fucked her tight anal channel.

He was definitely going to enjoy eternity with this magnificent woman.

His *Mate*.

29

The ding of the bell alerted Teagan to a new customer entering the café. It had been a long day and it seemed it was going to be an even longer night. She had been exhausted from the effort it took to perform the ward on the manor that morning, but that didn't give her an excuse to take yet another day off work. She'd had more than a week away already and unfortunately her boss, Orlof, didn't share the good will of most people during the Christmas holiday season. Unless of course it benefited him in some way, which it didn't. Teagan was sure the character of Ebenezer Scrooge was modeled after Orlof.

Which, in short, meant that Teagan's job was hanging by a tentative thread. It was either work tonight, or else…. It didn't take much to fill in the 'or else' part.

Pasting on a cheery smile she turned from the table she had begun clearing to welcome the new customer. Her breath caught in her chest and her heart skipped a beat when she realised who it was. His panty melting smile almost undid her.

"Saladin, what are you doing here?" Teagan asked, flustered. She shot a quick glance over her shoulder, making sure Orlof hadn't noticed her talking to someone who obviously wasn't a paying customer. Fortunately, the crashing of pots and pans in the kitchen seemed to have him preoccupied.

Orlof was unpleasant at the best of times, but when his waitresses slacked off by socialising on 'his time', he became a real arsehole. At the very least he would dock her pay for every minute she spoke with

Saladin. Orlof wasn't happy unless he was making someone else miserable. Regardless, Teagan still continued to work for him. What choice did she have? None. There weren't any other night jobs around, except in the nightclubs, and that really wasn't her scene. Too much noise and too many lecherous drunks.

Meg's Café had a high turn-over of waitresses, the hangers-on were all like her, desperate Uni students who couldn't afford to be out of work.

"I had to see you," Saladin told her, keeping his voice low.

"This is not the time or the place. Can't you see I'm working?" she berated in a whisper, steeling another quick look over her shoulder toward the kitchen.

For a moment Teagan continued to clean-up, almost frantically, as though finishing would get her out of this conversation. Saladin settled into the booth she was cleaning and crossed his arms over his chest and his feet at the ankles, a silent message that said he wasn't going anywhere until he got what he wanted.

"I apologise for my unannounced visit, but I haven't been able to speak with you since your grandfather showed up." Plucking the menu from the next table, he opened it to mindlessly flick through the plastic coated pages.

"Yes, well, he has my best interests at heart, even if he is a little too over protective," she answered defensively, although Saladin detected a hint of annoyance in her tone that for once, wasn't directed at him. Saladin kept that observation to himself. Whatever came out of his mouth about the old codger most likely wouldn't win him any brownie points with Teagan. As far as he was concerned, Richard was an aggravating old timer who had an over inflated sense of self-importance and an overbearing need to control his granddaughters lives. It really grated his gonads that Teagan seemed reluctant to stand up to him.

From outside appearances, Richard seemed to be the perfect doting grandfather, but Saladin wasn't born yesterday. Going by Teagan and her sisters behaviour around him, he suspected their grandfather ruled with an iron fist. The old druid maybe powerful with impressive bloodlines, but Saladin wasn't charmed by the man nearly as much as everyone else appeared to be.

Saladin had waited for two days for a chance to get Teagan alone, unsuccessfully. After they had finished the spell on the new ward on the manor earlier that morning, he had hoped Richard would leave, which he did, but unfortunately he didn't leave alone. Leaving Kaitlin at the manor as a private nurse to help care for the unconscious Raif, Richard decided to travel to London with Paige, insisting on delivering Teagan home himself along the way.

With his club only a block away from the café, the temptation to walk down to see her was too much.

"I really can't talk now. What do you want? I doubt you've come to sample the poison Orlof serves up," she commented as he continued to flick absently through the menu, her voice dipping low to avoid catching Orlof's attention.

"I wanted to congratulate you on your work on the ward," he answered. "And,...I,...I couldn't go another day without seeing you," he confessed, finishing in a rush, his anxious eyes eagerly searching hers for a glimmer of reciprocation. For a moment her eyes lit with joy and his heart skipped a beat, but almost as quickly she shuttered her emotions, her brow furrowing into a suspicious scowl.

"Is that because I turned you down, repeatedly, and you can't let a conquest get away?"

He had to admit that had been her initial appeal. But now,...she meant so much more. Did he dare tell her how he really felt? Could he even explain it since he was only beginning to understand himself?

The one thing Saladin knew for certain. He would need to lay all his cards on the table, if he had any chance of convincing her how serious he was about her. She had changed him on a fundamental level. He needed her like he'd never needed anyone or anything in his very long life.

Her fears of his womanising ways were well founded. Getting past those fears may prove to be difficult, but he was determined to show her he had changed.

While he was still human, he'd had several wives, simultaneously in fact. It was expected of him as a Muslim ruler in the twelfth century. Each wife had been hand-picked by his family and advisers for political purposes, but he never loved any of them. He had never felt an inkling of emotion toward any woman, although he had made chasing women into a kind of sport, like hunting. A new prey every day, none of whom he ever bothered to take the time to learn their names.

Until Teagan.

"No," he growled quietly, trying to keep his voice low too. "I would never degrade you by comparing you to the women of my past."

And, they really were in is past now. He had no interest in any other woman but Teagan, he doubted he ever would again. But how did he convince her of that?

Mine!

Rising to his feet he towered over her, cupping her face in his hands, he dipped his head and kissed her with seductive gentleness.

And he kissed her.

And kissed her some more, until he'd thoroughly scrambled her brain to anything beyond the way he tasted and the sexy sounds he made as his mouth dominated hers.

Then pulled back a fraction and bit her lower lip.

She stared up at him, her lips parted, her breathing rough and fast. Then she licked her lips. A slow, wet swipe of her tongue almost brought him undone.

Fire arced from nerve ending to nerve ending in Saladin's body as he pulled her closer to him, his lips devouring hers. He couldn't get enough. Her sweet taste and heated passion was eating him alive.

"God, Teagan, I *need* you." His voice was raw and husky, his eyes blazed with the honesty of his statement.

Her head fell back as pleasure bloomed inside her. Energy zinged from every point their bodies touched. Every instinct screamed at her to give herself over to him, take everything he was offering.

"Come to the club when you finish tonight. Please?"

His voice was a whisper, his words a plea. And they melted her like butter.

"You're going to get me fired," she chastised breathlessly. "Oh, crap. You're *really* going to get me fired. I can't lose this job," she said, her voice rising with the distress of seeing Orlof scowling at them, checking his watch to count the number of seconds he could dock from her pay.

"The obnoxious swine wouldn't dare," he growled protectively, as he locked eyes with the offensive café owner behind the servery counter in the kitchen.

"Stay here. I want a quiet word with your boss," he appealed, a mischievous glint in his eye.

"What are you going to do? You better not do anything that'll get me fired." Teagan planted her hands on her hips, her stern expression promising him severe retribution.

Fortunately for Orlof, Saladin's mission tonight was to win Teagan's heart, not her wrath.

"Have a little faith," he grinned.

Teagan huffed and muttered beneath her breath as she made of show of cleaning the table before her, which she had already cleaned. Doing her best to listen into whatever Saladin was telling her boss, unsuccessfully. The man was annoying most of the time, infuriating some of the time and unfortunately for her, adoringly addictive all of the time. She knew he was bad for her, just like chocolate. And, just like chocolate, she couldn't get enough.

"What did you just say to him?" she asked sceptically when Saladin returned a moment later.

"I just gave him a little pep talk, a word of encouragement to treat you nicely," he replied with a cheesy grin. Quite pleased with himself. He'd have to get video footage of the outcome, he thought with sadistic pleasure. Or, maybe he'd just play fly on the wall and hang around for a few minutes and watch for himself.

Much better idea.

"Well, my beautiful jewel, shall I see you later?" Saladin took her hand in his, her delicate fingers so warm and soft. Bowing a little, he lifted them to his lips for a lingering kiss, his sapphire blue eyes never leaving hers for a moment.

"Please?" he implored softly. Teagan's breath hitched in her throat at the look in his eyes, uncertainty mixed with hope and adoration. Was it her imagination, or had his voice held a slight tremor in it? His expression was open and honest, lowering his protective barricade around his heart and allowing her to see the man behind the façade of confident arrogance.

"Yes. Okay," she nodded timidly. Her pulse fluttered with the elation of hope.

Saladin's face lit up with delight.

He had two hours to prepare something amazing enough to win her over.

A wisp of hair had escaped her ponytail, falling forward across her cheeks. Saladin reached out to brush it back. Any excuse to touch her.

Teagan couldn't help but reward him with a shy smile. Nor could she keep herself from staring after him as he passed by the window as he left, he was fluid in motion and seduction on two legs.

There was no way she could deny even to herself, that she wanted to see him tonight.

Standing just beyond the light of the café windows, Saladin watched and waited, knowing that Orlof couldn't help himself. He was just itching for Saladin to leave so he could berate and verbally abuse Teagan. He couldn't hear the words, but his actions were very entertaining.

Orlof snapped at Teagan. A second later he slapped himself in the face. A shocked expression lit his eyes, his mouth dropping open in surprise. Quickly he rubbed away the sting. Teagan stared at him as if he'd just grown a second head, a look of amusement tipping the corners of her lips up. Quickly recovering from his bout of Tourette syndrome, he snapped at Teagan again with another tirade of degrading insults, shaking his clenched fist menacingly before her. A moment later, that same fist made a quick detour, punching himself in the jaw.

Orlof screamed and stared at his hand in disbelief, quickly crossing himself with the sign of the crucifix. A desperate gesture since he was about as religious as a Las Vegas nightclub.

"I'm possessed," he cried as he ran into the kitchen.

Teagan couldn't help but laugh. Her eyes wandered to the darkness outside the window to where she suspected Saladin was watching with great satisfaction.

She should get Saladin to pay her a visit more often. Working for Orlof might actually become tolerable.

Yes, she was definitely paying Saladin a visit tonight and maybe she wouldn't be going home afterwards, she thought with a flutter of nervous anticipation.

Saladin stared at the cozy nest of cushions, precisely arranged on the plush sofa in a private nook of the VIP room, well pleased with the romantic setting he had created.

When Teagan left the club tonight, it would be with him, as it would be every night after this one, he reassured himself.

"Ahh hmm..." Dray cleared his throat to get his attention. Saladin's mood took a sudden dip at the sight of the man standing behind his head of security.

"Richard. What a pleasant surprise," he offered with a false smile.

"Skip the insincere pleasantries," the old druid said, his eyes narrowing on the cozy setting before him, knowing all too well it had been prepared to impress his granddaughter. "I'm here to let you know that Teagan is off limits to you, vampire. You can never have her."

Saladin's fierce presence filled the space between them threateningly, his eyes flashing with the glitter of his fury.

"You don't control Teagan, *old man*, and even if you did, your human years are almost over. If you're not careful, I'll help you find eternal peace that much earlier," Saladin growled.

Richard didn't bat an eyelid at the threat. "You could try," he countered, staring Saladin down. "But, if you truly care for Teagan, as I suspect you do, then wanting me dead is the last thing you should wish for."

Saladin examined the man carefully, suspiciously. "What exactly do you mean old man, and make your explanation fast, my patience with you is wearing thin."

"When I die, Teagan will inherit our family's curse, she is the oldest of her sisters and the next in our bloodline. She will be responsible for protecting Morganna le Fey's immortality spell. At present the sorceress is hunting for me, not Teagan. As you know, Morganna is one of the most powerful magic users of all time, certainly the most powerful rephaim, and she desperately wants her spell back."

Immortality spell? That was interesting.

"If she gets it, she would become unstoppable," Richard emphasised slowly, letting the gravity of the situation sink in.

"She wasn't strong enough to defeat Merlin, a human druid," Saladin pointed out.

"She wasn't given a chance to use her immortality spell, and Merlin didn't defeat her on his own. It took the collective of druids, nephilim and even Alaric, to defeat her last time. She is stronger now and she is ageing, which means she's more determined than ever to get her immortality spell back, and her grimoire."

"But she *was* defeated. We can defeat her again. I assure you old man, I would never let Morganna get her hands on Teagan. I would rather die first."

"You see, there's the problem. You won't die. You won't age. But Teagan will. *That. Is. Our. Curse,*" he emphasised slowly.

Saladin struggled against the sensation he was standing in quicksand. "What the hell do you mean, exactly? You're not making any sense." His temper thinned to a tentative thread with every word the old druid spoke, taking him a step closer to the precipice of a dark abyss ready to swallow him.

"Morganna le Fey's immortality spell was hidden from her. When she was banished back to Fey her grimoire and her spell were kept here on Earth where she couldn't reach them. Her grimoire is well protected in Alaric's store room, and the spell has been protected by my family. Merlin was the first. I am the current protector, although when I die, it is Teagan's destiny to inherit not only the power of our ancestry," he pointed to the thick gold ring with a ruby set at its centre. "She will also inherit within her, the curse of carrying Morganna's immortality spell. She cannot become a vampire, and she cannot mate with a lycan, wyvern or nephilim and live to the age of her *mate*. If she tries, it will kill her. Part of protecting the immortality spell means that no one person can carry it for longer than a normal human lifetime, making it harder for Morganna to find the carrier, if she ever managed to escape her prison. If the druid dies of natural causes, the curse will pass to the next druid in our bloodline. If Morganna kills the carrier, she will regain her spell and can make herself immortal."

"What if I make Teagan into a vampire before you die, surely she can overcome the curse and live a vampire's life with me?"

"My dear boy, I admire your devotion to my granddaughter, but what you suggest is not possible. If she is already a vampire, the

306

moment she inherits the curse, she will die, and the curse will then go to the next sister in line, Kaitlyn."

Pity flashed in the old man's eyes, and wasn't that just the icing on his shit cake.

"Then we'll just find a way to use Morganna's immortality spell on Teagan instead."

"If there was a way to do that, don't you think it would have already been done?" Richard didn't want to mention that Morganna had used the spell on someone else once. Her lover, Marek. Nor was he going to mention that Morganna had bound Marek's soul to an artefact. Her lover would never age and could not be killed unless this artefact was first found and destroyed. Like Morganna, Marek had been banished to the Valley of Vardin in Fey and the artefact his soul had been bound to was hidden from him by other druids here on Earth. Richard had spent the past year searching for the artefact in the hope of finding clues to releasing his family from the curse. His efforts now would need to be doubled if he had any chance of succeeding. With Morganna hunting him, time was growing short.

"I can't protect my granddaughters forever but if you truly care for Teagan, break off your attachment now before it's too late, for both your sake."

Saladin stared in silence, his mind in a dilemma as he sifted through the information. Numbly he sank onto the couch, staring blankly at the rose petals scattered on the table around the chilling bottle of champagne and glasses glinting in the candle light.

"Sucks to be you," Dray sympathised as he watched the back of the druid disappear through the nightclub's exit. What else could he say? Emotional stuff wasn't really his strong point. Man, there were days you just wished you didn't get out of bed and this was one of them.

Saladin's world had just shattered into a million pieces.

What was he going to do?

Saladin paced back and forth through the club's VIP lounge, staring at the romantic setting he'd created in his private booth.

He could lie and tell Teagan that he didn't want her, that she meant nothing to him.

He could carry on with his plans for the evening, confess to her what she meant to him and pledge himself to her forever,...for however long that might be.

But how could he tell her how he felt, knowing his declaration could end up causing her more pain. Knowing that his love for her conflicted with her family curse, confining her to a short human life span. He would remain forever young, while she would be forced to watch herself grow older and eventually die.

Saladin frowned, a sudden sharp pain tore at his chest at the thought of losing her as his internal struggle continued between his conscience and his heart.

If he severed his ties with her now, her pain of unrequited love would be temporary, as opposed to a lifetime of emotional turmoil and regret by his side.

He could be selfish and pretend to want her just for casual, uncomplicated sex. After all, that's what he had done with all those other women in his sordid past. It should be easy to do the same with her. At least that way he could still keep her in his periphery.

Closing the door to Meg's café, Teagan turned in the direction of the Phoenix nightclub. Seeing the long queue of hopeful patrons outside she was tempted to turn around and run, far, far away, as her nerves began to sway her toward rational thought.

Saladin was more dangerous to her than any other man ever could be. She already felt a deep connection to him, more than she ever had for any other man and it terrified her.

It terrified her that her feelings for him were likely to deepen even further if she gave into his advances and her lusty body.

It also terrified her that she might lose these feelings and never find anyone else to share them with again.

Teagan craved his touch, drowned in his scent and on a level she couldn't fully fathom, she needed him. He filled a void inside her soul and made her feel whole.

She had to see him. She needed to resolve this once and for all.

Forcing breath into her lungs she willed her feet to take the first step forward.

Bypassing the cue, Teagan made her way to the barrier rope where Hawke awaited her. His steady, emotionless gaze following her every move as she approached.

"Teagan," he said, dipping his head slightly in greeting and removing the rope to let her pass.

Inside the club, Dray's Comm link announced her arrival.

Saladin's frantic pacing ceased as he realised his time had run out. There was no more time to debate his decision.

He had to do what was right for Teagan.

Walking a few paces from his private corner, Saladin approached another vampire's secluded lounge. "I need to borrow your dinner for a few minutes," he said, reaching down he grabbed the woman by the wrist. She was perfect for his cause. Her glazed eyes and the fresh puncture wounds to her neck still oozed their crimson nectar.

Dragging her to his private lounge, he draped her suggestively across his lap, wrapping a hand about her waist, the other along her inner thigh.

Saladin shuddered. Her touched repulsed him, burned him.

But this was all about appearances, for Teagan's benefit.

Teagan crossed the floor, a coy smile radiated her beautiful features, a glimmer of tentative hope lighting her bright eyes as she searched the darkened room for the dark haired vampire who pulled on her heart strings, overriding every thought except the one that compelled her forward.

Saladin watched her approach.

His entire body lit up at the sight of her, every nerve ending tingled and itched to touch her, to hold her.

He didn't need to make love to her to sense the powerful bond that had been growing steadily between them. But suddenly, that's all he wanted to do. To mark her, cover her with his scent.

Make her his for eternity.

Oh, God. He couldn't go through with his plan to drive her away. He needed her.

As he moved to displace the nameless woman from his knee, Teagan's eyes found him.

The colour drained from her face, her smile fading as her jaw fell open. Coming to an abrupt halt in front of him, Teagan's body stiffened, the tentative hope in her eyes dying. Betrayal and disappointment filled her as she glared down at him, stung by his blatant philandering.

Teagan fought to breathe normally, to still the hard, furious beat of her heart.

Something broke in her chest. A hollow centre of hope that she had begun to nurture. Dark, vivid dreams of Saladin holding her, touching her in love and gentleness, taking away the ache, the lonely core of misery that seemed to fill her. She felt it all shatter, and in its place a hard, cold core of fury replaced it.

"I guess I made a mistake. I can see you will never change," she said, fighting not to scream, to keep her voice calm, even, despite the tremble in it. She clenched her fists tight to keep from smacking the guilty look off his face. "Have a nice life, Yusuf Saladin."

Turning on her heels, her head held high, Teagan left without letting him see her face. She was going to leave with her dignity intact and tears didn't serve any purpose at this point. Her body shook with the effort to walk away calmly from him, to not break into a run and escape as fast as she could. Why was it that the ground never opened up to swallow you when you wanted it to? She thought dismally.

Saladin pushed the woman away from him roughly, back into the arms of the vampire he had borrowed her from. His eyes followed Teagan's every step, etching her into his memory with the burn of a branding iron.

"Fuck!" he cursed. Pain and fury shot through him like a knife, his heart breaking alongside hers, leaving an abyss in his soul.

It was the right thing to do.

He had to do it.

He had to keep telling himself that, needed to believe it, or he would go insane from the grief of losing her.

His *Mate*.

The grounds of the manor were landscaped to within an inch of its life, manicured to perfection and completely orderly. It resembled nothing like what it was four months earlier, after Alaric's epic battle with Ahriman, which decimated the gardens behind him.

The new landscaping contractors had done wonders with the damaged grounds, transforming them into a new and improved version of what had existed before, only the trees were much smaller.

Saladin performed his duty as Alaric's best man with style and grace, but he was oblivious to the happy couples on their most special day. The double wedding, Alaric and Cassie, who was now five months pregnant and proudly showing off her baby bump, and Alex and Abby. As the happy couples socialised and danced their way through the perfect spring evening, Saladin wallowed in a silent pit of misery.

Happy couples seemed to surround him. Besides the brides and grooms, Teagan's sister, Kaitlyn had become mated to Raif, undoing the spell which had struck him during Alex and Abby's rescue at the compound.

He hovered on the outskirts of the party, avoiding contact with Teagan at all costs, but he watched her covetously every moment.

As the party dissolved in the wee hours of the morning, Saladin watched Teagan farewell the guests.

Saladin refused to look back at the happy couples as they left the manor for their respective honeymoons. Anger and need rode him hard, arousal was a steady beat of blood in his cock, tormenting and torturing him.

She was so near, and yet so far away from him.

Gustav, lingered until the end, appearing almost reluctant to leave. He had spent the majority of the evening with Teagan and her sisters, singling out Teagan in particular, laughing and joking with her. His eyes too, constantly followed her every movement.

Gustav studied her carefully, betraying his affection he thought was so carefully hidden.

Saladin's body tensed with seething jealousy.

He had done the right thing, driving her away. He knew he had. But the pain of knowing she would never be his was tearing him apart.

She was his *mate*.

For him there would never be another.

The thought of another man touching her, loving her, was more than he could bear.

What could he do though?

Nothing.

He could only continue to pretend, as he had been for the past four months, that his life hadn't changed.

Keeping up appearances wasn't too hard.

Most of the time.

Who was he kidding? He was so totally screwed.

WAKING THE ETERNAL DRAGON

(Short Story)

Waking The Eternal Dragon

Kaitlyn approached the bed where Raif lay, still in his comatose state.

He was movie star material. His bronzed skin stretched over a heavily muscled frame, well proportioned for his tall height of seven feet, filling most of the supersized bed. His shoulder-length dark auburn hair fell loosely around his handsome face, graced by his strong cheekbones and masculine nose, and enhanced by sensually full lips, parted enticingly by the barest margin in his slumbering state. Every feature blended to make him highly seductive, she thought wistfully.

If only….

She couldn't finish that ridiculous thought.

Mine, a small voice in the back of her mind whispered.

Her heart began to beat wildly in her chest the closer she came to him, sloshing the warm water about in the basin she carried. This was the best part of her day.

His sponge bath.

For eight weeks she had cared for him, watching and waiting to see if there would be any change in his condition. She was after all the logical choice for the job. She was a druid, familiar with this strange supernatural world that others thought were mere fantasy. And, she was a nurse.

Over the past weeks they had tried everything they could think of to heal him, although they were hampered by the fact that they had no idea what exactly had been done to him.

The sorceress, Morganna, had cast a spell, intended for her grandfather, Richard. Instead, it had struck Raif when he attempted to

315

protect the old man. The spell had been designed to kill a human and trap his soul. It did not have the same effect on the wyvern, a dragon.

Druid magic had no effect, and Raif's sister's special healing ability and even modern drugs fared no better. Electric shock therapy, compliments of Alex, didn't even rouse a single twitch from his motionless body.

They had hoped to find a cure in Morganna's grimoire which gathered dust in their storage room, but as they discovered, not one of them could read it. Morganna had placed a spell on it, so the reader would only see the text written in a language unfamiliar to them. Where one person saw French, another perceived it as ancient Sumerian cuneiform, and for someone else it was in Chinese. The book was useless to them.

As the days turned into weeks his family's vigil by his side gradually decreased. They had their own lives to live and a kingdom in Fey to run in his absence. His sister had stayed behind but only visited him briefly a couple of times a day. All the while it was her, Kaitlyn, who stayed by his side. As the visitors began to dwindle, Kaitlyn's time with him increased. It didn't take long before she craved the time she spent alone with him. Each day she remained longer and longer by his side, drawn to him. She was quickly becoming obsessed with an irrational need to be increasingly nearer to him, as though she was a compass and he was magnetic north.

At first, she only sat by his side reading to him and telling him stories of her childhood, laying a fleeting touch on his hand or face, a lingering caress along his arm. It was her belief that part of a comatose patient's brain still registered physical touch and a soothing voice. It was essential that they not feel completely isolated in their non-functioning body, and by reading and touching them it gave that part of their mind which was still conscious, something to focus on. So, she persisted.

That is what she told herself, but deep down she knew her need to touch him stemmed from something far more primal within her.

The more she touched him, the more she craved him. Sponge baths became a daily occurrence, her guilt-free excuse to touch more of him and justify her illogical compulsion to caress every delectable bulge and crevice. Softly, slowly…thoroughly from head to toe, encompassing everything in between.

But still he lay motionless.

Raif listened to her approach with anticipatory excitement, the soft tapping of her strapless sandals on the timber floors announcing her approach. However, he caught her scent long before. A delectable fragrance of honeysuckle always preceded her.

His dragon once again stirred.

The dragon inside him was the physical manifestation of his soul, an essential part of who he was. Man and beast were so intertwined that one could not function without the other, which is how he had found himself in his current dilemma.

Although Morganna's spell did not kill him, it did succeed in separating the man from his beast, trapping that primal part of him in a purgatory of her design. A hex induced sleep left the man conscious, fully aware of everything around him, but unable to respond, his dragon having receded into enforced hibernation.

At least, that had been the case, until Kaitlyn.

Every day she came, and he looked forward to every minute. The nights were the hardest to bear, trapped inside his body with only the sound of his own breathing for company. Without Kaitlyn's constant presence and touch, his dragon fell more deeply back into its uneasy slumber.

There was no doubt in his mind that Kaitlyn wasn't just any female. Not to him.

She was his *mate*.

His dragon only responded to her. *He* only responded to her.

He remembered her clearly from their meeting at Brian Harlow's funeral a couple of months earlier. Even then he was mesmerised by her instantly. Her scent teased him, her beguiling grey eyes revealed her gentle nature, while her athletic body, curvy but strong held him awestruck. He was drawn to her like a moth to a flame. He'd wanted to touch her then, hold her, explore her body with more than just his imagination, but duty had gotten in the way.

Kaitlyn approached the bed, placing the basin of water on the table beside it. Her hands began to shake as she wrung out the cloth, steam rising from it in the cool air.

And then came that urge again. The one she couldn't quite define.

317

Over the weeks that strange urge had grown more and more intense, from merely feeling the need to touch him, to wanting to snuggle up next to him, to wanting to crawl inside his skin.

Kaitlyn drew in a sharp breath, desire curling stridently through her entire body and soul.

She was determined to keep her emotions under control. He was her patient, she was his nurse, she reminded herself sternly, taking another deep breath to steady herself. Her eyes however kept straying to all that glorious muscle exposed above the sheet and lower to what was hidden below it. A flaccid bulge between his thighs was clearly outlined.

She was his nurse, she justified quickly. It was her job to take care of him and to do that she had to see every inch of him.

Alright, maybe if push came to shove she would admit she had indulged in more than mere professional peeks. Maybe she had ogled him once or twice, perhaps gawked. Occasionally drooled.

It was okay to look, just not touch, right?

Except when she was bathing him. There was a very good chance Raif was the cleanest comatose patient on the planet.

But, suddenly that's all she wanted to do, run her hands all over his magnificent body, rub his scent all over hers, lick every inch of him from head to toe. Who needed a wash cloth when you had a tongue.

Kaitlyn's heart raced, her breathing became fast and shallow. Squeezing the excess water from the cloth her hand began shaking more fiercely. The need to touch him was overwhelming. Taking a deep breath Kaitlyn stilled herself before laying the cloth on his forehead, stroking it across his wide brow. The temptation was so strong she couldn't resist gliding her fingertips smoothly over his warm skin in the cloth's wake, tracing a finger over his brow, marvelling at his thick dark eyebrows, outlining their dark arches curiously. Her touch drifted over his well-defined cheekbones and along his firm, square chin.

Kaitlyn sponged his rugged face, his rough whiskers tickled her soft fingers. Her strokes with the cloth became bolder as she moved over his chest. He was all ridges and hollows, the thick bulk of his hard-used muscles beneath the flow of smooth skin.

Goosebumps appeared over his chest.

Kaitlyn paused, stunned by the occurrence. It was the first time his body had responded physically to anything. Reflexively, she touched the

318

small bumps over his chest, brushing her fingers lightly over his small male nipples. They hardened under her touch.

She was torn. Did she run and find someone to share this milestone with, or did she continue her exploration and see if she can elicit any further response?

Logic told her to find his sister but her feet weren't moving…yet her hands were.

Pulling back the sheet, she once again ogled the length of his magnificent body. His flaccid penis hung low between his thighs, larger than other men's she had seen, not that she had seen many. She was twenty-one years old and had only had two boyfriends in her life. Her over protective grandfather had seen to that.

Carefully, Kaitlyn spread his legs apart a little further as she sponged his inner thighs. Her fingers lifted his penis aside delicately, laying it on his abdomen so she could reach the space beneath, the sensitive strip behind his balls.

The heavy length began to swell.

Kaitlyn touched it tentatively with the tip of a finger to make sure it wasn't her imagination.

It swelled further before her eyes.

Kaitlyn stared, motionless, stunned excitement pulsing through her as he responded to her touch. And, it was her touch that was affecting him, she was certain of it.

Testing her theory, she skirted around the base of his thickening shaft with her cloth, her fingers edging closer with every slow pass of her hand.

Raif thought he would lose his mind before she touched him. Even through the cloth he could feel the heat of her hands gliding over his body, over his stomach, between his legs and…Holy hellhounds!

Suddenly the cloth slipped from her grip, falling onto the bed beside him, but her fingers remained touching him tentatively, so light he thought for a moment he was imagining it. Slowly she began to stroke the base of his cock, skimming her nails through the short dark curls at its base.

Kaitlyn watched as his heavy length continued to grow and harden. She couldn't look away, nor could she convince herself to stop her light, stroking ministrations on him. She was mesmerised by the feel of him,

319

the silky smooth outer skin covering solid steel. She suspected Raif would be large, considering his overall body size, but he wasn't just large…he was huge.

Kaitlyn could feel the silky slide of her juices moisten the throbbing folds between her thighs as her fingers continued to trace the length of the pulsing vein from its base to the flushed head, which was now a deep shade of pink. It throbbed and twitched in her hand.

Somewhere in the recesses of her mind she knew she should stop, but she couldn't. At some unknown point, her brain had detached from her body and now seemed to operate of its own accord.

The need to touch him was too strong to fight.

Raif inwardly groaned. With every touch she granted him, the more desperate he was to have it continue.

The beast within him continued to stir, closer to the surface than it had been for two months.

More. He needed more. He needed Kaitlyn's hands over all of him at once. He needed her full rosy lips wrapped around his cock, licking and sucking him into the moist depths of her hot little mouth.

Just thinking those erotic thoughts sent his arousal skyrocketing. His blood heated and burned in his veins. Silently he begged her to come nearer, to explore his body further, play with him, tease him, bring him the release he was desperate to find, preferably deep within her body.

As if his will were guiding her, Kaitlyn's fingers slipped beneath his balls, cupping them as she stroked the sensitive strip of flesh there, dragging them up, her nails grated lightly over the heavy sac before rolling them slowly between her fingers.

His fingers twitched.

Kaitlyn didn't notice. Her eyes were locked onto the bead of moisture emerging at the tip of his erection.

Kaitlyn couldn't stop herself from running her finger over the smooth weeping head, through the bead begging for her attention. Smooth and slippery. Her mouth watered. What would it be like to taste it? Warm, salty?

Kaitlyn dipped her head, his musky scent filled her nose as her tongue flicked out to lick away the bead. Her need intensified tenfold. Where before she felt like she was losing her mind from obsessing over him, now she felt like she would lose her mind if she wasn't possessed by him. The need was so strong to get closer to him, if she could crawl inside his skin, she would have. Her head felt light. His scent tempted her, his taste intoxicated her to point of torment.

Raif's fingers twitched again by his side, but still she didn't notice. She was completely lost in her exploration of his hard body as she took another swipe with her tongue over the head of his steely erection.

Kaitlyn's lips enclosed the tip, slowly, very slowly sliding down until the entire head was engulfed, wet heat sucking him deeper. Her lips tightened around him, stroking him with her tongue, lashing against it and stimulating nerve endings that sent his senses racing. She was pushing him to the brink of madness.

Raif's hands and toes curled in appreciation of her assertive attention as her tongue stroked the underside of his cock with slow, swirly licks, sucking on the mushroomed head, her mouth moving back and forth, forcing his hard length in and out of the snug grip of her lips and hands with tender force.

His dragon was almost fully awake now, finally, and Raif's body was beginning to move.

Kaitlyn moaned with delight, oblivious to everything but the feel of his cock pulsing and flexing in her grasp, as she feasted on his spicy taste coating her tongue.

Nothing could possibly be this good.

And be legal.

A stab of reality struck her.

With more effort that it should have taken, Kaitlyn released him from her hungry mouth. This wasn't legal, she realised with a horror filled gasp. She had crossed an ethical and moral boundary. He was a forbidden temptation she shouldn't have touched.

She was his nurse.

But she couldn't ignore that she was drawn to him in a way she would never have believed possible.

Raif's dragon fought to regain consciousness, lured back from the dark abyss by the maelstrom of sensation ravaging Raif's mind and body. Kaitlyn's touch, her moist mouth, hot breath and aroused scent acting as an anchor. Disoriented and barely lucid, it clawed its way back.

A growl tore from Raif's chest.

321

With lightening speed Raif grabbed Kaitlyn pulling her onto the bed, covering her with his much larger body. He simply relished the sight of her stretched across its sheets beneath him.

How many days, weeks had he tortured himself with this precise image?

This was far better than any fantasy.

Kaitlyn's dark hair spread about her with wild abandon, her pale face flushed with need and shock.

Guilt, fear and overwhelming lustful hunger raged against one another within her.

Raif growled again, scenting the arousal that rolled off her in waves. She was even more beautiful than he remembered.

"You're awake. Oh, God. I'm so sorry. I don't know what came over me. I shouldn't have done that. I'm really sorry," she croaked, her eyes wide with surprise and fear. She mistook the hunger in his growl for anger.

But it was his eyes that made her forget how to breathe.

They were....astonishing. The slightly reptilian slit-like pupil only made his emerald eyes more spectacular.

"Why did you stop?" he rasped.

"What?" That voice. That gorgeously sinful voice. She wanted to weave it into a blanket and wear it wrapped around her naked body.

Dark, intoxicating need threaded through him. Dipping his head to her raven hair, the scent of honeysuckle teased his nose, the warm silk of her rosy lips as potent as the finest wine tempting him to taste them. Never before had he experienced a woman who gave him such sensory depth, made his whole body ravenous for her touch, her scent and her taste.

But before he could wrap her slender body in his arms and quench the lust that had raged through him for so long, Kaitlyn lifted her hands and pushed them against his chest.

"What's going on?" Her voice was thin as she tried to drag a breath into her hyperventilating lungs, her heart pounding hard enough to break a rib.

Raif nuzzled her neck. "I believe it is what people call,...chemistry." He pulled her closer, although she doubted that the hardness jutting from his groin was chemistry. It was the primal call of biology.

Kaitlyn swallowed. Hard. She couldn't miss the pulsing hard-on currently pressing into her belly, the thick stalk trapped between their bodies making its presence known.

Gripping her hips, his lips curved into a slow, sensual smile that sent a shiver through her system, all the way to her toes and pooling in her belly. Kaitlyn moaned and wriggled beneath him, desperate to feel his heavy erection pressing as firmly between her moist folds as it was against her belly.

Lust, thick and hot swirled in the air around them. The scent of her sweet, female need was like an aphrodisiac, driving him crazy. On a groan, Raif's lips covered hers, his tongue pushing into her mouth to claim the velvety depths demandingly, unrelentingly, stroking and tangling with hers, sending tingles throughout her body. She tasted every bit as good as he imagined, as sweet as honey and just as intoxicating.

Kaitlyn moaned against him. A whimpering, needy sound that made his body flame. Never before had a man's touch made her body burn. But it wasn't just his touch, it was his lips and his tongue and the way he held her so possessively, as though he would die if he couldn't feel her body against his.

Taking a chance and letting her rush of need guide her, Kaitlyn ran her hand down his heavily muscled arm to grasp his hand. Slowly she placed his hand on her leg, bringing it slowly up her body, placing it on her aching breast.

A growl rumbled in his chest as his hand cupped her soft breast more firmly. He rubbed his thumb over her nipple through her shirt, raising it to a hard peak.

When she felt him hesitate, she pulled her lips from his to look him in the eye. "Please, Raif. I need you," she whispered.

"Sweetheart, I don't think you know what you're asking." His body was burning from the inside out, his blood searing his veins. "This won't be just sex. If I take you, it will be forever. I will make you mine," he warned, his voice hoarse from pent-up need and barely leashed impulses. "Do you understand what I'm telling you? There would be no turning back."

323

He'd felt her gentle touch for weeks, it had driven him crazy that his body refused to respond, that he couldn't return her caress with the care she had shown him.

Her brow creased. Somewhere in her hazy mind she understood what he was telling her, but she couldn't think straight from the desire tearing at her body. All she knew was one thing. She needed him more than she needed air to breathe. "I don't care what it means. Just touch me, please," she begged. She had never desired a man with such desperation and right now she was beyond caring. Kaitlyn felt helpless to deny what her body wanted. As though fate, destiny or some sort of mad karma had decreed that there would be no chance of avoiding this man.

Raif's large body corded with rippling, tense muscle. He should stop before things got out of hand. She had no true understanding of the consequences. But he couldn't make his hands cease their caresses, couldn't stop the moan of delight as her beautiful grey eyes pleaded with him for more.

He could feel his dragon within him coming fully awake at her touch, her musky scent of desire dragging the beast out of the hex induced abyss.

Only Kaitlyn could make him whole again.

Raif's hands slid to the hem of her shirt pulling it over her head in one quick tug. His hand then released the clasps of her bra, pulling it free and giving him free access to those soft, full mounds. Her breasts were exquisite. High and round, with perfect delicate, pink nipples that hardened as he watched them. Raif was in heaven, Kaitlyn's soft moans of pleasure urging him on. He loved what that sound did to his own excitement when he heard it and couldn't wait to taste the sweet buds, roll them between his teeth and massage them with his lips and tongue.

With every twist and tug of his fingers, he could feel her body buzzing with need. His body hummed in harmony with hers, his cock hardened painfully, pressing against the only remaining barrier left between them, her sweatpants. Raif swallowed tightly as he tried to hold onto his control.

Kaitlyn wanted him every bit as much as he wanted her, so what was the problem?

The problem was that as a man, his conscience battled against taking her, making her his *mate* without her full understanding of everything that entailed. But his beast wasn't inflicted with any such emotional constraint.

Mine! His dragon roared in frustration. The beast paced just beneath the surface, crying out to be free, to claim what was his.

Raif's body shuddered with the force of his dragon's demand. Never in all his long life had his control ever been tested in such a manner. He could not remember a time when he had been so filled with conflicting desires and needs that his body nearly crumbled under the weight.

She stared up at him, her lips parted, her breathing rough and hard. Then she licked her lips. A slow, wet swipe of her tongue, almost brought him undone. Kaitlyn couldn't hold still beneath him, grinding herself against the length of his hardened shaft, and nipped at his chin with her perfect little teeth.

Raif's will shattered. He went from restrained to dominating male in an instant.

In less than a heartbeat he had her fully naked beneath him, his eyes roving her full length. Drinking in the sight of her soft creamy skin that covered her slim, athletic body from the tips of her delicate toes, all the way up, lingering on the newly revealed small patch of short, dark curls that glistened with moisture over her glorious mound.

"You're so perfect," he told her breathlessly, his smouldering gaze hooking hers. "I will ensure you know only pleasure, sweetheart," he promised. "Only the most incredible pleasure you could possibly imagine."

His gentle, possessive words murmured against her flesh, soothed and released her tense muscles that bunched with need.

Kaitlyn's whole body quivered as he once again lavished attention on her full breasts, the tips so tight they ached as he toyed first with one, then the other. Raif shifted his weight as he teased, giving him room to insert a hand between their bodies, his fingers in pursuit of the moist heat between her legs.

A single finger probed her tight channel, seeking out hidden nerve endings deep within, sliding effortlessly through the lava hot cream. She cried out, nearly screamed his name. "Oh, God, Raif!" Gently he began to stroke her from the inside out.

Kaitlyn melted into his hard frame as he pulled her closer, tighter against him. She strained and arched into him, wanting more. Needing more. The desperate moan that escaped her lips almost undid him.

Raif kissed her with far more demand while he stroked and explored her body.

As his thumb rubbed over her sensitised clit, he added a second finger to her tight sheath, stretching her, caressing her. Kaitlyn groaned in pleasure as a third finger joined in the erotic invasion as Raif attentively prepared her for him. Her back arched as he applied pressure to that hidden internal bunch of nerves, her G spot.

"Oh, God. I need you inside me...now," she begged breaking the steamy kiss, lifting her hips higher, driving her aching slit closer to his torturously slow caresses. Her head was spinning from all the sensations overwhelming her. The only clear thought in her mind was the need to get closer to him, skin to skin still wasn't enough. She needed...more.

It should have frightened her, this illogical demand within her. He made her feel things she had never felt before, want things that she instinctively knew only he could give her.

She wasn't afraid. In fact, she was excited, as though she had waited her whole life for this moment. For him. An intimacy existed between them she had never known, with this near stranger who she had so diligently watched over and cared for, for weeks.

Raif hardened further at her breathy plea, though he had not thought it possible. "With pleasure, sweetheart," he growled as he shifted his weight above her.

Grasping her thighs with strong, gentle hands, he knelt between her legs, easing them apart further to accommodate his much larger body. Taking the length of his rigid shaft in his palm, he pumped it slowly in his grip a couple of times, his fingers spreading the beaded moisture over the mushroomed head before pressing it against her entrance.

His erection felt enormous against her, so much so, Kaitlyn wondered if she would be able to take all of him inside her. There were no training wheels with this bicycle. But she wanted him with a desperation that defied reasoning.

She gasped as she felt the head of his cock breach her opening and begin to stretch her wide. He was so big.

The first, sharp burn of her entrance blazed past pleasure, past pain.

A low throaty hiss escaped his lips as he thrust forward into her tight, hot sheath with his thick girth. He stilled for a moment to give her time to adjust to his size, to the slight burning sensation of his dominant entry. "You're so beautiful," he whispered thickly as his hands tightened on her hips. His cock slid in further by the slightest degree. "You make me hunger for you, Kaitlyn, like I've never hungered before. You've been driving me crazy for weeks." His voice was filled with desperate need. The rough rumble in his chest sent a deeper caress vibrating through her core. Kaitlyn shuddered. "Relax. Watch me, sweetheart. Don't close your eyes. Watch me as I take you, make you mine."

Kaitlyn was incapable of doing anything else. She was mesmerised by his reptilian emerald eyes, caught by the extreme emotions and power that filled his gaze, the grimace of sexual hunger tightening his face and the gentleness and care in his movements to ease her discomfort.

She knew in that moment, her entire life was about to change forever.

With short, slow strokes he worked her slick channel open, his thick length delving deeper with every thrust. Kaitlyn groaned. It was so good. Her body was on fire as he continued to push forward, filling her with a pleasure/pain so intense it consumed her.

"More," she begged, her head thrashing on the bed as she became lost to the sensations ravaging her mind, body and soul. "More, Raif. I...need...more," she breathed in short, rapid gasps.

She needed more? That was a red rag to the bull, or in this case, the dragon. Raif's dragon was bucking at his restraint to mark her, to claim her as his *mate*, and statements like *"I need more,"* only spurred his beast on, gave it more control.

Raif's face flushed, his eyelids lowered, his dark lashes casting erotic shadows along his cheekbones. Kaitlyn heard a harsh male growl as he began to fill more of her. He was pushing deeper, stretching further with each stroke of his hard length.

327

Kaitlyn moved beneath him, her hips thrusting rhythmically with his, taking him deeper, deeper, until every inner nerve was exposed to the caress of his hard length moving inside her. It was the most incredible rapture. It was ecstasy unlike anything she could have ever imagined.

Raif gripped her legs, raising her hips higher to allow for extra penetration. He was big, he'd thought maybe too big for her…but she was taking every inch of him.

"Sweet mercy," he cried. His exultation coincided with an abrupt relaxing of the muscles at her very depths, allowing the final few inches of his length to slide home, his balls coming to rest against her backside, as his hard shaft flexed and throbbed with surging excitement.

Kaitlyn gasped as he filled her completely, her gaze shifting to where their bodies met. Her clit was swollen and ripe, fully revealed by the folds of flesh parted around his thick stalk penetrating her.

She was impaled, on fire, consumed by the pleasure streaking through her. Raif's body went rigid when she gripped his shoulders and thrust her hips higher against him.

"Don't stop. Please, don't stop," she pleaded, moving against him, attempting to gain that final sensation that would push her past the brink, over the edge into complete ecstasy.

A furious growl rumbled through his chest. He'd tried to take it slow and be gentle with her, he really had. But she undid him with her hot little body and eager pleas. "You may just regret your words," he growled, pulling his hips back to thrust them forward once again. His growl becoming a moan of pure intoxication when her body once again stretched around him, accepting his full length. Her answering groan told him everything he needed to hear.

Together, in unison, they slowly began to move, her hips rising to meet his every thrust. His hard-muscled pelvis lingering after every stroke, rotating against her cleft to heighten her pleasure.

It was too good. His dragon roared inside him, fighting for release. It's desperation to claim her rising with every pistoning thrust into her welcoming body, merged with his own until both man and beast were fully one again.

Raif picked up the pace, burying himself deep inside her, pulling back almost to the point of withdrawal only to thrust forward again and again, until the passion grew so intense between them he could no longer restrain his need. He began to plunge harder…faster…each stroke more urgent, more possessive than the last.

Mine, his dragon roared.

Kaitlyn wreathed beneath him. Her fingernails dug into his shoulders as she clung to him, drawing blood as she scored his flesh, driving him into a frenzy.

He needed more.

He would always need more, he knew.

She was his *Mate.*

Raif was lost to the siren's mating call, eagerly plunging over the precipice of no return.

Raif roared as his dragon took control. His emerald green eyes glowed, his face contorted momentarily, elongating as his dragon pushed to the surface, its snout filled with razor sharp teeth bit down into the tender flesh between her shoulder and neck.

Marking her.

Claiming her as his for all eternity.

Kaitlyn barely felt the sharp sting in her shoulder, so lost was she to all the overwhelming sensations whipping through her body. It was like electricity gone wild, zapping through her blood, through every nerve ending, convulsing in her womb as it rippled around Raif's pistoning shaft. She pushed her hips higher, her inner muscles working his hard length with possessive need. A kaleidoscope of colour and light danced in her vision, brilliant fire bursts of carnal bliss blasted into her as her orgasm detonated.

The earth moved. Mountains shuddered…or did he? He wasn't sure which. All he knew was the violent release quaking through his body as her tight channel milked him, hot spurts of his seed filling the depths of her womb.

His dragon purred with satisfaction, as did the man.

Mine.

Raif collapsed over her, his strong powerful body shaking from his release, his breathing laboured and ragged, but he did not pull out of her body. He stilled. He stared intently into Kaitlyn's flushed face, studying her, assessing her for any injury. He had been rough, he knew, far more than he had ever wanted to be but he'd felt helpless to fight his nature, his need and his dragon's, to claim her as his *mate*. Leaning in closer, cautiously, he took in a deep lungful of her scent.

It was.....

He sighed with relief.

It was there. His scent was now a part of her. *He* was now a part of her. She had accepted him as her *mate*.

"Are you okay?" he asked. His watchful eyes lowered at half-mast and mussed hair made him look sexy as hell.

"Never better. And you?" she panted, lifting her shaking hand to touch his bristled face, his short whiskers adding to his roughish charm, before letting it fall back bonelessly beside her, utterly exhausted and sated,...and she felt something else....

Raif still filled her, not just with his body but with his soul. That niggling feeling she'd felt building for weeks, of needing to get closer to him, of never being close enough. She felt it now, the bond between them, bright and vibrant and intensely intimate.

Raif looked around the spacious bedroom. Alaric and his family had been more than generous to him over the past two months he had stayed here, but this wasn't his home. He had a kingdom to run and he couldn't do that from this bed, no matter how much he wanted to stay.

Kaitlyn's brow furrowed, the corners of her mouth dipped in a pout of understanding. She could feel the cogs in his mind ticking over, could almost hear them. "Now that you're awake, you're leaving aren't you?" she asked, quickly blinking away the tears that began to form.

"Yes," he answered in a whisper, his fingers gently teasing the knots from her silky dark hair as he nuzzled his nose against her cheek. Kaitlyn bit her lower lip and held her breath to quench the need to cry. "I've stayed here long enough, it's time to go home."

"I know." Barely a squeak of sound passed her lips, her throat closing over, her lungs burning from lack of oxygen as she fought to hold back a sob. If she took a breath now she would lose her battle and break down in a flood of tears. She'd just found the man of her dreams and now she was also about to lose him. Wyvern weren't permitted to live on Earth, he belonged in Fey.

Raif shifted his hands to cup her cheeks, holding her face to face with him until she raised her moistened eyes to meet his. It almost broke his heart to see the pain behind them. "Sweetheart, I think you misunderstand. It's time for me to go home, but I'm not leaving without my *mate*. Without you."

Kaitlyn stared for a moment, stunned by the sincerity in his words.

Her heart skipped a beat.

There was a long silence as Raif waited for her response. She could physically feel the weight of his searching gaze. His fate was already sealed. He had mated with her, marked her. For him there would never be another female, but that didn't mean that she couldn't reject him regardless of the bonding that had occurred.

They were from different worlds.

"This is crazy, we barely even know each other."

Raif chuckled. "True love defies logic. That's its signature trait, didn't you know?" he replied.

That was true, she admitted to herself.

Raif remained still as he watched her facial expressions change as she processed his proposal.

There were no rules forbidding druids from entering Fey, her own ancestors had done it. The question was, could she leave everything behind and go to Fey with him? Leave her job...*which she was unsure whether she still had after an eight week leave of absence.* Could she leave her sisters, particularly her twin, Paige? They had been inseparable since birth, where one went, the other always followed....*Maybe they could visit her, or she could visit them.* She had a life here...*living in a rundown apartment in a sleazy part of London.* She had friends....*who she couldn't tell who she really was or what she did in her spare time.* She had a cat...*who could maybe come with her to Fey?*

The ultimate question was, could she let this incredible man leave without her?

Her chest constricted once again. The thought sent a stab of pain straight to her heart.

No. No, she couldn't.

"Okay," she grinned.

Raif's eyes burned with gratitude, and he wished he could look away from her long enough to relieve his overwhelming emotion. But he could not. Did not. Instead, he simply let if flow over him, mingling and intensifying his pulsing need for her.

Kaitlyn had given him the greatest gift ever. She had awakened the dragon within him, reuniting them once again. But she gave him something else far more precious. The gift of peace with the touch of her complimentary soul.

He had found his *Mate*.

About the Author:

K.G. Inglis is the author of the Eternal series. When not writing about the sexy vampires and alpha lycans and dragons, she can be found reading about them and spending time with her family. Native to Australia, she lives in a beach town on the Southern Coast which many call a holiday destination. If you like your men hot and the action steamy, mixed with a heavy dose of humour then the Eternal series will find a space in your 'must read again' collection.

Follow her for updates at:
www.kginglis.com/
facebook.com/kginglis.official/#
instagram.com/KGInglis
twitter.com/KG_Inglis
bookbub.com/authors/k-g-inglis
goodreads.com/author/show/17230080.K_G_Inglis